BEING MY OWN WITNESS

Being My Own Witness may well become a signpost in Australian feminism. This fictional memoir vividly addresses the struggle faced by women and girls who suffer from the current instruments of a patriarchal society.

Females of all walks of life will surely be moved by the protagonist's strength and heroism in the face of overwhelming challenges: parental betrayals, men who exploit, abuse and suppress female rights, and other misogynists who wield power in contemporary societies. While using effective verisimilitude to describe shocking events in her life, author Violet Budd also applies insightful observations of gender politics.

Violet's literary processes explore how female identity is subsumed by predominantly male narratives within families. Despite government attempts at reform, unfairness toward females is still discernible in court judgements and the way police implement the laws on domestic violence, incest and other areas where sexual exploitation is rife. Society, and especially the mass media, must focus on raising awareness of the sexualisation of young women and educate youth about issues of consent and respect.

Violet's story urgently needs to be heard.

As a child, the meanness, cruelty and blatant sexism that Violet suffers at the hands of her parents and siblings makes us ask: How many more girls and young women are also 'out there' suffering in silence?

Violet's grief is downtrodden. Her silence is parentally enforced. Her story alerts us to the plight of such children, globally, who suffer post-traumatic stress disorders with little hope of either recognition or help. Through sheer determination and her observations on human nature, Violet reaches a pivotal moment that many women yearn for: in spite of the harm she suffers, Violet finds her voice to speak up against injustice.

Violet's story has universal application. It should inspire women across the world to protest the forms of societal advice that serve the dictates of men, both powerful and ordinary, who seek to marginalise, exploit and suppress women.

David Alpe
Art teacher (ret'd) and writer

To the invisible children, victims and survivors of child abuse.
May this book open doors for you to be heard and
validated in a society which has failed you.

Speaking out to be heard

VIOLET BUDD

Being My Own Witness: Speaking out to be heard
Author – Violet Budd

© Violet Budd 2025

A catalogue record for this book is available from the National Library of Australia

<h1 style="text-align:center;font-style:italic;">Acknowledgements</h1>

First, I would like to acknowledge our young, brave feminists who led the Women's March across Australia and on Parliament House in March 2021, and called out for victims of domestic violence and child and sexual abuse to write their stories and shared experience to bring about systemic change to our patriarchal society embedded with unchecked misogyny and toxic masculinity. Their strength, rage and grace inspired me to find my voice and contribute my story.

I also want to acknowledge my beautiful children and grandchildren, who I tried to keep my traumatic past from. Your beautiful presence in my life has helped me to be a cycle breaker.

Finally, I would never have written this book without the support and guidance of my editor, Neasa Nic Dhómhnaill. Well, I would have, but nothing like this final result. Words cannot express the depth of my feelings when she encouraged me to go deeper into my soul than I ever imagined and salvage my 'self' from the ruins of child and sexual abuse. The archaeological site has now been studied, and the broken parts of my psyche arranged for public exhibition and for society to learn from, lest history be doomed to repeat itself.

Floating like a magical
mist, risen from the ocean
depths, in dream works
both day and night,
it enveloped my human
consciousness and
rendered me a prisoner to
its malevolent machinations.
As such I was a shell of a
human being.
The sorrow passed
through me infinitely and
unstoppable like ocean
waves, powerless to its
insatiable, primordial
rhythm. Slowly, through
writing I waded the dark
waters, I looked into its
impenetrable depths,
drew a deep breath and
exhaled. I could do this.
Somewhere in this
darkness I could find the
other, its primordial
opposite, and learn to
speak its language
find my truth.

Into the mystic.

This was child and sexual abuse,
and how I learnt to speak out to be heard.

Violet Budd 2022

About the Author

Violet Budd previously lived in a seaside town of Tropical Far North Queensland where she completed her tertiary education as a mature aged student and worked full-time as a secondary school English and Humanities teacher. She first studied her Bachelor of Arts (Honours) in English Literature and was profoundly influenced by the provocative and illuminating voices of the Contemporary French Feminists of the late 1990s. At that time, she realised that core concepts of feminist writers were commonly rejected by the male scholars. From there she completed a postgraduate Diploma (Secondary) in Teaching. Determined to maintain a strong feminist approach to education, and to protect her students from harm, she held that people could learn to unlearn sociocultural constructs of language, such as gender constructs wherein men and women are expected to fulfil distinct and separate roles in society.

Today, Violet staunchly stands firm on her tertiary education experiences which inspire and drive her current works, alongside the deeply damaging lived experience of child and sexual abuse. When she moved to the ocean harbour town on the southeast coast of Queensland to retire, she was not bound by long work hours and mother duties and decided to write her memoir. This memoir, retelling child and sexual abuse, was her way of contributing to the prevention, intervention and response by society and its institutions, and to the recovery and support for child sexual abuse victim survivors. The release of *Being My Own Witness: Speaking out to be heard* coincides with an ambitious draft Australian National Plan to end violence against women and children in ten years and break down intergenerational trauma through targeted programs. Violet is passionate about connecting with communities and keeping up with pertinent topics in the feminist movement, including *The Grace Tame Foundation, Future* Women, *Me Too Movement* and Clementine Ford.

Contents

Introduction

I begin by acknowledging the land on which I write, from my coastal harbour home of the Traditional Owners, the Gubbi Gubbi people, to the far north land of the Yirrganydja and Tjapukai people. I pay my respects to all Aboriginal and Torres Strait Islander Elders past, present and emerging. I recognise that the Aboriginal land on which I have lived, worked and raised my children and grandchildren has never been ceded and the work of reconciliation is not yet done. I am committed to continuing the conversations about women and their work, including raising their children, that have taken place on this land for tens of thousands of years.

> *"We labour hard from morn to night until our bones do ache*
> *Then everyone they must obey, their mouldy beds must make,*
> *We often wish when we lay down we ne'er may rise no more*
> *To meet our savage Governor upon Van Diemen's shore."*

Anonymous from *Female Transport*, circa 1788[1]

How does one articulate child abuse fifty years after it has happened? Many would ask, "Haven't you forgotten about it?" I thought it was buried so deep it could never be spoken. That was the intention of my abusers – to intimidate me to never, ever speak of it to anyone. If I did there would be consequences; a beating, torture, isolation, humiliation. If I dared speak, they would say I was a liar and a 'teller of untruths'. It was all in my imagination. She's just a hysterical girl. A bad girl. Not quite right in the head. You know! My brain was so whitewashed with guilt and fear that I dared not speak up.

This book is my journey of letting go of my fears, being my own witness and speaking out about the abuse. It is about being heard for the first time. This book is also written for other victims and survivors of child abuse who are looking to find their own voices. There is no fixed answer about how and when to speak out because the child narrative of abuse rarely exists. It is drowned by fear, left out of the societal dominant male narrative and its underlying sexism. Child abuse appears sometimes in the public consciousness, occasionally in a court report written by an outsider. In some cases, after months of investigation of suspected child abuse, when a child is in need of support, the report becomes the property of the state. The abused child has still not been heard; they are silenced and unable to learn discernment to keep themselves safe in the world.

Where do you find stories of child abuse? I Google searched key words, child/abuse/memoir. I came up with a handful of stories, the most notable written by Dave Pelzer, *A Child Called 'It'*,[2] written some twenty years ago. This book is an honest and heart-wrenching account that explains how children can be abused. Since then, more memoirs have emerged to help writers find meaning and for survivors struggling to make sense of their own trauma. I noted one book was withdrawn from publication, caught in a legal battle claiming the author was a liar. This would trigger fear for anyone abused. I am not a liar and I am sure other memoirists of trauma are not liars. Writing my memoir meant meeting myself in the dark waters, wading through the murkiness to bring the truth to the surface. In the process, I have enlightened myself, and hopefully readers interested in these issues, to help explain why it happens and what needs to change in society for it to stop.

However, these handful of stories of child abuse do not compare with more than one million Australian children experiencing sexual abuse. In 2016 it was estimated that of the 5.7 million children in Australia, eight per cent of boys and twenty per cent of girls had experienced sexual abuse. That is a staggering near half a million boys and more than one million girls. Of those instances of abuse, ninety to ninety-five per cent were committed by men, the large majority being family members.[3] By now, writing in 2022, the numbers have undoubtedly increased. It is also known that rates of child sexual abuse are thirty times greater in studies relying on self-reports than in those based on administrative data sources. Most likely family threats, violence and intimidation stop children from speaking up. It was like that for me. I am only learning how to speak out about the abuse now. This is my self-reporting of the abuse to you.

Disturbing figures reveal that 109 children in my own state of Queensland were killed by their parents or carers over the past sixteen years (June 2022).

Death of any child is a tragedy but what is most shocking is that the warning signs were missed. According to Luke Twyford from Queensland Family and Child Commission, "More research was needed to better understand the phenomena of filicides and help authorities 'find the opportunities that will help us save a child from death.'"[4]

This is alarming.

The statistics of child sex abuse and filicide do not tell us why this happens to children or why the majority of abusers are caregivers/legal guardians whose moral and legal obligation is to protect children from harm. I too suffered near-death experiences. My sensory information was frozen by trauma, blocking the self-preserving actions of speaking up and writing. After many years of surviving the trauma in silence, I am driven to tell my truth.

To overcome the terror of my childhood and speak out about the abuse has been a highly challenging project. My healing agenda for writing about my trauma was to bring to life my deadened capacity to feel alive. I dug deep within mysef to write about those visceral feelings which were tragically blocked and frozen by trauma many years ago. In writing this book, I realised my conscious mind lacked a story that could communicate the experience. Consequently, I have reenacted the childhood trauma by creating a narrative of traumatic memories hidden under complex layers in my mind. I needed to stand back and observe my child's experience rather than be hijacked by trauma feelings. I have based each chapter on a significant memory of my present-day main character – my twilight self, an older woman, a grandmother who has arrived at her harbour home to retire and help care for her grandchildren. I hope to find grace in my twilight years, as well as write about the truth of the wrongs done by my parents and grandmother in my childhood. Throughout the chapters, my child-self tells the story of the child abuse. I then return to my present-day self to write my testimony, which up until this point in my life has been intentionally destabilised by concerted outside interventions inherent in patriarchal society, and to make sense of it all. Between the present-day voice and my childhood self, is my academic and teacher-self which I drew on for insights into the child abuse. Uncannily, but not surprisingly, all insights lead to misogyny and toxic masculinity at the core.

This is not a book where we can 'skip to the good part'. It's definitely not intended as child abuse porn or for voyeurisms. At last, I am not chasing down a job to keep myself and my family alive or running marathons to run away from the abuse which haunted me. Now is the right time to write this book but not without the inner struggle of anyone suffering from trauma. I found inspiration through my muses: writers, poets, philosophers and mythical goddesses, the current feminist's movement, nature, photography, raising my children and grandchildren, my honours thesis on medieval writer and feminist, Christine de Pizan and my local doctor. Even so, I suffered defeatism while writing. My internal battles often left me with writer's block. On the one hand, my desire was strong to hold my abusers to account. On the other, I was often triggered by memories and couldn't write for days. Each time, I overcame my fears and found strength in my writing muses because they challenged the patriarchal system and oppression of women and vulnerable people's voices which underpinned the central question of my memoir.

What causes child abuse and how can we change it?

My present-day self was driven to write my truth for all women who have been spoken ill by patriarchy in the past and present. Child abuse is inextricably linked to the ill-treatment of women and its underpinnings throughout history. The challenge is: Will I be able to clearly maintain my conscious level of understanding and at the same time interpret my dreams and subconscious level which speak my painful truth? In writing my truth, it was important for me not to ignore the foundations of humanity which are meant to give substance and meaning to our lives, since it was my humanity that was betrayed through the child abuse. That is why I must write for myself. I have been driven away so violently by the rhetoric of patriarchal society and its embedded toxic masculinity.

Through the layers of self-discovery, I am able to write the fine details of my own 'madness' without outside intervention, in my private feminine space and bring my story to the outside world. I lean on my intellect and writing about imagined goddess encounters through centuries of patriarchal discourse. This way I return to the goddess aspects of the feminine, bringing them forward to speak for change. Combined with my imagination, my intellect is my safe space, to cope with and understand the trauma.

In writing this book, my childhood memory and soul are on fire, yet I am determined to speak the truth that a universal mother's love is replaced by a burning wind of patriarchy, making the world unsafe. So I pressured myself to finish my story. Memories of child abuse continue to smoulder under the surface, triggering anxiety and trauma. However, I am determined to 'write' the wrongs so other families can learn and create a better and safer future for vulnerable children and other peoples.

As a trauma survivor I am easily triggered by certain sounds, smells and images. Any one of these can throw me off guard and take me back to the terror of my childhood. It lives in me and I'm sure other survivors of child abuse can identify. But I am getting better. Creating awareness of the triggers and then taking control of them has helped me to heal. There are throughout the book several motifs and recurring images which relate to the hypervigilance and survival patterns of my child abuse. The scents and images of flowers, tropical gardens and garlands recur as symbols of my vulnerability and my desire for women's empowerment in finding my voice. And there is the recurring motif of the knocking at the gate or garden latches being opened, the bird sounds, all warning me of the inherent danger. The latching sounds of my father forcing himself into my bed. The whoosh sounds of the ocean and the breeze through the she-oaks are an opposite force working to soothe me and help me through my writing. These sensory details help demonstrate the effects of traumatic stress for survivors of child abuse. Each one of these produced profound changes on my childhood maturation and throughout adulthood, making me easily thrown into an elevated state of hypervigilance, scanning for potential threats around me. Writing this book has helped me to draw back the veil of threats, which at times were all consuming. Some days they left me in a haze, not knowing why I felt this way. Now the fog has lifted.

I was grateful for my writing desk and safe space, after all the years of suffering complex PTSD caused by chronic child abuse that continued into my teenage years. It was a place to give myself permission to write my truth and seek my own identity beyond the abuse. My writing journey brought me to where I felt whole and present in the world and to where I wanted to protect other vulnerable people. There was no question that I needed to speak out through my writing. I was no longer afraid of the patriarchy or its backlash. My only desire was for society to be free of institutional toxic masculinity and misogyny. I was challenged to write my truth in a society where women's and children's voices, and some men, struggle to be heard. Now I am ready to embrace my presence in the world liberated from fears and emotional wounds and continue to write for much needed change.

In essence, I have written this book to serve as both a release from personal trauma and an invitation to dedicate ourselves to facing the reality of child abuse and the inherent silences which protect perpetrators, to explore best how to expose it, and to commit ourselves, as a society, to using every means we have to prevent it.

CHAPTER 1

The Arrival

2021 autumn
Ocean harbour home

"No coward soul is mine
No trembler in the world's storm-troubled sphere
I see Heaven's glories shine
And Faith shines equal arming me from Fear."

Emily Jane Bronte[1]

The *'shee'* sound of the she-oaks shuffled through the sturdy branches on which the butcher 'storm' birds had built their nests. I spied a storm bird fly back to feed its chicks with freshly caught worms from the undergrowth. They were kind to their young, who were helpless, and relied on their parents to care for them and keep them safe until it was time to fly into their adult lives. Juveniles followed their parents in flight and landed on my small balcony facing the sea. I watched them from the safe distance of my sofa. From their parents, they learnt how to sing for food and what to trust. That was nature's way. These watch-keeping birds warned of impending storms and sang for joy. Their innate calling dredged up dark memories of my childhood. There was never joy in my parent's home. Without warning, they brought their destructive storms upon me rather than protected me like the storm birds did for their young.

I sat straight in my chair to correct my stooped posture and swore to get to the bedrock of the events that had rocked my world to the core.

Amid a small pile of personal paperwork, I glimpsed the edge of my father's Last Will and Testament jutting to the side. My fingers turned, claw-like, as I slid it out from underneath. I wished I hadn't seen it. Its very existence tampered with the peace I had created in my new home. It left me cold to read it.

My father was gone, and I felt nothing except relief. I wished he could have owned the child abuse and crimes against me before his final breath. But he held on to his denial until the end. During his lifetime he had lived the hero's journey of attaining personal wealth and success while destroying me to the core of my being. The world was structured not to hear my truth and that's what I sought to change. At least he had left me enough money, combined with my own life savings, for a modest financial independence to make ends meet for the rest of my years. But no amount of money could make up for the fifteen years of abuse he dished out when I grew up. No one was held to account.

I shoved the will into the bottom drawer, wishing I had never seen it, and allowed my shoulders to drop, releasing the pent-up pain in my back and head. I hadn't realised how hunched they had become while reading the will. I breathed in the salt air and wiggled my fingers to calm my mind. I had to consciously unlock my fists, drawing upon my new confidence to tell the truth. I would hold him to account even if he was dead.

2021 autumn
Ocean rock pools

"count the troubles and
trace the ripples
back to the pebbles
that started them"

Kirli Saunders from *Kintsugi*[2]

The next day I was standing in the dimming afternoon sunlight at the rock pools near the beach not far from my house. I watched over my grandchildren, Summer and Tyrone, feeling grateful for the much-needed grandma time for them and for me. The ocean rolled in on the shore and with each wave, sometimes soft, other times strong, the primordial *'whoosh'* reminded me of the mother's heartbeat I had never felt. The loving hearts of my grandchildren were close to me now. I wanted to keep them safe and close to me so they could hear my heart beating for them.

"Grandma, can we look for hermit crabs?" Summer squealed with excitement. She let go of my hand and pressed her tiny palms to her cheeks. Then, clasping her little brother's hand, she led him to the pools.

The sun lingered over the horizon behind them as they fossicked for hermit crabs, rocks, shells and sea anemone. Their intent little faces were in the shadow.

Tyrone turned to me and gleefully held up a tiny crab. I smiled back; they seemed oblivious to how much of the afternoon had passed by.

In the soothing presence of the ocean side, I released an appreciative sigh. I walked over the rocks beneath the landmark lighthouse, barefoot like my little ones. We were anchored to each other like a pod of dolphins. Every now and then, squeals of delight were let out when a major discovery was made.

"I found a hermit crab", or "Grandma, I found a beautiful shell!"

It was my job to safekeep small treasures we might take home like small pieces of driftwood, sea polished shells and tiny textual rocks. These gifts of time were laden into my open palms from loving tiny hands. Grains of fine sand sifted through my fingers like stardust. I would keep them safe for their treasure chests, or vase trays as reminders of our connectedness to this place, the sea and to each other. It was important for me to keep my grandchildren safe and connected with love; a far cry from my own childhood.

I glanced up to the lighthouse with a smile. Its light would guide the boats through the northwest channel. The cliffs and boats had the guardian lighthouse to watch over them like I watched over Summer and Tyrone. My eyes remained steady as I traced a line to the craggy ancient orange and white rock formations of the cliff face below. They rested on the breaching whale carved and etched into the outcrops and under clings. As I gazed at it, my nerve endings tingled. I made the connection. It was all about belonging to a place and telling the story from generation to generation. My desire was to move closer and to touch it. But I remained anchored on the spot, admiring it from the distance.

It was in that moment when I knew I had to write my story and invite the world into the secrets of my past. By not speaking up and telling my story I was unintentionally condoning the secrets of the child abuse I had endured. I was helping to create a world where abuse was allowed to continue unspoken; a world my grandchildren would have to bear.

I watched Summer and Tyrone's high energy and demonstrations of hugs and kisses each time they found a hermit crab. This was the land of the Gubbi Gubbi people. I was filled with a deep gratitude for the Aboriginal people and their attachment to this sea country. The meaning of this beach was sunbeam, and the neighbouring beach was wildflower. They were named by their ancestors. Belonging to place meant understanding the connectedness of all living things – fish, shells, honeysuckle, cotton tree, mangroves, rivers and tidal estuaries of sea and land country. This was something I knew deep inside my being even though my own ancestors and land were far across the ocean in Ireland. With lightness in my chest, I took these beach names as a good omen, a sign of healing for my broken spirit.

I remember when my grandchildren were born, and even before then, I had made a firm decision not to be like my grandmother. The shadow of the seagull flying overhead and the clouds blocked the sinking sun. A chill ran down my spine, how could my grandmother have been so cold?

No, she wasn't cold, she was brutal.

"Come on kids, it's time to go!" I called out, swinging my arms as I walked toward my treasures, pushing away my childhood memories.

"We love it here, Grandma!" Their voices remained full of glee. "We don't want to go home!"

"Come on, the sun is about to go down. I need to get you both home safe and sound," I said, leaning in on them with a warm smile on my face.

2021 autumn
Ocean harbour home

I was ravenous after the beach combing that afternoon with my treasures. Outside the window in the twilight, the cicadas had begun their song. Hunger clawed at my empty stomach, it craved to be fed. The earthy baked-clay kitchen tiles were cool underfoot as I busily prepared an organic vegetable dish to satisfy my fresh eagerness for food.

The TV hummed in the lounge room. My ears pricked at the breaking news; a women's march had spilled on to the streets of Canberra. They marched towards Parliament House, demanding to speak to the Prime Minister, Scott Morrison.

I edged into the lounge room to get a better look. The people were furious over his inaction and lack of leadership on women's issues. Tens of thousands of people took to the streets to protest gendered violence and yet again, call for the equality for women.

"The Prime Minister insisted he was too busy, instead offering a private sit-down to the protest's organisers," reported the high-pitched journalist.

The Prime Minister was not putting these voices to the top of his social agenda.

"What do you think of the Prime Minister's response?" asked the journalist, holding the microphone out to a prominent domestic violence advocate.

"Make the protest stick!" she rallied. "Right now, the Morrison government is banking on the media losing interest, but we will not be silenced."

Immense cheers of support came from an ocean of heads in the crowd. They forced their placards into the air over the grounds of Parliament House.

The reporter leaned into prominent professor Ms Florence. "What do you think of Ms Payne, the Minister for Women not attending the rally?"

"By refusing to step outside the Parliament to answer women's justified concerns, the Prime Minister and Ms Payne have demonstrated callous indifference," she said with conviction. "It's as if women are starting the fight all over again, after several failures from government. The government's apparent inability to listen or respond to the serious concerns of women suggests a deeper underlying cultural reason for its policy failures." The professor was resolute.

I sat on the edge of my couch; my feet gripping the carpet in stride with the march. At least the Prime Minister was going to speak his point of view in a media conference, although he was already considered cowardly for prioritising media management and a flattering photograph, above humanity.

An advertisement blared across the TV screen, and I raced to the kitchen to prepare a coffee before returning to the sofa. By the time I got back the march was on again.

"Not far from here, such marches even now are being met with bullets, but not here in this country,"[3] Mr. Morrison told Parliament, improperly celebrating a notion of liberal democracy and trying to palm off his violent tendencies on a recent visit to Myanmar.

Didn't he get it? This was about violence towards women, children and some men. I leaned forward with my coffee in hand. He was completely out of step with what the protesters were saying. Surely it would be better for him to listen, have empathy, understand and then to act.

The aroma of steamed vegetables lingered in the air, reminding me to return to the kitchen. Seeing Morrison and his crony boy's club left me feeling sick in the stomach. I couldn't even think about eating dinner.

I lowered the heat on my cooking pot overladen with fresh vegetables and rice, wrung my hands dry with overly zealous twists of the hand towel, and set off to my office with one eye on the TV in case there were further updates. When I got there I sat rigid at my desk; the pink and orange glare of the sun sinking behind the mountains lit up my silver laptop. My fingers moved by themselves like when I wrote the last poem and the one before that. These events, particularly Morrison's response and violent subtext, triggered a swamp of recollections buried deep in the dark places in my mind. The best way I knew to face them was to write.

Leaning slightly back in my chair I reached for a poem I had written upon waking the other morning. I had started to write poetry again now when I was in my safe place and had the opportunity to renew my creativity. I had completed my education some years ago and the written word allowed me to express my childhood trauma; helping me to release the anxiety.

During that feverish night I felt like the ocean tides were being pulled by the moon and the sun. I was being wrestled out to sea; the pain refused to go away. I swam to shore, only to wade during the day through a blur of childhood trauma and survival. I read the first verse of *Sea Anemone:*

> *"I was always trying to figure out a wider intelligence,*
> *a truth, where it was hidden, and what shape*
> *beyond the subterfuge and secrecy of unspoken words—"*

I had to stop hiding in corners. All I was doing was repeating the abuses in my poems and tucking them away in a drawer with all the other poems. Each one was filled with pain and possibilities for transformation, only to be silenced by my childhood trauma once more. I was tired of making excuses in my poems for the terrors my childhood inflicted upon me. I needed to come out of isolation, my self-induced prison, guarded by fear. The Women's Movement was the perfect political platform upon which to raise my voice. Leaning forward, I put my loose-fitting poems away in a tidy box.

I then eagerly awaited the replay of the Women's March in ten minutes. My fluttering stomach was appeased by the vegetable dish I forced myself to eat, and a glass of cool mountain water I brought from the kitchen. I made sure the oven was turned off so as not to interrupt my viewing. I was in awe of these women and the few men who stood by their side for the cause.

The replay was on the TV. The crowd spun forward together, chanting like a sea of angry goddesses tormented too long by the patriarchy. Their faces were flushed, and their heads shook in unison as they assembled on the lawns with hitched chests and white transparent knuckles bulging from clenched fists clutching signs ushering change. This was Australia's fourth wave of feminism on the cusp, many women from the third wave in the 1970s joined their ranks, rightly espousing they were activists back then for the very same issues women and children were facing today, in 2021.

Their leaders, two strong and elegant young women in their twenties, were led to the podium by their posse of diverse women taking up their positions in the firing line of the patriarchy. The crowd was in expectation of their words. Sitting forward on the sofa, my legs followed suit, my feet crept closer to the screen. Upholding both respectability and rage they called out for victims of domestic violence and child and sexual abuse to write their stories to bring about systemic change to our patriarchal society embedded with misogyny and toxic masculinity.

I listened to their words; deep inside my soul I heard their call. This was exactly what I needed to do. The call was already conscious but hearing these women strengthened my resolve.

Leaning in on the podium with eyebrows raised on their faces, they offered questioning glares why toxic masculinity is prevalent in our institutions and goes unchecked by our leaders. Swallowing and nodding at the same time, I sipped the cold mountain water while maintaining an air of readiness created by these brave young women.

I had to write my story, but the risks were daunting. I could be marginalised, silenced and shamed as a teller of lies, told that these events did not happen and only existed in my head. I knew this reaction would enflame the wounds from when I tried to speak out as a child, but I was prepared to take the risk because I owed it to this fresh wave of feminists whose voices were heard across the country and the world. I owed it to my children and grandchildren. I owed it to my own child within to seek answers for the trauma suffered.

*"When the victim is already devalued (a woman, a
child) she may find that the most traumatic events of
her life take place outside the realm of socially validated
reality. Her experience becomes unspeakable."*

Judith Herman[4]

I awoke the next morning to the melodious song of the butcher birds. The bird's renowned grace and power prompted my resolution to write my memoirs. My feet hit the carpet as if I was marching against the patriarchy, ready to speak out. To safeguard myself I had already rung the clinic for a referral to a psychologist in case anxiety triggered by writing my childhood memories overwhelmed me. Still, the idea of risking telling my story to another therapist who didn't understand or tried to guide me in the wrong direction played heavy on my mind.

"May I see a woman doctor please?" I couldn't deal with speaking to a man in a position of power, my trust had diminished after too many painful experiences.

"Yes, Dr Nuha is available at 10am." I sensed the comfortability with my request, after all, it was not unusual for women to request women doctors.

"Do you need an extended appointment?"

My throat tightened, the less people I told what I wanted the better.

"I'm not sure," was all I could say.

"Well, what is it you want to see the doctor about?"

Whatever determination I found in the butcher bird's song deserted me.

"I'd—rather not say."

There was a pause on the other end of the phone, and I half expected her to reject me.

"Alright, I'll give you a standard session. Is 10am tomorrow suitable?"

I couldn't think straight enough to remember if I had anything on but decided I could move things around if I needed.

"Yes, that's fine, thank you."

I hung up the phone with my heart pounding in my chest. I only hope this one works out better than last time.

I entered the GP's waiting room. Thankfully it exuded calm. Hand painted pictures of the beach and hinterland by local artists hung on sea green walls and instinctively I connected to the sense of place. I sat down opposite the water bubbler, the sound of bubbles filling a micro space in my thoughts, inspiring me to escape my fear and follow my newfound desire to write my childhood trauma. Eager to hold onto my inspiration to write, I picked up a newspaper from the side table and flicked through it for articles on the Women's March.

I looked up just as Dr Nuha appeared from the corridor. She called my name and my gaze met with her sparkling eyes and I followed her to the consult room. "Please take a seat." Her voice was soft and direct. "How can I help you?"

She seemed like she was living in the moment, with no desire to be anywhere else but here listening to me.

"I have a history of child abuse and was diagnosed with complex PTSD. I am a rape victim, torture survivor, and I was brainwashed." The words fell out tangled and stained like the spoils of war. I waited for her reaction, but her face didn't change. I thanked heaven above; I didn't want to shock her with my previous therapist's diagnosis. I think she expected it, words and diagnoses that are spoken between practices but hardly enter the mainstream consciousness or if they do are washed over in 'we will do an inquiry' discourse until it trickles away into oblivion.

"I know a very experienced psychologist who can help you. I have heard only positive feedback."

I took the referral form she handed me out of respect but in truth I was reluctant to see another therapist. The first one didn't believe me and told me not to come back after one visit. The second one was friendly enough but wouldn't let me talk about my childhood trauma. Instead she preferred to use techniques to help me deal with the effects of trauma in the present, but it only made me feel more ashamed than ever of the memories forever lurking underneath the surface.

"I had a terrible childhood. I suffered growing up. My guardians abused me, my father, mother and grandmother. I've never really had anywhere to turn for help." I found myself confessing to Dr Nuha. She was an educated woman, committed to others unlike my mother who never stepped outside the home to gain worldly experience.

"I understand dear. I'm from Egypt. Women face a battle against patriarchy there too. It's very bad," she said pressing her palms together.

I was so relieved.

"Thank you so much Dr Nuha. I really appreciate your time and understanding."

My thoughts trailed off like a rambling brook. Quickly, I brought them back, out of the entanglement.

I studied the referral form, slightly twisting the top of it.

"I may not make an appointment with the psychologist for a while."

I wanted to find my own voice for healing my trauma.

She gauged me for a moment, perhaps about to ask me why I am here asking for a referral if I don't want to see a therapist.

"That is fine dear," her voice was gentle, "whatever you feel is best for you."

With open palms she gestured me to the door. I left with a sense of being in control of my life, no longer feeling compelled to keep my parents' secrets. The whole exercise in setting up the option of accessing therapy was about making my own choices. I was ready to acknowledge to myself and the world that my father abused me, and it was no longer acceptable to deny it. But I had to do this my way – writing my memoir was my destiny and my therapy.

CHAPTER 2

The City of Ladies

1996 late summer
Far north home

> *"I need not conjure you to look upon me as one of whom*
> *all links that once existed between us are broken."*

Mary Shelley from *Mathilda*[1]

Twenty years prior, I was living in the tropical north and raising my two children. It was my dream to live there, one thousand miles from my aging parents. We lived in a modest low set brick home close to the local primary school, near rainforest botanical gardens and waterfalls and sublime tropical beaches and palm trees fanning the azure blue sea and its coral inhabitants.

The corals were plentiful and colourful this year. No one foresaw that within one year the colour and life would be drained from them by global warming and chemical run-off. Crown of thorns starfish were released from the bilges of international boats. Nothing was protected, not even our precious, one of seven, wonders of the natural world. I was fully aware it was a result of farming and industry practices by local and state councils dominated by male leaders. I wanted to protect my children from it all but I couldn't even tell them the story of my traumatic childhood. I hardly recognised it myself.

I used to wait at the white picket fence; eyes fixed on the corner of the street for them walking home from school.

"Please Mum, can we walk to school on our own. We're not babies anymore." Jasmine begged with a heavy brow and wide raised arms as if I didn't have a clue.

"Yeah, Mum. You can trust us!" Johnny joined in the petition.

Jasmine and Johnny joined arms and wrapped them around me for a big hug. How could I resist? I loved them so much and at seven and eight years of age, they were able to make some of their own decisions. I wanted to give them independence but also the safety I was denied as a child. I wanted them to know I trusted them, but it wasn't them I was worried about. Predators were lurking everywhere, sometimes right in front of them.

"Our friends are allowed to!" Jasmine shone her bold blue eyes at me.

I tried to resolve my reluctance to grant her desire. The clock was ticking but in my head, time had slowed down. I questioned whether my thoughts were irrational, out of touch with today's reality? The long-repeated traumas of my childhood were clashing with the normalcy of my own children's upbringing. The memories I had pushed away confronted my decision making but I decided not to allow my loss and betrayal to be handed down to them.

"Mum. Are you listening?" Jasmine's voice jolted me out of my thoughts.

My pulse was racing with confusion but keeping my past a secret and pretending everything was fine was best for everyone.

"If you promise to walk with your friends, stick close together and talk to no one but them," I said, clasping my hands together to make sure they didn't shake. My resignation was met with exuberant cries and more hugs and kisses but deep down the dread gnawed at me.

'What if—'

That afternoon I watched them turn the corner, smiles and laughter coming from the pack of children heading up the street. I stood tall with pride.

"Hi Mum, we told you we would be ok!" Jasmine and Johnny spoke at the same time clearly delighted with their accomplishment.

"I can see you stuck together." I nodded an approving nod towards their friends for following instructions and responsible decision making. "You better be off since your mums will want you home on time too." My kids broke away from the little pack and came through the gate I had opened for them.

"Mum, is the cordial cold? I'm hot and thirsty."

They let out heavy sighs, pushing their way inside the house with school bags in tow. They dumped them on the floor and slumped in the lounge chairs from heat exhaustion.

"Please, Mum!" Johnny uttered above the grumbling noise of the air conditioner atoning for the relentless humidity in the far north of Australia.

"Thanks Mum," Jasmine said with outstretched arms for a tall glass of chilled raspberry cordial.

"Thanks for trusting us, Mum. We had so much fun walking to and from school with Daniela and Ryan!"

"I'm really proud of you both."

Snugly sitting between Jasmine and Johnny on the sofa, I rested one arm on each of their shoulders and gave them a congratulatory hug. I had given them a taste of control over their own lives, and they were grateful for that. My stomach roiled and I sipped my iced cordial to settle it. They didn't know how much their gratitude for self-determination meant to me.

I remember how I was unable to escape from my father's control. I was still plagued by the memories. For fifteen years he continued to demand that I conform to his selfish and unnatural needs of which I could not speak. I was grateful that my children would not have to keep a dark and malignant secret. A secret I pushed to the back of my mind every day, trying not to bring the painful memories up again.

"Now, before I lose you both to online chats with your friends while doing your homework," I jibed, reflecting on how times had changed, "I have something to tell you both."

"What is it Mum?"

The chilled red cordial had removed the gravel from their angelic voices.

"Remember how I told you I studied for two years at university before you were born?" I surveyed their unblinking eyes. "I'm going to the local university tomorrow to enrol to complete my Bachelor of Arts degree."

"That's great Mum," Jasmine said, and then with a sidelong glance, "Will you be here when we get home from school?"

"Of course." How could I not be? "The tutorials and lectures are three days a week. The rest of the time I work at home. I have a meeting with the dean tomorrow and will know more."

I fixed my eyes on their schoolbooks that spilled out of the bags and onto the floor. The odour of school desks and writing pens filled the air. The musky smell triggered memories that were worlds away from my children's reality. At school, as a child, I felt much-needed security when learning but these feelings were fleeting. When I went home, my father was distant and his affection was inappropriate, and my hostile mother blamed me for the family troubles.

At thirty-eight years old, I had not shed light on the child abuse, nor had I spoken of it to anyone. Perhaps the knowledge I would gain at tertiary level would help me. Maybe I would find corroboration and support in the literature to make sense of it all.

I pulled myself back to the present and tidied up my children's books now on the floor.

"Here you are. Get your homework done and dinner will be ready by 5.30pm."

"Ok Mum! But not tuna casserole again!"

Shaking my head, I walked to the kitchen and put the can of tuna aside, rethinking the meal plan. Salmon patties, fresh garden salad and chips it would be. Their favourite. But try as I may, my mind was racing through potential pitfalls for understanding my abusive childhood which I would embark upon the next day.

1996 late summer
Far north university

I stood looking at the newly opened university. It was a modest building, austerely sitting at the bottom of a lush, treed range; a mystic place drenched in rainforest and Aboriginal Dreamtime. The acidic odours of the fresh paint conflicted with the fragrance of the hibiscus flowers in bloom that lined the pathway to the administration block. The contrast in smells was overpowering like the nausea I felt as a child coming home from school. Pensively, I entered through the glass doors and immediately sensed the Aboriginal ancestors holding vigil over the universe and its creation. Even as a child, I was highly attuned to their troubles. Maybe it was because as an abused child I understood the concept of invasion and the destruction of identity. But unlike the Indigenous people of this land I lacked their connection to spirituality at my core. There were no Dreamtime stories for guidance and kinship. I was invaded by my own family and my colonial ancestors exploited and murdered the First Nation's people for their own greed. All I had was shame. I had no idea how to resolve my inner conflict. With a heavy feeling in my heart, I pushed on towards reception to seek information. Perhaps I would find some answers here.

By 3.00pm, I had an appointment with the dean, Dr Aurora Mayson. Inwardly I wondered if my child abuse would be drawn out of me given her focus in feminist studies. I mounted the stairs to her office on the second level and sat quietly, like a flower about to bloom. I clutched my study references and degree points I had accumulated in a two-year stint at university when Prime Minister, Gough Whitlam had opened the universities to everyone. Back in the '80s education was egalitarian and not just for the rich and privileged. Unfortunately, it didn't last long in Australia's history; perhaps too many women were getting an education. But there I was, points awarded to me in my hands, like the seeds of a flower about to be spread on my feather brain.

The door was open; apparently she never closed it, so no one was shut off from her. She beckoned 'come in' with a warm smile.

Sheepishly, I entered. I wasn't sure what to expect but her name gave me hope.

"I see from your previous results you did very well," she said in a positive tone from the get-go. "We are happy to have you here. What degree are you considering?"

"I'm thinking about a Bachelor of Arts since it covers the Humanities, things about life and how it works." My words fell out awkwardly.

"Sounds good. There are five strands of study, English Literature, History, Politics, Sociology and Critical Thought. After your first year you can choose which two streams to major in."

Dr Mayson's areas were History and Politics. There was an unspoken expectation that I would follow her subject areas, but I was reluctant about Politics. It was male dominated and I had enough of that in my life. She scanned her expert eye over my results and congratulated me on my high achievements in study from 1985-86.

"I can approve you one year credit for this work; therefore you can start Year Two with us. That way you can drop one subject. Would you like to think about your majors or decide now?" Her sincere stare spoke to me.

"I'm not interested in Politics," I told her upfront, despite the churning of my stomach. "Although I agree we need more women in politics to bring about equal representation of men and women in Parliament." I stopped there. I wanted to say: 'the system would remain oppressive,' but I kept silent. The oppression I suffered growing up was too much for me to speak up.

"Okay then, I have you down for English Literature, History, Sociology and Critical Thought. I look forward to seeing you in my lectures." Her voice was warm and sincere. "Please call me Aurora," she followed through with.

I sat straight in my chair and held her gaze with a smile. I liked the idea of being on first name basis with her. But it never detracted my respect for her place in the hierarchy of the education system. She was an amazing woman to have as the head of the university, it gave me hope that I could finalise my degree and gain knowledge that would let me into a world from which I had been shut out in my formative years.

2021 late spring
Ocean harbour home

I watched the warning birds from my home. The concept of women in positions of power and the hope I had from meeting Dr Aurora Mayson still left a bitter taste in my mouth. The ring of the warning birds echoed in the distance, rebounding across the blue autumn sky. The power structure in the natural world was equitable, unlike in human society. The male and female calls were a shared harmony, there was concern for all living things. Their tonal energy reminded me of the women's groups I belonged to at university. I knew equality there, at least for a while. We worked extensively with male scholars without denigration of feminist advocacy. Reaching upward and slightly elevated from my seat, I glimpsed some university papers in plastic sleeves for preservation. I pulled them down to me and held them like a shield to my chest, the protector of women's business.

The boiling kettle slowed and finished with a familiar click. I placed the papers on my raw-timber desktop, a place of safety, while I left for the kitchen to make the cup of Wildhorse Mountain coffee. Its distinctive earthbound aroma wafted through the air, creating a communal vibrancy between sipping coffee, reading feminist papers and writing my story.

I returned to my desk and placed my caffeine-effusing mug on the desk careful not to spill coffee on my preserved and deeply nostalgic university papers. Quietly sifting through them, I retrieved a history paper from its plastic sleeve – *The sealing industry in Colonial Tasmania and the abuse and exploitation of Aboriginal Women.* Before reading it, I took a sip of coffee and closed my eyes to recall the memories of my university life.

The outside air was still, and the songbirds hushed. Clumps of magenta flowers amassed on the hibiscus trees beneath my window and parcelled reminiscent scents from the far north rainforests. I replayed my meeting with Aurora.

"Keep striving," she would say to me when I struggled to meet the high academic standards I set for myself. "You will come to understand it. I sense a strong will in you. You can do this."

She had a keen sense for my educational wellbeing and the development of my womanhood. Her staunch feminism came across in her lectures in Revisionist History. When I wrote the paper I now felt my voice was heard, at least it was by my highly regarded Aurora.

Aurora pushed the boundaries of academic study, so I was so glad to be part of her pioneering contributions to Revisionist History. This paper, and many others like it, led me to fields of research that connected me to knowledge and understanding of the emotional and cultural burden colonialism and the patriarchy had taken on women, not excluding Indigenous women.

"A cogent and strong feminist argument, excellent work! High Distinction," were her comments on my paper.

I could hardly believe it was possible to speak out against the patriarchy. Only now do I dare to question whether the continuation of my study would one day lead to me speaking out against my child abuse.

With a heavy sigh I replaced the paper in its protective sleeve. My voice was once heard, at least to my small audience. But my university days were a long time ago, over twenty years. I wrote many feminist papers with passion, drive and absolute rage, based on critical thought and academic inquiry. My arguments were valid and strong and here they remained in a plastic sleeve on a shelf, hidden from the world. One day I vowed to have them published in honour of the 'blue stockings' of this period. Essays of significance, they gave voice to women writers and critiques supported by the radical French feminists who lay bare western philosophical and psychological thought of misogyny and reshaped it from women's perspectives, absent from the Western literary canon. I flipped through the papers.

Mary Wroth – Urania (1621) Urania Book 1 is not a novel depicting the pastimes of the Jacobean Court 'invented' by male writers, rather, it is Wroth's own invention of women's self-identity, an intervention into a cultural space closed to women as writers.

In line with contemporary trends, D.H. Lawrence recreates and focuses on female desire in *Lady Chatterley's Lover (1921)*. How does his treatment compare with later concepts of a woman's desire such as the ideas of French feminists Julia Kristeva or Luce Irigaray?

Christina Rossetti's, Goblin Market (1850) offers a feminist reading in terms of the poem's implicit exclusion of male practices, and the writing of codes and values of women back into literature,

Eighteenth Century Women Poets, An Oxford Anthology. Ed. Roger Lonsdale (1989) - Are the themes favoured by these women as philosophical or political or substantial as those of contemporary male poets?

Discuss violence and/or suffering in *Sir Thomas Malory's, Le Morte Darthur Tales VII and VIII (1485).*

Nineteenth Century authors reveal a tendency towards self-disclosure and the expression of personal emotion. Discuss how this tendency influences and shapes the writing of Mary Shelley in *Frankenstein (1818).*

Virginia Woolf's, Orlando (1928) – how does Woolf expose the dominant masculinist context of literary and historical texts?

Give a thoughtful account of *Aristotle's Poetics (325-323 BCE).* Poetics is only a partial analysis of human life with an inbuilt masculine bias. Aristotle believed that men were whole while women were but a by-product and lacked what man possessed, that is, reason.

Misogyny and Images of the Virgin in Christine de Pizan's *The Book of the City of Ladies (1405).* In the fifteenth century Pizan addresses the pervasive attitudes towards women in her society, challenging negative stereotypes and advocating for their dignity and worth.

I let the papers slip from my fingers and back down onto the desk. Such cultural prejudices against women have become embedded in western philosophical, symbolic discourse, beginning with Aristotle or before.

It was the support of strong women teachers and academics back then that held me together and taught me, through the study of History and English Literature, to see the wrongs done to women in the past.

Swallowing my last sip of coffee, I made a promise to myself to stop obsessing over why things happened the way they did. I shifted several clumps of hibiscus flowers in a vase, as if arranging nostalgia and hopefulness in my head. I knew I needed to do it. I had to make my voice heard once again. I had a duty not only to myself, and not only to those strong women who had come before me, but to my children and the future of humanity to speak up.

1996 early autumn
Far north university

University resumed in early autumn, 1996, when the hibiscus flowers were in full bloom. I remember the luscious flowers overhanging the pathways clearly as they brushed my shoulders on the way into the vast hall. Students of all ages thronged together for our first lecture in English Literature. The soft hibiscus petals fell to the ground around me as if a garland was dropped from above me by my spirit guide.

The number of women students clearly outnumbered the men. I caught up with Florence, or Flo as she preferred to be called.

"Hi Flo, so great to see you!" I fell into step and lightly rapped one finger on her shoulder to flick away a hibiscus petal.

"Same, how was your break?" she said, brushing her shoulders to remove the petals to the garland underneath our lightly stepping feet.

"It was great to spend the summer with the kids but now I'm looking forward to getting on with uni."

"Have you noticed the guys here?" said Flo spinning in a wide circle; the petals flew up to our knees.

"I have! They seem so comfortable in their own skin."

I followed Flo into the lecture hall with a smile.

"Lecture begins in ten minutes," a young male tutor ushered us into the hall with a reassuring tone. Other men entered alongside their female counterparts. Their postures were non-threatening. They were the good guys, lacking the hyper-masculinity that was so prevalent in our society and culture.

"Have you heard the news?" said Flo.

"No. What is it?"

"An exciting new lecturer has been sent by the main campus. All we know about her is that she has a doctorate in the study of the Ancient Greek lyric poet, Sappho."

"That is exciting news!" Just hearing Sappho's name gave me goosebumps, so much feminine mystery attached to it. I wanted to know about the archetypal feminine and not the feminine constructed by our capitalist media-driven society – the cultural construction my mother fell victim to and then threw me under its bus.

The lecture hall was full of English Literature students from all levels of study. I sat on the edge of my seat, eager to see our new lecturer, Dr Laura Wilmont. She was bound to be a feminist. There was so much babbling and talking over one another in the room around me. I was sure everyone was as nervous as I was. Flo's foot bounced up and down beyond the seats in front of us and our young tutor was up on his toes to get the first glance. I got it though, I was here to advocate for change, like most students, and Dr Wilmont would be a guiding light.

All eyes turned when she entered the hall as if she were Sappho herself draped in a flowing floral print dress. Her lightly tanned skin was adorned with delicate statement jewellery and her bleached blonde hair fell like exotic silk. She swayed on her red high heels as if on a romantic gondola ride, when she approached her place at the lectern.

"Good morning," she addressed the hall, "thank you for the lovely welcome. I am so glad to be here and the opportunity to be your lecturer in English Literature. As most of you know I completed my doctorate on the work of Sappho, the ancient Greek lyric poet from the island of Lesbos, during the seventh century BCE. I am a feminist and believe in equality between men and women in our society. In case you feel threatened by this information, I assure you that I am open to a wide range of theoretical and philosophical approaches to literature other than feminism."

Hands went up quickly, eager to hear more.

"Why did you choose Sappho for your thesis? Is her work relevant to us today?"

"That's a good question. She is an important historical figure who set a foundation for lyrical poetry, influential art and women's voices more generally."

Her voice and ideals surpassed all the stars as if Sappho was reciting her lyric poem, *You in Sardis*.

"Since her works were translated, women all over the world have used her expressions of love to enhance their own lives and the lives of others." She tilted her head leaving her silk blonde hair to fall to one shoulder, revealing her petal earrings like those of the Lydian women. It shone after sunset like the rosy fingered moon. I was encouraged to study hard by this beautiful woman's voice and to let my woman's voice be heard.

"Some people say she was a lesbian. Was that the case?" Jack couldn't help himself.

"Sappho's poems tend to focus on relationships among women," she calmly replied. "The focus has given rise to speculation that her interest in women was because she was a lesbian. The word lesbian comes from the island of Lesbos and the communities of women there."

"How did you get into study?" Sarah, a girl I didn't know well, asked.

"My husband was a tradie, and I was doing his bookkeeping from home. My kids were becoming independent, and I had more time on my hands. I enrolled in a degree and completed that. After a while my husband grew less tolerant of my study. I backed off, but deep down I wanted to continue to do a master's and possibly a doctorate."

"What did you do?"

"I left him."

Students shuffled in their seats; muffled voices could be heard around the room.

"I realised we had grown apart," she said without skite in her voice, "And I didn't want to live that life anymore. It was a difficult decision, but I am glad I did. I studied hard and gained a scholarship to travel to Greece as part of my doctorate study. They also paid for my Greek translator to go too. I learnt so much and here I am!"

"I have heard stories of husband's jealousy of their wife's study. It must be a real thing?"

Another hand went up.

"It certainly is. My case wasn't too bad. My husband took it well and we parted mutually. There was another woman in our year whose husband was so jealous of her study he burned her books."

The whole room let out a gasp. My hands gripped the seat, my father's raging face flashed in my mind. I pushed away the intrusive thoughts the best I could. I felt the poor woman's pain, being spat upon by her red-faced husband as he set light to her very essence. I had to consciously relax my grip on the seat, thinking about avoiding the common enemy – the fist-shaking, coercive, book burning maniacal male.

"She was petrified of him and gave up her study. The threat was real, and he may have harmed her physically. We couldn't do anything to help her; intervention wasn't possible."

I understood this feeling and was angry that men could do this to women and get away with it.

She ended the orientation lecture on a positive note, "I would like you all to address me as Laura, you can dispense with the formality."

Afterwards, we spilled out of the hall and into the café thirsty for coffee and to discuss our inspiring new lecturer.

I felt safe in my new university 'home' with Aurora and Laura championing me forward to realise my personal goal of self-realisation through study. It was important to me that domestic violence had been amplified in the lecture theatre and a gasp of collective empathy filled the room. Maybe one day I could share my voice, my story and it would carry weight and be authentic in society.

But at that time, my feather brain could not see the underlying biases about to emerge from the shadows.

1998 early summer
Far north university

*"Damn my woodenhead, my feather brain, why
I am waiting here at your closed door?"*

Nuala Ní Dhomhnaill from *As Fragile as a Shell*[2]

University was winding down in the early summer in 1998 and the hibiscus flowers were fading. It was the end of the last semester of my third year. I strolled towards the café for a coffee date with Flo to catch up on personal experiences of objectification. I pushed the glass door until it lost all tension and with an easy walk, made my way to the vacant table in the corner. I arrived early with time to kill, content to wait for her and enjoy the moment. My bag was conspicuously light on books, having returned them to the library for the year. With a satisfied breath, I placed it over the back of the wicker chair and sat leaning with one arm hooked over its bamboo fretwork. The chink of coffee cups mingled with the soft hum of voices and laughter; another study year finished. No more essays to write and no more exams or deadlines.

The wet season was early this year. Peering through the café window I traced a line with my eyes from the rainforest range below to the high-altitude tableland. A veil of mist blanketed the summits. The heavily watered gorge and river and the creeks that joined into it, streamed down the luscious woods and tree ferns that covered the slopes and spilled their way over ancient boulders and riverbed stones into the mother Coral Sea. A babbling brook could not hold up a palm tree fist to stop nature from dumping its rushing force upon it. The snakes and wildlife scampered for caves and other places of safety while the river and creeks surged towards the coast to the Dreamtime water.

Swamped with the euphoria of the mystical rainforest, I was aware of the Aboriginal Dreamtime story which lay behind the land and sea of this country.

"Can I help you with anything?" A young attendant woke me from my trance.

"My friend will be here in five minutes, we'll order together." My eyes widened vindicating me from daydreaming. "I'll stick to water while I wait, but thanks." I slinked further back into my chair.

Returning my line of sight to the rain-drenched range, I imagined the river carved out from the tableland to the sea like in the Dreamtime story of the carpet snake. He sang and danced on his journey between places while trading beautiful nautilus shells with different tribes for dilly bags, eel traps and other useful items. But then he was hacked to death by jealous marauders who envied him for his nautilus shells and peaceful community. They scattered his parts, the tail to the tableland and the head down on the coast to the Dreamtime waters on different bluffs and ranges.

"How long have you been waiting?"

I jumped and turned towards Flo, masking the deep breath I needed to calm my nerves. She slumped in the chair opposite me and eyed me with a flash of concern.

"Not long at all. I've been admiring the view," I said in more depth than I cared to explain. I sat upright to bring myself back to the present. "Let's order our coffee before you get too comfortable."

Gently holding her hippy bangled wrist I led her to the counter. The colourful wood beads jangled like a tambourine rejoicing us with praise.

We perched ourselves at the table and sipped locally grown coffee, in support of our growers and in protest of labour exploiting capitalist companies.

"How did you go with Stephens?" Flo probed.

"I suspect the novelty of my paper has worn off." I met her gaze in solidarity. My lecturer and medieval literature scholar, Dr Stephens was impressed by my paper: *Discuss violence and/or suffering in Sir Thomas Malory's Le Morte Darthur, Tales VII & VIII (1484).'* So much he suggested that it be published and that he would arrange for me to give a reading at the next meeting of faculty.

For a moment my eyes held hers and then I let them drop downward to my hands cradling the cup of coffee. "I've just come from his office. He said maybe next year because we're running out of time." But something deep inside niggled at me.

"Fiddlesticks!" Flo rallied, and my eyes lifted to meet hers. "These guys can't take it. As soon as a feminist deconstructs a masculinist author for asserting dominance over his feminised characters, they shrivel up!" The glow in Flo's eyes was like a beacon in the dark.

I didn't want to think that was the case, but she was right. I retrieved the paper from my bag and read his comments with a tremor in my voice. *"A thorough – indeed devastating – application and up-to-the-minute feminist theory to the question of 'literary' violence. If this wasn't so good, I would probably find nothing to argue with it. But it's thought provoking, and we must talk about some of the ideas here one day – HD 84/100"*

"And did he?" asked Flo.

"No." I took a sip of my coffee. "I mentioned it at one point, but he was busy, so I ran it by Laura."

"And what did she say?"

"Laura said he was unfamiliar with the philosophical and political diversity of French feminist thought, and it took him by surprise." The fact that I discussed the theories of Helene Cixous and Luce Irigaray in the light of their political ramifications in fifteenth century society was enough to disarm him. I giggled for a moment.

"Yeah, I get it. You were determined to use the French feminists to hold up your arguments in support of women in society and culture. If women don't support women, who will?"

I looked up at Flo, deeply appreciating her unwavering support. Where would I be without her?

"Of course! He manipulated the characters to suit his own purpose. Guinevere obsessively doodled love hearts with flower petals, Lancelot's identity was fragmented by the wheel of fortune and Arthur was escorted to the otherworld, by the ladies of the lake, never to return. Effectively, his characters were left without a place to speak."

"I know, right! And then the master narrator throwing doubt on possibilities for change in society. You know, giving women a voice and all that!" Flo was as keen on the French feminists' approach to deconstructing literature as I was.

"I don't know why Stephens couldn't rise above it. His world is not collapsing like that of his idol Mallory in fifteenth century England. Or it doesn't appear to be."

I took the last sip of my coffee. I still had time for another before collecting the kids from school. They would probably want to go for a drive to the lookout to catch the water gushing spectacle.

"Time for another coffee, Flo?"

"Sure. Flat white, no sugar. I'll mind the seats."

The café was full now; the chink of cups still in celebratory mode but something was different. I couldn't put my finger on it but I'm sure Flo would know.

"Here you go." I rested the full coffee cups on the table. "Have you noticed the guys in this place?" anticipating Flo already knew the answer.

"Yes, they're sitting apart from the women. And their backs are stooped hiding their bias against women no doubt." She said with a creased brow. "And that's not all. To answer your question before, Stephens' world might be falling apart. Rumours are circulating. The main campus down south is giving their northern campus a shakeup. Aurora is about to retire, and they are sending Professor Harry here to 'sort us out'. It's said the feminists have taken over."

Her news registered in my mind slowly. A chill ran down my spine and a heavy weight fell over my chest. I held my coffee in closer.

"Are you serious?"

"Dead set."

"What are you going to do next year?"

"I'm moving on. I'm getting a job. I have my BA now. It was a lifelong dream to gain a degree, but I've had enough of this place."

I could distinctly feel my pulse in my throat, and in that moment, a profound sense of solitude washed over me. I'm sure I'd been here before in another life. I shook my head, trying to break free of the dizzy feeling overcoming me, the thought of losing my feminist network was too much to take in.

"I will miss you. I've committed myself to honours next year. But Laura and Aurora were meant to be here for my fourth year." I gave Flo a sudden look. "Have you heard what is happening with Laura?"

"Her teaching position is up for tenure. Harry's also a Professor of English Literature. No doubt he will take up a lecture position as well as dean."

"If Laura is not going to be here—" I will become the carpet snake.

"Are you okay?"

"I'm not sure." I didn't want to voice my fears, but I was suddenly sure my head was about to end up on the coast and my tail on the tableland. I lost myself in the coffee swirling in my cup. I knew what was coming. Professor Harry envied our feminist philosophers and peaceful community. Growing up in a household dominated by toxic masculinity, I knew this only too well. My stomach dropped. Harry was coming here for one reason and one reason only. His mission was to destroy our idyllic circle of women. My spirit was still searching for a safe place; somewhere I could trust the people around me. I had hoped it would be here. I glanced through the window at the misty rainforest; perhaps it was not as bad as Flo was letting on. I fought the tightness in my chest and leaned in closer to her.

"Of course, I will be fine!" I threw her a cheeky grin. "Don't you worry."

"You're a strong woman. Keep speaking out and give those old boys a run for their money!" Her hippy bracelets rattled in tune.

I hugged her wanting to believe that everything would be all right without her in fourth year, but my feminist support network was disappearing, and I lacked the strength to resist the patriarchy alone.

I watched Flo walk to the carpark and my stomach sank. Instead of slinking home, I mustered the courage to face Laura to discuss a thesis topic for honours. I found myself at her office and gently knocked on the door. Her gracious elongated Aegean Sea blue jewel bracelet arm warmed me to enter.

I eyed her as I entered.

"Hi Laura, I just wanted to talk about next year."

She sat back in her leather swivel chair behind her desk and nodded respectfully.

"My marks were good this year – High Distinctions for nearly all papers. And I'm encouraged to do fourth year in English Literature."

"That will be great – you know you must choose an author who you have not written a paper on yet." The two candles in her eyes shone like Aphrodite to Sappho.

I wish I could have pursued a thesis paper on other tales of *Le Morte d'Arthur*. Elayne of *Escolat* needed to be rescued from the tower, and her wild feet stamping malady and despair, by a feminist academic. Surely there was a way to empower her artfulness of web and loom other than imprisonment and effacement because of Lancelot's unrequited love. I felt strongly to free Elayne from her subjugation in the same way I wanted to be freed from the silence surrounding my childhood abuse.

Laura passed me a list of writers and poets.

"I thought you might be interested in one of these."

I looked over her suggestions and leaned towards the French medieval writer Christine de Pizan, *The Book of the City of Ladies* (1405), a polemical work in the defence of women. My decision was strongly based on the precept that Dr Wilmont and Dr April would be there in my fourth year.

"*The Book of the City of Ladies* by Christine de Pizan looks interesting." Her candlelit eyes dimmed for a moment, looking like she lost focus of me. She then quickly averted her attention back to me. Her eyes flickered again, reflecting the Aegean Sea blue from her jewel bracelet when she spoke.

"Christine was a medieval female writer, left a widow at the age of twenty-five with three young children to support. She earned a living by the pen—she was extremely unusual and daring. In 1401 she joined in the debate about the vulgarity of texts because the male writers of the time were exchanging traditional antique beauty with raw physical facts of sexuality."

"Wow, she was unusual for her time. Women were considered intellectually inferior." My imagination galloped ahead; I could work with Christine de Pizan.

"That's right. Her contribution to the debate extended to moral concerns on the role and function of literature in society. She was a woman who was not afraid to speak her mind. Her book fell out of translation by 1521 and was not rediscovered until the 1980s." I loved the way Laura was passionate about feminist history and women writers.

That was it, I would choose this book for my thesis. She wasn't afraid to speak her mind, that sucked me in right away. I admired her strength and resilience, no matter what the stakes. If only I could have been half the woman she was but the words so desperately wanting to be expressed about my past were stuck in my throat.

2019 late spring
Ocean harbour home

I stared vacantly outside the window of my coastal home. Seated at my desk, I turned on my computer and tried to write but my mind and fingers were seized by the dreaded 'writer's block'. Perhaps the timing was not right. Or maybe I shouldn't…

My eyes honed in on two nautilus shells I kept with me from the far north as a reminder of the tablelands, rivers and creeks that snaked to the waterholes and ocean below. I couldn't write no matter how hard I tried, the last few days had me feeling like I was walking through mud.

I closed the laptop and decided it was a good day to arrange my desk. Maybe I should unpack the last of my papers. I moved the nautilus shells to the shelf above my desk. I cherished them because their distinct spirals reflected a much-needed order in my life after the chaos in an abusive and toxic household where I grew up. The shells were one of the oldest creatures to survive in the Earth's oceans, like me – a survivor. I needed to tell my story or when I die the lies and secrets would die with me. I brushed my fingers across their gold and ocean-blue spirals and my desire to write my truth was renewed.

Two more boxes remained unpacked. I eyed the boxed *Misogyny and Images of the Virgin in Christine de Pizan's The Book of the City of Ladies*, signed and dated October 1997. I hadn't yet laid my hands on my thesis. Part of me wanted it to remain at the bottom of the box, the negative memories it evoked were too hard to bear. The violent hierarchy of patriarchy at play, in both medieval European literature and late twentieth century, in their attitudes to women's writing and critical thought should perhaps remain hidden forever. I glimpsed the Virgin Mary blue binder and dug my hand to the bottom of the box – there it was, firmly packed.

Filled with mixed emotions of rejection and accomplishment, I pulled it out and read the notes from the Marker's Report – *"admirably broad in its reading, theoretically informed, and recovers a female ancestry, a line of mothers to think back through."* I read on, *"the thesis definitely makes its case and enables the pervasive presence of the Virgin throughout the city, and Christine as a matriarchal source."*

To this day I was shattered that it gained a distinction and not a high distinction. At the time my deepest desire was to apply for a scholarship for masters or a Doctor of Philosophy and I needed a high distinction for that. Not being able to go on with a PhD was devastating, triggering memories of being disregarded and silenced as a child.

I carefully placed the blue binder near my poetry books and made a mental note of its location. I had to think positively about the thesis and ignore the threat of patriarchy at my heels. If Christine de Pizan could challenge the misogynist writers of her day then I could too.

I made myself an aromatic cup of Wildhorse Mountain coffee and sat back at my desk sipping my drink and thinking of ways to approach my writing. Stargazing at the gracious nautilus shells above, I vowed to find my voice. My desire to be heard had to become stronger than my fear and Christine's legacy was a good start.

1999 early autumn
Far north university

By the time fourth year at university came around, Aurora had retired and was replaced by Professor Harry. A younger male lecturer, Dr Landsdown, took Laura's role. He was given tenure which meant a ten-year teaching position. Harry was here to 'sort us out'. The feminists had created a fleeting safe haven in academia and now the patriarchy had to take back power and control.

The dynamic was different as soon as the year started; I felt it in my woman bones. Helplessness overwhelmed me in this drastically altered learning environment. We were in our first tutorial with the professor; he was taking us for Australian Fiction for the semester. There were new faces in the class, notably a scholar from Sydney who had moved to the north for her honours year under the tutelage of this professor. She loved the traditional male writers and had specialised in the seventeenth century English poet John Milton. I shuffled through my bag and retrieved my notebook and pen, trying not to think about the professor having favourites, especially when scholarships for masters were at stake.

"Most of you in this room have voiced concerns at some time or another of the replacement of Dr Wilmont. I know you were all fond of her, she was an influential lecturer."

I wasn't sure what he meant by that, but it felt like a threat.

"You may have heard that I am anti-feminist."

I stared at him, feeling like I had just been kicked in the guts.

"Let me assure you I am not. I have much respect for our feminist scholars and their contributions to the English literary canon. I am looking forward to seeing some good papers from this cohort, but they don't always have to be feminist deconstructions."

I narrowed my eyes and placed my fingers over my mouth. Was he trying to warn us off taking a feminist approach?

His towering figure stood over us at the lectern, reminding me of the parental authority I was accustomed to in my family. My heart plunged into darkness and despair but I disguised it with a fake look of interest as best I could.

The list of novelists and books for the Australian Fiction course was out. There were limited choices to go around between fifteen students. *Tirra Lirra by the River*, a Miles Franklin Award-winning novel by Australian author Jessica Anderson was already taken by our new student. She must have been given forewarning since it was already gone when the list went up. With few options left, I chose Peter Carey's *Bliss* not having a clue what it was about. It turned out that the author was a close associate of our learned professor.

For Laura's tutorials, I used to wait outside the room, singing in my mind like a member to a Sapphic circle. For the professor's tutorials, I stood stiffly lined up and waited to enter, unsure of what was to come next. The professor was in deep conversation with his pet student when he turned my way and looked directly into my eyes.

"By the way, Peter Carey is not a misogynist," he said staring at me like a gawking owl.

I froze, heart in my throat, feeling like I had been ambushed. Fear gripped me like I was standing in front of my father, unable to escape his fist. My only option was to surrender. I dared not resist him and write a feminist rebuke of Carey. The violent hierarchy was at work.

Harry sounded like he was in the Middle Ages, colluding with Mallory, and he would not leave me anywhere to speak. Nothing had changed in seven centuries. I may as well have gone home and swept the floors than be out in the world trying to raise awareness of the wrongs done to women throughout history. In the twentieth century I was being shut down by the patriarchy just like the women's voices had been shut down centuries before me. Somehow, this stung harder than ever before given my tiny taste of freedom.

2019 early summer
Ocean harbour home

A thunderstorm passed over the coast. The skies were grey and the birds were hushed. Apart from the growling thunder in the distance, the silence was ominous. In my last packing box I had found my thesis bound in Virgin Mary blue leather. I kept it with me as a reminder of the days I strove to understand the position of women in society by the study of English Literature. The opening page was printed in capital letters: "Misogyny and Images of the Virgin in Christine de Pizan's *The Book of The City of Ladies*."

My head dropped to the side as the storm began to lull, my consciousness was fading. I was falling – falling into another place.

Thunder – crash – falling away – helpless to stop – my story – my flowers fell from the vase and ran away – I chased them – they found a new home – another flower bed – find my writing.

The flower bed was filled with annuals and perennials. The pink and pale blue butterflies fluttered between a blooming equestrian of flowers. I dug soft loamy soil between the zinnias and hollyhocks with fluttery hand movements, barely able to hold the spade. My eyes darted between the entangled flower stems and roots in an effort to find my writing. It had to be here because it was nowhere else to be found.

I dragged my nails through the dirt and let go as I espied a shimmering emerald light in the distance. A beautiful young woman came toward me. She was dressed in a forest-green velvet dress. The hem dragged on the floor; it was low in the waist with a scooped neckline. The sleeves ended at her elbows, and she reached inside her dress to a fitchet pocket. She swept back the head veil that covered her beautifully braided golden hair, coiled over each ear. She fossicked in her fitchet until she revealed a quill pen in one hand and a small piece of parchment in the other.

"Hello, I am Christine de Pizan," she said. "I have been advised by Rectitude to take my pen and go with her, to go ahead, and mix the mortar of my ink bottle so that I can fortify the City of Ladies with my tempered pen." She looked straight at me. "I see that you are troubled. Would you like to come with me?"

"I would love to come with you and learn from you," I grabbed my Pilot Frixion pen and notebook and followed her to the City. I hoped they would allow me entry with my daggy jeans and sloppy pink tee-shirt.

"You see," she said, "The auctors are getting away with hell. They are speaking ill of women, and I believe this could cause people to do harmful acts. In my City of Ladies such writing is not permitted."

We passed through the ornamental wrought-iron gates of the City and rested under the shade of a gigantic oak tree. She beckoned me to help her gather gall wasp eggs from the roots so she could make more ink.

"I have joined in the debate about the vulgarity of texts, in particular the Roman de la Rose. I am against Jean de Meun's contribution to the allegory because he writes of the raw physical facts of sexuality in the traditional love symbolism of the rose. It is important I write in the defence of women as a moral concern about such things. Writers like him have caused a conflict between Christian morality and sexual liberalism."

"I believe you, Christine, I don't think much has changed in the future."

She glanced back over her shoulder at me, as if gauging whether I was joking.

"Most of pop culture," I continued, "is based on the heroes' journey. He acts on the offensive and kills or tricks his way to victory. He loathes women because they get in his way – they build community just like you have built the City of Ladies".

We were connected by our experiences, Christine and I, and they spanned centuries.

"The character of the jealous husband in the Rose will surely encourage readers to emulate the violent and misogynist acts from the text. My concern is not only on literary topics but also for the moral concerns on the role and function of literature in society."

The soft summer breeze filtered through the bowers of the oak tree collecting the scent from the meadows steeped in lavender. Once again, I was inspired to write my story.

"Ecclesiastical literature is to blame too. They view women as vile and their writing anything as unthinkable. At first, I hated myself when I read 'God formed a vile creature when He made woman'. Fortunately, Reason rescued me from the debilitating self-hatred. She told me that anyone who spoke ill of women only hurt those who say it, not women themselves."

Christine was not afraid to speak her mind.

Thunder rumbled in the distance.

Stiffly, I raised my head from the desk. My Virgin Mary blue bound thesis was on the floor. It was covered in flowers fallen from my toppled vase, the realisation jolted me back to full consciousness. In the early hours of the morning, I rushed to save my thesis and collected the flowers and vase.

Christine's voice was still vivid in my mind, *"Don't speak ill of women!"*

Between wakefulness and sleep, a heavy yearning consumed me. I didn't want to be afraid to speak my mind anymore. I wanted to be like Christine and challenge the violent and misogynist acts I had experienced. I had begun to build my own *City of Ladies* in my ocean harbour home.

I placed my Virgin Mary blue bound thesis, now free of fallen petals, on the desk as inspiration for writing my story.

CHAPTER 3

Letter to My Brother

2020 summer
Ocean harbour home

"O Kypris and Nereids, I pray you to sail my brother home
unharmed and let him accomplish all that is in his heart and
be released from former error and carry joy to his friends
and bane to enemies and let no one bring us more grief."

Sappho from *Protect My Brother Haraxos*, circa 700 BCE[1]

The storm lifted and sky opened. A sea osprey descended from the heavens. Its wingspan, brown-grey feathers, gathered the blue sky and shawled the turquoise waves crashing softly on the rocks. Under the sea shelves, tiny molluscs tucked their soft bodies inside their shells, having evolved the hard shell by secreting calcium carbonate from their survivor glands. I stood barefoot on the sea rocks in awe of the harbour, feeling serendipitous with the molluscs. Like them, I was a survivor. I would grow my shell and write my truth from the inside. And when the time was right, I would raise my head and share my story with the world. I turned my mind back to my blessed grandchildren who were fossicking in delight for shells and hermit crabs.

"Perfect, just what we all needed," I said, delighted. Salt water was the cure for everything.

Summer and Tyrone ran ahead but knew not to leave my sight. The children were good like that and listened to what they were told. The rock pools shimmied in the early morning sun; the hermit crabs scurried inside their shells on our approach, another reminder of fight or flight congruent with my childhood memories of abuse. But unlike them, I had nowhere to run and no way to fight back, except in my mind. But now my head was filled with a beautiful dream of a wondrous garden because of my children and grandchildren; no longer would I run.

For now, I needed to put my feelings away and care for my little ones at hand. It was important to give them grace and nurturing in all facets of their life, including our journeys of discovery at the rock pools.

"Go away," my blessed girl yelled at her little brother.

He was three years younger and looked up to his big sister. She had separated herself from him. It was too much for his little heart to bear and he burst into fitful sobs. Swiftly, I picked him up and cuddled him until he gained his breath.

Summer looked at me with a cold stare. She was set on alienating her baby brother.

"Why did you send your little brother away?" I asked.

"I don't want to play with him."

"But why? You know he loves to be with you. What has brought this on?"

"He's a baby, that's why," she said with her hands on her hips.

"He may be a baby but that is no reason to be mean to him."

"Why, Grandma?"

I looked out over to the ocean's horizon, partly to give her the impression that my story had a mythical origin.

"Many, many years ago there was a girl called Sappho and she wrote a letter to her older brother. She begged him to amend his ways and come back from his journey on the boat." They had been on boat trips with their parents so she knew what this meant.

"Why did she want him to come home?"

I looked back to her with a serious expression.

"Because he had darkness within him which he needed to heal and by coming home she knew he could fix that."

"What was the darkness?" She asked, now captivated by my story so much she didn't notice her little brother leave my arms and plonk himself at her feet. "And why did he need to heal it?"

"The darkness was being cruel to those he loved, although he had many wonderful qualities."

"Did he come home, Grandma and get better?" Summer gently patted Tyrone's hair like she had many times before. She was good-natured but she'd had a long day at the childcare centre the day before and my guess was the meanness of other kids had rubbed off on her.

"Yes, he came back from his journey and mended his ways. He realised his behaviour was wrong and he wanted to keep his family safe."

"That's good," she said with a smile and reached out to hug her little brother.

My heart ached while being joyous at the same time. My father was an only child and grew up in a patriarchal society – a double banger which explained his lack of empathy for others. I caught my thoughts and steered my focus back to my blessed ones.

"He feels happy and sad just like you. We all share this world together, the rock pools and the ocean, the birds in the sky, the shells on the beaches, everything."

"Okay," she hugged him again. "Then, the letter that 'Sappo' wrote was to tell her brother to behave better?"

"Her name was pronounced with an 'ef', Sappho. And, yes, how you treat others is very important. It's also important to speak up if someone is being mean to someone else."

The culture of silence was embedded in our society. I averted my gaze to the evening star, recalling Sappho's poem, *Evening Star—'Bring home all the bright dawn scattered and to bring the child home to its mother'*. That was what I was doing now, bringing home my grandchildren to their mother freed from secrets and lies rooted in the past. I would no longer participate in the silence of generational trauma like my parents and their parents did.

The gale from the previous evening had passed and together, I walked home with my grandchildren in the fair wind, our heads held high.

1998 spring
Far north home

The far north rain was torrential. Cram filled gutters and spouts flooded down pipes and poured into the street, then made its way to the local creek tributary. I packed the kids' lunch boxes until they almost overflowed; it was their first day back at school. The air conditioner grumbled, taking part in the cacophony of beating rain on the tin roof. The humidity was stifling.

"Mum, we're ready to go to school!" Jasmine was excited to see her friends, most of whom she hadn't seen over the summer vacation.

"Are our lunches ready?" Johnny piped up, always grateful for lunchtime.

"Here you go." I squeezed their lunch boxes on top of the load of books in each bag. That familiar musky smell of schoolbooks lingered as I zipped up their bags. I tried not to think how lonely I would feel when they left for school.

"I'll have to drop you at school. The rain is too heavy!"

"Oh Mum, really, you don't have to. We'll be fine, Daniela and Ryan will be there."

"You have no choice; it's belting down outside. And it's not like umbrellas are going to work in that downpour." I sighed, looking down at their glares and frowns. "Okay, if it stops raining this afternoon, you can walk home with your friends."

Jasmine smiled and Johnny shrugged and turned towards the front door. The ping on Jasmine's phone made Johnny stop and turn back.

"Mum, Lucy texted. Her mum can pick us up. There's room for both of us in her car!"

It wasn't a question.

"Okay." I wasn't going to win this battle. "Tell her the gates are open. She can drive in behind my car under the carport."

Lucy's mum pulled up minutes later and the kids piled into the car with laughter, lanky legs and flailing school bags. They waved goodbye as the car drove out.

I stood there at the back door, my gaze fixed to the empty space in the carport, long after they were gone. Rainwater from a leaky spout splashed my face and woke me out of my trance. The teeming rain was not letting up. I closed the door with a heavy sigh and returned to the kitchen to clean up the breakfast dishes. With the kids gone to school the house was lonely, it reminded me of my mother at home all day. It must have been depressing but I didn't want to be like her – a victim of the patriarchy, deprived of self-fulfilment and a life of my own.

I glanced at the package on my desk, inside was the postgraduate secondary English teacher courses that I had enrolled in. This was my answer to the despair I felt from not going back to the university, I would become a teacher. I hurried through the dishes and housework and eagerly began my new academic studies. I sat in my study chair and sipped my cup of coffee, the self-renewing course material in front of me. I flipped pages of subjects with diligence and paused at Psychology and Education. The first topic 'How People Learn' urged me to write the paper immediately. The cruelty of the professor's attempts to thwart my feminist approach to literature left me dispirited but now I liberated myself from his hold over me and wrote freely.

"People can learn to unlearn sociocultural constructs of language, such as gender constructions wherein men and women are expected to fulfil distinct and separate roles in our society."

My ideas were boundless; my fluent fingers only just kept up. University might have been an unsafe place for me to speak up, but secondary schools would be different. I gently touched the spare school pens I kept for the kids and recalled Ms. Felucha, my Grade Ten French teacher. She was hip, dressed in her mini skirt, knee-high boots and colourful hippie bead chokers. Her dress code vividly rejected conventional constructions of masculinity and femininity of the time. This was what I wanted to give my students, the same confidence feminist teachers such as Ms. Felucha had instilled in me.

1999 late summer
Far north high school

My first teaching job was at a local high school. The school was previously a make-shift hospital during World War II for our returned soldiers in the north who, like myself, suffered their own form of PTSD, or shell shock as it was known back then. I related to the place with an uncanny sense of complex trauma. It had been a refuge for suffering souls; when I entered I could feel their anguish in the rafters. Built of fibro with sturdy wooden window frames, it remained in place for fifty years. Their memories were embedded in the school as was the patriarchy. Some new buildings were built in the square from the main building, comprising a quadrangle walkway and green space in the centre. Assemblies were held there each Monday. The teachers and students would stand in the hot burning northern sun while the principal stood in the shaded balcony above, emanating his authority within the school community. He would be buggered if he was going to hold the assemblies in the air-conditioned luxury of the school hall, or even in the breezeway of the shaded sports centre. I would come to know this man to be a sadist; I was sure his glassy blue eyes had been forged in Dante's hell.

But in the beginning I went to my classroom on the top floor, overlooking the quadrangle to the east and the highway lined with local businesses to the west. My students would often stare out the window, absent-minded as cars whizzed by, and then turn back to me and their work. My classes ran like clockwork; I took each and every student under my wing. I couldn't help but nurture them as well as teach them. I went out of my way to reach each one of them and to give them the best chance of academic success. I could tell the kids who had it hard at home. I would let them eat their breakfast they brought in, having got out of bed late and struggled to make it on time. Sometimes I would find a student sleeping on the floor at the back of the classroom if they had a rough night.

It was mid-autumn and school camp for the seniors was approaching. Administration was looking for teaching staff to go along and I knew my students would want me to go.

"Are you coming on our camp, Miss?" Johanna eagerly inquired.

"I would love to but my kids are too young."

"Oh, come on Miss, they won't mind." They would say. "I'm sure someone could look after them for five days."

I knew my kids would be supportive of me attending the seniors' camp. They expected it of me and thought it would be an opportunity to stay at their friend's houses. I sighed, my students were right, my children would be safe with Lucy's mum, so I added my name to the list of attending teachers and prepared my camping checklist. In foresight, the principal must have been happy to see me go since I had gained a reputation of being a popular teacher but in hindsight he would be anything but happy I attended camp. For me, it was good to have a ratio of women to men teachers. It always seemed that male teachers could get away from home more than female teachers and who would teach them the ways of the patriarchy if I didn't go.

The camp was up in the hinterlands where the mountains were shrouded in mist. The days were kept busy with mountain hikes, water activities on the lake and off-road bike riding. I remained fit with running marathons over the years and was able to keep up with the kids.

I was determined to keep up with the emotional requirement as well. Generally, senior students didn't get homesick and loved being out with their friends on school camp. However, there was something I didn't bargain for. One morning Rose stayed back in the dorms. I went to check on her to find she was crying, clearly in distress. I approached her and sat next to her on the make-shift bed.

"Rose," I said gently, "what is it?"

"It's Mr. Troy, Miss." She sobbed into her hands. "I've had enough of him. He touched me where he shouldn't have – I did nothing to provoke him." She looked up to me with a look I knew too well. It was the same look I must have had when I was her age. Her eyes searched mine to see if I believed her. Unlike the adults in my past, I gave her what she needed.

"Of course, Rose, you did nothing to deserve this."

She broke out in fresh tears; it was safe for her to continue.

"He gave me no warning – I hate him – he's spoilt my last camp with my friends!"

I felt sick to my core. I had heard the rumours of this teacher but my hands were tied, I had no firsthand evidence. Today that had changed. Now I had a duty to act.

"I'll tell the principal," I said trying to console her, "he's coming up here today."

I turned and saw Troy skulking in the background, sure he was there to cover it up. I shot him a look of disgust and he turned and walked out of the dorm. I couldn't believe he had the nerve to come in here after what he had done. He had no boundaries.

"I'll tell him, Miss." Rose's voice trembled. "I want it to come from me."

I held her hand, grateful she hadn't noticed Troy's presence.

"Whichever feels right for you," I said, "I'm right here if you need me."

It was not long before Luther arrived. I watched Rose telling him of her abuse by Mr. Troy from a distance under the silver birch tree. He shook his head and moved away to the next chore, leaving Rose standing there looking so very alone. I wasn't sure whether shaking his head was in disapproval of Troy's behaviour or if he was annoyed that she had reported it. A chill ran down my spine, an omen of what was to come.

I strolled up to Rose, tears streaked her cheeks. She stood there with her arms folded tight over her stomach.

"How did it go with the principal, Rose?"

"I told him, Miss. But nothing will come of it." Rose replied miserably. "Nothing ever does!"

"This is a formal complaint," I tried to reassure her, "they have to take this seriously."

Rose shook her head, facing the ground.

"He's been doing this to me and other girls since Grade Seven."

"What?"

I was shocked. How could they do nothing about it? I gazed into the distance, but with hollowness in the pit of my stomach I couldn't see the beauty of the rainforest. Everything became irrelevant except for the disgrace these students were bearing because of a school principal's ugly bias. What lengths had this piriah gone to cover this up? Was his precious school reputation more important than the students' safety? Without appropriate recourse predators like Troy would never stop.

A tremor ran through my body; I crossed my arms trying to hold myself together. I remembered when I was a small child I broke my father's secret and admitted the incest to Mum. Within a second I regretted saying anything at all. She hit me over the head with the back of her wooden spoon and screamed at me that I was a liar.

Like Rose, some thirty years later I still didn't know where I stood. Drastically, Rose had admitted a teacher's dirty secret to the principal, and it gave him a great deal of power to put her in her place and infer shame upon her.

Rose's face became flushed and she walked away as if lifeless. Her arms clutched around her body to shield herself from the toxic masculinity she had no defence from.

I snuck back into the sleeping quarters. All I wanted to do was hide under the bunk. I held on to the bedrail to steady myself, my limbs were ready to collapse. Nothing felt real. Surely the principal had to do something about it when he got back to school.

I reached for my port and packed up my gear, a lump wedged solidly in my throat. This can't be the end of it; I was determined to raise the matter back at school.

1999 late summer
Far north high school

"Can you hear the women who came before me
five hundred thousand voices ringing through my
neck as if this were all a stage built for them"

rupi kaur[2]

Assembly was underway at school like every other Monday morning. Only it wasn't just another Monday, not after what happened at camp. The principal stood in his shaded lofty tower while the rest of us, apart from his deputies and senior leaders, fanned ourselves with work booklets and straw hats to fight off heat exhaustion in the boiling far north sun. The principal's chin was lowered and his arms crossed. He looked down at us as if holding students and teachers in contempt with his patriarchal privilege. His devil-blue eyes hovered above our headline to appear as if he had made eye contact, but I was sure he feigned empathy for our heat suffering and for his smug sense of self entitlement.

I watched him, finding it difficult to not scream in his face. My listening skills were at a wit's end, especially when it came to him.

"Bleat, blah and grunt," followed by a "whoop" for the football team coached by Mr Troy. My blood boiled, this was an institution of male dominance. With one last "whoop" we were dismissed for class.

My sense of injustice was boiling over, spurred on by the child abuse I suffered at the hands of my parents. I was resolved to speak up. Baring my teeth, I ascended the stairs to meet him as he was about to exit the courtyard. Masking my readiness to fight, I approached with a smile just in case he would act against Troy.

"Mr Luther, can I speak with you?"

He turned to me abruptly and scowled.

"What is it, I'm busy!"

I straightened the books I was holding and tried not to hesitate. I didn't want to give him the satisfaction of showing him how he intimidated me.

"I want to speak to you about Mr. Troy."

"What about him?"

"Rose spoke to you and told you that he abused her on camp. I can't see anything has been done to reprimand him?"

"That was dealt with at camp," he said and strutted off to his office, shutting his door in my face and all the women in the school. The sound of it slamming rang in my ears, reminding me of my childhood home. I never felt safe and protected as long as my father lived and now this principal had exactly the same effect on me.

The hollowness in my chest haunted me and my breathing was shallow. I shuffled back to my staffroom, readying myself as best I could. I opened the door, hoping my colleagues would be in class and I would have the room to myself. But when I walked in Annie was there. She stared at me with narrowed eyes.

"I heard you spoke to the principal about the school paedophile. Nothing has been done about this problem for years," she said with an understanding nod.

"Yes." I longed for Annie to come to my rescue. "The culture of silence has obviously been running rampant in this place!" I was emotionally drained but I had to do something and maybe Annie was an ally.

"I'm so proud of you for speaking up. No one has dared to. We were too afraid of retaliation."

"Well then, it seems I am the only one." I replied with an ache in my throat. "I can see why it's not safe to stand up against abuse in this school but if we do nothing then the problem is just going to get worse."

Annie looked down towards her feet, her cheeks were flushed.

"You will help," I continued.

"I—um," she shook her head with an apologetic look. "I can't afford to lose this job." She turned and washed her cup before replacing it in the cupboard. I stood there and watched in silence. She then slid past me and out the door.

The conversation went no further; asking for support from anyone was like beating my head against a brick wall.

It wasn't even the end of the day before I was rounded up and marched into Luther's office and told to quieten down or be fired.

It was just like when I was threatened with the most dreadful consequences if I told on my father as a child. He would be put in jail, I would be forever punished, and my mother would never speak to me again. The only difference was that I was an adult but otherwise nothing had changed.

CHAPTER 4

In the Beginning: The Dark Night of the Soul

2019 early summer
Ocean harbour home

"… I call, I cling, I want — and there is no One to answer —
no One to Whom I can cling — no, No One. — Alone…
Where is my Faith — even deep down right in there is nothing, but
emptiness & darkness — My God — How painful is this unknown
pain — I have no Faith — I dare not utter the words & thoughts
that crowd in my Heart — & make me suffer untold agony…
I am told God loves me — and yet the reality of darkness &
coldness & emptiness is so great that nothing touches my soul …"

Mother Teresa, the 'Saint of the Gutters', undated[1]

I awoke, stretching like a cat and tugging at the blinds to reveal a sun-flushed morning. The wind remained fair from my walk over to the rock pools the day before. Melodic riffs of butcher birds filled the sea air. They brought joy to my ears. I had no desire to be anywhere else but in my harbour home, listening to the calming sounds of nature that connected me to life. Today I would continue to write my story, no longer bound by crippling fear and guilt. I spun my legs out of bed, landing on both feet and high tailed it to my desk. I wasn't in the mood for coffee and cereal. Not just yet.

A *Time* magazine dated September 3, 2007, lay on my desk. It was the only magazine I brought with me from the far north. The rest of my collection was left behind; I had no use for those memories. But this one was different.

On the cover was Mother Teresa, the Saint of the Gutters. I read this article many times before. She had suffered a 50-year crisis of faith which started when she began tending to the poor and dying in Calcutta in 1946. I traced my fingers softly over her frail image. She was dressed in her signature blue-bordered sari which framed her hollow, tiny face and self-abnegating eyes. In this moment, it reminded me of my fractured self-image as an abused child, unable to develop moderate virtues and tolerable faults. I was to blame for the family problems. I was at fault even though deep down inside I knew I wasn't. The 'double think' was coming back to me, spinning me into a place of despair and terror. I took a deep breath and averted my eyes towards the magazine. I held it steady; my hands had ceased trembling like they once did.

It hit me, I too was faced with an existential task just as Mother Teresa all those years ago. I too felt as if I had been abandoned to a power without mercy, in my case it was my parents. Like her, I had to find a way to preserve hope and meaning in life when the utter despair of child abuse was too much to bear. The environment in which I grew up demanded complete conformity with my abusers.

I meticulously studied Mother Teresa's image for empathetic likenesses. The body-cloistering sari enclosed her wrinkled narrow face as she leaned into the camera, revealing an arid landscape which her deity had disappeared. Inspired by the inconsolable face that appeared before me, I reached for my iPhone camera and turned it on to selfie mode.

Tilting my face toward the camera, I fixated on my weathered skin. The lines on my face were deeply ingrained like that of an old oak tree. I raised my eyebrows to remove them but they persisted, revealing my own arid landscape of child abuse. Each line signified a trauma I suffered and clung to ostensibly because I was unable to object that something was terribly wrong with my family. I straightened my shoulders and gazed out the window at the gracious old she-oak speaking her *'shee'* sounds in the gentle wind. Beside it was a tree stump cut at near ground level, concentric black and white age-telling lines were revealed by its destruction. The dark lines grew in winter and the light lines in summer. It was an uncanny reminder of my childhood. The concentric rings of my past were my existential task to suffer the malice of my parents, while at the same time preserving my faith in them as if nothing was wrong. The incongruence tore me apart.

I gazed at the sawn-off tree trunk, then to my camera and then glanced sidelong at Mother Teresa's image. This time I was triggered by the sari, covering her cut-off hair that she had gifted to her God. One hand free from the camera, I stroked my long-tangled locks that I kept below shoulder length since I left my childhood home. After more than forty years I was unable to let go of the power they held over me to grow my own hair.

My grandad's words came to mind.

"Leave the poor girl alone. Don't cut it, she has beautiful hair. My sisters all had beautiful hair and grew it to their bottoms. It was their pride!"

But Grandad's words fell on deaf ears. My mum and grandmother hacked at my pretty blonde eight-year-old locks. One squished a bowl on my head for the basin cut, while the other exacted the scissors in corrupt delight.

"Sit still!" Snapped Mum as I wriggled to get out of it.

"Please don't cut it up to my ears!" I begged.

But I could not defend my identity that was carved by an environment of abuse.

Mother Teresa's eyes were still focused on me when I wrote the title of my story, *'Being My Own Witness'.*

As a child I had no place to hide. Sometimes I'd try to find solace when sitting in the old tree in the back garden. I would sit alone and daydream of a life with caring parents who didn't abuse me. But under my parent's roof my only way to survive was to believe it was my fault. I wasn't conscious of it back then but it was too terrifying to think it could be them. So unable to escape the unbearable reality of the abuse I altered it in my head, keeping it a secret even from myself.

I turned to the she-oak once more and vowed that I was now conscious of the malice and indifference to my suffering caused by them. Like Mother Teresa, I would voice the dark night of my soul. It was as if her eyes were telling me, it was time to seek spiritual solace by 'learning to speak out' by writing my own story.

I sat on the lounge after eating a late breakfast, my head filled with my writing from earlier that morning. The birds had gone quiet and the sea air was still. The words, 'witness and evidence' repeated in my mind like a ticking clock repeatedly returning to twelve. It reminded me of the court system that holds greater protection for an adult perpetrator than the child who accuses them. But I was fully conscious now, after years of suffering from periods of amnesia, a symptom of complex PTSD, that had blocked aspects of the abuse from me. I would be my own witness for the prosecution because I was no longer dependent on their care and obedient to their authority.

I reached for pen and paper and reclined on the lounge, glancing through the front window. In the mid-morning stillness I summoned a court scene from the recesses of my imagination. From my mind to paper, I wrote down the court testimony of my defence.

Since I was representing myself, I chose my own court and jury.

A satisfied grin spread across my face. Christine de Pizan would be the presiding judge and Sappho and her circle of women and men would be my jury. The *Time* magazine article covering Mother Teresa's 50-year crisis of faith would serve and support my testimony. I would let go of the magazine when I had reached a sense of peace.

I could already hear my opening statement.

"Thank you Your Honour! This case is about the abuse of myself, perpetrated first and foremost by my family and more broadly, by the patriarchy".

Judge Pizan: Why are you appearing as your own witness?

Me: When I was a child my parents and grandmother abused me. They tormented me and abandoned me in a dark place. I lost so much of my life and soul. Since no one admitted to the crime, I am the only one to testify for myself.

Judge Pizan: What is the purpose of the *Time* magazine article you present here today?

Me: To show Your Honour and the jury that the dark night of the soul is authentic suffering.

Judge Pizan: Are you saying that you suffered like that of Saint Teresa of Calcutta?

Me: The core of myself collapsed when I was a very small child. I had nowhere to go, I entered a dark place in my mind. This is not to be confused with depression, I aim to show that the collapse was a direct result of the abuse. I wish to point out that I have been carrying this burden my whole life. Mother Teresa in her own way experienced this dark place too. Her written story is evidence this condition exists.

Judge Pizan: How do you expect to come out of it?

Me: I have been lost and unsure of the direction in my life for too long to remember. I started to rally against violence last year, to enter a new consciousness and way of living.

Judge Pizan: How is that?

Me: I no longer wish to conform to what is expected of me in a patriarchal world that has no mercy.

Judge Pizan: And what is that?

Me: I realise that my fear-based childhood no longer has a hold over me. So now I wish to write my memoir since the repressed memories have resurfaced. This time I will not surrender to the silence, I will speak the truth about the abuse.

Judge Pizan: I understand that Mother Teresa's intentions to serve the poor have been 'questioned' by the auctors, that is, male writers.

Me: That is true Your Honour. In 1994 a British writer named Hitchens and the Pakistani-British journalist, Tariq Ali, wrote a critical documentary on Teresa titled: Hell's Angel. In one part, they compared the conditions of her Missionaries of Charity in Kolkata to a Nazi concentration camp, along with a catalogue of criticisms. There were other critics too—

Judge Pizan: That will be enough. They are further examples of the sacred female narrative being framed by male-centred narratives. Teresa was no woman to be picked like a rose from her own fortress.

Me: Yes, Your Honour. This is my plea too.

Judge Pizan: This court will be adjourned. You will next appear before me when you finish writing your book supported by evidence collected to support your case. I will conclude today's hearing that you are finding your voice and will write your story.

After starting my account of the court case I arrived at an impasse. The wound of my childhood ran so deep; it was a crippling force that I needed to address from the beginning. The injustice of the abuse was enormous and my emotional shield of staying silent was about to be surrendered in the name of writing my truth.

I took a deep breath and armed with my pen, I wrote: *"In the beginning, the dark night of the soul."*

1962 summer
Elster

My first memory of my existence in this world was paradisiacal. It was a warm spring morning and I was sitting on my tricycle under the peach blossom tree. I rocked myself gently from side to side and gazed into the wondrous blue sky, sparsely furnished with soft white clouds. They were like the cotton balls on my baby blanket. The breeze brushed the tree branches and leaves. The warm spring sun sprinkled golden flecks upon the skin on my cherub arms, as if God was watching over me and procuring the light of the day. My mother's voice hummed in the spring air. It drifted across the fragrance of jasmine and filled me with a sense of peace. Then I remember she was chatting to our next door neighbour over our white picket fence outside our bungalow-style home in Robert Street, Glen Eira. In this moment, I existed. I belonged here. My heart was filled with wonder and love.

This was the last childhood memory without conflict or pain.

Thinking back on it now, no one would have suspected what was about to happen behind closed doors. My father was the head of the family, and my mother and older brother by thirteen months lived with me. It was 1958 and the city of Melbourne was rapidly growing as nuclear families spilled into the suburbs such as ours. Mum and Dad were a young married couple. Mum was nineteen when my brother was born and twenty-one when I was born.

My grandparents lived nearby in Wicklow. They had lived in the inner-city suburb of Yarra once upon a time, which was full of Irish-Catholic families, some the descendants of colonial immigrants and perhaps a convict or two. As post-war European migrants arrived in large numbers to Melbourne city people began to shift to the outer suburbs for affordable housing. That way, everyone had a chance to live 'the great Australian dream' and own their own home. Dad graduated as a police officer and we had a steady income. With a new baby on the way, we shifted to a three-bedroom brick veneer home in the suburb of Elster.

My second childhood memory was one of fear. My life went from living in paradise to living in hell. My older brother and I shared the back bedroom, closest to the back door and side entrance where Dad used to come in after parking his car in the garage most nights. We had separate single beds; mine was closer to the window and some nights the moonlight filtered into our room and cast shadows upon the walls and ceiling. On this night, I sensed something terrible was going to happen. I couldn't explain it, but the stillness in the room screamed inside my mind like a wild animal that had been let loose. The shadows in the moonlight played a vicarious game with my eyes; I thought I was being stalked by a demon.

"Can I sleep with you?" I begged my brother.

"Okay but don't move, I want to go to sleep."

We faced the wall to avoid the moonlight glow in our eyes. We settled in platonic security but for me that was short-lived.

I listened to the silence of the night. The air was warm and the humidity was thick. It lay like a wet sponge in the atmosphere and soaked up all living things. No sound could be heard, not even a night bird, until his car came up the road. The engine groaned like a monster stalking its prey.

The car droned into the driveway. Mum left the low, wrought-iron gate open for him so he didn't have to stop to open the gates. He pulled up in front of the wooden gate which sealed off the backyard from intruders and turned the engine off. I laid there motionless; my sweaty little palms holding the sheets. He was drunk, too drunk to park the car in the garage out back. My heart raced when I heard his first clodhopper footstep on the concrete driveway. I prayed he would go in the front door and sleep it off with Mum, in their bed.

The latch of the gate lifted in the still night, it sounded like a knife cutting the throat of an innocent bird. I hoped Mum heard him enter and waylaid him to their bedroom, but she didn't. She found herself enveloped in a chilling metaphorical snow, gradually vanishing into her personal abyss of darkness.

He dragged and slopped his copper boots along the path as he made his way to the back door. There was a pause which magnified the silence; it must have been witching hour. The veil of the night had become thin and his ghostly presence lurked outside my bedroom. It was unbearable. He must have stopped to urinate in the garden, as vulgar drunks do, and then his boots scraped the earth in an evil regime. He opened the back door and staggered into the sunroom. He still had time to go to his own bedroom through the kitchen door.

After another lapse in time, I felt his presence looming outside my bedroom door, his lips smacked with saliva. I ever so slightly raised my left eyelid to confirm my suspicion. Sure enough, his silhouette stood in the doorway, he was an overwhelming menacing figure.

"I'm going to give you a talk about the birds and the bees," he sniggered.

I hated him when he was drunk. Why couldn't he teach me my place in the world in broad daylight and when he was sober?

He grovelled his way to our bed and threw back the sheets. Lifting me out of my brother's bed, he placed me on top of my own bed. I was reeling from the stench of putrid alcohol on his breath. I tried to play dead, hoping he'd leave me alone but the knots in my stomach told me I had experienced this before. My mind must have blocked it out. My brother didn't flinch; he kept out of the way. I wished he spoke up and said, "leave her alone". I wished Mum had come to my rescue but that didn't happen either.

"Don't you know little girls shouldn't sleep with little boys?" he said slobbering his filth all over me.

I didn't have a clue what he was talking about as he pulled my pyjama shorts down and pushed me on the bed. He was kneeling on the bed, having already stripped himself down to his singlet and underpants. He began to rub himself between my legs, holding them by the ankles and hung me upside down like a piece of meat in the butcher's shop.

"This is what happens to little girls," he slobbered as he grinded his hard body into me for his own amusement. In the wildness of the shadows on the wall, I glimpsed my brother watching silently from under the blankets.

Afterwards he gathered his police uniform from the floor and the man who called himself my father skulked away, leaving me completely empty. I grabbed my clothes and slipped under my sheets. I don't know how long it took before I dozed off, exhausted from the grown-up things he shouldn't have been doing to me. I was his own daughter – his flesh and blood.

The next morning there were murmurings in the house.

"Mum, Dad came into our bedroom last night and was doing things to sissy," I overheard my brother telling Mum.

Mum went lock, stock and barrel on the rampage. She burst into my bedroom as I was dressing for school to confront me.

"Is it true? Did your father do things to you last night? Was he in your bed?"

I was speechless, my brain couldn't process the questions.

She grabbed me by the hand and dragged me through the house and down to their bedroom where the coward was lying on their white linen sheets. The sheets were partly pulled back to relieve him of the morning heat but certainly not to relieve him of his guilt. His eyes were closed, pretending to be asleep.

I was terrified of Mum, she was furious. Her questions weren't calm like Perry Mason on the television show; he was generally friendly and patient in his investigative interviews. Mum was flustered and her questions were all over the place; focused on minute details out of sequence. I didn't know what Dad had between his legs. She asked me if he put something, she gestured dramatically with her hands, between my legs in my private parts and then she pointed to my vagina. I only knew that I did wee-wee from there.

My father casually propped himself up on one elbow and acted dumbfounded at the proceedings. In no way were Mum's questions appropriate, they were never going to elicit the truth.

"Did he touch you down there?" she screamed. "What did he put down there?" She fired multi-faceted, closed questions and I could only counter them with a child's faculties and recollections. I dared not to fall into error with my mum.

"It felt like a paper ruler," I whispered.

"What do you mean?" She was red in the face, shaking my arm to bits.

"It was hard like a school ruler," I said louder.

My response infuriated her even more.

Glaring at my father she yelled, "How does this child know about these things?"

"I don't know what she is talking about." His rattlesnake eyes popped almost out of his head.

My heart sank so low I was sure it would sink through the floor. He was my dad. He should have stuck up for me and admitted the truth. Now Mum would hate me forever.

Mum took his side and glared back at me.

"I must agree with your father. The whole story sounds made up. You must be lying."

I was devastated that she blamed me for it. From that day forward, I was known as the troublemaker in the family.

2020 summer
Ocean harbour home

My father had forever deserted me, leaving me only memories which set an eternal barrier between me and my fellow creatures … [His] unlawful and detestable passion had poured its poison into my ears, and changed my blood, so that it was no longer the kindly stream that supports life but a cold fountain of bitterness corrupted in its very source. It must be the excess of madness that could make me imagine thatI could ever be aught but one alone: struck off from humanity: bearing no affinity to man or woman; a wretch on whom Nature had set her ban.

Mary Shelley from *Mathilda*, 1819[2]

There was still enough daylight for a walk. I approached the end of the beach track and my steps became uneven, causing me to sit on the sand dunes. Dredging up the history of my child abuse had brought me to think deeply about how it led me here. To this day I felt betrayal that rocked me to the very core. My father never admitted his abuse and my mother's alienation still haunts me. The parental abandonment was very real. It was not visible to the public but it happened in private behind closed doors.

I raised my heavy head to the sky and prayed in my heart that one day I would be able to forgive them. But all I could find were more reasons to hate them. I understood how the patriarchy, through sheer force and entitlement of men, can nullify the roles of mothers, wives and daughters but still, how could parents harm their child so completely?

The wind was light, creating a sense of peace in the morning. It drifted across the ocean and flicked sun-bleached strands of hair about my face. I pulled my polaroids closer and traced the coastline with my watery eyes until they rested on Old Woman Island, two kilometres out to sea. Aboriginal legends were well-known to locals in honour of our Indigenous people. I had been told that one version of the story was that the island came into being from an epic battle between two men, Coolum and Ninderry over a woman called Maroochy. Coolum's head was knocked off and ended up in the ocean where the island lies today.

I turned and focused inland to the flat top of Mount Coolum, over-lording the coastline like a dominant father, reminding me of my father.

The other legend had it that two women made a home on the island where there were *midyim* berry bushes. When one of the women could be seen on the island it became known as Old Woman Island. *In the beginning, the dark night of the soul* left me as the old woman marooned on the island. I was the outsider, socially isolated, shamed and put in my place. I attempted to become an independent woman without the guidance of a mother. She was the other woman who left the island, who left me for her husband wanting him to herself. Their minds degraded by countless Lolitas appearing in literature and media that I was to blame, I was the wanton daughter. Weaving my hands through my unruly hair, I pushed my shoulders back and stood upright. I no longer wanted to be the little girl abandoned by her parents. Now, I aspired to be the adult woman, conscious and able to determine my own life.

I walked back home, thinking of Rose who was abused at the high school camp. Then, I was a teacher trying to be the adult who spoke out against abuse to protect her. I wanted to be different from my mother who supported the perpetrator and then vanished from my life. She reappeared in the role of my judge, under which I collapsed under the pressure of interrogation, bullying, insults and humiliation.. When Rose told me her secret, I was overwhelmed with the trauma she must have been feeling. I treated her complaint with respect, knowing all too well how destructive it was to not take her seriously.

The call of the warning birds sounded in the distance. They reiterated my sense of being an advocate for child abuse, but this was a sound that the school principal and those he governed were not in tune with.

CHAPTER 5

Grandmother: Too Much Information

1999 autumn
Far north high school

"But there are those who see no colour, who will
not feel the beauty of this land – who wish only
to destroy the mother and themselves."

Oodgeroo Noonuccal (1920-1993), formerly Kath Walker,
and Kabul Oodgeroo Noonuccal (1953-1991)[1]

It was the beginning of second term and that meant a change of curriculum. The staffroom was a hive of industry; pens clicking, books shuffling and voices waffling off key words unheard the previous term. I entered the room and nodded to Annie when she glanced in my direction. Before I could ask about the holidays, she darted to the preparation tasks on her desk pretending to be too busy to talk to me. I took a deep breath, was I being too sensitive?

I turned to see her back, obviously avoiding conversation with me. I knew it was because of Troy. The principal ran a smooth ship and leaks to newspapers about school paedophiles were forbidden. I thought about going to the press but since Rose's parents were not pursuing the case it wasn't my place to go over their heads. It was no good pulling anyone else into this battle against child abuse so the issue was swept under the carpet.

I left the staffroom and strode past reception towards my classroom.

"We are introducing a new unit to the Year Ten English syllabus," the head of department uttered as I walked past. "Social issues."

I narrowed my eyes and turned to her. This was a deviation from the study of English literature leaning more on sociology. It was outside the scope of teacher training but education policymakers introduced it anyway.

"I don't think so," I muttered under my breath. It would damage young minds when professionals confronted topics with the same kind of avoidance as my mother confronted the incest. I unfolded my arms, trying to remain open to the idea.

"What issues will it be covering?"

"Sensitive topics such as rape, abortion and homelessness are some of them," she replied and then switched the conversation to Grade Twelve novel studies.

It was the first day back and already my stomach was churning. I thought of my grandmother telling stories when I was a child of her abortion, performed illegally in a backyard. I would hide behind my jumper, pulled over my face when she spoke. Her face was expressionless as if her life had been drained from her. The experience left her at the wailing wall of life. My dad was her only pride and joy. She joined my mother and would not tolerate my accusations of incest. Deep heaviness set into my bones as if I was listening to her all over again. I studied the course notes, resolved to be the adult in this institution and guide my students through this unit without letting my feelings of betrayal, trauma and abandonment overwhelm me.

I stood at the lectern, a newspaper article on the topic of abortion was screened on the overhead projector. My Grade Ten students sat stiffly at their desks, each with hands, knees and feet locked in a straight line. Their eyes were fixed firmly on mine. They were solemn about the content and relied on me to guide them through it. Abortion had not been decriminalised in Australia and several *Right to Life* groups opposed it. My students were confronted with a situation in which a person was torn between right and wrong.

Amanda's hand went up.

"So, what you're saying Miss, is that the explanation women often give for seeking an abortion is that the pregnancy was unplanned or unwanted?"

"Yes, if an abortion was performed in the reasonable belief that it was necessary to protect the woman's physical or mental wellbeing, then it was lawful." I was reading from the McGuire case which had been upheld by the Supreme Court of Queensland in 1986.[2]

"What kinds of beliefs were they Miss?"

"Lack of support from the father, poverty, relationship problems or the perception that she was too young—"

Amanda burst into tears. She sat in the middle row; her wide eyes had not left mine. Her cheeks blushed hot pink as she reached out to take a tissue from her classmate, Peta.

I stood there, unsure of the best course of action. The last thing I wanted to do was humiliate her.

"Are you okay, Amanda? Would you like some time out and we can have a chat after class?"

"No, I really need to tell someone. Everyone in the class is my friend. My uncle raped me when I was thirteen and this stuff has brought up the memory. I've never told anyone."

She broke down and sobbed into her hands.

The class was silent. I felt they wanted to hold her and tell her she would be okay and that her uncle should be castrated. This was exactly what I was afraid of. There are too many children who are vulnerable and have been subjected to abuse. The school setting was not appropriate for this information. They were too young to know how to protect themselves with healthy boundaries. I wasn't about to brush her off like I had seen too often in the school system. I referred her to the guidance officer and followed up on it the next day but inside I was furious at the ignorance of the school system.

Amanda came to see me when I was alone in the classroom. The midday sun bore down on us through the windows.

"I've seen the guidance officer," she said, "but I decided I won't pursue the matter." She looked awkward standing there in the middle of the room. "He's my mother's brother and I don't want to hurt her. He's left the area so it's best not to think about it anymore."

I nodded, trying to remind myself I had done the best thing I could for her, but this wasn't my decision to make. It was a good thing she wasn't pregnant or else she would be faced with the further moral dilemma of an abortion and after that class she was fully aware of it.

I smiled kindly to Amanda rather than make some clumsy attempt to comfort her any further. The matter had been resolved between her mother and herself. She turned and left the classroom, head held low. I attempted to continue my preparations for the next class but my hand ached from holding a piece of chalk too tight. I stopped it from scratching on the board. If only my mother had believed me and sent my father away like Amanda's mum sent her brother away. That would have been better than living each day tortured as a child.

With a heavy heart, I set the daily tasks and moved the class on to their new issue, homelessness.

1962 late summer
Elster

"Your silence exists as does my self gathering ..."

Luce Irigaray[3]

There was a familiar knock on the door of my parent's house. It was my grandmother's knock. I knew it was her by its obstinate hard-knuckled insistence. She was convinced my family couldn't live without her.

Clutching my hand-me-down jumper to my chest, I wanted to hide and disappear from her presence. So I huddled in the corner of my room, knees held tight to my chest.

Mum answered the door.

"Come on in," Mum said, her voice breaking into sobs.

"What's wrong?" Grandmother was onto her.

I heard their footsteps enter the kitchen. My mouth was dry from swallowing too much. The kettle whirled while Grandmother wheeled her two-wheel shopping stroller in the door. I knew she would be huddling an ugly, black handbag which bulged with cash, a rude, dark-red lipstick, a face powder compact and mirror which had belonged to Snow White's stepmother, *Viscount* cigarettes and a gas lighter. Inside would be her stash of bizarre looking liquorice all-sorts or other candy that she kept to herself or shared with my mum and brother, ensuring I was left out. I used to stare at her shopping trolley and imagined it as some grotesque object wheeled by the ferrywoman of the grim reaper. It held a dark and terrifying scythe and she was ordered to collect my soul for the grave. She was an agent of the devil.

"You're upset. What's going on?" Grandmother's voice sounded with entitlement, she had to know everything that happened in our house.

"She accused him of touching her up in bed last night." Mum couldn't hold it in. She was gasping like a cut snake that had almost shed its skin.

My fingers and toes went cold. I stopped myself from rocking so they wouldn't hear me eavesdropping.

"That girl is nothing but trouble. She suffers from the imagination. We cannot allow anything to get out to the neighbours!" Grandmother snapped immediately.

She was so grave I could feel the black shroud envelope the house. I would be cursed forever more, – spurned from my family and myself.

"We must keep her quiet! If word gets out about this he will lose his police job. He could go to jail. And all based on a child's lies."

"I don't know how to handle this," sobbed Mum. "She is nothing but a homewrecker, bringing shame on this family."

"There, there," Grandmother consoled her, lulling Mum to her side to ostracise me. "We will beat it out of her. She's not to be trusted."

Mum replied with an animal-like groan.

I squeezed my eyes shut, afraid of what was to come. I bolted out the door and fled the house unnoticed by them. With rasping breaths, I climbed the apple tree in the backyard and sat on the highest branch, crying. I grabbed onto a crisp apple, my only consolation apart from not standing before my awful grandmother's bulging glare. For now, anyway. I cringed to think about the revenge she would take out on me. She was already bitter with her life and now my mother told her the secret that made me the perfect target to take out her frustrations. The sweet juice of the apple helped my brain from shutting down.

I could think of nothing nice about my grandmother that gave me comfort. Her stories were vengeful and she didn't like anyone in her past.

"My little girl died in my arms when she was one day old," my grandmother groaned as she dwelled on the 'death rattle' of her baby girl. She would extend the anticipation by stalling for a second or two and then suddenly imitate the sound of the last breath of life with throaty chokes. It was as if she owned death. My legs would go weak and I tried not to look at her. She would stare at me with her boom-gate eyes when she made the croaking, death noises as if casting a spell for it to happen to me. I was terrified of her.

I fell backwards in the tree and clutched a jagged branch with one hand, launching myself upright into my curled-up position. My hand was bleeding. I pressed my other fist to my lips so as not to shout out in pain. The pain took me to the edge of my wits. I imagined my grandmother sending men after me with knitting needles and rusty coat hangers to stab me to death like the unborn baby from her story.

"They were butchers. They killed my baby and ruined me." Her lungs were half full, unforgiving of these bad people. I overheard her telling Mum the story one day. I could hardly comprehend what she was saying. How could a human being do this sort of thing to another human being?

"It was done in a back yard joint. I paid them twenty quid. I had no choice—" Her trembling voice drifted into the silence.

I clapped my hands to my ears to block out her nightmare stories but soon they called me inside to punish me for lying about my father.

2019 autumn
Ocean harbour home

"Our western culture cuts us off from our natural roots,
instead of contributing toward the cultivation of the natural
beings we are. This tradition, has, in this way, rendered us
extraneous to our environment, extraneous to one another
as living beings and even extraneous to ourselves."

Luce Irigaray[4]

Adhering to a daily routine of writing my childhood memories took its toll on me. Today, I felt tired and began to wonder if revealing my story would allow others to use the information against me. Held prisoner by my memories, my writing came to a standstill.

I didn't intend to develop tunnel vision but always being on guard, dredging up my past had brought up the trauma all over again. I needed to slow down to gain more insight and find the right words. When I waved both hands out in front of my computer screen, I could only focus on one thing – my broken and chewed down fingernails. They never recovered from my childhood trauma. I had always been embarrassed by them, they were a telltale sign of the abuse that no one took notice of. The emotional wounds and physical attacks brewed on my fingertips and spread beneath my skin. I couldn't escape them, they were too close to the surface but I didn't want to bury them so much that I could never heal. I was not beyond repair. Picking up my partially written manuscript, I held it to my chest and reminded myself of the good my writing could bring to the world.

I placed freshly picked sun-golden frangipani flowers on my desk to create a sense of calm. The television hummed in the background. I could hear news of the Women's March and went to the lounge room to turn up the volume. I was heartened to find a man, the Leader of the Opposition, Anthony Albanese, speaking out for women's rights, even if for votes. Prime Minister, Scott Morrison, had not met the women on the grounds outside Parliament House and Albanese took the opportunity to slam him.

"They said enough is enough," Albanese said, "And what I saw outside was passionate women who are angry. They are angry about what has happened to them, what has happened to their mothers, their grandmothers, their sisters, their daughters and their granddaughters."[5]

Watching the Opposition Leader, I was inspired to write again. I began by tracing what went wrong with my female lineage, beginning with my grandmother.

The heat of anger surged through my chest. From the distant past, my grandmother's out-of-one's-mind voice came back to me. She was recounting her backyard abortion with grotesque images of her body – her vagina and uterus being stabbed, scraped and poked. She uttered in hushed and secretive tones and jabbed in all directions as finger-painted penis-knives penetrated vaginas in the air. My parents said behind her back she was going mad in her old age, although it didn't stop them being persuaded by her to abuse me.

The feminist philosopher Luce Irigaray wrote:

> *"Each sex has a relation to madness. Every desire has a relation to madness. But it would seem that one desire has been taken as wisdom, moderation, truth, leaving to the other sex the weight of a madness that cannot be acknowledged or accommodated."*[6]

I discovered reason as an adult from Irigaray's work but as a child I was on my own. My academic self realised my grandmother and her unwanted baby were butchered by this backyard operator in a patriarchal world where only women and unborn foetuses could suffer this fate. As a child, all I longed for was to be loved by my grandmother but the abortion took a grave toll on her. Little did I know back then of the power and corruption of a political system run by men. Men controlled women's decisions about their own bodies and consequently there was an absence of the female perspective. The only way for my grandmother to become a legitimate person was to assimilate to male subjectivity, hence her pitiful devotion to her abusive paedophile son and her sadistic pleasure to beat me into submission. Consequently, I was subjected to rape and torture by those who were supposed to care. It left me with absolutely no guidance in the world. I was lost. Without their support, my faith in life was crushed.

Now, I was buoyed by the women's movement. The sounds of their voices, through gritted teeth, infused hope into my life. I was ready to bounce back and stand up for myself. I felt grounded again, supported by the feminists to fight the burden of toxic masculinity and get myself back on my feet.

That night I had a dream, undoubtedly influenced by my writings.

I was a child. The gag over my mouth was so tight that my veins popped a vulgar red. A tsunami was passing through me. Timbers snapped. Glass shattered from ruined buildings. I yanked off the gag for air and screamed. Rotten debris slapped me from side to side.

Despair.

I was drowning in waste. I gasped. I bellowed for air before being swept away. Unstoppable.

With each breath came a nightmare. A beating. A shaming. I screamed for help but no one heard me. I went under again. I was drowning in the deep and unforgiving water.

My heartbeat was arrhythmic. Dodging death. I choked. Breath escaped me. Please!

One more gasp. Please listen to me!

Someone!

I forgive Mother now that she was divorcing Father. But there was still danger! His new wife has two daughters. I won't have it! He can't just move on scot-free! He should be held to account. People had to listen to my story.

A burst of water wrenched me from the tsunami and lobbed me in a room full of women and children. He was there, bigger than all of us combined. I shared my story with his new daughters and told them of his sexual abuse. They held seashells to their ears, unconscious of me.

"Put the seashells away. Listen to me! Don't trust him!" His traffic officer eyes were fixed on them. "He will do the same to you!"

Mum came around to my side of the story. We moved into a new place with a fence around it to keep him out. And the tsunami. I didn't want to say he would still come for her. And me.

My heart and soul craved for my mother. We hugged. I begged her that together we could bring him to justice.

"I'm writing a book, Mum. I'm a woman writing for myself. I am returning to the body which was confiscated from me. I have found higher ground."

Mum's head bopped up and down. A fake mink shawl hung dripping wet from her frail body and its dead animal head hung limp on her breast. She too wanted him brought to justice for his violence and abuse.

"Did you hear him last night? He held me down and punched me! Didn't you hear the blows from your room?" Her ethereal voice was ushered by her ghost. She disappeared. Again, I was alone.

I woke with a start. My jaw ached from clenching my teeth. I pulled the bedcover back from the floor where it was tossed in midst of the nightmare. I rubbed the middle of my forehead, my tangled locks were damp. I had been sweating. I shivered lightly, caught off guard by my dream.

I glanced around my bedroom in amongst the shadows; I had faced the danger and made a tough decision. I was writing this book to reclaim myself.

I would awaken my inner power to heal myself, my mother and other abused women.

In those early hours of the morning, before the sun rose, I shrugged off the bedcover and my fears. I resolved in myself more than ever, to tell my story and influence change.

The sweet-smelling scent of the frangipani drifted across the room, feeding my inspiration to write.

CHAPTER 6

God is Dead

1999 winter
Far north high school

> *"A tearless mother, bowing down*
> *Prayed to her for her blind son*
> *And a voiceless hysteric thrashed about*
> *Lapping about for air on the run.*
> *And he who arrived from the South,*
> *A hunchbacked old man with dark eyes,*
> *Clutched the wall of the stairway, worn out,*
> *Like the door into paradise."*

Anna Akhmatova from *Autumn, 1913*[1]

It was my spare period and I spent my precious time in the staffroom preparing lessons for my Year 10 English class. I scuffed my chair closer to the desk and reached for the student textbook, thumbing the pages until I arrived at the *Poetry* unit. I smiled to myself, pleased to be teaching my topic of passion.

Over the other side of the staffroom, Annie was stacking her books a little too roughly. The books came down around her with a thud.

"Damn," she swore under her breath.

I looked up towards her.

"Do you mind if I borrow that teacher reference book?" I pointed to one of the many books at her feet.

She squinted at me.

"I only need it for five minutes," I said in a friendly tone.

"Okay, but I need it back before class." The sharpness of her tone implied, 'get your own and don't bother me'.

I stood up and grabbed the book before clambering to my desk to be sure to hurry up and give it back. The last thing I wanted was someone obsessing over every detail I did wrong. She started to remind me of my parents, controlling and critical. Quickly, I returned her book and concentrated on the preparation lessons.

Students would select a poem or song of their choice and analyse the poet's purpose for writing it. I scanned the question on the page in front of me: 'What message did the poet convey to the reader? Did the themes, favoured by the poet, challenge the dominant cultural, societal and political systems of their times and give voice to those who lived in fear?'

I thought the best way to ease them into the unit was to set up a trolley of poetry books in the library so they could spend a couple of lessons searching for a poem or song they may connect with. The librarian was happy to help and we spent two lunch breaks scouring the shelves for poetry books, carefully stacking them on an overloaded trolley. I immersed myself in the *Poetry* unit. My love for poetry had given me personal insights into the human condition. I hoped my students would gain from the study too as they did from *The Social Issues* unit. It had raised their awareness of the essentials of human existence including birth, emotion, conflict and mortality.

I waited at the library entrance, standing tall in readiness for my students. Some met me with crossed arms and the usual objections.

"I hate poetry, Miss! Do we have to?"

"It's not as bad as you think. Give it a try." I cajoled.

Once I got them through the language barriers of metaphor, simile, alliteration, visual imagery and more, they would be fine.

"Leave your bags outside. The books are on the trolley in Section B. Please come to me with any questions."

I left them and found a library space to set up my pens and teacher diary. I always kept my diary close to me, the front cover bound in a euphoric painting of Joan of Arc praying to her God. I was connected to the weighted feeling of the pre-Raphaelite artist Dante Gabriel Rosetti who painted it on his death bed.

I then turned my attention to my students, watching them flocked around the trolley and eagerly reading the titles. One by one, each student took their poem to a quiet reading space. One or two hesitated to select a book, preferring to sit in a library chair and obstinately repeat they 'hated' poetry. For these students it was best to suggest they choose a popular song, lyrics which spoke to them that only their generation could understand.

From the corner of my eye, I saw the principal mount the library stairs and walk through my class scowling at the students who lounged and read their books.

"What I would give to be an English teacher!" he sneered as he passed by. His devil-blue eyes destroyed the calm atmosphere. His background was manual arts; everything about him was man-made without emotion. Ever since the camping episode with Mr. Troy, Luther micromanaged me. I'm sure his file on me would soon say:

"Not in her classroom, found in the library, sitting around doing nothing, not engaged with her students—"

His mission was to destroy me as a schoolteacher and to destroy my passion for raising awareness of social injustice and human rights through the study of literature. The only way forward was to 'block out' his accusation that I was the school 'whistle-blower'. But the heaviness in my chest didn't let me forget he was just like my mother who had accused me of being the family troublemaker.

I collected the class, bunched in small groups in hideaway corners or at the book scattered round tables.

We made our way to the classroom like a gaggle of geese, trying to keep the noise to an acceptable level. Even the reluctant ones seemed happy with their exploration of poetry and popular songs. I should have been energised with the success of giving my students the gift of poetic appreciation but instead, my limbs ached with exhaustion from my brief encounter with Luther and the memories he triggered.

Back in the classroom, I allowed the students to sit wherever they were comfortable. Seating plans were useless and it was best they were responsible for their own choices. After all, most of them were fifteen and on the verge of adulthood. So it was important to me to provide them with a learning environment that encouraged them to make positive choices that shape their identity. It was unlike the family pressures I faced when I was fifteen which completely overrode my choices for healthy self-determination.

Without an inch of judgement for my students, I wandered through the rows of tables.

Sam did not like poetry but he had chosen a song from a popular album by Steve Vai, *Sex and Religion*.

"I like this song, Miss; I reckon I can do my essay on this."

"Okay Sam, what can you tell me about it now?"

"Well, the words are very powerful. Steve Vai thinks that two people find God when they are together, you know, in an intimate relationship. It says here 'it was the divine act of love whereas at the opposite end of the spectrum you get the perversion of lust'."[2]

Sam stopped reading from the article he had researched and looked up at me.

My heart became shrouded in my inner most thoughts. Sam was speaking about my father. My father had stooped so low to perversion and lust with his own daughter. I consciously forced my eyes to appear interested in Sam's words, disguising the deep buried disgust at my father.

"Keep going," I urged Sam.

"It was the same thing with religion because love was at its centre but when people and their egos get involved, it gets perverted." His voice was filled with respect for his idol songwriter.

"The 18th century philosopher, Friedrich Nietzsche was saying a similar thing," I replied, facilitating his historical inquiry. "Does this make sense?" Perhaps the themes were too troubling for a fifteen-year-old soul?

"It's fine, Miss, I really want to do this. I'm going to investigate this Nietzsche fella too. He was on to something."

I watched the teenage boy sitting there in my classroom. His blonde mop of hair was strung over his head and shoulders. He leaned intensely into the song verses and their philosophical underpinnings.

"Miss, what did Nietzsche mean when he said God is dead?"

How had Nietzsche begun his journey only to come up with the declaration: "God is dead." He had been misinterpreted by numerous critics as an atheist but his statement had reflected a more subtle understanding of God. "From my understanding, God had served people for over one thousand years and suddenly society grew secular. People stopped believing in God. He was alarmed by this because Christianity and its moral values had safeguarded people."

"What happened when people stopped believing in God?"

The rest of the class glanced up from their books to listen to Sam and myself.

"Once they stopped believing they reverted to the despair of nothingness. It's called nihilism, you can look it up." I wanted him to look beyond what was generally accepted.

Sam ran his hands through his long hair, pushing it aside from his face. His eyes looked away from me deep in thought. There was much for him to think critically about Vai's *Sex and Religion*.

Abbey too approached me, holding a copy of *Requiem* by Anna Akhmatova about the suffering of people under the Great Terror in the Soviet Union 1918-1921. She tilted her body toward me and tugged at her non-regulation hot pink knee-high socks, she was already rebelling against authority. I encouraged her, telling her she had the potential to create alternative visions of society and influence people.

"Miss, did you know that she wrote these poems in secret and in fear of being assassinated for speaking out against the regime and its purges?" She hesitated before speaking, apparently weighing up the gravity of Akhmatova's writing.

"I am aware of her work, Abbey. She was very brave to conceal her poems from the Soviets. She committed them to memory and the whole book was not published until much later, around 1987." Akhmatova was one of my favourite poets but I didn't want to influence Abbey too much, she needed to make the inquiry for herself. I was pleased that Abbey had chosen Akhmatova who had given voice to people who otherwise would not have been heard. "Is this the poet you would like to study, Abbey?"

"Yes Miss, I find her incredibly interesting. I never knew such things happened and I want to find out more," she said, appearing eager that she had discovered this courageous female poet. "The book says she waited for months outside Leningrad Prison, along with many other women, for just a glimpse of fathers, brothers or sons who had been taken away by the Soviet guards. She was worried for her son who had been taken." Abbey laid one hand over her heart.

I wanted to stretch Abbey as well, to dig deeper and investigate Anna's motivations for writing. My mind went to Anna standing outside the Leningrad Prison where her son was imprisoned, and how she praised the Stalin regime: the regime she had staunchly and secretly resisted. I knew that feeling of not speaking out against authority when all the while they were violating human rights.

There was the familiar sound of shuffling books, stretching out legs and enthusiastic zipping of pencil cases. The bell rang and my students left the classroom smiling at me while engaged in chatter and telling jokes. I watched them walk across the quadrangle and pressed my palms against each other. I prayed for them to be safe from people and institutions who would take advantage of them.

2019 early winter
Ocean harbour home

"You need a big god …. Sometimes I think it's getting better
And then it gets much worse …. Jesus Christ it hurts."

Florence + the Machine from *Big God*, 2018[3]

The sun-golden frangipanis stood tall in the handmade clay vase watching over me writing my story. I was love struck by their delicate petals and tropical scent that I rearranged them, each flower leaning on another like an eternal love song.

The sound of the ocean was close by, salt air wafted through my window. I felt myself flowing back in time on the hush sweeps of the swirling foam on the outgoing tide. Slowly, I flipped through a small pile of teaching memorabilia and came across my high schoolteacher's diary. There, she was glued to the cover – my arch angel, Joan of Arc who protected me on my teaching post from my adversary, the devil principal Luther. I released a sigh and my thoughts returned to teaching poetry and my Grade Ten class. I recalled Sam with his mop of blonde hair, studying Nietzsche and Abbey in her hot pink socks, taking responsibility for Anna Akhmatova and future generations to spur action for unheard voices.

Gently, I traced my frail fingernails over Joan of Arc's exquisite face praying to God. I found myself replaying the events when my grandmother visited in my childhood. Inevitably, thoughts of her left me rocking in my seat but I was going to write my story and have my child's voice heard. I lit my mandarin and rosewood candle to calm my anxiety. Its flame swayed in the ocean breeze and my breath fell into line with its rhythm. I remembered praying in secret on our front porch like a beggar child. I had lived a childhood of violated moral codes and prayed to Jesus to save me, in his purest form, to hear me.

"Dear Jesus, don't let my brutal and crazed grandmother beat me today!" My bare knees dug into the floorboards.

She would go to any lengths to save her son from going to prison. That meant every Saturday giving me a hiding with a thick leather belt to keep me silent. I wished that she had been noble like Anna Akhmatova, but they were worlds apart. I had to live with that.

Maintaining eye contact with my computer screen, my warrior fingers thrashed out words. It was time to lay blame on my grandmother for destroying my childhood. The wave of the unhurried candle flame relaxed my overburdened mind as I replayed the past.

I relived the moments in which I prayed on the front porch with my bare knees pressed firmly together, in touch with the earthen timber that felt like a conductor to heaven. I clasped my hands in an 'Excalibur-hold' like those of Joan of Arc praying to God. Kneeling in deep prayer, my whole body was in a stranglehold with the ceiling and heaven above. I hid myself from onlookers on the street because I didn't want my burning prayers to Jesus interrupted. I was afraid they might question why I was so deep in prayer outside my front door, it was something I couldn't explain to anyone. My eyes were tightly closed. I squeezed my little hands together in prayer and in consolation of each other, for there was no one to console me – no one.

I reflected on how these issues affected me as an eight-year-old child, my mind remaining steadfast in defence of the child within. To the best of my ability, I gathered the shattered thoughts of my childhood. All I wanted was for the grief to end, right now, at this desk with these words.

In this moment, I was at the crossroad between the moral ground upon which I stood and my innocent and childish belief in Jesus. The concept was real and my grandmother and parents were the liars. Reason was dead in my family. Life lacked purpose except for their desire to cause destruction.

My eyes rested on the frangipanis leaning together in love. That was what I prayed for as a child – to lean on my parents for love – but all I could do was kneel on the front veranda, deep in prayer.

I asked the very same question as Nietzsche once had: 'is God dead?'

My guardians had turned from me. I was of no value to them. They completely disregarded their obligations as parents. I was sure nothing remained for me to cling to, if Jesus didn't listen to me, I was doomed.

I hugged my teacher diary to my chest, along with the memories of Friedrich Nietzsche and Anna Akhmatova, grateful for their insights as an adult. With their help, I was finding the words to speak my truth.

1962 summer
Elster

"The misogyny is just so wild, and that underpins our attitudes to female victim survivors and we're a male dominated organisation."

A serving Queensland police officer who cannot be
identified for legal reasons, ABC News, 14 July 2022[4]

During the summer, my family camped on the foreshore of Shallow Water Bay. I didn't mind so much because my grandmother didn't come with us and punishments were relaxed. Except for one year when I had chicken pox and had to stay at home in my grandmother's miserable clutches until I could meet up with my mother, father and brothers.

I loved swimming at the beach and spending hours at the rock pools each day. Jumping on the floating car tubes, I felt a calmness I wasn't normally privy to. I closed my eyes and took a deep breath before diving into the sparkling blue salty water. I blew as many bubbles as my lungs could make under water. I spoke like a mermaid deep in the ocean, letting my anxiety go in one big bubble. I would then come up for air, filling me with satisfaction. While clinging to the inflated tyre, my loose legs waded in the salt water.

I heard Mum's shrill voice from the caravan one of those days. Even on holidays I never liked it when she called me, unsure of what she had in store.

"Coming," I called back, running hot footed up the sand track. "What is it Mum?"

"Your father and I have been talking and we want you to go to Sunday school." Her mouth was pinched. It was her way of showing me she was the authority.

"Ok, Mum. But where is the Sunday school?" I tried not to stutter. What was Sunday school anyway? She never did anything nice for me so she must want something.

"It says here on this pamphlet." She pointed her spindly finger at a piece of paper emboldened with a cross. "They hold it on the foreshore opposite the church down the road. It's for kids on holidays."

Her face was rigid. What I would have given for a smile from my mum.

"Are the boys going too?"

"They don't want to go – and they don't need it," she snapped. "They don't tell lies like you do. Sunday school might talk some sense into you."

I wanted to burst into tears.

"Okay, Mum," was all I could say.

My fingers fumbled together, clasped behind my back until she went inside the caravan. I was curious what this God thing was about and only hoped I wouldn't be punished there too.

The very next Sunday morning, Mum and I walked along the foreshore track until we came to the Sunday school.

"I'll be back in an hour to get you."

She didn't look at me as she walked away.

"Are you here for Sunday school?" A warm voice came my way. "My name is Rachel. I'm a helper."

I turned towards the voice. Rachel's eyes gleamed at me. A flush of warmth crept across my cheeks. I was too embarrassed to speak. Did she think I was a liar?

"This way." Rachel took my hand and led me to the inner circle of sun-tanned kids in shorts and midi tops. They were all here for Sunday school, talking over each other while colouring in pictures of a long-haired man dressed in a robe with hands wide open in a gesture of welcome.

"Here's yours." Rachel handed me colouring-in paper and a small box of colouring pencils.

I pressed my lips together unable to speak.

"It's a picture of Jesus. Isn't he the best?" She pointed to the picture of Jesus dressed in a simple hessian robe and sandals. "Those people around him are beggars looking for spiritual and physical healing."

"Thank you," I whispered, struggling to speak.

With a bowed head, I found a place in the circle and sat down with my paper and pencils. Perhaps it would be good for me here. I glanced at the picture of Jesus again. The beggars looked lovingly into his face. They were not afraid of him. The tension in my shoulders released and I joined in with the others. I coloured his peasant's robe in vibrant colours of orange and reds, his sandals an earthy brown, and the golden sun a bright yellow shining over him. The fields were rich with crops of corn and wheat, I coloured in earthy ochres. The trees under which the people sought shade, I coloured a new-beginnings green.

Rachel sat in the middle and told us more about Jesus with her affable voice.

"Jesus is our saviour. He climbed a mountain to gain insight into the oppressors below. When he came down from the mountain, he was refreshed and full of answers and mercy which he shared among the people. He fed the starving people, healed cripples, gave sight to the blind, washed the feet of beggars and forgave prostitutes and other sinners. He upturned the money tables in the rich man's temple and renounced worldly riches." She drew a deep breath and rose from the table, leaving us to our colouring.

My heart was full. I became overwhelmed with the spiritual love and humility of Jesus. I needed a miracle and Jesus was my only hope in hell. I began to believe in my heart that only Jesus could save me from my parents and grandmother. I wanted someone tangible to believe me, someone to hold me and be tender with me and love me for being their child – love me as instinct and nature would have it. I grinned at my picture, from now on I would pray to Jesus in secret.

When we got back from the beach holiday my mother didn't let up on her campaign to have goodness preached into me. But this time she insisted I go to church.

"Why can't I go to Sunday school?" I tried not to let on how much I liked it but it was too late. She had already cottoned on and insisted I go to church and stand alongside adult strangers.

"Church is more disciplined." Spittle flew from her mouth. "You won't be allowed to sit around gossiping with other kids. In church you will stand up and say prayers for being a liar."

It was no use, I was to go alone and be punished through prayer. My mother was above the entire goings on of the church. She was raised a Catholic and 'had a gutful'. In truth, she probably just wanted to stay home and smoke cigarettes.

"You'll wear this." She said shaking a pretty frock at me. "We can't have people thinking you come from a poor family." But I knew keeping face was to not let on to outsiders that I was being abused inside her house. Appearances were everything.

I put the dress on and Mum tied the pink ribbon at the back. It was probably a hand-me-down from a distant aunt but I didn't care. It made me feel like a princess.

"Thanks Mum," my smile wavered when I met her frown. The dress was beautiful but it wasn't for me. It was for her, to cover up her lies.

"And here's sixpence for the offering tray. Put out your hand." Her nostrils flared as she thrust it in my little palm. "Don't go spending it on your gluttonous gut."

I wanted to cry, her opinions of me were so misguided. It was the last thing on my mind to steal the money for myself.

"No Mum," I said, pocketing the small silver coin. I smoothed the dress down to make sure I kept up appearances for her.

"Now, off you go. You know the way to the church. It's only two blocks away." She shoved me out the door and quickly disappeared, I was sure she was glad to get me out of her sight.

"You seem lost. Where are your parents?" inquired the lady usher, staring straight at me.

I bowed my head, my voice was almost a whisper.

"They sent me to church on my own."

"Well come on in then. You can sit next to me."

I sensed kindness in her voice and sat in the pew where she directed me with a welcoming hand. Following the line of churchgoers along the highly polished wooden pew, I sat down and smoothed my pretty dress to keep up my mother's appearances.

I shared the prayer book with the usher lady. She proudly pointed to the prayer lines ignoring the book's time worn edges. I followed her cue, and my knees unbuckled and hands stopped trembling. I locked my eyes on hers. Her face beamed with expression as she said the prayers. The congregation stood up while the offering tray was passed around.

"Where are your parents young lady?" An elderly man spoke as he offered me the tray with one hand and hooked a thumb into his belt loop with the other.

"They couldn't come." My mind went blank, I didn't know what else to say, and I placed the sixpence in the offering tray.

"Oh, that's okay. We'll look after you." He proudly took me under his wing too.

Sitting down, I pressed my hands to my chest, relieved that the churchgoers liked me. But my pretty frock could not make up for the fact that my parents didn't accompany me to church. I couldn't help wonder if they would work it out, that I was here because I was a liar because I told the truth about my father. If they knew, I was sure they wouldn't be so kind.

The following Sunday I prepared for church but something was wrong. The muscles in my shoulders began to tense and I looked away from my pretty frock laid out on the bed to see Mum standing over me. Her eyes were narrowed and lips pursed.

"You're not going to church today! It was supposed to make you a good girl but you haven't been good, have you?"

She sidestepped me, holding her vicious gaze on me.

"What do you mean, Mum? I haven't done anything!" For the life of me I didn't know what she was talking about but I needed to be careful with my words in case I crazed her more.

"You are a liar. You have been talking about us behind our back at church! They rang up here wanting to know why you went alone and you told them we didn't care for you!"

My body stiffened all over. I tried not to twirl my sweaty fingers together or pick at my nails. Instead, I deliberately held my hands by my side. It was pointless arguing with her, she would never believe that I didn't start gossip against the family. I couldn't help it if the churchgoers thought it was strange that I was there without my parents, after all it was my parents who let me go to church unaccompanied.

"I told them I was too sick and your father was working. You begged to go alone," she said, covering her tracks with the church. "You won't be going any more, drawing attention to yourself and all that. You little liar! If only they knew what a bad girl you are!"

I dropped my chin to my chest unable to meet her eyes. Fighting back the tears, I had no choice but to comply. The lump in my throat was too swollen to talk. I reached for my dress but before I had time to pack it away, she tore it from my trembling hands.

"You won't be needing that anymore. I'll give it away to the St. Vincent's people!" She said through her clenched nicotine-stained teeth. She then curled her fingers like an animal claw on my frock and shoved it in a waste bag.

Pressure built up in my chest making it hard to breathe. I desperately wanted to dress up like a princess and visit church, surrounded by loving people and the soft sounds of prayer and forgiveness. That day, I started to hate her. But it did me no good. I had no one to believe in me, to adore me, to think anything of me except I was 'bad, a liar and a thief'.

"Go outside and play in the backyard." She grabbed my arm and shoved me outside and then spun on her heels and walked inside.

I sat in the tree for a while, watching the birds making their nests. The wind picked up and blew the leaves around me. The chill in the air went right through the hand-me-down threadbare jumper.

I climbed down and knocked on the back door. Minutes passed before Mum glared down on me through the crack in the opened door.

"When can I come in, Mum?"

"Go away. I'm not talking to you."

I watched her disappear and the door closed in front of me with the click of the lock. Tears stung my eyes, fixed on the weathered paint. She used the silent treatment to make sure I felt worthless and unloved. For some reason Mum not talking to me was worse than a beating.

I sat down, legs crossed, my back against the bottom of the door. I held my hands together, lowered my face, and said a little prayer to Jesus.

2019 early spring
Ocean harbour home

*"To live is to suffer, to survive is to find
some meaning in the suffering."*

Friedrich Nietzsche[5]

I lit the candle at my desk and stared at the computer screen. The calming aroma of mandarin and rosewood warmed my heart, a far cry from my cold mother when I was a child. The comfort created by the ambient flicker of the candlelight helped me to write. My lips were dry and I fossicked through the side drawer for the aloe vera lip gel, the more natural the remedy the better. Then I faced my computer keyboard again. My fingers wrote by themselves, the words came easier to me the more I wrote.

Out of the blue, my phone pinged. I glanced at the screen. It was my friend, Siobhan. She had recently moved to the area and was looking to catch up but her message was vague so I messaged her back to clarify.

"How are you going? Hope all is okay with you. Lunch maybe?" My text read.

Last time we spoke she seemed down in the dumps.

I returned to my writing. The candle burned. My lips responded well to the curative gel as I put them to my mug and sipped the locally grown organic Glass House Mountains' coffee.

'Ping,' the screen on my phone lit up again.

"I'm not well. I knew you would sense it."

"Can I help? Where are you?"

"I'm in *Bellview*, up on the hill. I admitted myself four days ago."

I stared at her message. *Bellview* was the private hospital for acute mental health with a good reputation for patient-centred care.

"I'll come see you. What's a good day and time, can I bring you anything?"

"I'll text you back after I run it by my doctor."

I wrote for an hour before I received the text that I could visit the next morning at 10am. I packed in my writing, distracted by thoughts of Siobhan and what she might be going through.

The next day I arrived at *Bellview* ten minutes early. Siobhan didn't ask me to bring anything but I purchased two lifestyle magazines for light reading and a bouquet of purple, pink and white carnations, garnished with baby's breath, from the gift store. I'd never visited a mental hospital before and wasn't sure what to expect.

Siobhan said she would meet me at the front doors, leading into the ward. She had been given certain freedoms that the other patients were not because she was self-admitted.

The sliding doors opened and I stepped inside the calm-green carpeted room. The walls were painted off-white and the furniture was sparse. The hallway must have rounded through the whole ward, starting and finishing in the same place. Siobhan emerged from around the corner and before I could stop myself, I gasped. She was frail and too thin, tears streaked her cheeks like a helpless child. I embraced her. I had bigger shoulders and she could use them.

"I'm sorry," she kept saying over and over again.

"Please don't be," I said holding her tight. "You've done the right thing. You need to be here until you feel strong again."

I walked her down the mysterious green hallway until we reached the security doors. The attendant waved his security pass for us to enter when we approached. Siobhan had clearly established bonds with the staff now that her relationships with the outside world had broken down.

When she opened the door to her room, I thought of van Gogh's bedroom painting: two colour contrasts, the blue walls and red bed covers, the lack of shadows that gave a distorted perspective of objects hinting that his mental health was not steady. Siobhan's room was the opposite with off-white walls, green carpet and soft shadows that fell through the gauzy white curtains. The room emanated steadiness.

"I had to check myself in," she sobbed, closing the door behind me. "It got so bad I felt like I was being strangled to death while my soul fled."

"It's okay," I said. "I understand. You did so well in training and then competing in your event. I was proud of you. And I'm proud of you now because you are seeking help when you need it. No one can do it all on their own."

Her sobs began to subside and she sat cross-legged on her bed, her hands wrung tight together until her knuckles popped purple and white. I arranged the flowers I bought her in a vase on the window sill and laid the magazines next to her on her bed. Her knuckles let go of death and reached out for one.

Sometimes I had these experiences for a whole day or more. My thoughts and feelings seemed unreal, like they did not belong to me. I understood depersonalisation disorder and maybe Siobhan was the one person I could trust to tell. "Once, I was outside myself for about a week. I had trouble coming back."

Siobhan eyed me, looking confused sitting there motionless on her bed. She was vulnerable in her own way, just as I had been too. Her soul was suffering just like the character in Anna's poem. "I couldn't believe it, but I've started praying," she said. "My pain was so unbearable, I couldn't stop crying. All I could think to do was to pray to Jesus."

"That's okay," I said. "You won't be punished for it. Sometimes our intuition will lead us to prayer when everything around us is chaotic. People have done worse – believe me!"

Siobhan wiped her teary eyes.

"We should go to the common room; the nurses don't like us entertaining visitors in our rooms. I just needed a couple of minutes to pull myself together."

"Maybe we could sit in the garden? It's a lovely place to have a chat."

"I'll take this with me," she said holding the magazine. "It may come in handy?"

I agreed although I was not sure what she meant.

We stepped into the hallway and walked to the hospital garden. The warm ochre bricks were lightly sprinkled with pink and gold rose petals. It was a beautiful spring day, the sun filtered through the all-knowing willow trees. Dappled light glistened on the few patients who were spread about sitting on wicker chairs. The side tables beared herbal teas and lemon myrtle biscuits.

Siobhan shadowed me as we walked towards a wicker setting under one of the willows, dew drops remained on their ends like tear drops, falling to the rose-petalled ground. An attendant brought out a jug of hot water and we chose from a selection of herbal teas.

I sipped my tea and rested back in the wicker chair. Siobhan was silent, caught in her own world, so I looked around the garden. The wind gently blew back my fringe. Before I knew it my imagination had lifted me to another realm.

I was tired when I glanced at a flower bed where a young girl was sitting picking off one flower at a time and making a garland. There was nothing remarkable about it except the floral decoration was giving her contentment.... my eyelids drooped in the warm sunlight that played on my face... they drooped to a close when I heard a voice.... the young girl was holding Siobhan's hand...

"Come this way," Siobhan beckoned as she led me toward a bent-over old man, sitting quietly in his chair. He stared into the willow universe.

"At first, I feared him. I could hear him calling out 'God is dead' and then silence. I met him the next day out here and he told me he was a writer and philosopher but most of his work was misunderstood. He was brought to the wards after starting a house fire. He was trying to burn his work so it would not be discovered." She told me lightly stroking her forearm.

"Oh dear, poor man," I said. "It's terrible to speak and have no one believe you!"

"Hello Fred," said Siobhan as we approached. "This is my friend, she brought me some magazines. Would you like to borrow one?"

"Thank you, but no thank you! The media numbs your brain and you become mediocre. We need to rise above all that hogwash of mass culture to become healthier human beings. It's very important for parents to understand this when raising their kids."

"*Well, I'm not a parent Fred, but I will certainly keep it in mind if I ever become one.*" *Perhaps Siobhan didn't want to stir up his anxiety any further.* "*Have a lovely day and I'll see you tomorrow.*"

"*The old lady over there,*" *said Siobhan. We walked in her direction, passing the young girl who had returned to the flower bed making garlands.*

"*Her name is Anna,*" *she admitted.* "*She is sad because she can't see her son. Apparently, he's in a Russian prison. Don't ask me how. She sits all day and recites words to herself. They sound very poetic. She says when the time is right she will leave here and have her book published. If she speaks up now, she will be assassinated.*"

"*Poor dear,*" *I said.* "*I sorta know how she feels, being persecuted for speaking out.*"

"*Right!*" *Siobhan agreed.* "*I knew you would understand even if those on the outside don't tolerate them.*"

"*Absolutely, as long as they give you solace being in this gorgeous garden, I'm happy for you.*"

The grace and majesty of Van Morrison's album, No Guru, No Method, No Teacher, became my reality. We were the masters of our own destiny. We were the creatures in all rapture and had the key to our own souls; I found a degree of tranquillity.

"*There is someone who is off-putting though,*" *declared Siobhan.*

"*Who's that?*"

I kept my eye on the garland-making girl.

"*That grey-haired old lady over there, the one with the hair net. She gargles out loud like someone is choking to death. At the same time, she rocks back and forth as if she has a baby in her arms.*"

I glanced from the corner of my eye, so as not to be rude. I saw this old woman cradling a baby. She looked like my grandmother swaying her baby girl back and forth. I agreed with Siobhan, she was peculiar unlike Fred and Anna who seemed human.

"*No one comes to visit her. She has a son but he's too busy. Too full of himself she says. But I don't like talking to her because she told the attendants I stole her funny looking lollies and that I was a liar!*"

"*You need to keep clear of her!*" *I said, nodding my head.* "*Her life is miserable and she makes everyone else around her miserable too.*"

My eyes returned to the little girl in the flower bed. She looked familiar, as if I was looking at myself.

She finished weaving her garland and sat smiling to herself in the warm sunshine. I considered helping her make another...

Siobhan's voice lifted me from my daydream.

"I need a nap," she announced, resting her head on one hand.

I recognised her emotional exhaustion and bid her goodbye with a warm hug.

"I'm here if you need anything," I reassured her.

"Sure," she said with a quick nod.

I left the mental hospital that afternoon with a deep knot in my stomach.

I was relieved to get home that afternoon. Sensitive to Siobhan and the other patients' inner suffering, I lighted my mandarin and rosewood candle. The delicate musky fragrance pervaded the room, calming my shaken sensibilities. I took a few deep breaths and reflected on my visit to the mental hospital and why I felt so shaken. It took me a moment to realise that when I dozed off in the garden and fell into that daydream, I faced a truth I was hiding.

Pressing my palms to my eyes, I recalled Fred, or Friedrich, setting fire to his work in fear of it being discovered. It had triggered my lifelong fear of telling the truth about the child abuse. But here I was, attempting to overcome that fear and write my story. I was safe right now, in my own creative space, but I knew one day I would have to face the world. I no longer felt the need to be subservient to my parents' threats and staying silent but deep inside still lived the panic of other people finding out. I knew I should overcome my fear of talking to God, as they once forbade me to go to Sunday school and church. After all these years, it was time for me to re-establish my spiritual connection to God and trust life enough to write my memoir.

I reached out and picked a frangipani from the vase and laid it on my desk above the keyboard. I stared at it while simultaneously touch typing and wrote a letter to God.

Dear God

Perhaps you would be amazed by this letter. You may be wondering why I am writing to you at all. I have not visited church since I was eight years old, except for a wedding or funeral. I apologise for being secular and less connected to you than I should have been. I am grateful for my children and grandchildren, and my presence. Today, I write to you with Jesus next to me and the collective of lost and unloved children.

I brought Your existence into question since I was living on the edge of the world where I was unable to protect myself from an evil regime in my parent's home. The atrocious conditions I was subjected brought me to the eternal question – does God exist?

I knew about God from Sunday school and my rare visits to church on Sundays. I was vaguely familiar with the Ten Commandments – the law of God – and that we should not break those laws.

As an abused child, I had no voice. I struggled to survive in an unimaginable world of suffering. Anna Akhmatova's and Friedrich Nietzsche's work presented me with the inspiration to write my personal story of suffering and grief. In my own way I can now find the words to describe my pain although in childhood I had been criminally and subversively silenced and oppressed.

My world was in conflict since my parents, my moral guardians, were in violation of the Ten Commandments. I carried this burden and anomaly of my abnormal family with me most of my life but the question of Your existence still permeates within me as I grapple with my upbringing. I am writing through litanies of despair and soul searching. I often think of my childhood home as a madhouse and my imaginations of the mental hospital were justified.

Thank you for taking the time to read my letter. Perhaps you have been there for me the whole time, in your own way. Please forgive me if I have had doubts.

Kindest regards

I looked up. The writing candle had burned to its wick. I extinguished the dying flame with my two fingers pinched at the tips. The computer screen faded and the room darkened. In the dim light, my eyes averted to *Macbeth* in a collection of Shakespeare's tragedies, my mind became locked on events while growing up.

I had an image in my head of the witches on the heath where they lived on the edge of the world. I needed to distinguish between what was real and the forces beyond the laws of nature. I kept digging to understand why my mother and grandmother could not love me, as instinct would have it. Perhaps the story of *Macbeth* will give me the answers I seek.

CHAPTER 7

The Outside Dunny

2001 winter
Far north high school

"Fair is foul, and foul is fair:
Hover through the fog and filthy air."

William Shakespeare from *Macbeth*, The Witches (Act 1 Scene 1)[1]

I raised my chin and observed my Grade Ten English class reading their textbooks. Engrossed in study, their lingering fingers carefully turned the pages. All of the students had eager looks on their faces. I ticked each name from the absentee roll, they were all present, and tucked it under my Joan of Arc teacher's diary. The class was well into Term Three and we were studying Shakespeare's *Macbeth*. I hoped by sharing complex themes of the work they would grow into thinking empowered individuals. There were moments when I was triggered by the abuse in the text but I hid my trauma reactions the best I could and pushed through. I wasn't going to let the strange house I grew up in hold me back from enjoying literature. Even if Shakespeare brought up themes related to child abuse, I was capable of stepping back into my professional self to analyse the text.

I stood next to my desk flicking through my copy of the book when Jessie's hand went up.

"Miss, do you have a spare copy? I left mine at home."

"Of course, here you are. I like your enthusiasm, Jess!" I handed him a copy from my desk and was no longer met with an eye roll.

"He's not as boring as I thought he would be Miss." Jessie grinned.

I watched him reading. His eager glances switched between the Modern English notes and Shakespeare's sixteenth century writing. The room was quiet except for the occasional soft chatter of students sharing interpretations of themes or asking to borrow a pen.

"You can stop reading," I said, proud of them for overcoming Shakespeare's old-fashioned language.

"There are several themes in the play, some which are relevant today – corruption of power, ambition and fate. Does anyone have questions?"

I kept strong eye contact with the class. Sara's hand flew up.

"What did the witches mean, 'fair is foul and foul is fair,' Miss? Isn't it confusing?"

"Yes Sara, it is. Shakespeare placed them in the first act of the play to set the tone for confusion."

I made sure my voice was steady, despite lingering anxiety in the pit of my stomach.

"Were they casting spells to bring up trouble for the people?"

Good question.

"In some ways they were. On a deeper level their presence was communicating treason and impending doom. Much of the confusion came from their ability to move between reality and the supernatural."

"Is that why they lived on the heath?"

"Yes. There they could act as both agent and witness to Macbeth's downfall."

"Then, why did they prophesise he would be king?"

"Shakespeare was setting the theme of temptation. The witches put the thought of kingship in Macbeth's mind so that he would either indulge it or reject it. Of course, Macbeth indulged it."

I was pleased with my students' questions, they were seeing the unpredictability of human nature and trusting me to guide their understanding of the text. I didn't feel the same way growing up under the care of my parents who left me alone and isolated, unequipped to determine my own fate.

"Miss, in Act 2 it says, 'Tis said they eat each other,'" Sara read from her heavily earmarked textbook. "The horses ate each other after Macbeth killed King Duncan, having been manipulated by Lady Macbeth." Her face grimaced. "That's awful, horses don't eat each other. What does Shakespeare mean?"

I stood tall in the middle of the room before them, having anticipated my students would make fun of this scene. But the topic left a sour taste in my mouth, the memory of my family turning on me was vivid in mind.

On the day I recalled, my grandmother and mother locked me in the outside dunny. They may as well have eaten me like wild horses. Small pieces of macular fell like spiders across my vision. I paused to centre myself until they disappeared. I stared over the class and retreated inward for a moment. I had to draw a deep breath and take a wide step between desks to ground myself before continuing the class discussion.

"Nature was out of sync because of King Duncan's murder. The balance between good and evil had been tipped in favour of evil with Macbeth's heinous crime against a divinely appointed King."

The realisation hit me as I stood there, Macbeth was strong but he was a bully and dictator. Ultimately, he came unstuck. I took a moment to clear my throat; the school principal was a living example of Macbeth. He too would ultimately come unstuck. Sooner than later I hoped, both for my sake and for the sakes of the children molested in the school.

"This theme is continued throughout the play. For example, when Lady Macbeth hears a voice saying that 'Macbeth does murder sleep.'"

The bell rang and our lesson came to an end. The class restlessness cut into the study of *Macbeth*. My students picked up their books and deep in thought, they shuffled from the room.

I collected the spare copies of the textbook and stacked them in the corner bookshelf, ready for the next lesson. The unpredictability of Macbeth's emotions played on me.

A worse for wear textbook fell to the floor splitting in two. The inside tore away from the cover. I gathered it in my hands, it reminded me of my mother and grandmother when I was a child, cutting me off from my natural roots. At the same time, they enabled the unbridled ambition of my father.

I tucked it inside my Joan of Arc teacher diary intending to glue it together that night.

I glanced at my watch. Damn, I was late for the lunchtime staff meeting. I cast one final glance over the classroom and locked the door behind me on the way out, dismissing the thoughts of my childhood. I prayed to God they would disappear but as much as I fought them, they never really went away.

1962 winter
Elster

"'What's wrong?'
'O, Mam, I'm scared stiff, I thought I saw the mountain
heaving like a giantess, with her breasts swaying,
about to loom over and gobble me up.'"

Nuala Ní Dhomhmaill from *Hag*[2]

The small brick veneer house I grew up in had an outside toilet, or dunny, as it was called. Mum said the brick veneers were modern and an improvement on the old bungalow we used to live in. But the lavatory remained built away from the house in the back garden. That was because the sewerage system was not introduced until the 1960s. Ours was a timber dunny, only rich people had a brick one. It was overgrown by a huge choke vine, providing a level of secrecy, and the turning of a blind eye to inside activities. I avoided going near it as much as possible, the sight and smell of it made me feel sick. Inside was the can that sat over the dug-in pit where the faeces and slime decomposed into a putrified mess. A pipe was fed from the dark pit through to the roof, lit by sunlight, where it was closed off by fly wire. Dirty blow flies broke into the dunny when it was unlatched, or over and under it, and flew straight into the can. They frolicked and buzzed in the sludge. Inside the dunny, it was miserably dark except for the slither of light above the air vent. The blowies were attracted to the light and would fly up into it, lured to their death.

"Come here, you jezebel!"

It was Mum's shrill. I took a gulp of air and met her on the garden path.

"Yes, Mum."

"The dunny needs a clean. Get to it."

She shoved a bottle of the foul-smelling *phenol* cleaner in my quivering hands and left me alone to carry out the worst job in the house.

Holding back a cry, I entered the dunny. I took one waft and backed up towards the choke vines. In the dark and mouldy corner sat a pile of last year's telephone books, both white and yellow pages, thick with addresses and phone numbers of people from the city and Elster. They served as our dunny paper along with used newspapers – *Melbourne Age, Herald* and *The Sun*. Grandad often sat in there and read them without a thought to the squalor he was in. The combined smell of week-old faeces and urine with the overpowering fumes of the toxic *phenol* nearly made me keel over.

I staggered outside and ran as far away from the dunny as my legs could take me, gasping for breath. But the smell lingered for hours.

Once a week, every week, I whiffed the dunny man coming a mile away in his dunny truck. There was collective appraisal among the neighbours for his essential comings and goings. He came to fetch the can and replace it with an empty one. It was taken to a heap, only God knew where, so the sludge could break down over time. That's what Mum told me.

I scratched my head, today the dunny man was coming, so why did Mum give me this chore? Avoiding eye contact with her, I fetched a bottle of beer from the fridge and placed it on the side entrance for the dunny man. The neighbours did the same since nobody wanted the dunny man to have an accident in their side entrance where he entered and exited the property.

A knocking sound got my attention. The hair went up on the back of my neck. It was that crotchety entitled knock of my grandmother at the front door. She was the giantess from the mountains come to gobble me up.

I edged my way to the apple tree to hide from her until she was gone. But before I had time to climb high enough, my mother's voice shrieked from the back door.

"Come in here now!" She rolled up her sleeves.

My body shook.

"Yes, Mum."

"Go and sit over there."

Her eyes were so cold.

I crouched on the damp linoleum floor in the corner of the kitchen. My grandmother sat stiffly in the chair at the table and swilled on her pain-killer cough medicine. Her hands fidgeted on the bottle.

"The beatings are doing no good." The wicked witch glanced down at me with a foul sneer. "This girl needs to be punished another way since she hasn't confessed to being a 'liar'."

I didn't understand, if I confessed to being a liar then that would be a lie. I was staring up at her but her wrinkled face blurred until I was not seeing her at all.

"Let's lock her in the dunny! It's dark and cold in there, fitting for naughty girls. And if we sit her there long enough the spiders will crawl over her and bite her." Her sneer turned into a gruesome smirk. "The spiders are large, black, hairy and deadly and they love to bite little children, especially liars!"

Her mouth went so wide the dirty blow flies would have no trouble flying in. I feared her mouth, full of dirty blow flies, would turn on me and eat me alive.

I shook uncontrollably, too petrified to fight and they pulled me by my clothes and ears along the path to the dunny door.

"Now get in you hussy and see if you tell any more lies."

They shoved me in and bolted the door shut from the outside. I was ordered to not bash on the door or else the spiders would find me faster.

I was clammy and bursting for breath. The stench and fear of spiders caused me to jerk my whole body from side to side of the dunny walls. I screamed and yelled at fever pitch, stopping to gulp filthy air to keep me alive. Eventually I stared into the darkness and felt for the dunny lid. I sat there quietly to think through how I was going to survive. I was helpless, so I prayed to God and Jesus that the spiders would not attack me. The darkness and cold was terrifying. I didn't understand how could they do this to me?

My silence must have been too much for them. I heard them scratching around in the garden which sounded more like them abrading for moral duty in the barren patches of their minds. Their broom and rakes scraped the ground like grimalkin witches conjuring malicious spirits aiding them to carry out their evil deeds. They were agents of my ill fate.

Swiftly, my grandmother appeared outside the dunny through the hole above the door. She hurled 'spiders' over the top of the hinged door – another small slither of light apart from the trap-wired vent on the roof.

"Go on, take that!" She squawked and darted leafy spiders over the dunny door.

Her shadow backed away, leaving me sitting there in terror.

I pressed my fists to my head and jerked about to avoid the leafy spiders falling on me and the traipsing spider legs on my body. I contorted my elbows to my face and hair in a pulse racing bid to flick them off. I had reached breaking point but I didn't know what my grandmother or mother wanted me to say before they released me. I was 'dead' in my heart, broken in my body and soul. I could hardly bare the stench of the *phenol* that overpowered my already tortured senses.

Their twisted entrapment went on for what felt like an eternity until I was finally taken out. The sun had dimmed behind the clouds, it would not be long before it was night-time.

They dragged me by my ears and leaf-ridden clothes into my bedroom. I was then locked inside like a prisoner of war from a TV show and made to lie there on my bed without food or water.

I heard them muttering in the kitchen. I jumped as a cough syrup bottle hit the table like a judge's hammer.

"Let's see if this changes her mind," my grandmother scathed.

I had reached my wits' end and began screaming.

I screamed so loud I thought my lungs would burst but I had had enough. I was only seven years old. The burden I carried was too much for a child and it was inflicted upon me so cruelly. It was still daylight outside and I pitted myself up at the bedroom window which was covered with a closed venetian blind to keep the light out of the room and keep me in the dark place.

Clawing at the venetian-blinded window, I yelled until my lungs would burst, poisoned by the toxic environment in which I was born. I desperately wanted the neighbours to hear me. My survival instinct had taken over my atrophied silence. Now was the time for someone to rescue me from my pitiful, intolerable and unspeakable situation. I screamed and I screamed and I screamed.

The two witch women had left the kitchen and were toiling away in the garden as if they were immune to me or to the neighbours latching on.

From my window I saw the lady from next door pop her head over the paling fence and inquire as to 'why a child was screaming?'

Both witches looked smug and innocent as they toiled away like 'good wives' and replied, "Oh, it's nothing. She screams over nothing."

The neighbour frowned and held onto the fence tight.

"Are you sure? She sounds so distressed and it's highly unusual to hear such dark screams."

Caged in my room, I pressed my ear up to the glass and listened to the conversation as my life depended on it. She was my only hope.

I should have kept it up – the scream from hell. Then any hope of being rescued was dashed.

"Oh, it's nothing," Mum said.

"She's always putting on a performance," said Grandmother. "Look, she's stopped as quickly as she started."

"She'll quiet down," my mother convinced my neighbour.

The neighbour's head disappeared from the fence top, as did my hope for survival.

My body was numb with fear when my bedroom door opened and my punishers stalked in, glaring at me as if I was the worst child on earth.

"You can scream all you like, no one will listen to you," Grandmother said in a tone too low for anyone outside to hear.

"Nor believe you!" Mum's tongue lashed.

She was worse when my grandmother was there. I hated them both but said nothing. I think I died inside that day.

They left and exhausted, I fell into a deep sleep. I dreamt the lady neighbour came knocking at the gate in a bid to rescue me.

Please open the gate. Knock, rap, strike, tap!... Why can't anyone hear her... Let her in. Help! Help me!

"I thought I heard her screaming."

The kind lady neighbour was standing over my bed. Her angel wings opened for embrace...

"Come here. I'll help you." She gathered me in her arms...

"Where are you taking her?" My mother screeched.

My mother and grandmother stood at the door, wielding garden rakes. They were devils with forks...

Wild horses driven by fear of being eaten ran through the house.

"We control her fate, not YOU!"...

The angel neighbour dropped me from her wings and disappeared. I fell hard to the floor... my back ached... my head split open...

I woke with a start. My bedroom was pitch-black. It was night-time and they had left me without food or water. I coughed to myself, keeping silent and wishing to have nothing to do with them even if I was thirsty and starving. Recalling the spiders from the dunny, I ran my hands over my body to check none had come in the house with me. The stench of *phenol* reeked from the clothes I still wore.

I lay there numb. They were becoming more evil as if they had eaten their own spells. Had I woken only to remain in this otherworldly place of torture?

2019 early summer
Ocean harbour home

"To bed, to bed: there's knocking at the gate.
Come, come, come, come, give me your hand.
What's done cannot be undone."

Lady Macbeth in *Macbeth* (5.1) by William Shakespeare[3]

The truth was my need to be seen and heard was still with me, despite how much my family tried to knock it out of me. I contemplated my camera, always aimed towards the ocean. Now I wanted to turn it towards me.

I needed to be seen and taking long exposure shots with my camera helped me do that. There was something unique about them. The rolling waves became smooth and soft, drifting clouds morphed and took on otherworldly forms.

My pictures were popular on social media; my addiction to Instagram gave me strength. I now have a thousand followers. I loved to scroll through the feed where I found validation, even if it was for shaming that which had happened to me many years ago.

I plonked my bag on my desk in my study and unpacked my camera gear. I mulled over the raw images and decided to set up for a morning shoot.

Then there was that sound again.

Knock, rap, strike, tap!

The sound made the hairs on the back of my neck stand on end, as if a troop of militants were barging their way through the door.

I thought of Lady Macbeth when she heard the knocking at the gate and spiralled into madness. Then I thought I heard the lady next door, knocking at our gate when I was a child, that day when my grandmother and mother sent me spiralling into madness.

I shook my head and reminded myself I was safe in my harbour home – no one could hurt me. And as for Lady Macbeth, she was an archetypal 'mad' female figure who suffered damnation at the scribe's pen just as I had suffered damnation at my family's accusation. I was the seductive daughter, it was all my fault.

I shoved aside the past and walked to the front door, somewhat shaken. I opened it a fraction. The delivery man stood there innocently, holding a box.

I almost broke out laughing; the camera filters I ordered last week had finally arrived. I opened the door fully and stepped out to take the box.

"Thank you," I said with a smile and took my precious filters back to my desk to finish assembling my camera for the morning's sunrise shoot.

That night, while I was lying in bed, I mentally ran through my camera equipment to make sure I didn't leave anything behind. Second guessing myself was all too familar. I sighed and turned over to face the window. The shutters were ajar. Sea air wafted inside, washing over me and cooling my body.

My eyelids dropped and I drifted into a deep sleep.

I was inside the stone walls of a castle. Cold floor. Bare feet.

A bedside table was in front of me and upon it was a flickering candle. It cast broken shadows on my leather-bound copy of Macbeth. The page was open at Act 5 Scene 1. Bluetooth speakers blared Florence + The Machine, 'Never Let Me Go.'

A bedraggled barefooted young woman giddily moved toward me. Her white cotton night dress trawled the castle floor and her long unkempt hair fell over her emaciated body.

Taking my hands in hers, she stammered.

"To bed, to bed; there's a knocking at the gate. Come, come, come, give me your hand. What's done cannot be undone. To bed, to bed, to bed!"

It was Lady Macbeth; I didn't think she was all that bad. Our hands remained locked together in a gesture of empathy. We were in each other's world.

"Why did you call upon the supernatural to 'unsex me here'?" *I couldn't help but ask.*

"Because women were not expected to kill. If I could be rid of my soft, feminine qualities and gain a more ruthless nature I could kill the king myself — my husband was weak," *she said, flicking hair from her ashen face.*

"That didn't work. Did it? After Duncan's stabbing, you became prone to fits of manic handwashing, sleep walking and ranting."

"I know, right! Shakespeare was writing me out of the text, as male writers do. I had suited the role of the 'madwoman' and then he had me commit suicide. My husband pursued his ambition in a heroic role until his final battle with Macduff."

She looked disappointed with the outcome.

"I get it Lady Macbeth. You were driven mad, annihilated by the scribe's pen, labelled the fourth witch, alienated from your environment and from yourself!" *I was off balance with her giddiness but I was used to that from my childhood.*

"True that," *she said, maintaining a spunk that Shakespeare could not write out of the text.*

"Similar things happened to me when I was a small girl. I spent much of my childhood and young adult life suffering insomnia. My world was turned upside down and my spiritual being was brought into question because of their devotion to my annihilation."

"What happened?"

She tightened her clasp over my hands.

"Too much to explain here. I was living on the edge, in a dark otherworldly place not connected to ordinary life. At one point they locked me in the outside dunny and hurled spiders over a small opening to scare me." *My voice began to falter.*

"Oh, I'm so sorry. Caregivers are meant to act as your agent and witness when you cannot speak for yourself."

The song was on repeat, 'never let me go...'

"Speaking of that. I'm writing my experiences of child abuse and intend to have it published. It's called 'Being My Own Witness: Speaking out to be heard'. I'm taking it to court, there's already been one hearing. Judge Christine de Pizan ordered me to find further evidence to support my case. Would you testify for me, your Ladyship?"

"Of course! But I'm not sure I will be of much use to you. I was complicit in killing a king."

She pulled our clutched hands tightly to her knees.

"I see that you were brainwashed to wish to be a man. Shakespeare wore you down until you disappeared from the text. My parents did the same to me. They wore me down with abuse and torture so I would admit to being something I was not. It's called gas lighting."

There was a crash. My copy of Macbeth fell to the floor. Its pages closed.

"There's no going back for me. I entered the gates of madness until my final undoing at the hands of a male writer. Although his writing did portray the patriarchy back then."

"Then and now! Not much has changed..."

The warning bird's early morning song made it through the window and into my dream. The candle flickered out.

"One more thing Lady Macbeth."

"Yes." Her head fell to the side, weighed down with the myriad of emotion.

"Please stop washing your hands so much and eat more otherwise your conscience will become narrowed and you will continue to live an impoverished life. This is exactly what patriarchy intends. Fight back dear Lady... rewrite your story from your point of view... for the sake of women and children... and others...."

I awoke and forced my eyes open, the dream was still vivid in my mind. Early morning sunlight filtered through the shutters and I breathed in fresh sea air. The warning birds were perched on the outside gate joyfully singing their morning song.

Why was I dreaming of Lady Macbeth? She didn't want to get out of bed. If she did, she would go mad.

Enough, I thought to myself.

What's done has been done but now I had to try to undo the damage and heal from the abuse.

I threw back the sheets and swung myself out of bed, making my way to the kitchen. I was hungry, which was a good sign.

I prepared organic cereal, fresh fruit, local dairy yoghurt and mountain grown coffee. The nourishment helped me to write my story, and overcome the destitution caused by toxic masculinity.

I paused for a moment and grinned, I couldn't believe I gave Lady Macbeth health tips in my dream.

I pulled my diary closer and made a note to bring the dream sequence into my court case later.

I then leaned in and began to assemble my camera. I placed my micro lens in the kit to capture the fine detail of budding frangipani on my way to the beach. The macro photography style lets the subject fill all or most of the frame, so that you capture an incredible amount of detail. I likened it to my writing, self gathering my inner petals and filling a once silenced and empty frame with rich detail. Detail that I chose in the moment without outside interference.

CHAPTER 8

Torture by Light

2001, September 11
Far north high school

*"Ah, I am worn out – I am wearied out – It is too much – I
am but flesh and blood And I must sleep. Though you were
dead again I am but flesh and blood and I must sleep."*

Edna St. Vincent Millay from *Interim*, 1912[1]

I was walking across the quadrangle to my history class when I became caught up in a sea of students making their way to class. I loved being connected to these brave young people in the simplest of ways. It didn't matter if we were walking and chatting about the weather, the heat that day or about how Miss Chimer had kept them overtime for music practice and there was no time to eat lunch. Of course, I let them eat their lunch in class.

A student came running over to the moving sea of adolescents. Their purpose must have been important enough to tackle us head on.

"What is it?"

"You must come quickly, Miss!"

"What's wrong?"

"A plane has flown into the World Trade Centre in New York. It exploded and the building is collapsing."

"What on earth?" Panic and confusion overcame me. "It must have been a terrible accident," I said in disbelief.

We all headed to the library where the news was screened live on the television. The event unfolded before our eyes in real time.

Then another plane flew into the second Twin Tower.

I felt sick in the pit of my stomach; we were witnessing firsthand a horrific attack. The crashing of the second plane into the next tower dispelled the theory it was an accident.

Jessie turned to me.

"Is there a war in America, Miss?"

I couldn't answer, I was as dumbfounded and shocked as they were. I only hoped this didn't mean war, knowing too well that Australia was in allegiance with America. If they were at war, we were too.

The principal passed by the library door and stabbed me with his blue-black gorgon eyes.

"Get back to class," he ordered. His shoulders were permanently hunched in never-ending suspicion. He shoved the class aside as if to get to his enemy – me.

I'm sure he would write in his 'highly confidential' file, 'late to class', omitting the gravity of the 9/11 disaster. Little did he know, the date 9/ 11 would speak for itself.

War or no war, it was another opportunity for him to mobilise his attack against me and demoralise and break down my will. With the power invested in him by the education system, he must have believed he had every right to consign me to oblivion. Without connection to a global political movement for human rights, I was powerless to fight back. I felt as helpless as the civilians fighting for their lives in the Twin Towers.

"Okay everyone, you heard the principal, it's time for class."

"But Miss, look what's happening" – "We can't miss this" – "How can you—"

I hated having to force them away from the screen but my job was on the line.

"Sorry everyone, we'll have to find out what happened at recess."

It was ridiculous but with Luther breathing down my neck I had no choice. My hands were shaking as I walked with my students to the classroom.

My thoughts shifted to my mother. It dawned on me then that her actions were in alignment with the gravity of war crimes that violated the human rights of innocent civilians. She was not that different from the terrorists who attacked the Towers that day.

1962 spring
Elster

"My relationship with Mom drastically changed from discipline that developed into a kind of lifestyle that grew out of control. It became so bad at times, I had no strength to crawl away – even if it meant saving my life."

David Pelzer *A Child Called 'It'*[2]

World War II ended in 1945 but eighteen years later the effects of that war revealed itself in my childhood home in a shockingly perverse way. I was abruptly woken from my sleep when Mum yanked me out of my bed and dragged me into her bedroom.

I stood there in my nightie, shivering in disbelief. It was freezing without my blankets.

"What's wrong, Mum?" I stuttered.

"Shut up and sit there!" she blurted and shoved me onto a stool.

She shook her fist in my face.

"This is what you deserve. You are a bad girl. I am going to punish you!"

"Please Mum!" I cried but she refused to allow me to defend myself. It only infuriated her more.

"I have learnt a few things they used in the war. By hook or by crook, I'll get the truth out of you!"

She bared her teeth. Her blue eyes turned black and her white face stared at me like a wicked witch. Her bombshell blonde hair was ablaze like a mangy rabid dog on its kill. It blazed in the darkness, highlighted by the side flares of an electric light globe which was shone into my face.

"You will sit there and stare into this light!" barked the rabid dog. "You are not allowed to go to sleep! This is what they did to the prisoners of war. It works! It broke them. You will sit there and stare into this light." She glared, hounded and forced me while her bony knuckled madwoman hands fidgeted with the convoluted lamp.

The hard wooden stool was precisely placed in the middle of the room at the end of their double bed. This was insane – the breeding chamber juxtaposed with the torture chamber. The double standard that filled the room was unbearable. Mum was relishing in her newly concocted scheme of near infanticide. The lamp was one of those free-standing adjustable things which she could manipulate within centimetres of me. She had turned off the main light and only the darkness of the room remained, apart from the torturous light aimed at my startled eyes. I was too afraid to cry, my body stiffened into a corpse-like position, barely able to comprehend the atrocity of the scene. My eyes were bone dry. I was sure I would suffer retina damage due to the intensity of the light.

Mum continued her violent attack.

"Don't you dare move. I will know if you move after I leave this room because I can see all the little things that change in the room, it'll give you away. If I find you have so much as flinched, you will be made to sit here every night and never sleep again. And I will beat you until you are black and blue!"

She looked like a madwoman, shaking her fist at me.

There it was, she had the key to break me. I was forced to assume this stressful position for long hours, deprived of sleep with an interrogation light shone in my eyes.

"Sit there and don't move. The light will burn your eyes out of your head you little hussy, adulteress, liar, schemer. You won't destroy my life, I will destroy yours!"

Her face twisted in vile contortion before turning on both heels and leaving me alone.

I wiped back tears, trying hard to sit straight as Mum had commanded but I was tired and wanted to go to sleep. My world spun around me.

Mum was out of control and I was helpless against her. Where did she get this idea from? She was obsessed with the war and often told us stories about Uncle Robert, maybe that was it.

"Your uncle was shot in the kneecaps by the Japs. He was carried out of the jungle on a stretcher and shipped back to Australia." Her nostrils flared when she spoke.

"They're the worst people on earth. Barbaric!"

Mum had a kind of sick pleasure in her voice as she recounted her stories of how the 'Japs' threw innocent babies into the air and bayoneted them to death. She took extra time to explain how the bayonets were attached to machine guns while she stood with her pelvis manically thrust forward. She then mimicked thrusting a bayonet into the air and expelling babies at whim. She never tired of repeating this sordid scenario in front of me. She raised her spindly arms to heaven holding the imaginary infant-child killer bayonet while her murderous blue eyes burned in hell fire. Her puny bum pointed to the ground, supported by her spindly legs. She glared at me as if to say I measured up like the enemy. I wasn't to be trusted.

My small body crumpled under the strain of sitting on the stool with the light burning in my eyes. The only sound was my heartbeat rushing through my ears. If I rocked on the stool I would fall off. I wanted to cry but my tear glands were dried up. Unable to hold the position any longer, my chin fell to my chest. My eyelids surrendered to sleep in the stark light.

But only for a moment.

Mum marched back into the room and my body flinched at her being nearby.

"Well, have you got anything to say to me?"

I looked to her. She appeared satisfied she had tortured me to breaking point.

My body shook uncontrollably and I burst into tears, unable to answer her.

She must have been tired and wanted the bedroom for herself. Clearly, she could not stay up all night to torture me. But I had nothing to confess, I didn't understand any of it.

I was worn out and weary. It was too much, for I was but flesh and blood, desperately needing to sleep. Apart from sleep, all I could think about was Mum trying to blend into our family as a kind mother disguising herself as an enemy soldier. Was I to forever be her prisoner of war?

2021 September 11
Ocean harbour home

"… a particular female officer at his station… was referred to
*as c***y Mcc*** face', that other women at his station were*
*referred to as c***s, f***ing b***h, f****ing slut and mole…"*

ABC News, from *The Commission of Inquiry into Queensland Police Responses to Domestic and Family Violence,* posted 18 August 2022[3]

I turned on the television for news of the Women's March, only to hear that the twenty-year war in Afghanistan had ended. The reporter said that peace can only be brought about by helping the Afghanistan people develop their own stable government. It was comforting to hear our soldiers were being sent home but it had been a while since there was an update on the Women's March.

I rubbed the back of my neck; I had very much hoped that our cause would remain in the mainstream media. The war on women worldwide continued in silence, too often ignored by the media and hidden from public scrutiny. There was no talk about reforming the misogynists in Parliament and developing a stable working environment for women.

I had to take my mind off the oppression of women, so I listened to the ocean waves outside my window. Distracted by the ocean and trying to take my mind off my fears of the women's movement fading into *Nike* ads, I lost track of time. I checked my watch. There was still time for a sunset shoot.

Despite the heaviness in my limbs, I collected my camera kit from the freshly painted sea mist cupboard and headed out the door.

The foamy waves crashed into sheets of pearl white water and met with their destiny on the shore. I found a dry place between the sand and rocks to set up my tripod and aimed my camera at the high-spirited ocean washing back and forth over the shore. The beryl salt water, drenched in golden shards of vanishing sunlight glittered on the sea. My breathing slowed to meet the pace of the ocean, keeping time with the frothy flow off the back of a rolling wave. I pressed the shutter button for a long exposure smoothing out the movement of the water and clouds.

In the review panel appeared an ethereal picture of another world untouched by war and enmity towards women and children. I created a utopian vision of a better world that I could only dream of.

Dusk fell and I came out of my seraphim trance. The incoming tide washed over my feet anchored on the ancient rocks to purge me of the childhood abuse. But my mental and spiritual peace was temporary; my lack of sleep from the previous night, coupled with the news of the end of the Afghan war, brought back memories of that terrible night when my mother tortured me by light.

She was a war zone under attack with an increased need for heightened security. In her paranoia, she perceived me as the enemy and planned future attacks on her eight-year-old 'hussy' of a daughter. Her anti-daughter hate-crimes went on the rise because my dad would not admit he was a paedophile.

The power of my beating heart, took me by surprise. I was ambushed by my own emotions. Vertigo took hold over me and I struggled not to fall into the rushing water. I couldn't feel how cold the water was over my feet or hear anything except the rushing blood in my ears. I focused on my breath until the sensation subsided.

Tears welled up in my eyes; they stung in the salt air. I refocused on packing up my camera. My hands were shaking and I decided I would ring the doctor's twenty-four-hour service for an appointment the next day. It was time I talked to my GP about this complex PTSD.

The entrance to Dr Nuha's waiting room was open; the sliding doors were bolted to the walls and only closed at night. It was a straight walk through from the chemist next door where people came and went freely. I checked in with reception and then took a seat by the plant box. I felt safe here, not like a prisoner held captive by my parents. I was an easy mark for them, a target unable to escape.

I knew writing my story had caused me to relive these traumatic events but now I was in a safe place and was determined to heal. I summoned the courage to talk to Dr Nuha about what I endured during captivity as a child that caused my parents to reject me so harshly.

"Mrs Budd." Dr Nuha called my name.

It felt good to be going to her and not running from someone in authority.

"Hello, dear," she said as I entered her office. And with a gracious outstretched arm, she welcomed me to take a seat in her surgery. Apart from a family photograph, her desk and walls were bare of decorations. It was her kind voice and willingness to understand that made me feel better.

"Hello Dr Nuha," Already I was smiling and my body was relaxed.

"Have you been well?"

"I'm going okay, but I'm having some trouble sleeping. Can you please write me a script for the tablets we discussed in our last consultation?"

"Of course," she answered in a warm tone, her body turned toward me. "Have you seen the psychologist yet?"

"Not yet." I didn't want to sound ungrateful for her referral but I didn't want to see a shrink. I still wasn't over the previous ordeals with psychologists.

"There's no hurry, when you feel ready."

"Last time we spoke you told me you were from Egypt; that it was hard for women living in Egypt?"

"Yes, I remember our conversation. I was fortunate to leave Egypt more than twenty years ago and come to Australia. I brought my husband and family with me. More of my family travelled over but I still have two sisters living there." A frown fell across her forehead.

"Withdrawing the troops from Afghanistan and the September 11 anniversary, I've been thinking about my childhood. Mum used a form of military torture to punish me for something I didn't do," I said wisely because it happened so long ago.

"That is awful, I am sorry to hear that. In Egypt there is much tension in families. Egyptians struggle for freedom. There is a sense that controlling family behaviour or venting frustration at women close to them has become second-best for many who feel dispossessed of control over their own lives."

Dr Nuha used words I wanted to hear. She was on my side.

"Our women marched on Parliament House to protest the culture of misogyny in the parliamentary system. Our Prime Minister didn't go out to meet them and put their cause on the backburner."

"It was similar in Egypt. In January 2011 a women's march took place but, in its wake, it was considered not important to protest for women. Since then, many young women had tried to seek independence and agency in their own lives, but it is very difficult for them." [4] She stroked her crossed arms, her attention fully upon me.

I related to what Dr Nuha was telling me. Australia was meant to be a 'civilised' country but the patriarchy disguised itself in many forms.

"Probably you feel like most women in Egypt," Dr Nuha was empathetic. "Unfortunately, they are subject to control that mirrors the military regime; they rely on relationships and power structures of force and obedience."

"Thank you for understanding," I said with tears in my eyes. I wanted to reach out to her and show her I was there rallying with her too. "In my teen years my parents didn't let up on their controlling behaviour. They said I could leave home only when I got married."

"It's much the same for most girls in Egypt. They may leave the family house only when married. Marriage is a compulsory institution that perpetuates the patriarchal system." Dr Nuha prepared my script as we spoke. She smiled and gave me the script. "Get yourself lots of rest and sleep. Your blood tests came back clear; you are a very healthy woman."

"Thank you so much Dr Nuha. I appreciate how you take the time to talk to me, especially about such important matters. Men's complications seem to come first in social systems worldwide. It's lovely to honour the issues women face with you."

"You are very welcome, my dear," her tone was calm and reassuring.

"I won't take up any more of your time, I know you are very busy."

She nodded, listening intently.

"I am writing a court case as part of my story. I would greatly appreciate if you agreed for me to include you as a witness?"

"Yes, dear. What do I have to do?"

"I am spending hours, finding data, doing research and talking to experts. May I quote you that it is highly probable my family mirrored a military regime like most families in Egypt?"

"Do you want me to testify as an expert witness?"

"Oh no," I said with a smile, "it's part of my story."

"Of course, dear." She smiled back. "It is important to inform the world we live in." She clasped her two hands as if in private prayer for me.

"To support your case, you may say that you have presented with symptoms consistent with complex PTSD much like those suffered by many from the armed forces after returning from their deployment."

"Thank you so much," I said, grateful that she agreed to involve herself in my story. My case was mounting.

Dr Nuha opened the door with her gracious outstretched arm. I left knowing that she understood me.

By the time I returned home, the fire-ball sun had sunken beyond the horizon. Its orange phosphorous glow ordained the transition from day into night. In this place, my ocean harbour home, I was safe. My security was justified by Dr Nuha's support of my search for answers. The rich burnt-orange afterglow of sunset nourished my soul with a sense of belonging, the same sense I felt at school when I was a little girl. School was my safe place away from the violent house in which I was abused, except for the day my mum came to visit my teacher.

CHAPTER 9

The School Visit

1963 autumn
Elster

"There is a dark line between the lips in the outline of several waves in a turbulent storm - it says don't kiss me, don't fool me I'm a dancer who cannot dance."

Marilyn Monroe, poem fragment, *Roxbury Notes*, 1958[1]

The tiny piece of security I found for myself as a child was at primary school. I enjoyed my schoolwork, playing with the other kids in the playground and I strived to please my teacher. Parents came to school on parent-teacher day but the playground was one boundary they didn't cross. Well, I thought it was until the day my mum marched across my school yard during playtime. She walked with her beak nose jutting out in front as if it was a radar on a submarine navigating her mission. When they saw her, my friends looked excited and panicky at the same time.

"Your mum's here," my friend Michelle whispered in my ear.

The other kids flocked around me. My body stiffened and, with a dazed stare, I watched her march toward my detachable classroom, set apart from the main school buildings making it easy for her to stride straight in.

"Why?" I said to myself, humiliated as my school friends barked with laughter.

I crept towards the classroom, shadowed by a few other children and looked through the door from a distance. My eyes widened when I saw she was wearing her mink-fur stole. The tiny head of the dead animal drooped from her shoulder. Her lips were fire-engine red, an extra curve applied to her thin upper lip. I didn't know whether to feel embarrassed or proud of my movie-star mother. I squeezed my eyes shut. Was this real?

She wasn't meant to be here in the playground, this place was for kids only. It was not for Mum's wanting to look like Marilyn Monroe, her peroxide blonde hair style and her ciggies tucked away neatly in her tuppence clutch. God knows why she was dressed up like a movie star. Marilyn had died; I saw it on the newspapers on my way to school. All I knew was she was a famous actress and beautiful. Everyone knew her, even the kids at school.

My school friends continued to gather around. With wide grins they chirped at the cocky bird and then at me.

"Your mother is here!"

"You are so lucky, she is so pretty."

On and on they went like they had never seen a Marilyn Monroe look-alike in the flesh before. Perhaps their mothers were plain compared to my mother. She caused shock waves through the school yard, parading in her Tinseltown get up. She was startling like a model from a fashion glamour magazine but it was also improper.

My mother didn't make eye contact with me, rather she walked straight past, preferring to regale, swagger and glide on her imaginary red carpet. The kids in the playground would never understand my mistrust of my mum's visit. I tried to keep my chin up and think positively as to why Mum would come unannounced to my playground. But her bizarre antics caused me to think she had thought up another torture for me. Dread gnawed at me even though my school friends were abuzz with excitement.

Once she entered my little outcast classroom, her and my old spinster teacher, Ms Crabapple, went head-to-head for the entire lunch break. I wished I could hear what they were saying but they were too far away.

My mother then teetered off, refusing to acknowledge me and we peeled back into the classroom. I shook with embarrassment, sure that everyone knew something was very wrong. We sat at our desks for a few seconds before Ms Crabapple addressed the class.

"Everyone be seated except for you," she looked directly at me, "you can come up here."

My legs felt like jelly as I walked to the front to the class. The little security I had was being taken from me. Red veins throbbed in my teacher's neck and her wrinkled mouth curled up, berating me in front of my Grade Three class.

"Look at this girl!" She pointed her gnarly-knuckled finger at me. "She is a thief and a liar!"

Some of my friends gasped while others just sat there at their desks, mouths ajar.

She shoved my lunch pass in her top drawer with a bang.

"You are no longer permitted to get fish and chips at lunch time. You can eat sandwiches inside the classroom."

Everyone sat there, unusually quiet in their seats. Even Bobby Jones refrained from making some joke about it.

I hung my head and ghosted back to my desk, without any idea what I supposedly did to deserve this treatment. All I knew was that my reputation was ruined. I had lost everything I built at school because of my mum's hatred for me.

After the school visit, I resented my mother even more. Like church, my safe place was stolen from me. Any opportunity to belong away from the clutches of her madness was gone. She had broken what little peace I had and I didn't recover until the next year when I was promoted to Mr Parker's class in the main building, upstairs on the top floor.

I assumed she wouldn't make it up the two flights of stairs in her ridiculous high heels and nicotine reduced lung capacity. There would never be anyone else like Marilyn for her to emulate.

And Marilyn was dead.

2021 late autumn
Ocean harbour home

> *"You must suffer—*
> *to lose your dark golden*
> *when your covering of*
> *even dead leaves leave you*
> *strong and naked*
> *you must be —*
> *alive — when looking dead*
> *straight though bent*
> *with wind*
> *And bear the pain & the joy*
> *of newness on your limbs*
> *Loneliness— be still"*

Marilyn Monroe, poem fragment,
Waldorf-Astoria Stationery, 1955[2]

The breeze was cool, its late summer fragrance drifted north and lulled from its recalcitrance. The reddish autumn hum slowly shifted it southward. I sat at my desk, the adjacent window open and the Indian summer breathed its last warm sigh on my skin hinting at cooler weather. My book order had arrived and I eagerly unwrapped it after collecting it from the delivery guy. It unfurled into my waiting hands, *Fragments: Poems, Intimate Notes, Letters* by Marilyn Monroe. The blurb read, "for anyone who truly wants to know the depth and complexity of Monroe's feelings, this is a must have book." *New York Daily News*.

I wanted to know more about this movie star than what I could get from a Google search. Memories of my mother were linked with her since Mum tried so hard to emulate her—her blonde bombshell hair, hourglass figure and a tendency to walk with her hips to name a few. My legs were stiff from my sunset shoot the previous night, so I sat on my snug lounge for a close reading of *Fragments*.

Everything about Marilyn's cover photo was appealing. Her gorgeous platinum hair was curled like ocean waves about her beautiful face. She glanced sideways and a shadow cast over her glamorous features, her dreamy eyes, heavy with mascara, created the feel of a faraway place. Perhaps she was looking out to sea, an implied mystery to her being. The inner corners of her arched eyebrows were angled upward which signalled sadness and suffering that her writing strived to rise above.

The balmy autumn breeze found its way into the lounge room. Leaning back into the sofa, my eyelids drooped – my iPhone dropped to the floor – the record button snapped on – click – Marilyn's beautiful face was foremost in my sleepy mind.

A golden mist filled the room, Marilyn sat opposite me on the sofa, our toes were pointing toward each other. I stopped my hands from trembling, not wanting to give away my anticipation... her smile was beautiful... a forced confidence, bending to the will of society... ten thousand cameras pointing at her...

"Hi Marilyn. I'm sorry to interrupt you but I just wanted to say I love your handwriting." This wasn't just a good conversation starter, I meant it.

"Thank you! That's so kind of you. I must admit I never dreamt the public would read my poems and notes. I'm so glad I carefully self-edited them with those cute little dashes and strokes. What do you think so far?" She raised her legs and bare feet onto the lounge and hugged her black leather-bound notebook to her bent knee. Her white three-quarter casual pants wrapped firmly to the most famous body in the world.

"You are so much more than a sex object Marilyn. I suppose you are not familiar with the term since it arrived with the modern feminist movement not long after you died."

I hated to break the news to her.

"Well, I sort of knew. One of my close friends and actor, Tony Curtis, said that 'sex was, then as now, the only way to achieve anything'. I mean, I

read books to understand myself and my own desires. But I tried to keep some distance when approaching the books... literature belonged to men. I guess a sex object and a damsel in distress are the same thing?"

"You are right, Marilyn. Sexism objectifies women and ruins their lives. In your time, women's roles were to serve men. Equal rights were not in public discussion."

"I've worked hard to succeed in acting. I even opened my own studio in New York, Marilyn Monroe Productions, but most men in the industry never forgave me for that." Her bottom lip dropped and she sighed. It was that look of silent suffering that endeared her to the feminists. "How did the feminists change things?"

"They marched to give women options apart from being a housewife or sex kitten."

"That would explain why Laurence, the lead actor, was disdainful and haughty of me on my production of The Prince and the Showgirl. He was unable to accept my cultural, artistic side I had developed in New York."

"I know, right? And he was awarded a knighthood, Sir Laurence Olivier, by the queen for his contribution to the film industry and theatre and all you got was a bottle of sleeping pills for yours. No offence."

"None taken. The media didn't help me either. They created a joyful 'Marilyn image', making me out to be a dumb blonde. I was never allowed to express myself, not really."

"Your death was not in vain. You became a martyr for the feminists."
She looked at me in disbelief.

"There was a stage when I became pessimistic about love and the passage of time." She held her notebook tight to her chest. "When Arthur and I stayed in London, I stumbled over his diary and discovered he was disappointed in me. He felt ashamed of me in front of his intellectual peers and he had doubts about our marriage. I was devastated... betrayed." Her coral pink fingertips prophetically glided over her notebook and I imagined her as Inanna, the mythical goddess of love, war and sex, the decider of the fate of her ungrateful husband.

"You remind me of Inanna. She was enraged with her husband and threw him to the demons for his disloyalty, lack of love and his unwillingness to give to her like a husband should.[3] She punished him for separating himself from her like Arthur did to you."

"I guess so. I respected his work and loved reading his plays, *The Death of a Salesman* and *The Crucible*. When I read his diary, I discovered he was isolating me in pursuit of his own superiority."

"There is no greater betrayal than an act of isolation. I understand completely, my parents did the same to me."

My feet dug deeper into the lounge, empathy overwhelmed me because I understood her.

"Yes, I was torn apart by greed, lust and coercion by the men in my life," she said as if quitting a team.

"They were not forgiven by the feminists. They put your face on the hardships that women face every day, sexual abuse, abusive relationships and sexual objectification."

"Why were you isolated?"

I was surprised she would be interested in my past.

"Mum was a victim of the times too. My father was cruel to her and ran after other women. She was isolated and powerless to throw Dad to the demons. If she had only tried to understand her darker side, she may have stopped him from hurting me too. They joined together to subjugate me into silence and not speak of him being a paedophile."

"My mother was an alcoholic and abandoned me."

"That's another reason the feminists adopted you because you spoke out about child abuse, victimisation and a mother's madness." I paused, this was the right time. "I'm building a court case to bring my perpetrators to justice in my memoir. Would you testify for me?"

"Of course, I must be a part of any movement that supports women from being isolated and forced into sex! I know the pain of toxic masculinity in my own life, like 'a dark line between the lips of waves' trying to control me into something I wasn't. One last thing?"

"Yes, anything."

"Do you feel that your book will have an impact on your society today? I mean you are including me and I was fifty years ago." She pressed a finger to her famous lips.

"The feminists marched to Parliament House last month. The leaders appealed to women to write their experiences of toxic masculinity and misogyny. The more of us who contribute, the more they can inform the systems of power how to change. Governments may change and society may move forward *but, nothing has really changed, sexual politics presents differently, that's all. Your voice is as relevant today as it was back then." I felt like bowing to her in gratitude.*

"I am so proud of you." She leaned towards me with that beautiful smile that charmed the world. "We have so much in common. I didn't go to premieres, previews, or parties because I was doing courses in English literature. I read Dostoevsky, Whitman, Beckett, Hemingway and Kerouac. I can't write like them but I was motivated to write my stories, poems and notes because I was unhappy. Writing helped me to seek the truth at the heart of both events and people." She tapped her elegant fingers while listing her readings and the consequences.

"Women's writing is different from men's writing," I told her. "We seek to integrate a harmonious society whereas men often seek to dominate society. You would like Margaret Atwood's The Handmaid's Tale. The message is that the control of women's bodies is wrong, she communicates examples of objectification and violence against women. It was first published in 1985."

"I sure have missed out." A shadow of sadness fell across her face. "But it's wonderful that more women are writing books. Perhaps my death somehow contributed to this change. I hope they carry similar messages to Margaret's book."

"I promise you, your life and your death have inspired so many to raise awareness of sexual objectification. I'm sure Judge Pizan will be delighted to read your testimony. She wrote a book too, The City of Ladies, to protect women from the male writers. Those men isolated and betrayed women's images in their books and Christine opposed it."

Marilyn appeared tired so I ended our conversation by taking her hands in mine.

It was time for her to head back to her studio.

"I thank you from the bottom of my heart," I said to her.

She smiled and her beautiful goddess figure transcended above the clouds into the violet mist.

My eyes adjusted to the purple pre-dawn sunlight filtering through the window. My iPhone lay on the floor, peering out from the cosy sofa rug. I was sure it would be out of battery.

Before rising, I remained drawn to the vision of Marilyn. Her presence awakened something inside me. Marilyn's departure from this world shook everyone to our core and a new understanding of violence to women emerged in her wake. I was beginning to understand my departure from the school and why the school principal punished me for men's mistakes.

CHAPTER 10

The Strip Search

2003 early summer
Far north high school

"If you have a mother, daughter or a friend
Maybe it is time, time you comprehend
The world that you live in ain't the same one as them
So don't punish me for not being a man."

Marina from *Man's World,* 2020[1]

It was the last day of school. The air was filled with the chanting and singing of students as they fist pumped each other farewells. They were glad school was over until next year. It was part of growing up, for them to be independent. They were tired of following policy and they welcomed the holidays. They were gone by lunchtime.

Before they left, my students were waiting with bated breath.

"Miss, will you be our teacher next year?"

They gathered around me, eager looks on their faces.

"I don't know. I'm sorry, we don't get our timetables until the New Year."

I loved my classes and hoped to carry as many students forward as possible.

"Whoever your teacher is next year, I'm sure they will be great and I'm grateful to have been your teacher this year."

I gave them a warm grin but inside my heart was heavy.

"But there'll be no teacher like you. Trust us, you are one of a kind. You are our friend and care about us besides being our teacher."

I stood there receiving the gifts and Christmas cards they gave to me with affectionate notes of gratitude. I held back tears, hoping to get another chance to be there for them next year.

"You're on holidays now. Go and have fun. Keep safe everybody!"

Deep down I felt the same bond to my students as they did to me, I would miss them terribly. They spoke highly of me and I trusted them. Our student-teacher relationship was one that was free of toxicity, unlike my child-parent relationships that I desperately wanted to leave behind in the past. But I didn't want to leave these kids. Keeping my own pain bottled up inside, I gave them a group hug and bid them a happy holiday.

The English staffroom had shed its mountains of marking and reporting. Dislodged textbooks were replaced on shelves and temporary neatness was restored until school resumed next year. I headed over to the sports hall where long trestle tables were set up with Christmas decorations. Flies buzzed over the party food and swarmed when mesh covers were lifted. The humidity was stifling, barely reduced by the hard-working air conditioner. A mixture of relief and excitement filled the air.

The hum of jovial voices was met with the chink of glasses.

"Cheers, here's to a happy holiday and a good year well done." The voice came from the corner across the hall.

Avoiding eye contact with anyone, I scanned the celebratory group. The principal moved himself between the teachers. His blue magnetic eyes took charge. I was left on the outside.

I slighted him, knowing he was going to get me back. I wasn't sure how or when, but retribution was coming. Clearly, I was not one of his attractions, the least said between us the better.

I tried to block out his joviality with others. All I could think of him was that he silenced me from speaking out about the school paedophile. I imagined myself taking him to the highest cliff and throwing him to the demons.

Over the years, I had observed his toxic masculinity, taking his temper out on underprivileged and mostly female students. One time he balled out my pregnant senior student for not complying with school uniform. I remember her sitting in the library catching up on her studies when he confronted her, obviously pregnant and out of uniform because it didn't fit her anymore.

"What are you doing here dressed like that," he scolded her. "Sit up straight. You look disgraceful. You have no respect for this school."

He ended up severing any connection with the school community she had, leaving her without an education and isolated. He depersonalised her viciously and once, she came to me crying.

"Why is he like this to me? I knew it wouldn't work. I can't come back here."

Her tears spilled over her flushed cheeks.

"I'll arrange for the work to be sent to you and you can apply for special circumstances to sit your exams. Don't give up now."

I didn't want to solve her problems but I wanted to protect her with what little I had to offer.

I had worked hard to stop her from falling through the cracks, to realise her senior year education before the birth of her child and in a fit of manic rage, Luther had destroyed all the work I had done to nurture this beautiful, fragile young woman. He had completely undermined the pilot program of inclusivity of teenage pregnancy, when our social workers, parents and teachers supported it. Her parents were not influential in the community so his behaviour went unchecked.

And then there was the incident of Sarah, a Year Ten student with cystic fibrosis. Her life expectancy was twenty-five years. Between severe bouts of illness and hospitalisation she tried to attend school.

"Miss, can I go to the bathroom please?" she piped up, a lollipop stick protruding from the side of her mouth. I allowed her to suck it in class because the sugar probably kept her 'up'.

"Sure, be as quick as you can," I said and before I had a chance to suggest she leave the lollipop behind, she hurried off out of the classroom.

I watched through the open door and caught sight of her across the quadrangle. Then my stomach sunk.

She was bailed up by Luther.

"What are you doing out of class?" I could just hear him from the classroom.

He had planted himself firmly between her and the ladies toilets, feet wide apart leaning his tall, stooped, skin-cancer ridden body into her frightened face so she couldn't escape or speak for herself. He dominated her to the point of cruelty.

"Get that thing out of your mouth! Who's your teacher?"

She said something, I assumed it was my name.

"Thought so! Look at your uniform! You're a disgrace to your school."

An explosion of seemingly little things blasted out of his mouth. He held no compassion for her condition and ordered her back to class.

She went scarlet and burst into tears. Visibly shaken, Sarah sat in my class for a while and then she went home early. I didn't see her for a few weeks after that. I'm sure the trauma with the bully principal brought on a severe bout of her illness.

The clank of a mug on the bench jolted me out of my thoughts. I turned to see Annie making herself a coffee. She never warmed to me since the incident at camp. I looked around the room for Troy. The little magnetic field had disbanded, Luther was nowhere to be seen.

I nudged my colleague and whispered, "Where's Troy?"

"He's not here. There's a rumour he's been transferred to another school out west. Already left the area, wife and kids gone too."

I then remembered not seeing him around the last few weeks, as if his transfer was inevitable, along with the transfer of his paedophile behaviour. Heat surged through my limbs and a sick feeling churned in the pit of my stomach. He was free to do it all again in another school. More children would be vulnerable to his harm, something that would damage them for a lifetime. God Almighty, I knew the consequences as clear as day and I was helpless to stop it.

Like all terrorists Luther used the strategy of surprise. He stormed the stairwell to my staffroom, feet wide apart, his tall skin-cancer ridden body stooped over me, blocking my way as I tried to leave.

"Here's something for you," he said and shoved an envelope into my hand.

I was forced to take it. The letter contained a list of points he had gathered to prove my teaching incompetency and thus a demotion and pay reduction or a forced resignation. Either way, it was pay back for being the 'whistle-blower' on his paedophile buddy.

He had 'handled that problem' by himself without drawing attention to it and protected the school from legal, financial and reputational risk. Now he had to tie up the final loose end.

He smirked and bore those blue eyes into me, knowing full well he had diminished my capacity to earn for my family.

He then turned away and strolled sure-footed back down the corridor like I wasn't worth his time.

The content of the letter loomed over me. It was like I was under a dark spell from which I could never regenerate. It reminded me of the Greek goddess Demeter who was refused help by her brother to return her abducted daughter Persephone from the underground. Luther ruthlessly and deliberately put high school students in harm's way since Troy remained in the education system. He shielded the perpetrator and projected harmful accusations about me, the woman who spoke out. My sources tell me the principal didn't remain long at the school after that but the damage had been done. I left my teaching position, having had enough of the wilful disregard of perpetrators getting off scot-free.

My incestuous father, mother and grandmother had had enough corroboration and support throughout literature to put blame on the wanton daughter, just like the principal had enough support throughout the education system to put blame on me. Whether the abuse was in the home behind locked doors or in plain sight in the education system, it left me devastated and destitute.

I gave up teaching and the toxic masculinity that went with it. Like an abused child, I fled a powerful force with nowhere to go. The antagonistic forces were too strong and I was forced into the underground. My soul had been 'strip searched' and I needed to find my way out again.

In the confusion, a dark memory resurfaced with analogies to the Greek myth of Persephone, daughter-goddess of agriculture and her abduction by Hades, God of the underworld.

My first memory, *In the beginning*, was the scent of flowers. After that I was spirited away to a sunless world, as was Persephone by Hades. In this dark place my grandmother sought me out to conduct a strip search to punish me. After all, she had adopted the values of toxic masculinity.

1963 early winter
Elster

"Persephone herself is but a voice or a darkness invisible enfolded
in the deeper dark of the arms Plutonic, and pierced with the
passion of dense gloom, among the splendour of torches of darkness
shedding darkness on the lost bride and her groom."

D.H. Lawrence[2]

I was getting ready for school when I heard my grandmother in the kitchen. It sounded like she was hissing in my mother's ear. She was a wild snake that slid down Jasper Road from her house in Wicklow, under our front door and into our fake-happy family home in Elster.

I pulled on my worn black leather school shoes. They were two sizes too small and the soles were filled with cardboard to cover the holes the size of golf balls. With some luck I found a pair of matching socks, even though they needed a good wash. Most often, the socks were irregular and with holes in them. They would fall below my ankles, causing me discomfort and embarrassment, coupled with my ragged shoes.

Hopefully this morning I could find a blouse to wear, dirty or not, other than the floral, flannelette pyjama jacket I had worn the previous day to school. I had hoped it would pass as a pretty blouse but the other kids were not convinced. They jeered at my face and behind my back, "look at her, she comes from a poor house."

Mum, whether she was too lazy or whatever her reasons, had not done any washing for days and she convinced me the pyjama jacket would pass as a blouse as she shoved me out the door. This morning I found one, crumpled under my bed.

It wasn't usual for my grandmother to visit before school. I wanted to leave the house before she saw me. My temperature started to rise as I fumbled to tie my straggly shoelaces but it was too late.

"Come here." Mum's voice shrieked. "Your grandmother has something to say to you!"

Trying to keep my breathing under control, I followed orders.

"Today you will come home at lunch to be strip searched."

Her face tightened into a snarl.

I held my elbows to my side keeping as small as possible. I didn't know what she meant.

"Are you listening to me?"

I looked away from her, blinking my eyes. Inside, my tummy was in knots that were so tight I would never be able to untie them.

"Look at me while I'm speaking to you!"

Her arm muscles started to bulge, so I ducked, scared she was going to hit me.

"Yes, I'll come home at lunch." I whispered, unable to speak any louder.

Whatever a strip search was, I hoped it wasn't going to hurt.

"If you've been stealing lollies from the corner shops or the other kid's colouring pencils, we'll catch you red handed!" Her voice went at a wild pace.

What on earth did she mean? My head began to spin, my little heart fled into a panic. My mother sat in silence, nodding her normal obedience.

"That's what they do in prisons to the liars and cheats of criminals." The words spouted from Grandmother's frothy mouth. "They get 'em to take all their clothes off and search 'em for stolen goods."

They're taking my clothes off? My palms started to sweat, I hoped to God my father wouldn't be here.

Grandmother was raving but she had the power to control me and my mum. She would do anything to console her son that I was a liar and he had nothing to worry about. To make me guilty, she would prove that I was a thief.

"You're a thief and I will prove it!" her blinking eyes quickened. She twirled her *Viscount* cigarette, smouldering to its butt. I too would be reduced to ash when she was finished with me.

I made my way to the school bus stop with my brother. I was beside myself the whole morning. How could I be myself when I had to disassociate from the real world and conform to these unreasonable grounds of crazy?

Most mornings I caught the bus to school and in the afternoons I walked home. Mum wanted to save the money from the bus fare for cigarettes—her nerve sticks. Thoughts raced through my head, too many to handle at once. Firstly, I only had one hour for lunch and the walk from school to home and back again would almost take up that time. I was nervous about getting back to school on time, they were strict about the bells, and I would be punished if I was late.

And second, kids never went home for lunch. We didn't wander the streets at lunch time unless you had a pass to buy fish and chips at the corner store which was a five minute walk from school and I was banned from that since Mum turned up at school that day.

The teachers would stand at the front gate and monitor your safety to and from the shop. When I asked my grandmother about this, she said the school wouldn't miss me and the strip search was far more important. She had it all worked out in her crazy mind. I was being forced to act like a criminal to be punished like a criminal—which I was not. Strip searches were used by police for criminals, not for little kids. But there was no way I could assert my rights and object to their unlawful conduct.

Negotiating the best route to the house and back to school was another problem. The shortest and quickest route was by the flasher's house. When we walked home from school we always walked in groups or pairs.

One afternoon the girls were on high alert; giggling, pointing and grabbing each other as they passed the flasher's house. He would be waiting for us on his veranda, naked from the waist down, his whopping penis straddled over his legs as he spread them apart and stretched himself enticingly across his filthy sofa. Oh my, I had no idea this sort of thing went on until the girls explained to me, he was a pervert to be avoided. We were to never walk on his side of the street. But there was safety in numbers, so we clung to each other and laughed and cried at the dirty old man.

The dirty old man with his penis hanging out, on display for all the schoolgirls to see, brought me to thinking. The schoolboys never worried about him and thought we were hysterical for carrying on such a treat. They said that dirty old men didn't like the boys and the thing between his legs was meant for the girls. Somehow the exchange of information about men's penises between girls and boys my age, I realised that all boys were born with a penis and all girls were not.

I realised that this was the object my father had rubbed between my legs as he dangled me upside down, like a piece of meat, in my bed in the middle of the dark night. I figured my mum knew about his penis too and she was angry with me that I had told lies about my father rubbing his penis into me, hard like a classroom ruler. Contrary to Mum's accusations, since I didn't know what it was then, I wasn't lying.

I made the association between penises and being naughty—and dirty— and that dirty old men should put them back in their trousers where they belong and not between little girl's legs. Inwardly, I felt terribly embarrassed. I wanted to climb into a deep hole in the ground and never come out. My father had used his penis on me when it was widely known in the community that it was taboo.

This insight made me even more sceptical that our family secret would be revealed to others since I gathered that it didn't happen in other families. If the kids at school found out I would be further ridiculed and made to feel ashamed. As it was, I didn't belong at home, so I desperately wanted to belong in my school, even if I didn't fit in some times. My sense of belonging in my school was my only hope to survive in the world.

Having to plot my lunchtime break-out to run home and be strip searched by my evil grandmother was the most obscure thing a child should have to think about. As I sat on the bus next to my brother, I wrung my hands together in the grip of death itself. I was flushed and confused by the moral dilemma set before me, tears rolled down my face.

My brother caught a glimpse of me.

"What's wrong with you?"

How on earth could I explain to him the horrors I was being subjected to? He wasn't at home most of the time when the torture and brainwashing took place. Of course, they timed my punishments when no one was around to witness them. If an outsider heard anything, my brother may have been able to corroborate my story.

I avoided his question and sniffed my tears back up my nose, wiping it at the same time.

"It's just a cold," I said. I couldn't tell him because he wouldn't believe me. No one would believe me.

I sat in my Grade Four class that morning, my attention drifted in and out of what my kind teacher, Mr Parker, was saying. If only I could tell him about my predicament and ask him if he would adopt me, I could live happily ever after in a normal home and Mr and Mrs Parker would love me and be kind to me.

Then my thoughts switched to the horror events of 1963 that saturated the media. For a moment I thought I could self-immolate, by running downstairs to the school courtyard and setting myself alight. I could burn myself to death in protest of my family's persecution of me just like the Buddhist monk in the Saigon Street protested the South Vietnam Government's persecution of Buddhists. With the newspaper stands, television, radio and *Time* magazine covers, even an eight-year-old child could not escape the stark images flashed over the screens, pages and protesting voices of these turbulent times.

In my soul, I was already on fire.

The school bell rung, foreshadowing the coming of my strip search and a symbolic death 'knell' to match that of King Duncan at the hands of the murderous Macbeth in Shakespeare's play. Mr Parker had read us the kid's version. My fear was projected on the bell, it was my summoning to a grim destiny.

I descended the school stairs and hurriedly made my way to the school gate which was never used by students during lunch break. I had been commanded by my grandmother to leave the school regardless of the rules. Despite how deeply troubled I was by this I would not dare disobey her. I exited the gate and slipped away into the brash unknown realms of the strip search.

Walking briskly, I kept my back straight so as not to display weakness to the public who may be watching me. I made my way down Wheatley Road to avoid the flasher's house. It was longer by a few minutes but I couldn't bear the thought of him. My anxiety was already beyond what I could deal with. Gradually, my steps increased into a jog as time was tight and I had to get back to school on time. My mother, along with the whole of Australia, idolised Betty Cuthbert. She was Australia's golden girl who had won three gold medals at the Melbourne Olympic Games in 1956 for track running. Mum was always on about Betty Cuthbert and her long and fast sprinting legs. She said that Betty was one in a million and I could never be like her because my legs were too short. But it didn't matter, if being like Betty Cuthbert right now was a way for me to get through this terrible business then I would run. Keeping my head held high, I forced my legs into a noble jog in the hope of convincing the passersby and street walkers I was undertaking a permissible role.

The streets were bustling with activity: people were coming and going in all sorts of activities: shopping, deliveries, visiting or just strolling. The roads were busy with traffic, mostly Holden and Fords. Traffic lights had been installed on the intersection of Elster Road where I had to cross, go past the corner shops and the newspaper stands, and then turn up towards my house.

There was an older pedestrian couple stopped at the red lights, waiting for their cue to cross when they turned their gaze on to me. I thought that if I pretended to be Betty Cuthbert, they would be convinced I wasn't out of the school grounds without permission but rather I was in training for the next Olympic Games. My hair was golden like Betty's, I lifted my knees and tried to let my blonde hair bounce in the wind just like Betty when she ran. I also tried to keep my breathing controlled although on the inside I gasped for air so much because my sorrow was so deep, I was drowning in it.

After an uncomfortable pause, the couple looked away and the lights turned green. I walked briskly across the road and then ran up the hilly slope of Elster Road. Finally, yet most ruefully, I made my way to our street. Distraught, I went through our small wrought-iron gate, past the flowerbeds of thorned rose bushes and stepped onto my secret place of prayer on the veranda. I knocked on our front door, dreading what lay ahead.

My grandmother opened the door with her thrust-out chest.

"Go to the kitchen. Your Aunt Dot is here for a visit!"

I was so pleased to see my great aunt in anticipation that the strip search would be called off but to no avail.

Aunt Dot's visit was a time waster, even though she showed me kindness. I was so anxious about what was going on, and that I had to be back in school, that I could not stop shifting in my chair. I was made to sit and eat with them. My mother hardly let out a word. Grandmother quickly put Aunt Dot in her place and told her why I was home from school at lunchtime.

"She is not what you think Dot. You shouldn't fill her head with praise. She's a very naughty girl and she steals things. She's a thief!"

Aunt Dot looked surprised, I could sense her objections but that didn't stop her sister.

"Don't let her fool you. We've had no end of trouble with her!"

I was ordered to finish up my sandwich and to go out onto the front veranda for the strip search.

I walked down the hallway in our little brick veneer house, it felt like the earth was dying around me and the great famine had crossed our house. Any seed of love was bound to failure. Even Aunt Dot's protests fell on deaf ears. My grandmother stood over me and ordered me to strip my cardigan, blouse and skirt.

"Go on, get them off. And it's no good looking at your Aunt Dot for sympathy because she can't help you."

Standing forlorn, stripped to my underpants and singlet, she went through the sleeves and parts of my clothes with her gnarly, witch-hands. She deliberately shamed me to no end, especially with Aunt Dot looking on.

I thought perhaps the search was over when her grinding voice shrilled, "Take off your shoes!"

Didn't she know I had holes in my shoes the size of golf balls and if I had anything concealed in them it would be a miracle. Frustrated that she found nothing she said for me to take off my socks too.

"Come on Mary, leave the poor girl alone," Aunt Dot objected.

"Stay out of it, Dot!"

By this time, I was sitting on the floor and peeled off my socks. There was nothing to be found in my socks either, but my grandmother insisted I was still a thief.

She ordered me to get dressed and get back to school without one ounce of empathy in her crotchety voice and not one ounce of love or moral support from my mother. My grandmother's ego was puffed up but mine was at rock bottom.

Bewildered, Aunt Dot stood on the veranda like one of the three monkeys: see, say and do no evil. She was the closest person to observe my mistreatment but nothing came of it. There was no intervention. Choking on my words, I begged to get back to school before the bell.

I tucked in my shirt, lunged for the front gate and bolted up the street towards the school as fast as I could. My eight-year-old mind could not comprehend the link between the voyeuristic strip search and my grandmother's preoccupation with me taking my clothes off. She certainly derived enjoyment from seeing the pain it caused me baring myself to the world almost naked.

She was just like my father.

They both liked looking at my bare body. All I felt was shame, standing there almost naked in front of Aunt Dot. I didn't understand how they could enjoy deliberately torturing and humiliating me. It was an adult thing I didn't understand but I knew it was not right, and was very, very rude.

If I was to get back to school before the bell I had to take the quickest route by the dirty old man's house. Panicked that I wouldn't get to school on time, I ran as fast as I could along the streets. I tried to keep up the Betty Cuthbert appearance to survive the humiliation of it all. Lucky for me the flasher wasn't on his porch but he could have been hiding in the bushes to grab me as I went past. Adhering to my girl friends' advice, I avoided his side of the street and ran furiously past, expending all the energy I had left.

Once in the school yard, it was evident the bell had long since rung. Silence hung thick in the air over the playground. It was as sombre as King Duncan's courtyard after Macbeth had slain him; the only sound was the owl that marked his death. A small bird in the distance was droning a hollow sound in the heat of that summer afternoon. My spirits were so low that I paced myself across the school oval and along the path to the girls' lavatories. If I was caught outside of class, I would say I was going to the toilet.

I had barely stepped foot on the path when the sick bay attendant came from behind me.

"Are you all right?" She asked with a concerned expression.

Speechless, I looked at her and felt myself collapse to the ground.

When I came to, I was lying on crisp white sheets in a sick bay bed. I looked at myself in the steel framed mirror on the wall. Sweat beaded on my forehead and my face had turned blood-pumped scarlet.

Deep down I hoped the sick bay ladies would see through my charade and send the police to my house to arrest my grandmother and parents. I had exhibited so many signs of child abuse: my dirty old shoes with holes in them, inappropriate clothing for the hot weather. I was the girl who wore a pyjama jacket to school. My body odour from the exhaustion of running stunk, my fingernails were bitten to the nail bed, my hair was hacked up to my ears, and if they looked under my trouser pants they would see welts and bruises from the frequent beatings. And I was emotionally bereft—I was a mess.

The ladies were full of questions that I found difficult to answer. As a child, all I thought about was avoiding getting into trouble.

They felt my forehead for a fever and at first were convinced I was very sick. They inquired as to why my mother sent me to school when I was full of temperature. I wanted to tell them about the strip search and leaving school without permission, but I didn't think the ladies would believe such a wild story, and I was afraid of retribution from my grandmother. I sipped the glass of water the ladies had given me and my temperature, or overheating from the running, began to drop.

I walked back to Mr Parker's class and tried my best to get my schoolwork done that afternoon. However, my heart was full of shame and my head full of gloom. The coloured chalk on the blackboard shed only darkness before my eyes. I was lost. I prayed for someone to give me a torch light and show me the way out but I didn't know how long that was going to take.

2019 early spring
Ocean harbour home

"Spring appears when the time is right
Women are violets coming to light
Don't underestimate the making of life
The planet has a funny way of stopping a fight."

Marina from *Man's World*, 2020[3]

I figured it was a full moon the time my grandmother came up with the idea to strip search me. I was stuck on the idea that people went crazy during a full moon. The repression of its gravitational influence brought about bizarre results in people and took me back to my childhood abusers.

The last full moon shone bright between the clouds through my bedroom window. I remembered it distinctly. Silver rings surrounded it, giving it an ethereal appearance. Just the thought of it made my pulse race.

My phone pinged.

It was on the coffee table next to my camera and head lamp. I reached over, careful not to spill my freshly brewed Glass House Mountains' coffee and read the screen. The message was from my friend and photographer, Sage.

"There's a full moon next Thursday. Meet me at the bluff 5pm for a 5.40pm moonrise, ten minutes before sunset?"

I was excited to hear from Sage but the idea of filming the full moon made my skin crawl. All the same, I had moved here to heal myself from the negative effects of the moon on my psyche and Sage was my sister goddess showing me the way. I no longer wanted to fear the moon. To the contrary, the moon held the promise of helping me to start fresh and realigning my heart with new beginnings. Seeds are best planted in a full moon and then the nurturing, mulching and growing take place in the moon cycle.

I tapped on the photographer's app for moon path, and when it waxed and waned, and was satisfied it would rise close to the lighthouse on the cliffs opposite the bluff. The conditions would be perfect to capture the moon in its full phase, closer to the Earth, an illuminated galactic treasure. I imagined the moon in her fullness, shining on the ocean, lighthouse and rocks reciprocating a halcyon-pink glow bringing home 'the bright dawn scattered' like in the poem by Sappho.

"Yes, love to meet you then. Can't wait! xo."

Sage and I had met on social media through our shared passion for photography. Our friendship was an important part of my networking that I required to complete my personal quest. She loved moon photography and was eager to drag me into it. Sunrises, sunsets, flowers and birds I was comfortable with, but the moon was never my thing, until I met Sage. Perhaps it was a blessing in disguise.

On Thursday morning my phone pinged and this time it read, "I'm so sorry. I've come down with a cold and I can't make our shoot tonight."

I was disappointed because I loved sharing these special moments with my friend.

"That's okay. I'm sorry to hear that you are unwell. Get well soon. I'll message in a day or two to check on you."

I left it at that. I let my mind drift on its own, an opportunity to ponder the calamities of my childhood in my safe place where I was writing my truth. The Greek myth of Demeter came to mind and into my prose.

That evening I was determined to step out of my comfort zone and photograph the moon by myself. It had become a new milestone in my healing. I parked the car as close to the bluff as possible and set off on a near one kilometre walk along the beach path and then up the steps leading up the cliff.

The wind blew offshore and brought a coolness with it, adding to the mystique of my solo journey. Something felt off but I couldn't work out what. Perhaps the light was too bright for the evening or was it that this place looked strangely unfamiliar. Fortunately, I packed a head lamp and pulled it onto my head. Coming out here in the dark might be difficult because the pandanus and she-oaks sentries would obscure most of the moonlight.

In the distance, a torch light.... hovering over the path.... flashing into the trees and then back on to the path... I was curious... was this the answer I was looking for?

It came closer and I squinted my eyes looking into its brightness. I wondered who it could be since I was only aware of one other person in the area, a photographer below. As we came shoulder to shoulder, I caught a glimpse of the torch bearer. She was an old, grey-haired woman who seemed to be quite beside herself.

"I am searching for my daughter, Persephone, she has been taken from me," she let out.

I assumed she was talking to me since I was the only one there.

"Oh, that's terrible!" I felt alarmed for her. "Who took her from you, shouldn't you call the police?"

"A notorious gangster from the underworld has taken her. His name is Hades, the boss of death. Helios, my brother, saw it with his own eyes but he is afraid of the underworld and the godfather Zeus. I pleaded with him to tell them I want her back but he refused to help me. I have no idea who your 'police' are but I am sure they will deny me too. No sane mortal would dare face Zeus.."

She darted her blazing torch light from tree to tree as she spoke, I guessed for any sign of her missing daughter.

"Oh dear, I know how you feel. Many years ago, my child was stolen from me too and I am still searching for her."

I tried not to shine my torch in her eyes out of respect for her grief and emotional withdrawal from the world.

"What stranger stole your child from you?"

"It's not always committed by strangers in dark alleyways. He was much closer to home. It was my father, the truth has been shrouded for the best part of my life. Now I am writing a book to tell the truth about him and his allies."

"What did your mother say?"

"My mother was an ally. She was told about him but she wouldn't accept it. She took it as my fault and tortured me many times."

The old woman looked shocked.

"Are you saying you had no loving and responsible adult to guide you?"

"That's right. They continued the abuse, along with my grandmother, and convinced me it was my fault! I wasn't a bad person but they made out I was."

"Then no one looked after you and protected you?"

"No, they punished and abused me for many years."

My eyes began to well up with tears. I wiped them away and confided to my new friend.

"My brother was a witness but has not spoken about it since. He saw my father in the shadows steal my child inside away. I am now an aged woman but I still grieve for her. I must come to peace with it before I die."

"Men have turned from me but I am a woman and mother myself, I would have never stood for that. Has the world gone mad?"

"The world has fallen into silence and denial," I said as if the earth had opened into a great chasm and humanity had fallen into the underground.

Her eyes didn't leave me except to check the trees for signs of her daughter – a broken twig, scattered flowers, a maiden's headdress.

"I have read about you. You are Demeter and have much power. Your throne is on Mount Olympus where you preside over your domain as goddess of almost everything – the harvest, food, agriculture, fertility, seasons and the cycle of life?"

"Yes, now I am crownless until I find my daughter. You must not give my identity away."

"Don't worry," I assured her. "I won't blow your cover, you are safe with me."

"And you with me," she replied and passed me some pumpkin seeds for nourishment. "I am disappointed the world has not become more enlightened since my time. It seems to be worse since this happened to you in your own family and the instinct to remain silent is part of the foundation of society."

"That's right Demi. May I call you Demi?"

She nodded with a beautiful smile that reminded me of the statue of Flora.

"Nobody wanted to see what was happening and even if they had a hunch, they didn't want to know." I was feeling depressed but talking to Demi helped me to keep perspective. "There were fun family outings that I held onto but it also created a false sense of a loving family unit."

"All children want to belong and need to be nurtured." She passed me her flask of lemon water and urged me to drink. "It can be so strong that we make excuses for mistreatment by dissociating from what is really happening."

Demi was all-knowing and I was pleased we met on the path. It was our destiny.

"You must not give up searching for your child and I will not give up looking for mine," she said.

I nodded in agreement.

"What is that sound?" Her eyes widened.

We walked to the end of the path. High on the bluff I saw far into the cloudless horizon. A family of migrating whales breached intermittently close to the shore. I heard their low frequency song bounce off the waves as they pulsed, clicked and navigated their way south for summer.

"Don't worry Demi. It's the whales migrating south." I was enthralled by their majestic grace in the ocean. "It's a positive omen of strength, protection and truth."

Demi gave a sigh of relief.

"The bluff will be my new temple and I will meet you here next full moon for news of our daughters."

We clasped hands and made our pledge and then she disappeared into the violet light.

I woke up on the sofa with a start. I must have fallen into a deep sleep not long after arriving home from the moon shoot.

For days the sensation of speaking to Demi remained with me. I grasped it all. Male domination had underpinned societies for centuries, as far back as the emergence of the goddesses from Mount Olympus. Patriarchal societies have disregarded the voice of women simply because they were a 'woman'.

Understanding how women disregarded other women's voices was more difficult. Ironically, it was the disregard from a female psychologist, who I turned to for guidance, which gave me unexpected insight.

Shopping Day

2004 late summer
Far north

"I was going to die, sooner or later, whether
or not I had even spoken myself.
My silences had not protected me. Your silences
will not protect you.... What are
the words you do not yet have? What are the
tyrannies you swallow day by day and
attempt to make your own, until you will sicken
and die of them, still in silence? We
have been socialised to respect fear more
than our own need for language."

Audre Lorde[1]

I avoided people seeing me enter the health centre that hot late summer afternoon. I didn't want anyone witnessing me accessing a psychologist, it would only compound my sense of failure.

School resumed in the New Year and I was left at home alone, having quit my teaching position. The absence from teaching and how it happened hit me hard.

I cracked under the pressure of Luther finding fault with me, even though I knew his real agenda behind his false accusations. I didn't have the confidence to apply to other schools for work, undoubtedly he would have blacklisted me. I suffered frequent panic attacks after that. High doses of adrenalin flooded my blood stream, causing me to shake uncontrollably day and night. It seemed the only way to win in life was to break the rules like the principal, my parents and grandmother. But I wasn't like them. It was better for me to fail at everything than to become a perpetrator of abuse.

My life was a constant string of failures, perhaps I needed a shrink. There was no one else to reach out to who would understand what I had been through. I was referred to a young woman psychologist whose office was in the main street of town. Discreetly, I went through the waiting room doors and took a seat in the corner.

I filled in the necessary forms and after some time a young woman half my age, shabbily dressed, presented herself to be the psychologist. She signalled me to come into her office. I followed her to the consulting room, feeling uneasy.

She sat on the second-hand leather seat opposite me. Her knees locked together as she carved her fingernail into a hole in the worn-out leather. The seat was defective, but I wasn't, although she looked at me like I was.

"Why are you here?"

"I don't have a job. The principal bullied me and I had no choice but to leave. It wasn't safe there anymore." There was a long pause. Was she being indifferent to me?

Her gaze wandered across the room.

"I feel humiliated now that I am unemployed," I continued.

"Yes." She managed a glare and dug her fingernail deeper into the hole.

"I really want to be a teacher. I love the job. But I couldn't work under his scrutiny. I felt like I was being punished like when I was a child." I hinted at my secret. I knew it had to come to light but I was petrified of further rejection.

"What happened?" She looked down at her notepad but didn't bother to write anything.

I felt awkward with her as if I had an undesirable label on my back that I thought she wouldn't want to deal with.

"My father sexually abused me. My mother and grandmother punished me for it, they said it was my fault. I feel the same resentment now as I did then." I tried to gain her eye contact, I really needed a supporter right now.

She gave me a short stare but didn't say anything. I assumed she wanted me to continue my 'talk therapy'.

"I am a shameful person to everyone around me."

My social alienation was getting to me, so I sought her eyes out for some mercy.

"Is that all?" She said giving me a sideways eye and pulled her fingernail out of the hole.

"Yes." I didn't know what else to say. I wished she would engage in the conversation with me.

"Okay." Her attention was withdrawn. "Wasn't your mother there?"

"My mother made it worse."

"Maybe you misunderstood her, this sort of thing can be hard on the mother too."

I stared directly at her; my throat was so constricted I could hardly swallow. Did I trigger something inside her that held a bias?

The conversation continued like that for another forty minutes until she finally closed the file with only a couple of lines written on it.

"Well, time's up. I'll send a follow up letter to your GP."

My legs felt too weak to stand up, an awkward heaviness hung in the air. I held back the tears as best I could.

"Don't you want to see me again?"

"No." She got up from the couch and stiffly waited until I left the room.

I was near rock bottom, my whole body felt numb. I walked away feeling completely rejected. My parents were undesirable and didn't meet society's norms, and nor did I. How could I be healed if a trained psychologist judged me to be hopeless, or didn't believe me, or both? I may as well have been talking to my parents.

I left the building feeling disillusioned and aimlessly crossed the road. I was unsustained, no, I was drained, by the dried-up branch extended to me by the so-called psychologist.

I recalled how much I put myself in the shoes of my students, willing to be their support. I was a teacher, not a psychologist, how could this be happening?

My heart ached, I missed my students so much.

I stopped at the local fruit market and selected some fresh leafy spinach for dinner. Its dark green leaves promised me a little grounding that I desperately needed. I packed it in my shopping basket, along with some other organic earth-coloured vegetables, and continued towards the counter.

There, I noticed a little girl around eight years old paying for purchases from her mum's wallet. It was a big task for such a small person. She thanked the shop keeper and carefully balanced the wallet, the bread, milk and fruit in her small arms and made her way out the heavy swing door to place them in her tricycle tray. She reminded me of when I was little and did the shopping for my mum.

1963
Elster

"… a detective with more than 20 years' experience wrote
he believed '90 per cent' of sexual assault complaints made
by women were 'completely fabricated or the women have
a misunderstanding of rape or sexual assault'."

ABC News, 18 August 2022[2]

On this day, my mother sent me on an errand to the corner shop. We would often run out of bread and milk or other things. I remember some deliberation by my parents as to whether I was old enough to go alone. She decided I was. She was a lazy mother who was preoccupied in the home, mostly smoking cigarettes in between patchy household chores. She really could have walked to the shops with me and my brothers if she wanted to but she chose not to.

The suburb of Elster was flourishing. Our small postwar brick veneer house and its low set brick fence, dotted with a rose bush or two, was a symbol of the perfect nuclear family which was simultaneously being shattered by the tumultuous events of the sixties.

It was 1963 and I was eight years old. I gauged this with the shock-belief news of the assassination of America's President John F. Kennedy. The news of his slaying affected everyone. It was splashed over all the newspapers, black and white television sets and radios. We even discussed it in class at school. It reverberated in the public consciousness over and over as if by saying his name enough times it didn't happen. His gunning down in cold blood in front of the whole world shocked everyone into disbelief.

How could America's beloved and respected president be shot dead in broad daylight, in his own cavalcade? By a person from within his own country?

He was a sitting duck – pinged off like a mechanical duck in the shooting row at the carnival. One shot went into his back, the other clear through his head.

Presidents and even the Pope did not ride in open cars after this, instead they rode in armoured vehicles. Fear was instilled deep into society after President Kennedy was assassinated. Everybody was a suspected communist and a liar, no one could be trusted.

That day, I was sent trundling on my three-wheeler bike with its tray to the store for groceries. My little hand clutched Mum's purse which was filled with cash for the purchases. In some ways I was proud that Mum trusted me to undertake this chore. It involved a level of responsibility and I craved to prove to her that I was a good child so she could love me.

I set off on my little tricycle and arrived safe and well at our corner shops located on Jasper Road, about two to three blocks from home. I felt a certain freedom I had never felt before, trundling along the foot path and negotiated roads and turns. They brought me to the busy little hub of local shops, including a milk bar and delicatessen. I carefully placed my tricycle outside the shops so as not to disturb the newspaper stands filled with news of President Kennedy's assassination. I held tight to Mum's purse together with the shopping list, which had been filled out by Mum in her neat Stott's College handwriting. She was forever telling me she learnt shorthand at Stott's College as if she was trying to outdo me.

I entered the delicatessen and there was a line up of people waiting to be served.

The shop owner was delighted to see me and greeted me with polite conversation.

"How are you today? Shopping for Mum, hey?"

My skin flushed a warm pink as he paid me compliments. I remember an older girl standing in line behind me or to the side of me. I imagined that she liked me too as she looked on fondly.

I felt important clutching Mum's wallet and paying cash to the shop owner for the groceries. I carefully undid the little twist lock and the coins and notes entrusted to me were displayed. Once the change was safely placed in the purse, I twisted the lock closed and went outside opening and closing the heavy delicatessen door on my own. Here, I carefully packed the groceries into the tricycle tray.

Suddenly an arm swiftly crossed over me, like a bird swooping down on its prey, and snatched Mum's purse clear out of my hands.

The young woman wasn't being nice to me at all.

Clearly, she had been casing me to steal the purse and its cash. In that split second, I was ruined. My happy day and feelings of optimism had turned into a catastrophe. I cried my eyes out all the way home for being betrayed by this kleptomaniac stranger, and worst of all, for the fear of what was to come.

I sobbed while retelling the story to my mother. She immediately called my father and not long afterward detectives, dressed in grey foreboding suits, arrived at our house. After a whispered exchange between them, my mother stood at the front door, and they were ushered in for the interview. We sat in the lounge room and they put me through a series of questions which I had difficulty answering. I underperformed as a witness and did not live up to their expectations. Detailed descriptions of other people didn't fit into my childhood matrix since I was only conscious of the fact that any young woman looked like my mother except that this young woman had brown hair unlike my mother's peroxide bleached and curler-rolled hair.

The detectives left our home without much to go by. They told Mum that children's evidence is often viewed with 'scepticism of outcome'. And this was one outcome that was not going to play out in my favour.

I was going to be blamed again.

The next day there was that same gnawing knock at the door.

I made a run for the apple tree but I didn't get very far.

"Come inside right now!" Mum's shrill voice called out.

My grandmother was standing in the kitchen, arms crossed over her chest. Her jaw was clenched. Her handbag was open on the kitchen table and a packet of cigarettes jutted from the top. Lipstick-stained cigarette butts smouldered in the ash tray.

Why did they smoke all the time? Why didn't they come outside and sit in the garden and enjoy being with me? There was nothing I could do to be accepted by them.

"What's this your mother tells me about some woman stealing her wallet from you?" She said, baring her false teeth.

Mum stood rigidly behind her. They were both of one mind to destroy me.

"It's true!" I blurted, hardly able to speak.

"You're lying!"

I could only shake my head, adamant of my denial.

"There was no such woman who stole your mother's purse, was there?"

My eyes bulged. I was unable to blink in case she hit me while they were closed.

"You made the whole thing up!" Her voice shook so much that her false teeth nearly fell out. She shoved them back and snarled at me.

"How dare you bring this whole thing upon your family!"

I couldn't back away. There was nowhere to run.

"You will go to any measure you little liar and thief! How dare you waste the detectives' time. And they are your father's work colleagues!"

Her mouth curled in hatred.

All I could do was shake on the inside. I was paralysed with fear. She was bent on carrying out yet another form of punishment. The hurtful accusations kept coming. She spat them out like rapid fire. My mother backing her with flared nostrils.

"You spent the money on lollies!"

"Where did you throw the purse?"

"We'll beat the truth out of you!"

"How dare you bring shame to your family like this!"

"Why were you ever born?"

My legs tightened and my body was ready to run but I had nowhere to go.

I was the sitting duck at the carnival. They were taking their shots and they weren't going to miss. It was stupid of me to think that the detectives would prove that I was not a liar. I was sure they had been clued up by my mother that the description I gave of the woman was 'fuzzy' since I was prone to 'lying' and for them to not waste their time. I was sure they needed to deny me contact with the detectives, after all, they had the power to intervene and monitor domestic violence. At no time would I be given the opportunity to express my concerns about the daily cavalcade going through our brick veneer house in Elster.

Not only was I discredited in my home but my falsely accused reputation of being a 'bad girl, liar and thief' and you name it, was being spread among the entire police force, local shopping proprietors and my school.

I wasn't safe in my own home.

I wasn't safe anywhere.

No one would believe me.

Jesus, save me!

Here I was being driven to my own death, however, unlike President Kennedy, I was too young to write my own inaugural speech before my own funeral.

My insidious grandmother thought it was a good idea to prove me to be a thief and a liar, which she frequently proclaimed and brainwashed my poor unfit-to-be-a-mother into believing. If it was said over and over then it would be true, just like President Kennedy's life and death but with a twist.

Her desire to bring me down overcame any tiredness she may have felt. She stood over me filled with anger and hatred.

"I saw you at the shops near your school. You stole lollies and hid them under your shirt." She snarled as she reached for a packet of liquorice all-sorts from her handbag. "They were just like these," and she shook them wildly in my face. "You just don't know when to stop. Do you?"

I was rooted on the spot in fear. How could she make up such lies about me? A bead of sweat ran down my forehead. Sheepishly, I raised my arm to wipe it away and snuck a glance for Mum's reaction. Her face had tightened into a snarl to match my grandmother's.

Mum took over.

"You must bring home some stolen lollies tomorrow as proof you are a thief!" She was all cocky with me and shook her fist at the lolly bag.

"But..." My lips trembled so much I couldn't speak.

"You are a liar! There is nothing you can say that will convince me otherwise." She reached out as if to throttle me.

If I brought home lollies, I would be beaten. If I didn't bring them home, I would also be beaten.

I stood there, on the hard kitchen floor. Silent. There was nothing I could do except try to stop the images of getting a beating with the barber's strop from flashing through my mind. The tension was unbearable. My tummy was in so many knots I thought I'd vomit.

There was no one to protect me.

The next day I went to school, silent and seized by dread. Without a doubt, I feared that if I didn't take home proof to my mother then she would beat me. And if I did take home lollies, which I didn't have access to because I didn't have any money and I didn't know what shop she was talking about, I would be beaten anyway.

I didn't leave the school grounds ever at lunch time – I didn't have a pass to go out. Fear gripped me all day. I felt like my heart was being wrenched from my body by some unseen and uncontrollable, unnatural force of nature, as if I was born in the time of warlocks and witches and was lost deep in the dark forest without a way out.

On the way home from school, I found a half piece of white lolly bag in the gutter. In a petrified state I placed a few puny pieces of small rubber I had hacked off at school during the day. I had tried to remain inconspicuous and undetected by my schoolteacher and classmates.

How terrified I was sitting in school that day, anticipating what awaited me at home that afternoon. I thought about my mother and wondered if she was apart from my grandmother would she love me and not be able to bring these brutal acts down upon her only little daughter. Curiously, I loved my mother in a strange, human, instinctual way. I loved her and wanted so much to be loved and trusted by her.

When I got home I knocked on the front door. My legs were as weak as jelly. She pulled the door ajar to expose her kettle-like, long-beaked face, embellished with crazy blue eyes which glared at me in hostility.

"Well, where are they? Show me what you have stolen!" She squawked like a mad bird in its frenzy but not quite at its peak.

I pulled out the small white bag filled with rubber and one or two small pebbles that I picked up from the gutter on my way home. God why didn't some kind, natural-spirited soul stop me and ask me what I was doing?

I passed them to my mother, shaking with anticipation from the bottom of my grave heart that she would 'believe' me.

She took one look and then viciously set upon me.

In her rage she flung the door open, grabbed me, pulled me in and set upon me with a huge strap and belted me hard. I remember being buckled over and sent flying onto the floor. My small body whipped from side to side at any angle to avoid the severe and heartless blows.

"You liar!"

Whack!

"Liar! You are a lying hussy!"

Whack! Thrash! Whack! Smash!

She was like a crazed demon screaming and yelling and accusing me of everything asunder while callously beating the living daylights out of me.

My parent's house was not a natural place; I had surely been born into hell. The brick veneer was exactly that, a veneer, a cover-up of the unforgivable and inexplicable sins taking place inside.

The pleasant aroma of roses drifted into the hallway but I lay there broken and bereft on the floor. Even beautiful roses in full bloom had thorns.

I never knew the feeling of childhood joy. My parents could not give this to me because they didn't have it in themselves.

2021 early summer
Ocean harbour home

"By giving
good fame
your beauty and nobility
to such friends
you sicken me with pain

Blame you? Swollen
Have your fill of them
For my thinking it is poorly done
and all night I understand baseness

Other
minds
the blessed."

{3}

Sappho from *To My Brother Haraxos*, circa 700 BCE[3]

"Can you touch the sky with your hands, Grandma?" Summer cried in delight with her outstretched arms reaching for the sky.

"If you touch the sky, can you pull down the rainbow-coloured scarf? It will look pretty with your new dress!" I laughed.

Her little brother, Tyrone joined in and tried to touch the sky too. They were filled with joy as we descended to the calm waters and golden sands of the Azure Conservation Lake which connected to the ocean at Azure Surf Beach.

Shady trees hung over the water and an early summer was fluting its own song. The shrill cicadas scraped their tiny wings together. Bright sunlight filled the salt lake as if all the evening stars had gathered in one place to rest until night fell.

We wore hats and lathered our skin with sunscreen for protection. I set up an umbrella and placed our gear in the shade while the children played in the shallows near the sand banks. Tyrone was looking for hermit crabs, a favourite pastime on the beach, and Summer was determined to watch over him.

"Don't poke at them." Summer urged as he nudged one with his small piece of driftwood.

"You can't tell me what to do!"

"I'm only trying to help."

"You're a girl! You're not the boss of me."

He stopped poking the hermit crab and waded through the water back to me.

"Do you have any grapes, Grandma?" His blue eyes beamed innocently at me.

"Of course. Summer, come over and share some grapes with us."

The three of us sat together while a summer breeze looped under the umbrella and kept us cool.

Unable to keep her frustration to herself Summer asked, "Grandma?"

"Yes, Summer?"

"Do you think Sappho would write a letter to my little brother and advise him of good behaviour and to respect me and Mummy? He says I can't tell him what to do because I am a girl. That must mean Mummy can't too."

Tyrone looked at the grapes in his little fingers intently and didn't say a word. He knew it was wrong but he didn't quite understand why. My daughter raised him to not hold sexist views.

"Why won't you listen to girls, bless?"

"My friends at school said that girls are weak and boys shouldn't listen to them." His head fell into his chest as he spoke.

"Well, to answer your question Summer, I'm sure Sappho would write a letter to your little brother and she would write to our members of parliament too!"

"Who are they, Grandma?" Summer asked.

"They are at the centre of power in our country but it's dominated by men. They formed a boy's club and don't like it when women speak out or seek leadership positions."

"Is that what happened to me at school, Grandma? But why would I not be in a boy's club? I'm a boy."

The poor little fella was confused.

"It's okay, sweetheart. You don't have to agree with those boys. You can be a strong boy with your own opinions, with the wisdom to listen to women."

"Why don't the boss men in parl-ment stop being mean to the ladies if it's wrong?"

"Because they haven't woken up to themselves. They are acting like larrikins. Hundreds of women from all over Australia marched to Parliament House in March this year. They held up signs and protested to the prime minister to listen to women. And there were lots of men and boys there too. The smart ones would never disregard a woman."

"What's a larrikin?"

"It's a rowdy young man but some of our prime ministers are old and they still act like larrikins. Bob Hawke bragged about sculling pots of beer and running our country at the same time. If a woman leader bragged about that she wouldn't last long."

"Grown ups should act more responsibly," said Summer and took her little brother's hand. "I'd like to go for a swim, Grandma."

"Yeah. Come on sis. Can we talk about this later, Grandma?"

"Of course, I'll come with you."

My heart swelled at the thought, I was helping my blessed ones sail safely through the storm of misogyny.

"How long ago did Sappho live again?"

"About three thousand years," I said stretching both arms as wide as infinity would take me.

"Then how do we know that her letters mean the same today as when they were written?"

"Well," these children were going to stretch my mind. "She lived on a beautiful Island called Lesbos and it was just like here. It had grapes, sweet-smelling orchards and saltwater estuaries spotted with little coastal towns. And it commanded its harbour from a large sea rock, like the lighthouse near my place. It has been said that to know the meaning of Sappho's writing is to see the light, sea and land of ancient Lesbos in the modern day."

"She's just like us then."

"Yes, she felt responsible for her family and that they upheld proper community values. She was sickened with pain and wrote a letter to her little brother, Haraxos, because he traded wine from the family estate and wasted it on sailing trips abroad. She told him to pay more respect to his mother and sister, and come home to contribute to the tending of the crops."

"What would she say to the men in parl-ment?"

"She would say their behaviour toward women is poorly done and is filled with baseness."

"What does baseness mean?"

"It means there is a lack of moral principle or just bad character. She would say to them to speak better of women. That they should refrain from using wrong words such as 'liar' when they are telling the truth, and much nastier things I can't repeat. Our former woman Prime Minister, Julia Gillard, was called 'Ju-liar' mostly by the men in politics. The opposition leader stood in front of a sign which said, 'ditch the witch' in his bid to take over leadership."

The thought of how they treated Julia made my skin crawl.

"Why did they call her a witch, Grandma?"

"The word 'witch' is a disparaging word to put women down. A woman was holding the placard, meaning that some women have adopted the men's values. Women are further disadvantaged if both men and women continue to treat women as inferior."

"Has anyone called you a liar, Grandma?"

I stopped dead, heat flushed my cheeks, but I was determined to overcome the shame of it.

"Yes, quite often," I heard myself say, "And it hurt me deeply because I'm not a liar."

Summer looked at me, shocked.

"Whoever said that to you is mean, Grandma. We know you're not a liar." Tyrone followed suit; I imagine because he saw how it upset me.

"You're not a liar, Grandma," he echoed.

"I want to be like Sappho when I grow up," said Summer and she poured lime nectar into our water bottles.

"And I don't want to be like her brother," declared Tyrone. His blue eyes beamed at me, their innocence giving way to experience. "I never want to sicken you with pain, Grandma."

"Me too," Summer joined in with the voice of a nightingale to herald a new era.

Love was alive during these summer days with my darling grandchildren. My heart fluttered with a joy I was never allowed as a child. I was motivated to push forward and find my voice to create a safer world for my children and my grandchildren.

CHAPTER 12

Keen's Mustard

2020 spring
Ocean harbour home

"I tell you, ghosts in the ghosts of summer days,
you are dead as though you never had been.
For time has caught on fire, and you too burn:
leaf, stem, branch, calyx and the bright corolla
are now the insubstantial wavering fire
in which love dies..."

Judith Wright from *The Two Fires*, 1955[1]

A news alert reminded me that the world was still not a safe place. In Minneapolis, Minnesota an arresting officer forced a defenceless African American, George Floyd, into a deadly position. His head was facedown on the hard bitumen road and the police officer pressed his knee, supported by his whole body weight, to Floyd's neck and throat.

Floyd cried out, "I can't breathe"[2] as he gasped for air.

A few seconds before he became motionless, he begged for his life.

"They'll kill me, they'll kill me."

In eight minutes and forty-six seconds, he was dead.

My book by Australian poet, Judith Wright, *Collected Poems fell out* of my hands. I opened the window for air, unable to breathe myself. I was suffocating, even my clothing became too hot and restrictive. The associations with Floyd's murder and my childhood abuse cut to the very heart of the child-wound inside me, like a wild bush fire.

No one was able to protect Floyd from a hate-motivated attack. No one was able to protect me when my parents aided each other and almost killed me in a similar hate-motivated attack. The sight of it on the television flared my trauma and I had to escape the room for a reprieve to change into something cooler.

My hands shook when I made a cup of green tea to calm my nerves. My breath burst in and out and I jammed my hands underneath my armpits waiting for the kettle to boil.

I returned to the lounge for updates on Floyd. The news reporter explained the officer had refused to lift his knee somehow thinking that Floyd was a killer or a threat to society for allegedly using a counterfeit bill.

The cops treated Floyd like the 'naughty boy' who could never be trusted.

It was not the first time a black man or woman had died in custody, or while being taken into custody, in America or Australia, or in other parts of the world. This incident caught the eyes of the world only because a young woman was filming the tragedy on her mobile phone. The attending police were completely aware of the public presence while the young woman yelled out, "let him go, he can't breathe," amid the crowd of sympathetic and helpless onlookers.

It reminded me of Aunt Dot watching me being strip searched and doing nothing about it. She let my grandmother get away with torture. She should have done something to stop it. She needed to take it personally. She needed to interfere as if it were happening to her. Showing sympathy was not enough.

Clearly it wasn't enough in George Floyd's case.

I picked up the poetry book from where I left off and read more lines of the life-affirming poem, *The Watcher* from Judith's *The Gateway* written in 1953; her daughter was three years old.

"I am the garden beyond the burning wind,
I am the river among the blowing sand,
I am the song you hear before you sleep…"[3]

I imagined Judith was my mother when I was growing up, she held me tight each time I had a fever or was scared.

The tragic image of George Floyd struggling for breath under the policeman's knee played over in my mind.

I felt his fear in those last minutes of his life.

My pulse was racing, and I wanted to let out a primal scream. I kept hearing his cry for help. There were significant parallels with my experiences as a child: the chokehold, I can't breathe, the consequent burning down of the city. What happened to Floyd cut across barriers of race, gender and culture.

I grabbed my pen and notebook set aside on the coffee table by the sofa. I could hardly breathe or get rid of the smell of Keen's mustard.

1963
Elster

*"Silos is like a volcano lava, burning
everything that stands in its face,
its embers painting a symbol of a lost people,
who burn every day by all means,
surrendering under the weight of profound pain,
after their impactful fall, turning into ashes
erased by the near history! Surrendering
people, including the reckless! Reckless
with the pain of another, reckless in neglecting the
value of their land, drowning in themselves
and their own desires, far from any belongingness,
living on another planet! Oh, how sorry,
we are for what our ancestors built, and for what
we have forsaken, from our sacred land
and the home of the homeland! Only God almighty
can save us from the disgrace of this history.*

Nidal Majdalani from *Silos in Beirut,* August 18, 2022
Human and the Environment[4]

I was eating lunch at the kitchen table when Mum had made a fresh batch of Irish mustard stew. You could bank on every household in Australia keeping a tin of Keen's Mustard on their kitchen shelf, alongside the jars of Vegemite, golden syrup and homemade pickles and jams, but I had no idea what the fuss was about.

I didn't like the taste of mustard. When Mum wasn't looking, I dared to spit it out. I couldn't stand it burning my mouth and throat. The taste was too bitter.

"Don't spit it out you ungrateful girl," she snapped while shoving the bowl under my chin. "You're lucky to have something to eat at all. I should starve you, then you'd be grateful for what you're given."

It wasn't unusual to be sent to my room without a meal. I closed my eyes and took another mouthful, but it was too late.

"Go to your bedroom. Your grandmother will be here soon, and she has something for you," she spluttered and crossed the knife and fork on her plate of stew. I looked behind me to make sure she wasn't already here. I didn't want to see her. I managed to gulp down some water to ease my burning throat and hurried to my bedroom. I had barely eaten anything except one piece of potato, saturated in mustard gravy.

It wasn't long before the familiar thwack on the door made my stomach churn. I looked around my bedroom for somewhere to hide but there was nowhere. So I pressed one ear to the door and listened, flinching when I heard my grandmother speaking to Mum.

"It's no point washing her mouth out with Velvet soap," my grandmother cut my mother off from speaking.

I clearly remembered the days when she forced a bar of *Velvet* soap into my mouth and madly scrambled it around my tongue and top palette as punishment for my supposed swearing. I tried to resist but she was a big lady. Her brow furrowed in madness as she plied her muscles with an added testosterone beneficial only to heavyweight boxers. She had made it up that I was swearing but her mission to punish me at any opportunity she could find was out of control.

"I will hold her down and beat her with the strap while you feed the mustard into her mouth!" Her voice was full of bitterness. Anyone would have thought she had walked on to a battlefield, hell-bent to kill the enemy to survive herself.

The humidity mingled in the air. Everything felt hot, my skin, their talk, the adult force unleashing like a wildfire in a cruel and calculated frenzy.

My body was numb.

I could already feel the hot mustard being forced down my throat. Rapidly swallowing, I kept my ear pressed to the door in the hope they would change their minds. Instead, they scratched around in the pantry like a pair of rats looking for the Keen's Mustard.

"Here it is!" I heard Mum say.

My grandmother's footsteps then marched down the hall. I backed off to avoid being hit by the door.

"There you are, you little liar," she growled and grabbed me by my arm, dragging me into the kitchen.

My mother was standing there holding a spoon piled with mustard. "No, that's too small," snapped my grandmother. "A teaspoon won't do. Get a bigger one than that!"

"But it won't fit in her mouth!"

"Well, bring both! We'll start with the dessertspoon and if it doesn't work then we'll use the teaspoon!"

Rats communicated in a pitch that humans cannot hear but I could hear these creatures, more sinister than rats.

"She must be stopped from spreading lies about her father. She will ruin his reputation and his life – and ours too!" She was convinced her son was innocent and I should burn for spreading lies. Even the way she pronounced 'father' came out searing and hot-tempered as the fires in hell.

"Put her back in her room," my mother urged, "You don't know who might walk in here."

Grandmother dragged me back down the hall, my feet hardly touched the carpet.

Sunlight glared through the small gaps between the blinds, illuminating stripes in my dim room. They shut the door and pulled down the old, rattling venetian blinds. My bedroom was in lockdown so no fresh air could enter and the whacking sounds and screams could not escape.

"Now, take your dress off and lay on the bed!" My grandmother's eyes bulged from her head.

I was petrified. The anticipation was unbearable. I wanted to rebel, to defend myself, even just a little, but I had no hope against their sheer size and brutality.

I stared at the mustard on the spoon.

"Why?" I cried. "I don't want to!"

But my protest only aggravated her more. My grandmother stood over me with the strap and beat me hard behind the legs, just below my knees, so hard and abrupt that my legs buckled, and I fell to the floor in pain.

"Get your clothes off now and lay on the bed!" she screeched like an old shrew dashing through the streets of old London town before being locked away in the madhouse.

Trembling, I removed my dress.

"Lie there, face up," she ordered, pointing to my bed.

I was dressed only in my undies and singlet. My mother came at me with the dessertspoon filled with putrid mustard and aimed it straight for my mouth. I clamped it shut, numbed by the thought of its taste. It would be like swallowing nerve gas.

Since I refused to open my mouth, my grandmother belted me with the barber strap so hard the noise rang off the bedroom ceiling.

I wailed blue murder, upon which my mother took advantage and shoved a spoon of the nerve-gas mustard into my mouth.

My body was on fire. My nerves exploded into a million neurons and my spine, heart and lungs buckled under the strain.

I lashed out, it was a fight or flight response. I writhed, screamed and spat whatever remains of the foul mustard back into their nauseating, screwed-up faces. I didn't care anymore; I was the naughty girl who could never be trusted.

"How dare you, you little bitch," howled Grandmother as she wiped the spattered, moistened mustard seeds from her face. Her ego had taken a bruising from my retaliation, the hatred burned inside her so much that her face turned scarlet.

"What shall we do with you?"

Her evil eyes narrowed, looking through me, and then she directed her frustration to pointy-nosed Mum. Mum reacted like a stubborn, dumb mule. She wasn't going to budge to help me out of this spot, too stupid to think it through for herself.

"You'll have to get her father. It's our only chance. She won't dare fight him back – he's too big!"

"If you think so—" Mum cocked her head, listening for God knows what.

I pulled my hands down over my body as if covering myself up with clothes I didn't have on. I could only stare at the ceiling, too terrified to lift myself off the bed and run to the back door to scream for help.

Then I remembered the neighbour, no one would help me anyway.

My body was burning up. It felt like the house was on fire.

My father met the witches in the outside room after being summoned. I watched him through my door as he listened intently to their plans with his burly arms crossing his chest. He was dressed in his navy blue, copper trousers, fastened by a thick leather belt and buckle. The lazy sod had been lounging barefooted in the lounge room keeping his family at arm's length. Deep down he would have detested my grandmother for invading his well-defined boundary.

"You must help us out here. Things can't continue as they are in this house. That girl must be stopped!" Grandmother sniped with her bony finger pointing at me.

He didn't ask them what had to be stopped because he knew he could not, and would not, defend me. He would rather let all hell break loose than admit he was a paedophile. He knew it was better to just shut up and toe the line.

"What can I do?" He pretended to help them to make the hard decision to torture me.

But I wasn't some street criminal he was dealing with. I saw pictures on the news stand of police arresting the Mutilator. But I wasn't one of them. I was his daughter, but he didn't care. He was concealing his own criminal activities.

"You'll need to take off your belt. We'll use that. It's thicker than the barber's strap and you could use the buckle if needed!" Grandmother's veins stuck out of her neck as she glared wildly at me.

He spat on his fingertips and wiped them on his white cotton singlet, a sign that he was not going to break the generational cycle of child abuse.

My head was spinning. The room was claustrophobic before they came back with the 'heavy hand' that was about to be unleashed upon me. I knew this was all happening because he was keeping secrets, not me.

"Why, oh, why," I cried to myself.

For a moment everything went static like a breathing space had opened, but it was a false sense of security. It was like taking a deep breath before someone forced your head under water. You never knew if you would come up again.

There he was, bent over me, the whole twenty stone and six foot three of him. His bulky knee was forced into my chest. He brutally pinned me down into the asphyxia hold, the belt wrapped around his fat, bulging white-bone knuckles as he clawed the buckle.

Raising his arm high into the air, he let go with a wallop like he was riding the Melbourne Cup winner home but would be fined after the race for whipping the horse too hard. The belt hit my hip and thigh flesh and my body went into a spasm. I was having a seizure. He had me pinned down so hard I couldn't move. My mouth opened wide, and Mum shoved a spoonful of mustard down my throat. I gagged as I choked on its burning bitterness in more ways than one.

"You bad girl. How dare you tell lies about your father." My grandmother's voice threatened me like a knife at my throat. "You will bring shame to your family. You must not speak to anyone about this or of your father. Do you understand?"

At that moment her screeching demands were the least of my worries, I was having trouble breathing. My father's dead-weight knee was flattened to my chest. My vision was becoming cloudy.

"I can't breathe!" I said to them in a feeble and desperate cry.

I mustered up enough wind to let out a huge scream hoping that the neighbours would come, or Grandad, bless his old soul, may have dropped in for a visit to save me.

"Gag her. Shut her up or the neighbours will hear!" Grandmother screeched.

My father clasped his fat hand over my face, like a tarantula spider on steroids. His thumb clenched my jaw, his fingers were spread blocking my mouth and crushing my eyes and cheeks. He let go, his horse whip beat the living daylight out of me again. His dead weight pushed lethally down upon my small body. Did they know then, in the police force, that chokeholds kill a person in eight minutes and forty-six seconds?

They were getting frustrated, the three of them. Their gruesome punishment was going nowhere.

I couldn't take it anymore, my survival mode was on its death bed, I needed oxygen fast. I bit as hard as I could on the fleshy part of his hand between the thumb and forefinger. I drew blood. I didn't care. I felt relief for what I had just done, they would kill me anyway.

"You fucking bitch," he roared, frothing at the mouth. He pulled back and sucked on his bleeding hand.

They didn't care about the abuse they inflicted on me. I didn't matter at all. Why did they even have me?

I bit him so hard so he would feel the void of love and not the other way around.

He had reached his breaking point. Shaking all over and with tear-drenched eyes, I watched him leave the room sucking on his injured hand. Through blurry vision I saw the stack of newspapers Grandad left near my door for the outside dunny. The heat haze in my eyes met with the photograph of firebombs being dropped on villages in a place called Vietnam. There was a war going on, our country followed America. Mr Parker said the firebombs were called napalm.

But tonight the war was marching down my throat. I wanted to run from my burning bed, run down the street, my body on fire, in the hope someone would help me to put it out.

2020 spring
Ocean harbour home

I woke up hot and bothered in the middle of the day, my writing pad and pen had fallen to the floor. I had gone to bed unable to put them down until I finished drafting my memoir chapter, *Keen's Mustard*.

The rhythmic sound of the waves outside my window eased my fears. I was not caught in a global holocaust – well, not anymore. Last night my mind drifted in ether: time and space were illusionary. My post-traumatic stress had resurfaced in a dark dream of chokeholds and burning cities. My inner child was being tortured and she was beyond rescue. The burden of living weighed heavily on me.

The only thing that kept me going was being so driven to write my memoir. Telling my story was taking its toll on me but I had to keep up the pace and present my story for the women's movement. That I was repeatedly reliving my past was something I was determined to conquer.

Now fully awake, I reached for Judith's book of poems and read from *The Two Fires.*

"And now set free by the climate of man's hate,
That seed sets time ablaze.
The leaves of fallen years, the forest of living days,
Have caught like matchwood. Look, the whole world burns…"[5]

I was inspired to write like Judith in a bid to express the atrocities of the abuse to help other children and women who were abused in a world dominated by men's voices and political opinion. Judith had stepped up her activism on the Korean War 1950-53, later the Vietnam War and fears of global catastrophe. Human rights are a basic right for us all.

"Article 5. No one shall be subjected to torture or to cruel, inhuman or degrading treatment or punishment."

This was not granted to me as a child.

Nor was it granted to George Floyd.

It was not granted to village children in the Vietnam War.

Children should not burn in their beds.

I needed to be brave and step up my writing even if it was considered just another 'feminist' voice that had the audacity to criticise toxic masculinity and the patriarchal order of society led by war mongers.

The heat of the day reminded me of my friend, Sage. The last time we spoke was on text message. She was feeling unwell and couldn't make the moon shoot with me. I missed her company although I was happy to meet Demi on the bluff on my own. I haven't told Sage I'm writing my memoir, but not from fear of her being a critic, accusing me of sexualised hatred which seemed to be a growing norm for many women who published today, particularly online. The truth was that I wasn't ready to discuss my past with anyone.

To write, I needed to have a friendship with Sage independent of the abuse from my past to feel like I was emotionally whole. It was self-care. I had to have one foot planted in the toxic stew and face off the destructive fire alone.

As if she read my mind, my phone lit up, followed by the familiar 'ping'.
"I'm much better, let's meet for lunch?"

"Sounds wonderful. I'll meet you at Wildflower Kitchen at 12?"

That was our favourite place to eat. The eatery was very popular with the locals largely due to its variety of organic food-based meals and delicious coffee. My headache started to disappear and my body temperature felt normal. Thank God the fire inside me abated.

'Meet you at the Wildflower' had a certain ring to it, a freedom of movement untouched by human intervention.

It was the perfect place for friends to meet.

Sage was there before me and had acquired a seat by one of the quaint flower gardens in a rectangular raw-timber box between the tables in the open-spaced room. Sea and mountain air intermingled under the eaves and dropped in gently on those giving patronage. I sat down and tapped her elbow in gratitude of acquiring the table and her friendship.

A tall glass of iced water, fringed with a lemon slice, was waiting for me.

"Oh my, that is so refreshing," I said, sipping the simple chemical bond of two hydrogen atoms.

"Oh, mine too," she agreed, and we chinked glasses in celebration of meeting up. "How have you been?"

How could I tell her I had written a chapter of my childhood memoir and that my parents had militarised against me for all those years. They had tortured me and put me in holds like George Floyd before he was killed. Through my nightmares and the lived experience of child abuse, I had drawn the conclusion that both napalm and the atomic bomb were symbols of the criminality of warfare – and the unpredictability of parenthood.

Surely, Sage would think I was crazy for saying such a thing—

I would have to tell her how my mother poured mustard down my throat while my father held me down like a criminal, unable to breathe and beat me. I felt like I was on fire like Napalm girl in the Vietnam War. It was over all the newspapers in the early '70s to combat the harbingers of weapons of mass destruction and expose the complex moral and legal algebra that informed the management of life and death.

I would have to tell her that my grandmother was the main collaborator and yelled out wonton overkill 'beat it out of her' like the modern nation state which gave birth to violent verbs: "Nuke 'em!" and "Napalm 'em!"

I would have to tell her I was reading Judith Wright and that I strongly identified with her poem *At a Poetry Conference, Expo 1967* and that I would love to quote it on social media.

> *"Rockets!" the crowds cried. "Wars!" and every window*
> *opened, every poet began to burn with napalm flames,*
> *and fires detached and fell into the crowds, fires of a human flesh.*
> *here a hand fell, opening like a flower,*
> *a firework breast, a glowing genital" …*[6]

And that was the end of human love, and all the poets lost their voices, and the fire of destruction overcame the fire of creation.

But sitting there now in the café, I couldn't tell her.

"I missed your company on the moon shoot," I said, leaving out the part where I daydreamed meeting Demi on the path.

"Yes, I saw your picture on the gram. You did such a good job of capturing the moon between the horizon and the lighthouse. I loved your quote, Mary Oliver, *The Pond* and the pink moon bit."

Sage loved reading my quotes on social media. I usually kept them apolitical but often more than not they were women writers and carried a symbolic feminine message.

"Yes, I love Mary Oliver.. I'm so glad you appreciate my quotes. I wasn't sure if many followers read them."

"Oh, I do. I always read them," Sage dared to admit. She dared to be the flower and lift faces without the grey ash.

"Thank you, Sage. I love your support and appreciation. I like to quote poets and writers who mean something to me but not to cause a stir. I find the media and opinion polls are dominated by men and they are scathing of women's issues. I noticed that eighty per cent of my followers on the gram are male! Honestly, I was shocked when I saw the stats."

"Oh, I never knew. I must check mine. That's such an interesting point."

"On my last sunrise post I used an accompanying excerpt from Nuala Ní Dhomhnaill's poem, *The Bond*. This one here," I said as I opened my phone app and showed Sage the post.

> *"A boat comes up the river by night,*
> *With a woman standing in it,*
> *Twin candles lit in her eyes*
> *And two oars in her hands."*[7]

"Yes, I saw that one too. I noticed Christopher commented on that. He said you were getting in touch with your Celtic past."

"I guess so. She was writing in the tradition of a strong Irish woman who placed three bans on a woman. I had several comments from women on that one too. And I only put that one verse up. It's the two oars that stand for the equal force of women against the death-dealing patriarchy."

"That's powerful stuff. Thanks for telling me."

Sage was always supportive of my ideas, even the subversive ones.

"Well, it's my way of getting a woman's voice over. That's why women liked the quote because they intuitively preferred and identified with the feminine perspective rather than the normalised masculine perspective. Nuala's poetry gives legitimacy and importance to women as they once were in Gaelic culture."

I kept the conversation balanced without going overboard but the memories of my childhood kept going around in my head.

Thunder rumbled across the sky warning us of the approaching storm.

"Oh dear, I have washing on the line. We should get out of the storm before she hits."

"It sounds like the Nuala is about to unleash her fury again," laughed Sage.

We gathered our belongings, keys, phones and bags and headed to the cars making a pact to meet again for lunch soon.

CHAPTER 13

Washing Day

2020 late spring
Ocean harbour home

"For you Kleis I have no embroidered
headband and no idea
where to find one while the Mytilinian rules

These colourfully embroidered
headbands

These things of the children of the Kleanax
In exile memories terribly wasted away"

[98b]

Sappho from *Her Exile,* circa 700 BCE[1]

The storm gained momentum as we made our way to our cars. I raised my chin to the sky before closing my car door and waved goodbye to Sage. I enjoyed our lunch dates and her feminine support; she was completely unlike my mother's toxic antagonism I had grown up with.

Heavy clouds moved across the sky like a Norman invasion, hell-bent on taking over of the new land. The humidity was at its peak, around ninety per cent and the car air con was on high. I drove out and waited for the boom gate to rise when a call came from my daughter. I loved my new car and the advantages of a hands-free car phone.

I pressed the little speaker button on the steering wheel.

"Hi Mum, where are you?"

"I just had lunch with Sage at the Wildflower Kitchen. I'm on my way home to get the washing in before the storm hits."

"Okay, great. Can you do me a favour?"

"Yes, what is it?"

"Can you please call by my house and bring in the washing? I put some on the line this morning. This storm is unexpected."

Domestic duties were not on her nine to five job description.

"Yes, sure." It would be easy enough for me to do. "I'll hang it inside and check your windows just in case."

"Thanks Mum. I hope you get yours in time too."

"No problem. I'll see you on Thursday when I pick up the kids."

Thursday was Grandma's Day. I shivered at the thought of hiding behind my door or under my bed every time my grandmother visited. What a different experience my grandchildren had with me, they were always so full of beans and excited on my day with them.

I pressed the speaker button and hung up, thanking God my relationships with my children and grandchildren were as healthy as they were after what I had been through. The sun was about to be swallowed by the Viking clouds, fierce fighters descending from the southwest. I could make it in time.

I arrived at my daughter's house as the rain was about to bucket down. On the way to her laundry, I passed the dining table with a stack of folded washing ready to be put away. Next to it was a drying rack of clothes which she had arranged the night before. This morning there was another load done and hung out and then the process would be repeated when she got home from work.

I gave a sigh, but this was no time to be resigned that history was repeating itself. Washing was considered women's work and not culturally accepted as men's work, as was mothering children, house cleaning, preparing meals and bath and bedtimes rituals, all the while working a forty-hour week. I strengthened my posture and picked up the washing basket with steady hands and arms and opened the back door.

The line was full of nearly dried unpegged clothes, sheets and towels.

Quickly I pulled them off. No time for pegs. The washing was thrown over the lines in doubles and they balanced precariously when the wind gusted.

The gale was mounting, bolstering the white beards over the ocean hitting land. I yanked one lot of clothes from the dryer and threw the damp load in. Washing was everywhere. Organised chaos. The children's clothes dropped easily into my working hands; the momentary touch brought to memory washing days of my past.

The memories took over, but my feelings then were not the same as I felt now, helping my daughter get through her washing days. I was the responsible one here, unlike my mum. She was so absorbed in smoking cigarettes and in her own life, that she forced the family washing on to me. As far as she was concerned, I didn't deserve happiness anyway.

Instead of mulling over the past, I folded the children's pyjamas for bedtime, leaving them on their beds for when the family arrived home from school and work. Closing the front door behind me, my thoughts turned to my writing.

Washing day was worthy of writing a chapter.

I was stronger now. Now when I was living in my harbour house, and could mentally return to the place where the humiliation took place and bring to light my awareness of the meanness of my mother.

I kept my head down as I ran to the car, staving off the rain drops and my over confidence to return to my dark days. But it was better to tell the story than to remain silent on the sexist attitudes towards housework.

*"What the housewives of Australia need to
understand as they do the ironing…"*

Tony Abbott, Former Opposition Leader
and Prime Minister of Australia[2]
February 2010

I parked the car in the undercover area and grabbed my own washing off the line just in time before the rain fell. The warning birds abruptly finished their calls and with drenched feathers, fled to their nests for shelter from the storm.

Tossing my damp clothes in the dryer, I decided I had enough of this dreary washing day work. My movements became slower and I shut the dryer with an extra nudge. The box of soap powder fell on the tiles with a thud, white powder dusted my feet. The thick smell travelled straight to my brain, triggering memories of washing day when I was twelve.

The washing powder was called *Persil* back then, but it had that same strong sodium sulphate odour and guaranteed the same whitest wash ever, as if performing a ritual of magic. My eyes followed the soft powder as I swept it carefully back in the toppled box and fixed it back on the shelf. My eyes began to water up from the soap powder acid filled air and I set off to the lounge to rest. On the way, I checked the window shutters were latched down to keep out the marauding rain and the air con on low to dissipate the life-sapping humidity.

I sat on my comfortable sofa inside my safe harbour home as the storm took its course overhead. But the memories of my past wouldn't let up. My eyes filled with tears and I reached for a tissue. My hand was shaking as I wiped them, overwhelmed by the caustic memory brought on by the washing powder.

Exhausted, I let my body rest rather than force myself to keep going. The days of forced labour were fading into the past. Relaxing my body helped and I stopped shaking. The Viking clouds opened and drenched the land with rain. It poured down the outside gutters like water filling the washing machine without stopping. Rain fell outside and I drifted off to a faraway land...

Where was I in time? .... who was that coming toward me?

I thought it was Demeter because she was holding something like a torch in her hand with her arm raised high, but I was mistaken. This woman was very beautiful, not a crone like Demi. She was dressed in an immaculate white gown, three quarter length with beautiful low, white heels to match. Her shoulder length Scandinavian blonde hair was held back from her high cheekboned face by a ribbon tied in a rune knot on her crown. It revealed her sparkling, soap bubble, blue eyes that spoke of loyalty, faith and eternity.

"Hello, I am the Goddess Persil," pearly water rained on her exquisite face as she spoke.

"That explains the bottle of Persil you have in your hand."

She was the most beautiful dream I had ever had.

"Yes, my desire is to care for others," she shared.

"How did you get here?" My mental concept of her was challenged. Was she the Great mother or the water maiden?

"I have come from Mount Olympus where I was created by the gods."

"Which gods?" I asked, sagging further into the sofa.

"The gods of capitalism." Her voice swished like soap suds gently beating back and forth in the washing machine.

"Oh dear, whatever for?"

"I was in exile; I had lamented for my colourful embroidered headband. There was nowhere to find one while the capitalists ruled."

"What happened?"

"Such memories were terribly wasted away."

I waited patiently while she reminisced about her colourful headband.

"*The gods agreed to give me a rune knot in its place on the provision that I became the goddess of Persil.*" *Her voice was losing its power. I don't know if I pitied her or if I was more appalled.*

"*And so, you agreed?*"

"*Yes, but at the time I wasn't aware that they were capitalising on my 'God's police' image. And I'm sure not a 'damn whore!' And there were no spaces in between for me to express myself as in the time of the matriarchs. It's so sad. I think I struck a deal with the devil.*"

She released a heavy sigh.

"*When I was a little girl, you appeared in television advertisements for Persil soap powder?*"

"*Yes, that was me. My little boy praised me for the care I gave and that it was worthwhile since it gave the wash a purer whiteness,*" *her voiced raised slightly.*

Persil was still holding the bottle of Persil. I assumed it was part of the contract. I pushed up my reading glasses.

"*Where was your little girl?*"

"*She was in the wash house boiling up the gas fuelled copper. The Hoovers had arrived but not in our house.*"

"*They call themselves the media gods now. They have signal towers all over the world. The closest one to you is Eagle Hill.*"

She pointed to the hinterland through pearlescent soap bubbles floating about us. "*You'll get no interference from up there.*"

I was impressed, Persil knew her technology and geography.

"*They've toned down their marketing. It seems they've steered away from their sexist attitudes to housework,*" *I said but I knew deep down there was an angle to it.*

"*Yes, they have changed their image because of the feminists' anger about gender stereotyping, but women are still trapped! They have taken my image off the packaging and replaced me with a dad holding up his baby boy. There's also an archetype blue symbol of caregiving beside them and the caption, "dirt is good". Good for women to clean up, I say!*"

Persil was as angry as any feminist. She could see through the marketing strategies of the media, an industry dominated by male executives.

"*I guess you've been silenced?*"

"*Yes, I'm the black box of the family, the fundamental infrastructure of our society. And I have been made invisible.*"

Her voice trailed off.

"You are not invisible to me, dear Persil. I will always see you even if most of society can't. I'm sure the feminists relate to your multilayers and nonlinear existence," I reassured her. "I'm writing my story of my childhood trauma and abuse and am using it as evidence for my court case. Judge Pizan has ordered me to gather testimony. Would you consider writing an expert witness statement for me?"

I watched her chest rise in surprise at my request. She clasped her hands under her chin.

"Of course, dear. What would you like me to testify to?"

"You could testify to my claim that I shouldered most of the unpaid work at home, washing and cleaning for the family and carried on the scarcely acknowledged patriarchal tradition."

I stood motionless in expectation, hoping to God – or the Goddess – that she would agree.

"Of course, I will do that for you. After all, I am to blame for being the stereotype your parents exploited for their own purposes."

Persil spoke with strong eye contact.

"You are not to blame Persil. The media gods were male writers and constructed you that way to keep women in their place. Judge Pizan will understand, she has empathy for women who challenge misogynist patriarchal discourse," I assured her with an air of readiness. "Society is lucky to have benefited from unpaid housework for so long, we cannot rely on it forever." Weighing up the cons. "Besides that, Persil, it was one of the factors which contributed to the arrest of my initiation process into womanhood. I was trapped in the home and the wash house. There was too much hardship especially since I did not have a 'good enough' mother!"

I exhaled and peeked over my glasses into her bubbly blue eyes.

"Well, let's hope we can give the Court something to engage with and set a new precedent for change in caregiving roles."

Her eyes glimmered back at me, giving me hope for change.

I reached for another tissue before turning back to speak to Persil.

She was gone.

The Viking storm had passed and the light through the window was still dim. I had no idea what time it was.

I lay there for a moment, recounting my dream and remembering the beautiful goddess who had come to me with a tremendous spiritual aura about her. We shared our stories, but she was much wiser having lived through centuries of female banishment and survival along with her feminine aspects.

Click.

It was the clothes dryer turning off.

Caw! Caw! The warning bird's song filled the air.

I stood slowly from the sofa and folded the clothes from the dryer while viewing the storm battered garden from the window. A tree branch had broken from the main trunk and fallen to the ground, reminding me of the atrocities of my parents. They had fallen from grace in managing my childhood physical, emotional and spiritual needs. No wonder I turned to the goddesses for knowledge and understanding. I was the broken branch lying shattered on the ground outside.

To make matters worse my father moved us from the city when I graduated primary school. I looked forward to attending high school in the city with my friends, but he took that opportunity away from me as carelessly as he stole the core of my being.

1967
Shallow Water

"Come, Muse and sing the dreaded washing day."

Anna Barbauld (1743-1825) from *Washing Day*[3]

I couldn't escape the dread of washing days back at the house halfway up the hill.

Our house was built in a street with a long slope which flowed into the dense, tea tree lined foreshore. The sun spackled golden sand enticed me to swim and frolic on those glorious, yet few-between, beach days. Brightly coloured vintage boatsheds lined the sandy front, all pretty on the outside yet rarely a human thought of care on the inside. Maybe the new generation didn't see the same value in them as the old folk once did, except for the odd occupant here and there. They reminded me of the darkness inside myself while on the outside I kept up appearances.

My father had forced our family to move to a sleepy seaside town of Shallow Water far from city life. I was twelve years old and not happy to move. I loved my city school and friends, but my protests fell on deaf ears. So we shifted into a half-built jerry house that Grandad had put his heart and soul into for us to have a better life.

Poor Grandad had no idea of the traumatic events I was subjected to. He just assumed I was safe in my own house. I wish he was my caretaker and then my experience of care would have been founded on trust rather than terror. In all his innocence, Grandad's attachment to our family was to help out the best way he could which meant free labour and building a house for us.

The 'wash house' was downstairs, underneath the house facing the backyard. I was to spend every Saturday there until I was eighteen years old. Mum hadn't broken my will enough in our city house. Here, in our Shallow Water house she preyed on me further, deciding it was my job to do the family washing.

"It's too much for me!" She said puffing on her cigarette and filling the room with smoke.

"But Mum—"

I had school five days a week and homework and I was only twelve years old. It was Mum's job, not mine. I wasn't a little mother or substitute wife! But what did Mum know? All she cared about was making my life a misery.

"Don't give me that," she cut me off. "You need to pull your weight around the house!"

"I already wash the floors, make beds, mow the lawn, do the dishes, the ironing and put the rubbish out."

But she wasn't listening.

"There will be no ifs or buts. You will do as you're told."

"What about the boys? They don't do anything!"

I tried not to clench my fists or else she'd get even worse. Maybe if I died, I would be free of her.

"It's women's work. You need to learn to be a good housewife, grow up, marry a man with a trade, have kids and be like me. The men of the house need their rest!"

"That's not fair!"

I had no way of putting my dreams or aspirations first, she would only say I was selfish.

"Stop being self-centred. There's no need standing up for yourself with those Hollywood actress eyes. It won't work! You'd never make it in Hollywood."

"My girlfriends asked me to go riding on Saturdays," I said longing to belong to their group, riding my bike around the beaches and hiding places only kids and young teens know about.

Mum puffed on her cigarette; the smoke stung my eyes. I waved the smoke haze from my face and went on to convince her, only wanting to grow up like other kids.

"Their mums have electric *Hoover* washing machines," I said. "They get the job done much easier and quicker than the gas boiling copper and handwringer."

"Don't start on me with airs and graces. Your father is working hard enough to put meals on the table. We can't go affording those things!" She stubbed her chain-smoked cigarette into the glass ashtray full of dead lip-stick-stained screwed-up butts.

I wondered how much three packets of them cost a day. Add that up with the amount of grog Dad brought home and I was sure we could afford ten *Hoover* washing machines. But it was no use laying that argument on the table. Mum clung to what she knew and never trusted me or anything new.

I stared at the piles of washing strewn throughout the house with a scowl. I held my jaw closed tight. There were flannelette sheets and pyjamas for five people, heavy bath towels, school and work uniforms, tea towels, doilies, soiled underpants – everything needed a wash.

I wanted to cry.

The only meaning in life was to make men's needs my priority. Wasn't Mum watching the television or reading the newspapers?

"Times are changing, Mum. Women are marching in the streets for equal pay and rights."

Watching them gave my life meaning.

"They are hippies. Now get your mind off those brazen hussies. They are not homemakers but loose women. Your father says so!"

"But Mum, it's the women's liberation movement, they are trying to make it better for all women."

Mum was a victim of the patriarchy too, but she wouldn't have it.

"That's enough from you, you're a brazen hussy like them. In the morning I'll show you how to do the washing. Now get to bed and no more television, it's rotting your brain!"

I sighed and turned towards my bedroom; no amount of reasoning could change Mum's mind.

In the wash house the next morning was a copper boiler fuelled by a gas bottle burner, two cement troughs, a handwringer and a box of *Persil* soap powder, guaranteed to give the whitest wash.

In the corner was the copper stick to agitate the wash while it boiled and then for lifting heavy, soaked loads into the trough filled with cold water for the rinsing. With the veins visibly throbbing in her neck, Mum led me through the ropes of the washing labour, and most frightfully, how to light the gas burner with a stark warning that it would blow up in my face if I wasn't careful.

"Stand back as soon as you light the burner," she said, waving a dead match in her witch hand. She was too frightened to light the mercurial thing herself.

Petrified of the menacing gas bottles exploding in my face, I nervously placed a lighted match to the skull and bones, charred, gas-leaking effluent.

The dreaded gas burner lit up and the water boiled in the septuagenarian copper. Carefully, using the copper stick, I heaved the clothes in, ensuring the whites were separated from the colours and cautious not to scald myself with the red-hot water in the shoddy process.

"Put your back into it," Mum shouted at me with flaring nostrils.

I turned to her as if to say, 'help me' but she had already walked off, refusing to have any more to do with it and leaving me to the hard labour.

Wearily, I heaved the washing from the copper to the rinse trough. Piece by piece, I wrung it through the handwringer until it fell into the dry trough. My arms ached and my body was limp with the strenuous work. I couldn't help but entertain intensely dark thoughts. I wanted to expose my mother for her ignorance. She didn't deserve me.

I pushed the copper stick into the second load causing the boiling water to sear at me, just like my mother's savage hatred.

Wringing my water shrivelled hands, I watched the freshly laundered clothes hanging on the line, held together by wooden pegs and child slave labour. The line was full, but my heart was empty – powerless to stop the hate crimes against me.

I packed away the copper stick and put the soap powder on the shelf for the next wash. I dragged my compulsively bitten, water-logged fingernails down my caustic red cheeks and glimpsed the lowering sun losing its spackles.

My mind turned to the beach; it was too late to go swimming. And I would be lonely swimming on my own without the company of my girlfriends. I was like the abandoned boat sheds, a fringe dweller living in silence. How was I going to learn to stand up for myself when all I knew was slavery? Sickened to my stomach, I kicked the washing basket under the troughs and closed the wash house door behind me, wishing the loneliness away.

CHAPTER 14

What He Brought Home

2013 autumn
Far north home

"The stain on your
Gauze Ku Klux Klan
Babushka
Darkens and tarnishes….

How you jump -
Trepanned veteran
Dirty Girl,
Thumb stump."

Sylvia Plath from *Cut*, 1963[1]

I was lonely at home on my own.

Seven years had passed since I resigned from full-time teaching and I knew I had to move forward. I traced my finger over the desk calendar and spotted my upcoming teaching contract. It would start next week. Good, I missed teaching even after all these years. That it had been taken away from me by the school principal for speaking out about the school paedophile made my trauma worse. I left the school branded an incompetent teacher while the paedophile walked away scot-free. It was exactly the same as when I grew up, I was to blame for everything. I don't know why I expected anything different. It was my feather brain no doubt, a kind of brain hole that followed me around, a weary veteran survivor of abuse.

I pushed aside the yearbook from my old school and entered the teaching address of the contract school in my phone. This would be better than not teaching at all, even if I didn't form the same close attachments to students.

There was a familiar drop of a bag on the floor and I turned around to see Jasmine enter the kitchen beaming her beautiful smile. She leaned on my shoulder as if to say, 'I'm all grown up and taller than you', and 'I love you, Mum'. If it wasn't for my children's love, my sense of belonging in this world would have long been shattered.

"When's dinner ready, Mum?" she asked while checking her phone for messages from her friends.

"Ten minutes, chickee."

I couldn't stop using her childhood nickname even though she had graduated from high school last year.

I rummaged through the kitchen drawer for the chopping board and knives to prepare a garden salad, not noticing the red liquid dripping from my finger. Blood ran down the cupboard door to the floor, my feet squelched in its rivulets. I stared at it like a door hanging from its hinge, just hanging on, like my emotional state. My son had already left home to live in the city and pursue his career. And my chick was leaving for uni this evening. I tried not to think about it but I was about to be an empty nester.

"Mum, what have you done?"

Jasmine grabbed the cotton tea towel and covered the flap of skin hanging from my finger.

"Here, hold it tight to stop the bleeding and I'll get some gauze," she said and raced off towards the bathroom.

I'm lucky she was there to help me stop the bleeding and bring me around.

The bandage did the job.

"That's better, thanks," I said and began to arrange the plates and cutlery while my daughter finished chopping the salad.

"Will you be okay, Mum? I'm heading to uni tonight and won't see you until semester break."

"I'll be okay." I tried to reassure her even though I wasn't sure myself, but I wanted the best for her including a tertiary education. "You concentrate on your studies and enjoy uni life. I'll start a teaching contract next week. I'll give you a call and let you know how I go."

"Bye Mum, love you," she said, giving me a big hug.

"Love you too." I cleared my throat, trying not to cry and watched her leave the nest, proud that she was choosing her own path into adulthood. She had more tools to survive in the world than I had. Laying my bandaged hand over my chest, I closed the front door and headed off to bed.

Sylvia Plath's restored edition of her *Ariel* poems lay on the bedside table. I rested my gauzed finger on a raised pillow to slow the blood pumping straight from my heart. In my other hand I held *Ariel* and read Sylvia's poem, *Cut*.

There were a series of strange and foreboding images which filled Sylvia's mind after she had cut her thumb. She compared her injury to a scalped pilgrim, a member of the Ku Klux Klan, a dirty girl, a stump and a trepanned veteran. I focused on the words with an understanding of the juxtaposition of these distasteful figures. I imagined the Babushka was my bitter and abusive grandmother and the dirty girl was me, the name my parents called me as a child. Sylvia's feeling of alienation spanned the entire poem bringing up memories of my own alienation beyond the school principal. The words took me back to my childhood abuse.

The next morning, I would ask for a referral to a psychologist. This time I wanted a different kind of psychologist, one who had more experience with trauma patients than the previous one who turned her back on me. I was feeling quite the trepanned veteran and I wanted help.

2013 autumn
Far north home

I was lucky to get an appointment with Dr Hannah Wise before I began my new teaching contract. When I lost focus cutting my finger at home, it was the last straw. I needed to make money and survive in the world. Teaching required my proper attention for the students and curriculum. Shuffling my way to the front door, I entered the quaint heritage building painted an off-white that highlighted the traditional cornices and decorative moulding. It was beautifully restored, its problems of the past addressed and resolved. I only hoped they had the same ability to restore me and my neglected past. Her practice was furnished with bright and colourful fabrics on soft chairs, surrounded by artwork created by grieving and traumatised patients to show their gratitude for her counselling to overcome the anxiety caused by specific traumas.

The receptionist was pleasant.

"Take a seat and Dr Wise will be with you soon."

She signalled for me to sit on a bright pink hessian and silk covered comfy chair. Next to it was wellbeing magazines arranged like a stack of bibles. Two candles burned on the shelf opposite, the flames dispelling my edginess.

A voice came from behind the receptionist. Dr Wise called my name, her voice had the same ambience as the soothing candles. Her floral dress matched her stylish Italian sandals. She had thick auburn hair which was tied back in a soft bun at the nape of her neck. She wore vintage bead necklaces and bangles that connected her to someone else's past. It gave them a sense of place on her elegant body and professionally trained inquiring mind.

"This way," she beckoned me with a smile.

Her vintage blue-beaded bangle chimed a protection song. I entered the consult room in my perseverance to follow a new path, leading to insights and truths to heal from my childhood trauma.

Fixed on her vintage beauty, I watched her reading my information form and my admissions of suffering childhood sexual abuse and related traumas.

"I'm so sorry," she said as if she were the representative of all of humanity for the injustices inflicted on me in my childhood.

Against my will, my eyes teared up. I had finally met a person, a kind soul, who believed me. I had been looking in the wrong places or perhaps this was just my time.

"Please call me Hannah," she insisted.

"One of my coping strategies is to write poetry. Would you like to read some, Hannah?"

I uncrossed my hands on my folder filled with poems and brought them out in anticipation of being read. They were my only narrative to date of the child abuse, even if written in mysterious symbols and metaphors unintelligible to a utilitarian patriarchal society.

"It's wonderful writing helps you through your trauma. However, I won't read them. What you have written here will do." She pointed to the few lines that described quarter of a lifetime of abuse and torture on the information form.

"My approach for survivors is to teach mindfulness strategies. You must focus on the present and not dwell on the past. I will teach you how to deal with the pain and grow emotionally and spiritually from now on."

I stared down at my hands. If this is going to make my anxiety and depression go away then I will go along with it. After all, Hannah was the professional. I was merely the survivor trying to tell her story. If my story was to go back into isolation while I was being treated with mindfulness, then so be it.

"But first you must try and reach inside yourself and find your inner child. Can you do that and rescue her from her dark place?"

"I'm not sure she is alive." I was convinced my parents and grandmother had murdered her long ago. I was also puzzled how this was not me 'dwelling on the past'?

"When you find her, bring her to your present for hugs and reassurance that she is no longer in danger," said Hannah, convincing me I carried my inner child inside myself. She wrote on the reverse side of a prescription pad and then outstretching her elegant arm, she handed me a nicely calligraphed note: "You don't have to do this day alone" and "I love the way you feel unthreatened – running, photography, loving mother tasks".

She hadn't missed anything from the information form.

"Live mindfully, be focused and engaged in the here and now and not distracted by the past," she said looking me directly in the eye.

I nodded. All would be well and good if learning to live in the present moment would contribute to my mental wellness and true happiness.

"You are visiting Melbourne shortly?" she spoke with light breaths as she read from the information sheet. "For the Melbourne Marathon?"

I stared at her with a furrowed brow, puzzled why she would ask.

"Yes, the course entails running past the suburb of my childhood."

"Being in the physical place of your childhood abuse will connect you closer to your inner child. I suggest you plan to rescue her from that place and bring her home to be safe with you."

I was running to resolve my trauma, with no cognition, to make sense of it apart from the fact the neurochemicals improved my mood. My mouth opened but I forced it closed. I struggled to find the words to respond to Hannah's suggestion. I enjoyed running because it took me away from my past and now I was going to run a marathon to my past.

"I'll try."

"Wonderful." Hannah glanced at the door. "Please book another appointment with me when you get back from your trip."

We stood up at the same time and hugged.

"Goodbye, Hannah. Thank you so much for the session."

I offered her a tiny wave on my way out and made my appointment with the receptionist as requested.

2013 autumn
Far north home

Once home, after my session with Hannah, I focused on setting my goals for teaching and running.

I wasn't sure of Hannah's plan. I fumbled with her calligraphed note, placing it under a paper weight. Running was enjoyable for its simplicity. A run on the trails before work cleared my head from the all-too-common nightmares. It helped me to exude calm and focus throughout the teaching day. Running helped me to stay employed. I had a mortgage and bills to pay like everyone else and didn't discuss my personal life or running at work. I kept my head down and worked hard, wanting to remain employed in contract work. Sitting upright at my desk, I set to organising my trip to Melbourne ensuring my return flight was late Sunday afternoon so not to disrupt the teaching timetable. Momentarily, my mind went distant and I stared out the window, pushing aside Hannah's plan for me to rescue my child while running the marathon. I would deal with that when the time came.

I leaned on my desk and studied the term planner for the teaching contract. The *bildungsroman* novel *Looking for Alibrandi* was the set text for Grade Ten novel study. I was familiar with the content having taught it before and knew the students would want to know the meaning of *bildungsroman*. It was a novel dealing with a person's formative years. I went over the student booklet and planned what to do. I was always interested to teach a writer's chronicle which looked back at the events leading to their loss of innocence and journey toward adulthood.

One day I should write a *bildungsroman* book about the unspoken forms of emotional abuse while growing up, for victims of family violence to find corroboration.

My thoughts returned to Hannah's plan. I trembled at the thought of visiting the Elster house where I grew up.

2013 autumn
Far north home

I waited outside Hannah's consulting room on the same comfy chair, reclaiming my inner child in Elster proved more difficult than she told me. The two candles burning opposite me in the waiting room lacked the same illumination as my first visit. I didn't want to look at them, so I kept my eyes fixed on the floor. I felt like I was the child arriving home without the candy, beaten by my mother. Dread gnawed at me, warning me to run or hide.

I heard my name and snapped out of the arrhythmia arresting my mind and followed Hannah to her room. I uncrossed my arms, we shared a hug and Hannah motioned me to take a seat.

"How was your race?" Hannah asked, bouncing one of her Italian shoes in my direction.

I shifted in my seat, unable to get comfortable.

"It was a disaster."

"Oh."

She pulled a loose strand of auburn hair into the knot behind her nape.

"It started out okay," I said, "I ran light in even strides along the freshly tarred St Kilda Road. The smell got to me first and I was suffocating in its thick stench. It reminded me of the pungent phenol smell of the outside dunny and I was consumed with darkness. My stomach began to churn and my legs lost their even stride."

I hugged the brightly coloured cushion as I spoke.

"Go on." Hannah crossed her legs at the ankles. Her Italian style shoes were asymmetrical with the rest of her body.

"As I passed the Moorabbin baths, not far from my childhood home, I thought of the Aboriginal poet, Oodgeroo Noonuccal's poem, *Municipal Gum*." [2]

Marginalised people's poetry helped me to understand the pain of not belonging.

"That's interesting!"

She wrote something in her folder. My stomach sunk, maybe she thought I was crazy after all.

"I recalled her use of the word 'bitumen'. The hard syllables are a metaphor for her people suffering a forced identity." I clutched the soft pillow higher under my chin. "My panic got worse when I ran through Black Rock. The syllables hit me harder and my mind fell into the abyss. I barely made it to the finish line."

"What do you mean hard syllables?" Her Italian shoe bounced again.

"My parents beat – choked – cruel – striked – tortured – broke – and nearly killed me—"

Did I have to spell it out for her?

Hannah maintained eye contact, except when taking notes.

"I tried to bring my little girl home. I dragged her by the hand through Black Rock, along the new bitumen road, and then we lost our grip and she disappeared."

I looked to Hannah for reassurance. She adjusted her vintage bracelets, making them align with her elegant arm and changed the topic. Her head tilted to one side.

"Have you thought about laying charges against your parents?"

Again, I was lost for words. That would be the worst-case scenario.

"I have thought about it but these cases go nowhere," I said, shaking my head. "It was so long ago and I don't have any witnesses. And they would deny it anyway, they always have."

"What about your brothers?"

She stroked her blue-beaded vintage bracelet.

"I have never discussed it with my brothers. Most of the abuse happened when they were not home. If they suspected anything it would be that I was a girl and it was normal behaviour. After all parents know best." I let go of the cushion and clasped my hands together on my lap. Any concept of connecting with my inner child was now history.

I left the session feeling stronger than ever that therapy was flawed. These sessions were going nowhere except for some temporary 'feel good' and take-home clichés. So far, the chronicle of my child abuse was a narrative written by me in ten minutes on an information sheet held by Hannah. And my poetry folder wasn't worthy for her to read.

This therapy was not working. I had to move forward and bring balance to my life in my own way.

The only way I knew how.

I would summon the courage to write my story even it terrified me. I would 'tremble, redden and bleed'. I knew deep inside that I needed to find my own voice and express the wrongness of the abuse but I had kept this idea to myself for so long. It was no good telling Hannah; she was invested in mindfulness – in being in the present. I would explore my past without Hannah or anyone else. I didn't need anyone to correct me. After all, I was used to being the odd one out to follow what I knew was true.

2013
Far north home

*"The only book that is worth writing is the
one we don't have the courage or
strength to write. The book that hurts us
(who we are writing), that makes
us tremble, redden, bleed."*

*"Explore the idea of what the language that women speak
would really be like if no one were there to correct them."*

Helene Cixous, French feminist/philosopher/writer, born 1937[3]

Substitute teachers were treated as if they were missing a limb. I set up the English classroom before the students arrived so not to give them the opportunity to discuss my differences from their regular teacher. They assembled outside the door and peered in while pulling out books from their bags.

"She's a bit on the wrinkly side," one criticised.

"But I like her dress and boots. She might be cool!"

I couldn't help but smile, I had a barracker. I raised a copy of *Looking for Alibrandi* in the air.

"Please come in," I said. "And don't forget your textbook."

They entered without a word and made their own seating plan. Standing in the limelight, I pressed on with the lesson, not giving them more time to find flaws with me. They were a mixed bunch of typical Grade Ten students. Long hair, short hair, hitched skirts, nose studs, shirts hanging out, nearly all breaching the dress code. Fifteen years old and on the verge of adulthood, in the middle of their very own *bildungsroman*, even if they didn't know it.

One hand flew up with a copy of *Alibrandi* in it.

"Why do we have to study this book, Miss?"

"Because it's on the curriculum."

"Our teacher said we could choose another book while she was away."

I dismissed the challenge to my authority with a friendly smile.

"What will we learn from it? Seriously? It was written like twenty years ago," another student joined in.

I was pleased they were speaking to me at all and embraced it as an opportunity to teach them.

"It was written by Melina Marchetta in 1992. It is the story of her final year at school, a year she sets herself free."[4]

"What does that mean? Was she in prison?"

"No. The novel is written in the style called *bildungsroman*. It is a German word which cannot be translated into English in one word. Write this definition in your workbooks and it will help you to understand as we go through the novel and its themes," I explained while writing the definition on the board.

"*Bildungsroman* is a story of the growing up of a sensitive person, who looks for answers to his or her questions through different experiences."

"What does that mean, Miss?"

I wrote on the board.

"The novel starts with a loss or tragedy that disturbs the main character emotionally. He or she leaves on a journey to fill that vacuum."

My hopes rose. They wrote down the definitions with intent looks on their faces, already involved in the discussion.

"The main character Josephine Alibrandi starts out being overdramatic about her Italian background and illegitimacy. She faces several challenges through her senior year and at the end she begins to achieve her emancipation." I spoke with ease and my confidence rose. I was a good teacher, my student's reactions were all the proof I needed.

I watched them sink back in their chairs, resigned to reading *Looking for Alibrandi.*

"These are your student guidelines to the novel." I said while handing each a booklet. "You have four weeks to finish reading the novel and complete the questions in the booklet. Then you have four weeks to write an essay due last week of term." I led them quickly through the lesson. "You have reading and activity time for each lesson. For the other part of the lesson, we will discuss the major themes Josephine Alibrandi is going through."

"Can we watch the movie, Miss?"

I smiled; I expected that.

"After you hand in your booklets and finish reading the novel."

The bell signalled the end of class and they left quietly. Satisfied I made a good first impression, I followed them out the door and listened for any small talk about the substitute teacher.

There wasn't any.

Two days later I arrived at the classroom before the Grade Ten English class, determined to be prepared for their novel study. The more I showed that I valued their lessons, the more they did too. Quirking an eyebrow, I set up the overhead projector with the themes of *Looking for Alibrandi.* I planned the theme of 'identity' for the class discussion. This was a big topic which would challenge their inhibitions. It was our second lesson and most of them were still shy with me but I hoped this would help break the ice.

"Miss is already in the classroom," a student's voice came from outside.

"She has the same boots on today. Cool!"

It was my barracker.

"Come on in," I said in a bubbly tone.

I waited for the students to take their seats and then completed the attendance roll. Checking them off the list, I quickly wrote a seating plan using first names in the hope of building their confidence with me. Apart from some intermittent throat clearing, they read their novels quietly. One or two raised their faces at me with a questioning look but declined any offers of support. Their guideline booklets were open but no one had attempted to write answers to questions.

The themes lit up from the overhead projector.

"If you would stop reading and look to the board."

"Miss, that's a lot," Breda croaked in her thick Irish accent.

"I agree. We will start with the first one, 'identity.'" Without overreacting and reading from the board I said, "Identity – all through the book the main character Josie is trying to find her identity and how she fits into society."

"Someone calls her a wog!"

Breda giggled.

"And how did that affect Josie?" I encouraged students to answer their own questions. After all, it was about them identifying injustices they witnessed or learnt about.

"She gets really upset because she is Australian and has Italian blood. Her nonna believes strongly in keeping their culture alive. It causes Josie to struggle with her identity and how she fits into society."

"Very good, Breda. Often people in the real world feel this way. They feel like outsiders. If there is something different about us, people will use it to discriminate against us or make us feel like the odd one out."

"Well, I can speak from experience on that one," said Breda in her thickest Irish accent.

Her and Abigail clutched each other while more laughter came from the class. Squaring my shoulders, I switched off the overhead projector and let them read for the last ten minutes. Some had begun to write responses.

Watching Abigail write, I noticed her pen stop and start. She hesitated and stared out the window.

My eyes followed her line of sight but my mind arrived at another place and time, when I was their age at school.

I was the odd one out at high school.

"Don't even think about going out with her," boys said to each other.

I often felt like crumbling and disappearing on the spot.

"Her parents are strict and won't let her go out with boys."

Word got out quickly.

My father said I wasn't allowed to date boys. He said I must stay in the home until I got married.

I wanted to be like the other girls my age and hold hands with a boy on the school bus. They were all doing it. Except me.

"That's not fair." I pleaded with Mum because my father wouldn't discuss it with me.

He passed it on to Mum to deal with. Of course, she agreed with him.

"Holding hands leads to other things," said Mum, the disabled wife who was deprived of fulfilling her own life, let alone help me to fulfil mine.

My father was a hypocrite. I had more faith in the boys at my school conducting themselves appropriately than how my father was with me when I was eight years old.

My father had forcibly detached and estranged me from life outside his own being...

"Miss, that was the bell," Abigail's words jolted me back to the present.

"Of course. You may go. Make sure you read more at home. See you all next lesson."

"Thanks Miss. Don't forget it's a split lesson," came the friendly reminder from Abigail.

I smiled.

"Thank you, Abigail."

Amid a flutter of chatter, they packed up their books.

"Thank you, Miss," each one nodded on their way out.

"Thank you," I acknowledged with lightness in my chest.

When they had gone, I wrote in my diary. *Year 10 English Split Lesson, Part 1 Theme - Love, Lunch Break, Part 2 Theme - Relationships.* I tidied my desk and locked the door on my way out. It was the end of the school day. Time for a run after work.

"Miss, can we come in?"

I looked up from my desk in front of the classroom to see Abigail and Breda standing at the door.

I smiled.

"Yes, of course. You're early!"

"We left Maths early," Abigail said, clambering into her desk. "We thought you would be here."

I frowned, concerned for them to follow the school rules.

"You mustn't leave your classes before the bell."

"Just this time, Miss. Sir said it was okay because we had finished our work. He trusts us. We're his favourite students."

They let out a chuckle.

The bell signalled the exchange of lessons and the rest of the class arrived not long after. They settled into their seats and began quietly reading while I marked each one off the attendance list. I browsed their first names and seating plan, watching them reading comfortably next to each other. The keen readers had nearly finished their novels, the pages bending with brightly coloured sticky notes. That was most of the class. A few laggards were a quarter in with a sticky note here and there.

"Miss, do you have any sticky notes?"

It was James. His name fit the seating plan.

"As a matter of fact, I do James," I said, passing some spares I had brought from home.

"Thanks Miss. Our other teacher gave them to us. We didn't think you would be nice but we were wrong."

"Teacher's pet," the freckled boy yelled from the back row.

The class burst into laughter.

Abigail and Breda were clutching each other. Taking the comments as a courtesy, I switched on the overhead projector and the themes lit up the white board.

"I see you have stopped reading, please look to the board," I said leaning in to talk to them.

"Do we have to talk about this, Miss? It's embarrassing," James blurted out.

"Love is a major theme of the novel and growing up," I addressed the whole class. James and other students were on the edge of their personal evolution and I didn't want to shame them. Holding my shoulders square, I read from the board. "Love was a stranger to Josie until she got to know Jacob Coote. She didn't know what it meant to care for someone so much when they weren't related to each other."

"It's taking Josie a bit of working out. She thinks she's in love with him but also there is the love from her parents," Abigail said, displaying emotional maturity.

"Her mother has always been there for her and she loves her a lot. She meets her father for the first time when she is seventeen and he moves to Sydney for her," I said, encouraging the students into the meaning of love in the character's personal space.

"All right then. If he loved her so much, why did he only get to know her when she was seventeen?"

James' face went red and his acne flared up.

Abigail shook her head.

"Because James, he didn't know Josie was his daughter. Her mum never told him about Josie until she was seventeen. Haven't you been reading the book?"

"All right, all right," said James, resigned to reading his book.

"Questions on the theme *Love* are on page twelve of your booklets. If you need help, raise your hand and I'll get to you. Work independently for now. We will share ideas later."

I watched James rub a hand through his untidy hair while he read. His eyes went back and forth across the sentences and he hesitated to paste a sticky note on an important page. He kept his eyes down and focused on reading. I looked away and my mind went back to when I was their age.

I was in love with Simon. He was so handsome and my age. I watched him on the bus each day and hoped he would hold hands with me.

One day I sat close to him.

"Can we hold hands, Simon?" I asked. "I like you a lot and I'm pretty sure you like me too."

"I do like you but it won't work out. Your parents are strict and don't trust boys. Why should I be any different?"

"We can make it different. If we try," I begged.

"Your parents will get in the way. I'm sorry I can't be your boyfriend."

Simon turned away from me and we never spoke again.

I saw him the next day holding hands with Marian. I couldn't blame him. He was upfront about his feelings but I was miserable. I desperately wanted to feel that kind of connection with somebody who had a better way of life.

My parents had rendered me invisible to boys my age. I wanted to learn how to care for someone else I wasn't related to. My parents didn't love me. Their way of thinking was warped and strange. I had no gateway into new thinking about the different perspectives of life.

The only decision growing up afforded me was to find a male protector in secret. That was a mistake.

I started dating older boys behind my parents' back but only to repeat and relive the secrecy of the incestuous relationship. As the 'other woman' I had little power to define the terms of future relationships and content myself with boyfriends who were capricious and unavailable.

Mum didn't shy away from her views, she tried to make it rub off onto me.

"Old man Hurt has been doin' things to his daughters up there on the farm. It's official police business but your father said you ought to know."

I knew what she meant when she said 'things' because my father was just like him.

They brainwashed me to believe their perspective on life. My father was guilty of doing things to me and yet he continued to convince Mum I was a liar. Now he was dealing out punishment to incestuous men like Hurt. He scapegoated old man Hurt as an opportunity to discuss with Mum the seriousness with which the taboo is regarded in society and culture and absolve himself of any wrongdoing.

"That girl is no good!" I overheard Mum tell my father on many occasions. Mum had abandoned me a long time ago and was implacably cold toward me. The punishment of old man Hurt was just the thing she needed to align herself with my father. She wanted to keep her man and make sure she came first.

"Yes, dear." My father went along with it to support his entitlement to love, service and to sex – and to hide his implicit use of his own daughter in the structure of the incest taboo.

"Miss, that was the bell," Abigail spoke as the bell rang.

I looked up at her, embarrassed I had let my thoughts consume me again. I had to get it together if I was to earn their respect.

"Of course, leave your books here and I'll see you after lunch for part two of the lesson."

"Thanks, Miss," the class said in chorus.

"Thank you," I said with a smile, I hadn't lost their trust.

Amid a flutter of chatter, they left the room.

I watched them walk across the courtyard. James and Breda held hands. Abigail walked behind them; her arm linked with another boy from the class. They were experimenting with love with boys and girls their own age. They were caring for someone else and learning other perspectives on life other than their parents'. I gazed away from their happiness. I felt a rising discontentment with my past and my mind wandered back to when I was their age.

"Your father said a woman drowned her three kids last night at Shallow Water Beach but she didn't have the nerve to drown herself."

I didn't know what to say. Mum said it so casual, like the time she told me the neighbour drowned a sack of helpless kittens.

"He's working overtime. He must write up the report. He said he feels sorry for the mother. She was driven by madness."

I didn't know what to think. This was my perspective on life. The snippets of drama he selected to bring home and share with me through Mum's voice. Was he telling me this because he thought I was lucky not to be drowned as a kid?

I never walked alongside my father, proud like Josie with her father in the novel. I wasn't proud of him at all, he terrified me.

His domestic battery demanded obedience and loyalty by sacrificing all other relationships. His control over me played into his sexual fantasy of power over me, not in fantasy but reality.

The classroom grew chilly and I put on my jacket to shield me from the dark memories. Averting my eyes to the window, I watched my students eating lunch on the lawn. I pulled out my salad sandwich from my lunch box and ate it. A cup of hot coffee, poured from my flask, boosted my focus and I welcomed the bell signalling the students back to class.

"Can we come in, Miss?" It was Abigail and Breda.

The boys not far behind them.

"Of course," I said with my shoulders held back.

The students entered the classroom.

Feeling warmer already, I removed my jacket and placed it over the chair and then turned to the projector.

"Miss, can we read a bit longer, please?" James asked. He was reading to catch up with the others.

"Ten more minutes."

With easy breaths, I completed marking the roll. They were all present.

"Okay, I'm up to Chapter Nine." James rallied. "Can I turn the projector on for you, Miss?"

He offered to help along with his witty commentary.

"Thank you, James," I said, leaning back in my chair.

James looked up at the themes lit on the board.

"First 'love', now 'relationships'," he said.

"What's wrong with that?" said Breda cheerfully. "Sit down James."

"Throughout the book, Josie's relationships with other people changes her way of thinking on different issues," I said, reading from the board.

"What does that mean, Miss?" James' face went red again.

"At first she didn't like being Italian, but she grows and learns to accept her family and heritage."

James slumped in his seat. He was getting the idea about making 'growing up decisions'.

"Yeah, like when Josie and Jacob split up at the end. Josie is focused on moving and not straying behind while the rest of her life moves forward," Abigail joined in.

"Like when Jacob goes on to be a mechanic and Josie a lawyer?" James said without looking at Abigail.

"Go to page fourteen in your booklets. You have the rest of the lesson to work on the 'relationship' theme questions," I said, leaning in and keeping eye contact with them. My gaze remained focused until they resumed reading and notetaking. Some spoke to each other in a quiet voice, telling stories of their own growing up decisions like those in the novel.

My mind went back to when I was their age and growing up decisions, I didn't get to make.

"Stop poking at me!" I cried.

My father was sitting on the side of the sofa. His overweight bulbous body sunk into it while he poked me in the ear with his fat penis injecting finger.

"He, he, he!" He sniggered and kept poking me.

"Let me go, let me go," I cried but it only incited him further.

"Little girl, little girl... you're a good little girl... he he he... do you like this little girl?"

My ways of thinking on any issue was controlled by him. He wouldn't let me go out with boys but here he was keeping me for himself, to poke and tease me as if he had never grown up.

Many nights he came home rotten drunk. I shuddered when I heard the car door close and his fat heavy body stumbling up the stairs. The jerry-built house shook. Mum ran away and hid in the wash house. She didn't want him to bash her.

"Where's your mother?" he roared.

"She's gone to the shops." My brothers lied to conceal Mum out of his sight. Then silence.

I would clench my fists and the room would spin around me. Nausea rose in my throat, I knew exactly what that meant.

He turned his big, beer-bloated body toward me. Stumbling and dragging his beast feet across the worn carpet, his hands in the pounce position. I quivered in fight or flight response but I was one third his size and there was nowhere to escape.

"Little girl, I will show you what it is like to have a lover!" He was snorting, dribbling and ranting.

I wasn't a little girl. I was a young woman. Our society forbids him to be my lover but he was unstoppable.

"Stop it," I screamed and cried at the same time.

He persisted by grasping my head with his fat funnel web spider hands on either side of my face, swallowing my ears and restricting my jaw movement to speechlessness. Shockingly, he planted his fat, salivating, sex-addicted lips on mine.

"Ahherrrraaa," I tried to cry out but his physical force overpowered me. Forcing his large body, half dressed in his police officer uniform onto me, pushing me hard onto the bed. He pulled up my dress and rubbed himself where Mum told me 'never let anybody touch you down there'.

But I had no ability to fight that I had given him no consent... I was his victim.

Did my brothers think I was asking for it? They stood by and didn't help me, like they helped Mum hide from him. Did they think it was a sex lesson? Didn't they realise I couldn't move? And Mum knowingly left me in the house alone with him... she would sacrifice me to save herself.

No one called the police and no one called out for help.

A hand raised in my peripheral vision. It was James. A sticky note protruded from the open pages of his novel.

"Miss, can you help me please?"

"Yes, James, of course." I forced my thoughts back to the classroom and took interest in his question.

"The characters in this book help each other a lot," he said, tapping the sticky note.

"Yes, that's true. In real life too."

"Can I write my essay on that theme? I know we haven't covered it in class discussion yet. Just thinking ahead, Miss."

I smiled, James was a helper.

"Of course, if it resonates with you, James."

"What does resonate mean, Miss?"

"You respond to other people's needs, like helping me with the projector. It's a musical note you strike that appeals to someone in a personal or emotional way."

"I like how Josie and her mum help each other even though they fight on and off. They're always there to support one another and love each other whether they like it or not." His eyes were fixed on mine.

"Exactly. Help is taking a confused, sad, or lonely person and picking them up to lead them in the right direction. It can change someone's life and possibly inspire them to help other people." I kept my eyes on James but at the same time I couldn't help but think about the lack of help from my own family when I was his age.

'Clang, clang!' The bell sounded the end of the lesson.

The students gathered their books. Amid the chatter, they left the room thanking me on their way out. Abigail was going too fast and dropped her books. James stopped and helped pick them up.

"Thanks James, for looking out for me," Abigail said, laying her hand over her heart.

Tucking my books under my chin, I left the room, locking the door behind me.

2021 late autumn
Ocean harbour home

"Unless our leaders take full responsibility for their own failings
Abuse culture will continue to thrive… it rots from the top."

Grace Tame, child sexual abuse survivor and advocate, born 1995[5]

The warm days of autumn crept their way into my ocean harbour home, replacing the summer which had blazed like a cheerful fire at my grate. The days were becoming noticeably shorter and the temperatures cooler. Autumn sunrises were filled with soft, reddish-coloured clouds from the east, creating exquisite frames in my camera.

I grinned. Which sunrise photo would I post to social media today?

I tilted my body closer to my iPad and observed several photos from my morning shoot. I was undecided, perhaps Sage could help me. She had a new camera and needed help setting it up. I jumped at the chance to help her and to enjoy a chat over coffee. I glanced around the room at the books put back in the bookshelf and the candles straightened on the coffee table, she would be here by 10am.

Change was in the air.

The women had marched on Parliament House to bring change to Australian society. Autumn was ripe with life; a unique mellow beauty punctuated by brilliance. I likened it to our women's movement which was ripe and punctuated by the brilliance of its young leaders marching for change to help women live better lives and to speak their truth, without the threat of toxic masculinity.

There was a knock at the door.

"Come on in, Sage," I called out from the lounge while switching on the TV. "You're just in time for the Women's March update."

I beckoned her towards a seat when she came around the corner. She was dressed in a light turquoise jumper and jeans, always ready to impress. She was as excited as I was about the women's movement and sat herself comfortably on the sofa.

"Oh great. I hope they are getting somewhere with the Prime Minister," Sage said, placing her camera on the side table for later.

I smiled and held up her favourite cup.

"Coffee?"

"Yes please. Quick, it's starting."

"The defence minister has called the alleged rape victim a lying cow,"[6] announced the update on TV.

"What?" Sage and I shrieked together.

"How dare she say that! Why isn't she trying to help her instead of calling her a liar?"

Sage held her coffee mug indignantly, nearly spilling it all over herself.

"An interview with the security guard regarding events which took place in Parliament House on the night of the alleged rape."

More breaking news.

A picture of the defence minister, flashing a cold smile at the camera, was enough to cement her contempt for the victim. Quickly the image shifted to the security guard, a youngish woman with a stiff posture refusing to be baited by the reporting journalist that there had been a security breach.

"Let me make it clear there was not a security breach,"[7] the words spilled from her hard jawline.

"You watch it Sage, and fill me in, I need to get my camera-fixit kit from the car." I turned my head from the screen and closed my eyes, thinking about when I was young. My mother and brothers left me alone in a room with my drunken paedophile of a father who had one thing on his mind. I couldn't watch it anymore.

"What happened?" I probed Sage when I reentered the lounge room.

"The security guard said she followed procedures." Sage went on.

I rolled my eyes. I didn't want to hear how others could explain away accountability.

"Are you okay?" Sage sensed my frustration.

I was edging on angry.

"I will be when I fix your camera." I said with a smile. Sage was dear to me and I didn't want to impact her with my violent history which had been triggered by the young feminist who was speaking out to be heard.

I wanted to keep one foot in the real world and write my memoirs of child and sexual abuse. This news update compelled me to continue writing this afternoon – after I helped Sage assemble her new camera.

CHAPTER 15

Leaving School

2021 late autumn
Ocean harbour home

"I love a sunburnt country,
A land of sweeping plains,
Of ragged mountain ranges
Of drought and flooding rains.
I love her far horizons,
I love her jewel-sea,
Her beauty and her terror -
The wide brown land for me!"

Dorothea Mackellar from *My Country*, 1908[1]

It was autumn and the golden afternoon sun shimmered low in the sky. The sun's rays filtered through the shutters and warmed me. With agile fingers, I pummelled the keyboard, selecting my words to hold my parents and grandmother accountable for their actions, refusing to cover up the family secrets anymore. I sniffed out the truth and called into question the security guard on the breaking news this morning who defended her position. She reminded me of my mother who subversively helped my father from being impacted by revealing the abuse. Lies and deception had become second nature through my childhood. I would no longer be an accomplice to those who forced me to keep dark secrets.

The culture of silence must stop here.

'Whoop. Whoop.'

The warning birds sang out from the she-oak as if completing a victory lap of the sky. I joined in their call of joy; the horizon was clear without the immediate threat of a storm. My sparring fingers tapped assertively on the keyboard, no longer stepping on eggshells.

A wave of cool autumn air filled my room and I leaned forward to close the shutters. The late autumn sun was departing the horizon on a euphoria of red and golden clouds. Storm birds flew to their nests with last calls of exuberance as they gathered their families to safety for the nighttime. I closed my computer and saw the dusk liturgy was complete.

I settled on my sofa with a plate of warm organic rice and vegetables, washing it down with Wildhorse Mountain mineral water. It was delicious, satisfying my need to keep my body healthy so I could continue my writing journey. Flopping back into the sofa, my hand brushed Dorothea Mackellar's book of verse. I brought it to my lap and began reading *My Country*.

It was the most recited poem in our country, written by a woman. I reclined back on the sofa, my eyes looking heavenward. Dorothea not only wrote poems for the nation from the core of her heart, but she was also a suffragette way back at the turn of last century. She was just like our women who marched on Parliament House for systemic changes in our institutions today. I snuggled under the sofa rug and rested my skimming fingertips on Dorothea's book of verse.

Daydreaming helped me to think deeply about the issues of my child abuse. Why did I tell Hannah it was no good taking my case against my parents to court? I let my mind go to a place in my imagination that soothed me while I grappled with this question.

The book of verse in my hand fell to my stomach, my eyelids drooped. Hannah's handwritten note that I used as a bookmark, fell to the floor like a tawny leaf falling from an autumn tree.

"I love the way you feel unthreatened – in the environment you created."

– my country – the core of my heart – tell my story – the truth—

Judge Lear: Read out your arguments.

Me: Our women are marching for systemic change. Our Institutions are embedded with misogyny and toxic masculinity.

Judge Lear: Prove it!

Me: Christine de Pizan is an expert witness. Here is her written testimony, *The City of Ladies*. She was in debate with male writers who wrote violent and misogynist acts committed against female characters. She feared they would encourage others to do the same in current life.

Judge Lear: This testimony has no relevance. It was written in 1472.

Me: Children are taught not to speak up about those filled with darkness. Sappho says we should teach them to write letters to instruct those of wrongdoing to behave better.

Judge Lear: This testimony has no relevance. It was written almost three thousand years ago. Anyhow, children should be seen and not heard.

Me: For the large part of my life, I have suffered an existential crisis.

Judge Lear: Another soul-searching hippie!

Me: My family placed a gag order on me since I was a young girl – from around seven years of age. They intimidated me not to speak of the sexual abuse and violence in our home.

Judge Lear: That's ridiculous! Only a court can place an order like that and I have no record of that here.

Me: I am of sound mind to give evidence.

Judge Lear: That reminds me, I shall order a psychiatric report on you.

Me: I was brainwashed by my parents and grandmother to believe I was bad. My psychologist will confirm that I have symptoms consistent with complex post-traumatic stress disorder, a condition caused by trauma or abuse.

Judge Lear: That's a big word for a little girl. Only our soldiers held in captivity are subject to post-traumatic stress disorder. We are not a military court.

Me: But my GP, Dr Nuha, said that it happens to women in Egyptian society.

Judge Lear: We are not in Egypt. This is Australia, 'the lucky country'.

Me: Your Honour, with respect, I am not just a dumb blonde. Women are as intellectual as men.

Judge Lear: I wouldn't know. I only read books written by men. I'm a facts man and I'm not seeing any facts before me!

Me: I have other witnesses. The sick bay ladies can testify to my anxiety and stress after I arrived late to school from the strip search. And the delicatessen man saw the thief snatch my mother's purse.

Judge Lear: These people are nowhere to be found. They must be in your imagination.

Me: But I am swearing on the Bible!

Judge Lear: A child is not a reliable witness.

Me: I was beaten black and blue.

Judge Lear: You don't present with any marks.

Me: They have long disappeared but the psychological damage still exists.

Judge Lear: We must have hard, physical evidence.

Me: With respect, Your Honour, you seem to have a bias against women. This whole trial has been filled with baseness.

Judge Lear: That's not true! I was only telling Bob over a beer last night how much I liked women.

Me: May we take a recess please, Your Honour? I feel like I am on fire and my evidence is being destroyed.

Judge Lear: All right! But not because you are 'feeling' anything! When we return, I will consider the independent report done on this case.

Return fifteen minutes later.

Me: I am unable to present the report, Your Honour.

Judge Lear: Why is that?

Me: I requested it in terms of the Freedom of Information Act, but my request was denied.

Judge Lear: On what grounds?

Me: My father had to sign it first.

Judge Lear: And he hasn't yet?

Me: No. He was buying time, fifty years of it. He's dead now. All I have is my word, I am my own witness.

Judge Lear: You say you were raped. Do you have evidence of penetration?

Me: No, Your Honour. My psychologist has termed it rape[2] from the information provided to her.

Judge Lear: That's not good enough. I need physical evidence.

Me: With respect, Your Honour, if there was full penetration I most likely would have bled to death. I have here an updated definition of rape which supersedes the common law when rape was defined as carnal knowledge of a woman against her will and was subject to narrow and restrictive definitions of 'sexual intercourse'. The new penetrative sexual offence law includes penetration of genitalia to any extent, by a penis, object, part of a body or mouth.

Judge Lear:	All these new fandangle laws! I can't see what was wrong with the old ones.
Me:	The last definition was outdated and narrow. It only included male penile penetration of a female vagina. The new definition includes any gender of the victim and perpetrator. It sends an important message to all victims that what happened to them matters and to perpetrators that they will be held accountable.
Judge Lear:	You have no case. The court will rely on the retrospective law.
Me:	But Your Honour—
Judge Lear:	You have run out of time to bring admissible evidence to this court. I declare this court a mistrial!

'Thud!'

Dorothea's book of verse fell to the floor.

I wasn't ready to wake up. I was despairing for the patriarchal understanding of abuse in the court system. The justice system in my dream served to uphold and protect the authority of the father. My only witness was me, a child, dependent on my guardians' care, obedient to their authority. But that was then. I was older now and I wasn't going to collapse to the pressure of court case interrogation bullying, insults, humiliation to supposedly test my testimony and a lecture from Judge Lear.

I needed feminist support and intervention.

It was necessary to overcome institutional bias in favour of fathers within the criminal justice system. Otherwise, my trauma would remain underground, festering deep within my body only to manifest in some other way. To reclaim my present and future, I needed a feminist movement like the current one where understanding psychological trauma begins with rediscovering history and widespread crimes against women and children which normally go unspoken. I had been silenced for a lifetime and a new creative energy was released. The barriers of denial and repression were lifted in this window of time.

The sofa rug was caught up in the book, it too had fallen to the floor. Reclaiming it with one hand, I spread it over me, tucking the soft edged trim under my chin. My eyelids flopped – I never felt safe or able to defend myself as long as my father lived. I was an outsider – seeking a new dimension – travelling back in time – explaining my 'being' in another dimension – herstory – find Christine – Christine who was relentless in changing the attitudes of men who enforce the law, the all-male club abysmally ignorant and careless of women and children's reality—

Dishevelled, I left the courtroom and found my way to the inner-city botanical garden to cry away the pain of Judge Lear's rejection of my testimony. I wanted to tell the truth and have my voice heard but this court system was biased against women's issues. Ahead, was an inviting wooden bench with flower pattern wrought-iron trimmings beneath a bountiful, green-leafed oak tree. As I approached, I noticed a familiar figure bent over the gnarly oak tree roots which had pushed themselves from the dirt for air. It was Christine, dressed in the same long rich green velvet dress and fitchet pockets. Her golden braids coiled over each ear. She was busy gathering gall wasp eggs for ink. I suspect her work was not done.

"Hello Christine, I'm so glad to see you!"

"Oh hello, dear." She blessed me with a warm smile. "How is your story going?"

"I have to admit, I've hit a low point." I was grateful she had remembered me but I was sad to disappoint her.

"Tell me, dear, is it those auctors again? What bad things are they saying about women?" Her fighting spirit gave me hope, but even so, I dared not trust it.

"It's the judge, Christine! I took my story to a traditional court, as advised by my psychologist, and it was a disaster!"

"It was?"

We sat together under the protection of the oak tree. She was interested in how I felt.

"There's a number of things. For one, Judge Lear is stuck in his ways, he is patriarchal to the bone. I heard rumours that he is mad. He suffers from narcissistic personality disorder, not that he would ever admit it."

"Yes, I know the play well. In the first act he recognises his own fragile psychological state, 'O let me not be mad, not mad, sweet heaven' But he clung to power until the end. I'm sorry you got stuck with Lear as your judge."

"Each time I put forward an argument he suffered his psychotic disorder and was intermittently explosive!"

"Give me an example, dear."

"He was treating me like I was some stereotypical dumb blonde when I challenged him, saying women are as intellectual as men."

"Good on you! What did he say to that?"

"He said he wouldn't know because he only read books written by men. He was stuck on binary opposites – men stand for reason, strength and knowledge, and women are the opposite, emotional, weak and unintelligent. He was treating me like I was a hysteric when he was the hysterical one."

"Yes. The auctors reacted the same way to my objections to their misogynist writings."

"I'm sure he would have recited 'I love a sunburnt country' at school like we all did. I wonder if he knows that Dorothea Mackellar wrote Arms and the Woman."

"Oh, I know that one, dear. I love the first verse."

She fluttered her veil to the side like a white-winged chakra butterfly and wrested a copy of the poem from her fitchet pocket. It had been neatly copied onto parchment paper with her quill pen in anticipation of our meeting.

"What if I do go armed?" she said.
"Where's the law that you say I've broken?
Firearms, yes—but my weapon's steel,
A two-edged dagger, and more by token
Its supple keenness that seldom slips
Is mostly quiet behind my lips."[3]

Christine continued, "Dorothea was defending herself against the tyranny of men in her time. It was considered not normal for women to be intellectual although she did have success at writing. The Melbourne Literary Club was established in 1916 and included women writers and their values. However, it was short-lived and literary clubs became exclusive to men for some decades afterward."

Christine shrewdly kept track of women writers through history. It was her job to keep the record straight – over time.

"That is why Dorothea felt the need to defend herself with her sword, metaphorically speaking."

"Yes, I agree."

"And you must do the same, my dear. Do not be despondent because of Lear's resistance to your testimony. Continue to write your truth. Together we must write our own universal chronicle about women's experience. We must unleash the creative energy elsewhere held in check." Christine was inciting me to take moral action.

"Thank you, Christine, for your strength and constancy. Lear's bullying had reduced me to tears and metaphorically invoked a non-speech. I will not be a victim of these oppressive structures any longer. I have fought hard for my education to express my childhood abuse. I will not give up."

"Goodbye, dear," Christine clasped my hand; the tip of her green velvet sleeve fell into my palm for one final soothe of my senses.

"Goodbye, Christine. Until next time I meet you in my dreams."

I let go of her hand, knowing that she was always there for me, even when she was hundreds of years in the past.

'Coo. Coo,' the night bird cawed.

I woke and brushed my hand through my messy hair. The night went hush. I reached over to switch on the lamp to gain my bearings. Dorothea's book lay on the floor and my sofa rug still covered my chest. Under the lamp was my Frixion pen and notebook.

Compelled, I wrote down the dream while it was fresh in my mind. The world of my dream unfolded on paper; I knew then it would be a part of writing my past in the hope of changing institutions in the future. With newfound empowerment, I was determined to write my truth and shed light on the coercive methods of my clandestine upbringing. No longer would I allow this abuse to disempower and disconnect me from the world.

One such method my parents used was to render me captive to the house because of dependency. My barriers to escape were invisible, no bars on the windows or barbed wire fence. I was made captive by psychological and legal subordination, and at times physical force and threats. They forced me to leave school and forgo an education at age fourteen. They told me it was normal – that girls' education was not important, and I should contribute my income to my place of captivity under a man's authority.

1968
Shallow Water

*'Women are not naturally inferior to men, but appear to be because
they lack education."*

*"Taught from their infancy that beauty
is a woman's sceptre, the mind
shapes itself to the body, and, roaming round its gilt cage, only seeks
to adorn its prison."*

Mary Wollstonecraft
A Vindication of the Rights of Woman (1792)[4]

*"To the person in the bell jar, blank and stopped
as a dead baby, the world itself
is a bad dream."*

Sylvia Plath from *The Bell Jar*, 1963[5]

It took me some time to settle into Shallow Water State High. It was so
different from the city and a city school: initially I was the different one to
the other students in my new school. In Grade Seven, I was withdrawn and
internalised my academic interest. Everything I studied in Grade Seven was
a repeat of Grade Six in Wicklow State School. I was nearly dux of Grade
Seven but a whiz girl, who was exceptional at Maths, pipped me at the post.
I was disappointed not to get dux that year – it would have made amends for
the loss of my less than adequate education in the sticks, and my more than
inadequate home life.

By Grade Eight I had had enough of trying to be smart and began to
level out to most students around me. I remained savvy in some academic
education but at the same time, I started hanging out with the disruptive kids.
By Grade Nine I had a good group of girl friends who remained my friends

in school but not on weekends or holidays. We mucked about, pulling faces behind the teachers' backs, yarning and cussing in the playground, being inattentive in class, that brought down my grades.

Funnily enough, my parents encouraged me to be good at my schoolwork despite their lack of vision for my future. In primary school, I received excellent grades and was continuously awarded gold stars for my projects. I loved getting recognition for my intellectual accomplishments from teachers, friends and even on occasion, from my parents. In retrospect, my parents encouraged me to be a good girl at school because it deflected from them being negligent parents.

They bragged to the occasional visitor, "our little sissy is the one with the brains in the family." They showed off my book work with carefully illustrated portraits of Australian explorers. It was neat with precise handwriting, depth of research and beautifully scrolled titles and borders etched in black fountain pen calligraphy. It flourished and splayed out on the corners of each page as if they were tipping out of this world into another universe to be discovered – on my own without my parents.

Education gave to me value. It was my ticket out, my stronghold, even if I mucked around with my friends in Grades Nine and Ten. Grade Ten was my *bildungsroman* year, cut short by two years. My personal journey to fill this loss was fraught with coercive control, I was unable to fill the vacuum. I resisted my parents' tyrannical behaviour the best I could.

In the depth of my soul there was only one way out of this hell. Deep in the abyss of my mind, despite the trauma, I could use it to earn myself a teacher's certificate, an independent income and identity. Most importantly, I could escape this hellhole in Shallow Water. I could move to the city and live in a trendy and modern part of town, be a beatnik teacher, anywhere away from the grip of terror where I was being held prisoner.

I formed a circle with my friends. Leaning in we made a pact: "let's not muck up next year. We've had our time acting like silly kids. In Grade Eleven and Twelve we will knuckle down and get our matriculation certificates. Let's make something of ourselves in the world."

We knew we were on the cusp of something great in our lives. The feminist movement had such an impact on us; we were emerging young women who wanted the liberation, as well as sexual freedom and equal pay.

We'd had enough of these double standards that had ruled our society for hundreds of years.

Most of our high school teachers were 'with it'. They were moving with the times too. We had a couple of graduate women teachers who were among our favourites. Ms Colburn, my sports teacher, encouraged me to get the best out of my body in physical strength and not to be intimidated by the boys who would leer at us.

"You are just as good as the boys," she would assert.

She wore trendy clothes, including casual but stylish tracksuits and shorts and hung out with us on breaks. She answered our questions about how she got on at college and what it was like to be a teacher.

I liked Ms Felucca too, she was my French teacher. She wore miniskirts with long leather boots, her hair was teased into a bun on top and long wisps fell around her shoulders and over her hippy-bead necklaces – strands of tiny psychedelic-coloured beads glittered and jingled jangled together like the sounds of the sexual revolution and women's rights. I loved her so much; I was her star pupil and achieved one hundred per cent for French. The French language was amazing, it fell off my tongue like croissants with melted butter. It was foreign, sexy and completely unobjectified. I wanted to run off to France to reinvent myself as a person with rights. In class, the boys dropped their pencils while Ms Felucca was writing on the blackboard. As they bent down to pick them up off the floor they would perv up under her dress.

"Get up off the floor you pervs." The girls would berate them.

They made me sick, I had so much respect for this second-wave, pioneering young feminist in our midst.

My parents reneged on their word. I couldn't believe it. I stupidly thought that they would trust me with my own education. Toward the end of Grade Ten our class was abuzz. The Grade Twelve class was going on to graduate and we were getting closer to becoming seniors. Instead of discussing our favourite pop singers such as Michael Jackson and the Jackson 5 at lunch break, we were bent over in huddles, zoned in on our subject selections for senior and our career options.

Mum was on to it straight away.

"No good you bringin' any form home for me to sign. You're leavin' school and gettin' a job like I did!"

"But Mum, you know I'm good at my schoolwork, I want to be a teacher!"

Propped up on her stool, behind her kitchen bench, the dugout trenches of her world made by men, she looked down her long nose and snarled with her bigoted knowledge of the world.

"No good you goin' on like that with your airs and graces. None of the women in our family ever did anythin' like that. You will go out to work at legal age, fifteen and earn a livin'. Your father and I can't keep on keepin' you. You gotta bring your wages into the house and put them into my kitty. We've been payin' out for you all these years. Now it's time for you to pay us back. It's your duty!"

She was the authority on the subject, the most powerful person in my life. Her psychology shaped by the beliefs of the perpetrator, my father. Mum had been consumed by the unnatural way we were living; content to be chained to the kitchen with slavish obedience to his unethically driven, amoral and narcissist behaviour. At the same time, she stubbed her cigarette out in the tray as if I were at the end of the smouldering butt.

My teachers were up in arms too.

"Why won't your parents let you stay on at school – it's unfair. Young people go on with their education today. That sort of thinking went out in the old days," said Ms Colburn when she heard the news.

"I don't know, Miss. Mum wants me to leave school and get a job," I replied with dejection in my voice.

No adult, outside our home, had ever gotten this close to me regarding important decisions; those that would impact my life in a positive way as opposed to my parents' constant drowning me since birth. I was a helpless kitten in the dark hessian bag clawing a way out to save itself.

Here was my dear Ms Colburn beside me and offering me support.

"What about your dad? He's a police officer, isn't he? Surely, he would listen to reason!" She was trying to rationalise the incomprehensible situation.

"I'm not sure, Miss. They pretty much stick together when it comes to me," without trying to give too much away because Ms Colburn would never understand the gravity of the abuse.

This belief was so deeply entrenched by now. If Ms Colburn could not come to terms with this crossroad in my life, which was merely a coalescence of all my strife, she would be up in arms beyond measure to hear the truth.

She had freedom, she was liberated and she had an education; we existed on opposite ends of the universe, although I loved her.

"Would it help if I came to your place and reasoned with your mum?" She asked me as if she were writing the Freedom Plea Agreement in her head.

"No, you can't do that!" I tried to stay calm but the idea terrified me. By this point of the conversation, I had to cut Ms Colburn's life raft from the sinking ship.

Mum's voice was ringing in my head like the bell of the Titanic.

"Don't have any of those teachers of yours takin' your side either. Don't have 'em comin' around here, or you'll have hell to pay!" She hollered. "If you don't leave that school I will come over and drag you out by the hair on your head!"

She intimidated me with some kind of 'hair pulling out madness' and although she was tormented by the problem herself, she would rather tear my hair out and shun me from my peers rather than attend to her own deficits. Even though I was fourteen years of age and as tall as her now, I was still unable to stand against her. She had legal right over me. I wasn't, by law, able to make this decision for myself, and Mum did not respect, or even acknowledge, that I had a point of view. My feelings didn't matter.

My last resort was to call my father at his workplace – the station. He was an avid reader. On his days off, or to do nothing around the house, he would lounge around on the couch and in bed and read books and newspapers.

"I only read non-fiction," he would expound with pride. "I'm a man of reason! That fiction stuff is for women, all that romance and emotional make-believe rubbish! No truth in that!"

Of course, men were the subjects, the brains of the world; women were the objects, passive and emotional run-off of the world. For all I know he had his *Playboy* magazine tucked up in his newspaper; the centrefold informing him of world politics.

It was weird pleading to my father since he was my subjugator, but I was desperate and he was my last resort. Maybe, just maybe, he would use his so-called reason to persuade Mum to let me stay on at school.

"Why are you ringing me at work?"

I couldn't explain his expressions since narcissists lie all the time.

"Can you please ask Mum to let me stay at school? I want to go on and be a teacher. I thought you wanted me to be smart at school?" I forced the words out of my mouth. It felt like I was plotting with the enemy.

"All right, I'll try. I've got to go now."

It was strange me reaching out to the adult in him when he was a child who had never grown up. He was camouflaged in his role as a police officer, few people would believe he was a paedophile.

I moped around the house for a couple of days, waiting for him to bring up the topic with my mother. He had many opportunities but was silent. It was the same as when I was a little girl. If he asked Mum to fulfil my request, he would have admitted his guilt that we spoke in secret. We never spoke at home except for when he was drunk and blubbering on me and I was screaming for him to get off me.

Seriously, what was I thinking? Silence meant complicity. Neither one of them were going to let me continue my education.

I was forced to leave school at fourteen and farewell my friends and teachers. I was the only student leaving, or one of few, and was completely embarrassed. I was alienated from the world that could save me from the bell jar in which I had been imprisoned.

There was to be no tenderness in this house.

2021 spring
Ocean harbour home

"Mother nature's dying
Nobody's keeping score
I don't wanna live in a man's world
Anymore."

Marina from *Man's World*, 2020[6]

Placing the half-filled coffee mug next to the keyboard I told myself, 'I must stop drinking so much coffee. Two mugs a day is enough.'

I was drinking twice as much caffeine now that I wrote several days on end. The coffee kept me 'up' but it also exacerbated the panic attacks. My childhood abuse was in the forefront of my mind. I was in a hurry to get the story out and relieve the trauma. It was essential to document the anthropology of my past, it was my commitment to future generations to overcome toxic masculinity. I didn't want my children or their children to live in a constant state of fear as I did.

I was stuck to my desk chair, barely able to break away. My concentration was bent on freeing myself from the brainwashing and submission of my own free will. The remnants of my memories were stuck in my mind like charcoal at the base of the fire.

I went to bed exhausted from writing. My Frixion pen and notepad, full of scribble, sat on top of Sylvia's restored edition of *Ariel*, on the bedside table. My precious poetry books were the very few possessions I had brought to my new home. I was reading *The Moon and the Yew Tree*, a poem defining Sylvia's relationship with her parents.

> *"The yew tree points up. It has a Gothic shape.*
> *The eyes lift after it and find the moon.*
> *The moon is my mother. She is not sweet like Mary.*
> *Her blue garments unloose small bats and owls.*
> *How I would like to believe in tenderness-"*[7]

I was open to reading about women's experiences growing up, anything to help shed meaning on my trauma. My eyes flopped – I was sleepy – the book fell from my hand – thud – it fell to the floor – find meaning – disempowerment – disconnection – why?

I was walking in a cemetery.

Alone.

He was there. My father. He was dressed in his police uniform. His shirt was hanging out.

He was drunk.

"Blab blab blab..."

"Get away from me," I cried.

There was nowhere to run. No one could hear or see me, except for him and his battering eyes.

He didn't need to beat me to control me.

"Don't even think about running away. Look at this!" He leered, pointing to his police emblem.

I froze in fear. He was not content with submission; he was after total control over me.

"If you run, I will report you. There is only one road out of here and I have roadblocks put up. Don't spin tears at them too. You won't be able to act your way out of it. I'll say you have been running around with boys behind my back and need to be kept at home for your own safety. They will believe me. After all, you are cheap like all women."

"Stop it!" I screamed.

No one heard me.

Voracious bats and owls unloosed from a blue untender moon, and the pine needled branches of the cemetery trees pointed up to prey upon the night sky madness...

Wake up... A beautiful woman was standing near me... It was Demi... Wake up...

I shook myself out of the nightmare and was compelled to write it down while it was fresh in my mind. Fervently, I wrote in my notebook alongside my account of the dream the night before where I met Christine under the oak tree. I tried to figure out why I was ambushed by my father in a cemetery.

My father's desire was to have control over me. His threat of trauma was piled on top of many traumas, to keep me a prisoner under his domination – a man's home is his castle. Was it a universal condition of dependency that Sylvia felt too?

The themes of the moon and the yew tree spoke of the lack of a relationship between her parents and led to her abysmal childhood and depression in adult life. A depression I was familiar with and was trying to analyse through my writing. I wanted to share my lived experience with the world to help prevent violence in the future for other vulnerable children and women.

The phone pinged.

There was a message alert on the weather app that a full moon was on the rise that evening. My attention shifted to the lunar activity but not for its nefarious mother symbolism alluded to by Sylvia. My feelings towards the moon had changed, now I valued its embodiment of the rhythm of nature. I jumped out of bed and placed the camera batteries on charge. Preparation was the key to a successful shoot.

Sage sent a message that she couldn't make it. I was pleased in a way because I would have more time to think about the issues of a global nature which had been playing on my mind. The flooded roads had cleared and I packed my cameras and lenses in readiness for the journey ahead. Along with my gear, I placed in a compartment of the camera bag, David Attenborough's latest book, *A Life on Our Planet: My Witness Statement and a Vision for the Future*. I would leave early enough to give myself some reading time before moonrise.

Once my packing was completed, I peered out the window to check the sky for clouds which may impede my much-anticipated lunar shoot. Soft streams of mist silked across the sky like a delicate Persian scarf that swore an oath to wrap the moon in its glorious delicate mystery. I drove to the carpark beneath the bluff and headed up the track with my camera pack firmly clipped on my back. My head lamp was fastened to my forehead.

The she-oak hummed their familiar 'shee' sound. The light sea breeze wound through the branch's fingertips. Further up the path I was greeted by the priestly pandanus trees, their twisted stems and spiral tufts of long spiny leaves shed bounties of sweet edible manna dew fruits beneath the stilt roots. The ocean churned its kaleidoscope of life to and from the rocks below, a mysterious vast body of salt water that covered seventy per cent of the Earth's surface.

I picked up the pace. My mind began to drift to another world. Why was our planet suffering? Why did women and children suffer? The common link was the patriarchal order.

Someone waved to me from the bluff but I couldn't make it out. It couldn't have been Demi because she was an old crone when we met. Low burning torch lights encircled the bluff, revealing a beautiful woman in the dim light. I studied her face, visible through the soft sheer veil over her head. She wore a crown of pink and gold plumeria interwoven with harvested wheat stalks. A sweet gardenia fragrance frolicked amongst the sea mist and I swooned over the scene.

I squinted into the mist and she threw off her disguise.

"Oh my, is that you Demi?"

"Yes, my dear. I'm very glad to see you, you have honoured our pledge," she spoke softly, without the anxiety of our last encounter.

The bluff was the ideal place for her new temple, a picture of what she represented, the Earth and its oceans.

I gestured toward the bluff's edge and my prefigured coordinates for the moonrise.

"May I set up my camera here?"

"Of course, dear, and then come sit with me while we wait for the moon to rise. It brings a high tide tonight but few fish, they are becoming sparse."

She sighed and shook her head, looking towards the ground before her.

"That is true, Demi."

I placed the camera on the tripod and did some practice shots in the fading light.

"How do you know this?" she asked.

"Here you are," I replied and gifted her with David's book, 'A Life on Our Planet'. "David says that the loss of fish populations is directly related to the Great Acceleration since the 1950s after the war."[8]

"Please, continue," she commanded with a grace that only a goddess could pull off.

"The rise of carbon dioxide in the atmosphere is causing the planet to overheat. Environmental destruction is worsening at a rapid rate and our Earth is becoming like a sealed dish with no food – ruined, hot, acidic and toxic." The words fell out of my mouth like fire from a spit, it was the tragedy of our time.

"But I have an agreement with the godfather, Zeus. He would return my daughter if I took pity on starving humanity and taught them the secrets of agriculture and the seasons. He then sent word to the underworld to bring Persephone back. Before she left, his no-good son fed her pomegranate seeds and bound her to him for the winter months. The rest of the time she spends with me, here on our bluff temple. My only choice was to compromise, although I am glad, she is with me most of the time." Her beautiful face dropped, some wheat stalks and plumeria fell to the earth in sympathy. *"Now, from what you tell me this deal with Zeus has been at terrible cost to humanity."*

"It is not your fault, Demi," I reassured her. *"You were hoodwinked!"*

"Yes, I was!" With each sigh, wheat stalks and plumeria fell from her crown. *"Thank you for bringing David's book for me. He says that we must restore everything we have removed. It is the only way out of the crisis we have created for ourselves."*

She was reading from the blurb on the back cover.

"Unfortunately, at the recent summit the world's biggest economies failed to agree on winding down coal production and any other significant issue when it comes to climate change. These economies are run hand-in-hand with male dominated governments and companies."

I glimpsed the moon as it peeked from the horizon, a reminder of the perfect home our planet could be.

"How can this have happened?" Demi cried with a heavy frown. *"How could I have been so blind to not see the cunning of the gods? How could they have deceived me? To think that they valued our mother-daughter relationship and returned her to me! They twisted my sense of reality and I fell for it. All they care for is greed and corruption. I should never have trusted the patriarchy!"*

She sobbed with tears of rain and showered the fallen wheat and plumeria, her crown almost destroyed.

"I understand your grief, Demi. Our prime minister was a laggard, he did not make any commitment to climate change policies despite the mounting

evidence. He is the same man who refused to meet our women who marched on Parliament House for change to systemic abuse and misogyny within our government. While the patriarchal order remains in power, we and the environment remain objects, we are silenced by them to the detriment of our very existence, and our children's existence."

This is not the conversation I wanted to have with Demi but I had to tell her about how desperate the situation was. I had hoped our future would be optimistic, especially since Persephone was returned to her. But time had moved on and our Earth was undergoing accelerated climate change. David had the statistics; he was the scientist and key world leaders ignored him. By 2050 our fisheries will be destroyed, and a ready source of protein would disappear from our diets. By 2080 global food production will be at crisis point and fertilised soils would be exhausted and lifeless. This was Demeter's immortal reign; she had control over the harvest and the growing of grains. Did our mortal governments think they were more powerful than her?

Demi's gaze focused on the moon, it shone pink and floated over the gauzy water. She lived forever, she could not fight it anymore. Her body began to relax and she removed her crown to replenish her garland of wheat stalks and fragrant plumeria buds and blooms.

"History has taught me some useful but dark lessons." Her heart beat strong in the descending darkness and her voice echoed from the cave of water which was formed by the tides below the bluff.

"There is always crisis, fluctuating economies, manners and moral shifts. David is right. Our world is on the verge of collapse but we will pull through. These horrendous leaders will be replaced by honourable governments. Tomorrow I will make my way to Mount Olympus and negotiate with godfather Zeus to end all agreements with these greedy magnates."

She spoke with despair and yet there was determination in her tone, now aware of the shambles of mortal existence.

Her gaze refocused to me as I tapped the auto shutter for my last shot.

"How about you, dear? Have you found your lost child?" Again, she passed me her flask of lemon water and urged me to drink.

"I am sorry to say she is gone – she's dead!"

"Is that how your search ended then? You must tell me."

"I talked to my therapist and she said I could contact her at my old neighbourhood and bring her home. But the mission was unsuccessful. At one

point I held her hand but she let go. There was nothing we loved doing when we were young, we were not loved and our childhood was a lie. She was isolated for too long and was unable to find acceptance of the trauma."

Telling Demi brought tears to my eyes but I was determined to be brutally honest.

"The healing of your inner child is essential to the wellbeing and growth of all!"

"I have been down the wellbeing path, Demi but now I am resolved that healing my childhood is lost to me. Unlike you and Persephone, she was never allowed an opportunity to cling to life, I am unable to connect with her. I can honour her now by giving her quiet and calm."

I allowed my eyes to shift towards Demi's soothing face.

"You have shown me how to accept the shambles of my existence with grace. I will write my story as a matter of satire rather than with rage or bitterness. My parents and grandmother will be an exemplar of madness well-handled and absorbed."

The good parent in me spoke without terror but with a basic trust in my capacity to write my story...

Demi disappeared into the violet mist, petals from her crown drifted away in the moonlit sky...

I turned my lamp towards the cliffs, I would have no trouble making the descent in the dark.

When I arrived home I unpacked my camera gear. Fumbling with the camera, I nearly dropped it. I was jittery and set my mind to understand why.

Apart from drinking too much coffee!

My childhood trauma left me vulnerable to so many people and institutions. At the bluff, I opened my feelings to my imaginary Demi – The Great Queen of the Beginning of Seasons. In my daydream, I figured out my truth.

But fear lingered like the stench of dead fish washed up on the beach. What if I reveal my emotions to the wrong people? Writing my story put me at risk of being cut off from the world. On the other hand, being vulnerable and sharing my truth about the abuse helped me to heal. This same vulnerability allowed me to experience great new avenues of thought. Our planet was as vulnerable to the patriarchy and toxic masculinity as was women, children and other marginalised people. It was important to continue to write and not let the perpetrators silence me, leaving me and others who have been abused without defence.

CHAPTER 16

Crying: A Child is Dead

2022 summer
Ocean harbour home

"The Vision, then, is a kind of interior journey,
where Christine hopes to find
meaning for her country and her own life
by reviewing past successes and
failures with the help of authoritative
allegorical figures. Like St Augustine,
she strives to connect temporal history with
a higher providential scheme.
That Lady Philosophy is recognised to be
Lady Theology at the end underlines
the ultimate spiritual nature of Christine's quest."

about Christine's Vision translated by Renate Blumenfeld-Kosinski
from the new edition of a *Vision of Christ*[1]

> *"Those who plead their cause in the absence of an*
> *opponent can invent to their heart's content,*
> *can pontificate without taking into account*
> *the opposite point of view*
> *and keep the best arguments for themselves,*
> *for aggressors are always quick to attack those*
> *who have no means of defence."*

Christine de Pizan[2]

Writing my truth was my defence.

I knew this now when my manuscript was near completion. I had worked hard to summon the strength to write critically and analytically and confront my own past. And I related my experiences to social, cultural, spiritual and political contexts of the western world ruled by patriarchal forces and toxic masculinity. I had come into opposition through my writing and was fearless to not back down. Often I expressed my memories in dream imagery and fantasy but I remained very much self-aware. If I fell into despair, I would not be able to fulfil my promise to my lost and tortured child to tell her truth on her behalf.

The funeral atmosphere was disappearing. It was time to stop crying over the past. I created my hard-won safety in my home and coastal lands. My children had grown up. No longer did I have a devil principal breathing down my neck, protecting the school paedophile. Nor did I have coercive threats from an English professor that I should write in alignment with toxic patriarchal values that destroy women's identity and safety in the world. The long painful process of writing was finally granted to me. Soon, I would lay down my pen and pursue aspirations for the future with renewed hope and engagement in an ordinary life free of abuse.

I set aside my manuscript, deep in thought about how much I had encountered during the writing process. I had nearly reclaimed my history. The descent into mourning my childhood and teenage years was an endless surrender to tears. But it will stop soon – the crying.

I needed to write about that too or my story will not be complete.

'Ping,' the phone lit up. It was a message from Siobhan. She was released from the mental hospital and looked forward to a meet up.

"Can you meet me today?" read her text.

Sirius occupied the sky the same time as the sun. It was in the same constellation as the *Canis Major.* Intuition told me that Siobhan was feeling dog days, a dull lack of progress after major upheaval.

"Of course, I can. Where would you like to meet?"

"You choose."

"How about the community edible garden?" I suggested. "It's lovely there!" And I was happy to support the local community efforts who had taken steps toward a more sustainable future.

The garden was grown on rich soils of the hinterland foothills, nourished by rainwater run-off from the waterfalls above. I parked in the tree-shaded carpark and scanned my surroundings. A myriad of eucalypts, banksias and melaleucas provided a fecund woody, green leaf and wildflower canopy for the distinctive Buderim holly bushes growing beneath, all of which had, so far, not succumbed to capitalists' bulldozers. The harbour lands had grown substantially since the building of the first wharf at the turn of the last century. It was now one of the most populated cities in the state, its biodiversity was increasingly at risk of overdevelopment and corrupt liveability strategies. Nature's vulnerability triggered my hypervigilance, swamping my veins. I checked it for danger but then quickly tempered my fears to meet Siobhan. I didn't want to set off her anxiety, not after her stay at the hospital mental health ward.

I entered by the restored iron gate. The latch was made of strong metal and took a sturdy hand to lift and open it. Masses of marigolds were in full bloom, their sun-blushed petals attracted bees essential for crop production. Herb and vegetable gardens were dotted about the park, growing in shade and dappled sunlight. Sage, thyme, rosemary and lavender were clumped together, carefully separated from the mint due to its invasive tendencies.

Basil grew in pots and preferred the company of sturdy iron-enriched silver-beet and other dark leaf vegetables.

The picnic basket was filled with a flask of hot aromatic Wildhorse Mountain coffee, lemon myrtle crackers, organic seeds, nuts, dried fruit and local dairy feta cheese. I lay the rug on the lush grass beneath the shade of a banksia, brimming with fruity cone protea flower heads. The perennial sound of the metal latch being opened alerted me to Siobhan's arrival.

"Hi!" she said with a smile, walking down the cobblestone path to our picnic rug. "I love this place!"

I imagined her reaction to the community gardens was connected to the beautiful yet fragile environment. I stood up and we hugged with shared understanding of our meeting place.

"I knew you would!" Siobhan looked well having gained a small amount of weight, enough to take her off the 'at risk to health' list. A single golden braid began at her crown, tethering blonde strands to it and fell in muse-like fashion over one shoulder. The bespoke hairstyle drew attention to her hidden eyes diverted from my gaze.

"You look well, I love the way you braided your hair!"

"Here, sit down and have a bite to eat." I gestured to the picnic basket. "How long have you been out?"

"About two weeks," she said with her gaze still averted from mine.

"How do you feel?"

"Well, as you know I was crying a lot."

I nodded my head and caught a half glance from her.

"How did that go with your therapist?"

"She prescribed me antidepressants to stop the crying – tear blockers I call them. We talked some about my tears but she couldn't find a file on them. I guess the pain of my tears got lost in the psychobabble. At least I'm not crying anymore."

"Did she ask you why you were crying?"

"I could only remember raking the garden in one spot for hours on end – when I was a little girl. I couldn't get past that moment, I think the therapist lost patience with me." Siobhan sighed. "She said I had OCD and depression and that the antidepressants would replace any overwhelming sense of gloom with emotional blunting, which means I can't cry—" She finally looked directly at me. "But I can't laugh either."

This explained her averted gaze and lacklustre eyes. When she passed up her picnic plate, barely a mouthful was taken.

"What coping strategies has your therapist given you?"

"She helped me with strategies to deal with anxiety and to identify unhelpful thoughts which distort reality. It's up to me now to end this crippling battle," she said as she leaned into a basil pot, picked a stem and smelled its pure organic aroma.

I listened carefully to Siobhan, not sure if I agreed with her therapist. It was life-limiting constantly searching for ways to avoid the fearful experiences. If I was looking for distractions from the events of my childhood abuse, I would never have written my story or dug for answers about why my abusers threatened my very existence. But I couldn't say that to Siobhan or ask: "Why were you raking in circles when you were a little girl?" Maybe she will read my story one day and begin her own search for answers to her tears.

The basil stem effused a freshly floral and crisply herbaceous scent, vibrant and uplifting. I became reminiscent of the story of *Lisabetta and the Pot of Basil*.

"Then you've been dealing with this since you were a child?"

I was curious without pushing her too hard.

"Yes, Mum has memories of me too, endlessly raking the same circle patch in the garden."

"See the pot of basil where you picked the stem from?"

"Yes."

"There are many ways to tell a story about the same pot of basil."

Siobhan's brow furrowed while staring at the basil.

"How so?"

"It's a story which has been handed down in time and changes from one storyteller to the next. First, it was told by a medieval writer, Boccaccio in *The Decameron*. A young virgin from Messina, in Italy, secretly loved a young house servant, Lorenzo. Their relationship was forbidden because she had to marry a noble. Her father dealt out harsh punishment and ordered her brothers to kill Lorenzo and conceal his body in the household garden. By misfortune Lisabetta discovers the dead body, severs its head and plants it in a pot of basil to secretly mourn her lover's death. She sat over it and cried all day."

"Heavens above, that's awful!" Siobhan let out. "How brutal on all levels!"

"Wives and daughters were the property of fathers. That was the law and Boccaccio was telling it that way." I kept going. "He delighted in telling the story in conventional style, presenting a mass of details like: 'Lisabetta planted several sprigs of the finest Salernian basil and never watered them except with essence of roses or orange blossoms or with tear drops,'" I said, waving two stems of basil in the air before landing them in my lap. Siobhan's eyes followed them in a trance.

"He was cynical of Lisabetta's power to regenerate life by providing a backdrop of blossom in springtime, the most joyful of the male poets' conventions. And worst of all, employed images of roses which were nothing more than a symbol of women's virginity waiting to be plucked."

"Oh dear, I feel sorry for women born in those days. Poor Lisabetta." Although Siobhan's medication had rendered her emotionally blunt, her ability to feel empathy was intact. "How was it written differently?"

"Christine de Pizan told it from a female perspective – Lisabetta covered Lorenzo's head with her kisses and placed it in a beautiful scarf and buried it in one of the large pots for violets. Over it, she planted five shoots of sweet-smelling basil. Grief-stricken she nursed the pot for days, watering it only with her tears." I paused in case Siobhan wasn't keeping up.

"Go on," she said.

"That's the difference between Boccaccio's and Christine's telling of the story. Christine describes the memorial pot only in terms of violets, well concealed beneath the basil. This restraint draws attention to Lisabetta's emotional wounding and the suffering caused by her lack of female agency."

"That's so clever. I didn't know any of this!" Siobhan motioned for me to hand back her meal plate. She was suddenly hungry.

"I know, right! Although Christine's text was somewhat secretive, she managed to evoke meaning which transgressed the patriarchal social system," I explained, passing her plate and then ate some more from mine.

"In Christine's version, Lisabetta appeared as a figure of woman as 'mother', her tears were like those of the Virgin Mary, evoked for the sorrow of humanity. Although her tears were non-verbal, they were still a process by which women spoke and empowered themselves, back then and today."

I hoped the semiotics weren't too much for Siobhan.

"I see it now. I'll remember this story next time I need to recount my garden raking memories." A smile escaped her lips and her eyes softened. "Perhaps there is meaning to my tears."

She leaned on one arm and gazed into the canopy of fruity protea flower heads.

While Siobhan drifted into her own world, I pondered the story of Lisabetta and the parallels to my own upbringing. My father catered only to his paedophilic needs and cast me aside to where I had no rights to my own virginity. Without any evidence, apart from his own fantasies, he thought that I was loose with boys. His 'model of life' for me was as brutal as anything the Fathers of the medieval churches had propounded about women. I was the construction of his masculinist discourse and my mother had yielded to it too. I was not allowed to go out with boys or have any relationship other than within our dogmatic and abusive household. I had to go out to work and come straight home, bonding me to his tedious biological teleology.

I kept this to myself and shifted my attention to Siobhan who now sat upright, straightening her golden plait in readiness for departure.

"Thanks so much for meeting me here and for the beautiful picnic lunch. We must do it again sometime." Her voice was the sound of flutes playing Sappho's tune.

"You're welcome, dear friend," I said, shaking the picnic rug and packing the almost empty food basket.

We picked stems of dark green, leafy silverbeet and mixes of herbs and bid each other farewell with one last sounding of the metal latch.

I arrived home in time to prepare dinner using ingredients from the community edible garden and set it aside to marinate. The aroma drifted into my study where I put the finishing touches on the photo album I was creating. I rummaged through my desk drawers for some glue and glimpsed the Last Will and Testament that I shoved out of the way two years ago when I began writing my memoir.

Again, my fingers retracted and turned claw-like as I slid it out from underneath. That reaction told me I was still angry with my father. Somehow I needed to let go of the anger and revenge. I had almost liberated myself from his hold over me – the crying was nearly over. I was no longer wordless and static, I had written the unspeakable.

I loosened my fingers on the document and let go of the horrors of the past.

My father was gone.

I not only felt relief but a sense of empowerment that I had almost integrated my childhood and teenage trauma into a life narrative. Finally, I was holding him to account for the abuse, causing the loss of my identity. And he was responsible for forcing me to leave school at fourteen and start work at fifteen.

Giving up school shattered my assumptions of growing up and sense of belonging. I was deceived by him and obliged to live by beliefs I didn't share.

1969-70
Shallow Water

"I am in favour of radically reimagining
what our societies should look like,
including ways in which masculine ideas
of power and leadership are
absorbed as natural and normal."

Clementine Ford from *Fight Like a Girl*, 2016[3]

Mum did my father's bidding.

She set up her own employment agency at the kitchen bench, hell-bent on getting me into the workforce. Mum ran her eyes over the 'positions vacant' in the local rag. It took her no time to find the job that came up at the Commonwealth Bank, Australia's leading bank.

"There's a job goin' at the Commonwealth Bank!" She was sounding off from her dugout fortress, working from behind the scenes to support the shenanigans of men and their swinging dicks. Bookkeeping was a subject I was good at. I liked the double ledger system: because it was intellectually challenging. I also wanted to please my altruistic teacher, who had removed me from my rowdy, disruptive friends. He gave me an adult choice to sit away from them, which I did. He said that I was a capable student and I should not fall to peer pressure.

"Okay Mum, what does the ad say?"

"It's for a school leaver and they will train you in the job!" She tried to sound professional but she failed to convince me that she would ever fit the image of a campaigning feminist in the left-leaning parties. I rang the bank and set up an appointment for an interview with the Bank Manager – and yes, he was a man!

"What did he say?" Mum barked, looking down her nose at me.

"He said I can come in tomorrow. There's me and a boy my age sitting the entrance exam."

I assumed his parents thought it best he should leave school too. With some luck he would get a job in a bank and then move to managerial level: an up-and-coming head of power.

"What about that job with the sign writer?"

"No good!"

Jobs for women were all the rage and women were entering the workforce in jobs which were traditionally only for men. Becoming a sign writer may satisfy my personal desire to be creative as well as a compromise with my parents' demand for me to get a job. I thought why not talk to the local sign writer. I'm sure he'll be liberated and give me a chance.

He agreed to an interview and we drove by my local 'artworks'. We went by the Spanish dancing lady I painted on an A Frame board at the local hairdressers. The price list ran down the side. She snapped her canastas with long sensual fingers at the budget perms and styles. Her wild flaming red dress flicked flirtatiously in the air, arousing seductive excitement. It was the price to pay to transform yourself into an erotic, sex-slave housewife, or a newly empowered woman entering the workforce at lower salaries to men. She was so happy with her sign board, it became a talking point with her customers.

"Such a talented young girl, she'll go far in life!" they would say.

"Then what did he say?" Mum's tone was impatient.

"He agreed that I had talent and he could certainly use someone with my artistic flair to grow his business."

This could be a way out for me. Once I had enough experience, I could set up my own business in the city and grow it from there – away from my prison guard parents.

"Then why hasn't he employed you?"

"He said I won't be able to lift the stepladders."

"What did you say to that?"

"I told him I was strong. I lift stepladders around our house. I said I helped my grandfather build our house."

I refrained from saying it was jerry-built.

I didn't tell Mum he said: 'I was young and good-looking and his wife might get jealous.'

This second-wave of feminism was making a lot of noise on the surface but underneath, on the subterranean level, the patriarchy was rife and enabled by insecure women. The underlying assumption that 'women are asking for it' because they turn up to work and climbed stepladders. This was entrenched in the social and cultural consciousness. It wasn't his wife's fault; she was constrained by the same power structure with the man at its apex.

"Well, I've never heard of a girl bein' a sign writer. So that's the end of that," rattled my employment officer mum.

"There's another job in the paper which will suit you!"

"What is it, Mum?"

By this time, I was getting into Mum's swing of things but for different reasons. I needed to prove that I could create my status from an inferior woman to a powerful female representation of myself.

"It's in a real estate office in Shallow Water." She took another drag on her cigarette. "Ring them up!"

It wasn't a request to see if the job appealed to me. It was a command. She was getting desperate. The school holidays had almost passed and I hadn't got a job. She wanted my pay cheque.

I dialled the real estate office and it was quickly answered by a man.

"Is the job still available?" I enquired.

"How old are you?"

"I'm fourteen but will be fifteen in two weeks."

I could hear him thinking on the other end of the line, 'cheap labour'.

Before I had time to get changed out of my beach shorts and midi top, Mum had me in the car and whisked me off to the impromptu job interview before I turned into a pumpkin.

"But Mum, I should at least wear something respectable – a dress!"

My plea fell on deaf ears.

The real estate business was just starting up in the area, a father and son business. The father met me at the office counter with a polite greeting; his son stood in the background trying to avoid eye contact with me. He was there to listen in and offer up his opinion when I had left. The father enquired as to my experience which was none but I told him my marks at school were good and I liked bookkeeping.

"How is your phone manner?" he asked.

"Good, I suppose but I have had no professional training."

"If you were so good at school, why did you leave?"

The question left me begging. Could I possibly tell him that my father was a paedophile and an alcoholic and that I had been subjected to abuse from a young age which had effectively stolen my voice: that I had no space for regeneration and my symbolic representation was unknown in the dominant patriarchal discourse?

"My parents want me to get a job," I said bluntly.

"What does your father do?"

"He's a police officer."

You could have heard a pin drop. His face went red and his hands jittered with excitement. If he employed me, he would get that 'blokey' police protection. Overwhelmed by the thought that he would become one of the boys, there was no room to consider that my father was a paedophile or that he was corrupt. Why else was his wallet bulging with cash which he was willing to bribe me and my mother after a violent domestic dispute so that we would forgive him, only to do it all over again?

That sealed it, I had the job.

Not only would I provide cheap labour but my father was an officer of the law – only I thought about him more in terms of the reinforcer of deeper structural sexism in our home and society.

Another contributing factor to getting the job was my physical presentation.

I wished I had time to change into a dress and at least comb and brush my hair. Instead, Mum rushed me out the door in her anxious state and almost pushed me into the real estate office as if I had walked straight off the beach. My hair was sun bleached white-blonde and it was stiffened by salt and sat like the sunshine itself on my head. My skin was tanned a loquacious brown which spoke of sunbathing in a string bikini. My bronzed navel poked out from between my shorts and midi top: it was impossible for me to practise my female agency. I was transformed into an object to be considered only for my sea siren beauty; the object of desire to be placed behind the receptionist desk. It was up to my prospective employer to imagine me in a tidy blouse and skirt, groomed hair, with proper shoes rather than thongs.

I hated the way the way he looked at me but even more, I hated my mother for setting me up like this. First impressions stuck.

The job in the real estate office wasn't too bad. My boss taught me telephone manner and protocols. Gradually, I learnt about the trust account bookkeeping, writing rent receipts and taking notes from tenants about rental repairs and passing them on. It was mundane work but it kept me out of the house. Mum had her hand out for the pay cheque each week. I was pretty much miserable and depressed but my gaslighting parents had already annihilated the thing most important to me – my education. They had worn me down by manipulating my relationships and socially ostracized me from school, as well as boy and girl friends my own age.

I sat at the reception desk, daydreaming about my friends at school – what were they studying, their conversations about life and boys, their dreams and hopes for the future and what parties they were allowed to attend.

The phone gradually rang itself into my consciousness. I picked up the receiver and put forward my best phone manner.

"Good morning, *The Real Estate Company*. How may I help you?"

"It's the Manager of the Commonwealth Bank here. Hello, dear."

I knew that voice. The last time we spoke on the phone he had rejected my job application: I wasn't smart enough for the job.

"Who would you like to speak to?"

I'm sure he had plenty of money to buy a house.

"I want to speak to you," he said timidly.

What on earth did he have to say to me?

"What can I do for you?"

"I want to know if you would reconsider coming to work for us?"

"What do you mean – do you need another clerk?"

"I don't know how to say this, but I apologise. The boy who sat the exam with you didn't work out. Admittedly, you did better than him in the exam and I regret not employing you," he confessed.

I had to ask.

"Why did you choose him over me?"

"The bank has a history of employing male clerks and even though he didn't pass the exam I felt pressured to employ him over you. Would you accept the job now? I think you would be great for the job." The double standards were pouring out of his mouth, I was flabbergasted.

"Leave it with me."

I felt a sense of loyalty to my new employer; however, I was tempted to work in the bank. I thought about it for a few days, and finally decided: 'no'. Even though he had come clean, he was a liar and a hypocrite. Why was he trying to seduce me into the job now? This sexism culture was rife everywhere. Deep down, hidden where my parents wouldn't find it, I savoured my tiny moment of triumph. After all, the bank paid more and Mum would have forced me to leave real estate for the paycheck.

As the real estate business grew, my boss hired more salesmen to cater for the demand in housing – the suburban sprawl wound its way down the highway from the city. Shallow Water was becoming a popular place for retirees and yuppies looking for holiday homes. The salesmen were nice to me and I began to gain self-confidence in the workplace. Their eyes seemed straight enough, unlike my father's eyes which had deviated down the garden path a long time ago. At lunch break everyone left the office for an hour and went home for lunch. Of course, I was too young to drive myself home for lunch and wouldn't want to go home anyway. My boss said I could have lunch in the office, just be sure to keep the door locked and hang the closed sign near the door handle.

In this space, in the darkness of the salesman's cubicle – the office lights were turned off – was where I began to mourn my inner child. Now that I had left school and was working in the adult world, her memory began to surface in my waking thoughts. It was a painful reminder of the abuse carried out on her. My fractious nerves said she had been killed by my dysfunctional family; that they buried her deep in the earth without a sacred burial. I was the poor Lisabetta when her brothers killed Lorenzo, his ghost informed her in a dream. She dug him out of the disturbed soil in the family garden and buried his head in a pot of basil which she tended obsessively, while she pined.

My inner child's world of pain welled in my trembling body. Tears rose as if from a fountain and streamed down my face. I dug deeper in the archetypical garden and discovered her body. In great sorrow, I mourned her beyond measure just like my timeless sister Lisabetta.

I knew that I could not keep crying in this space for fear of being discovered. So I covered her up and placed her in the garden of my heart and buried her there, covering her with violets. Grief-stricken, I nursed her in my bosom during my lunch break, watering her with my tears but doubtful they would regenerate her.

The salesman Alwin returned early from lunch break. I heard the front door rattle; the jiggling of the office keys was a dead giveaway. Absorbed in my suffering caused by my lack of female agency, I quickly pulled myself together, closed my heart off to the outside world and stepped from the cubicle as if I were as fresh as a daisy.

He turned on the lights and stopped dead, staring directly at me.

"What is wrong with you?" he enquired earnestly.

"Oh, I'm okay, just a bit of a cry." I replied, wiping fresh tears from my cheeks pitifully. I desperately wanted to divert him from my emotional experience to the preferred male-centred narrative that women cry over anything and nothing at all.

"Did someone die?"

"No!" I said as I drew back the tears – the water impounded by a landslide of torture and terror, held in the reservoir that would last for one thousand years in my soul. How could I explain my feelings to anyone: I was bound and gagged in the archetypical garden, my psychic nature considered to be weak and subservient to men. It was already determined by the 'original sin', handed down in generations of laws, writings, literature and art.

"Well, you must do something about it. It's just not right, crying like that."

He abruptly ended the conversation and got back to work.

There seemed to be no place for my emotions. There was no place of secrecy and sacredness for me to evoke meaning of my identity, other than that which transgressed and threatened the patriarchal social system. There was no precedent or a future: I was not authorised to compose my identity by my own efforts.

CHAPTER 17

The Final Judgement

2022 winter
Ocean harbour home

"A woman must have money and a room of
her own if she is to write fiction."

"The history of men's opposition to women's emancipation is more
interesting perhaps than the history of that emancipation itself."

"When, however, one reads of a witch being ducked, of a
woman possessed by devils, of a wise woman selling herbs,
or even of a very remarkable man who had a mother,
then I think we are on the track of a lost novelist, a suppressed
poet, of some mute and inglorious Jane Austen,
some Emily Bronte who dashed her brains out on the
moor or mopped and mowed about the highways crazed
with the torture that her gift had put her to.
Indeed, I would venture to guess that Anon, who wrote so
many poems without signing them, was often a woman."

Virginia Woolf from *A Room of One's Own*, 1929[1]

The sea breeze hummed through the office window as I sat at my desk, writing my almost complete manuscript. Finally, after all these years, I had a room of my own to write.

I was grateful.

Many women in society continue to suffer toxic masculinity and misogyny and never find a place to write or speak with honesty. I arranged my precious sweet-smelling frangipanis in the vase next to my computer screen, leaning upright on each other, representative of my presence in the world. All parts of me were once broken like the stems, now standing side by side, together and whole. No longer was I absent from this world, unauthorised to compose my own identity. It had taken a long time, but I survived the secrets and lies to write this truth, prepared for the patriarchal backlash. In fact, I was ready to look it straight in the eye and bring the patriarchy to accountability.

There were no more tears to sniff back, only nature to embrace when I walk the rock pools and beaches with my grandchildren and continue to write positive outcomes for the future of vulnerable people, those on the outside of the dominant patriarchal discourse. There was only one more thing to write, for now – the precedence for a court case, a guideline for women to be addressed by a court, rather than the convoluted traditional patriarchal laws that protected the abusers rather than the abused.

Judge Pizan: Why did you move to your coastal harbour town?

Me: I needed a place to write. A room of my own; just like Virginia Woolf. My coastal harbour home provided me with the space to engage in my writing without interruption. I rarely enjoyed this luxury during my lifetime. It provided me with a new beginning to write my truth and contribute to the new feminist movement. My goal was to share my experiences of child and sexual abuse to bring about systemic change to embedded patriarchy and toxic masculinity in our society.

Judge Pizan: Did your mature age university studies provide you with the language tools to write your story?

Me: Not at first, Your Honour, Christine. That came later at my new home. At university I wrote my thesis under the veiled threat of patriarchy.

Judge Pizan: This veiled threat of patriarchy followed you to your high school teaching days?

Me: Yes, Your Honour, Christine. There is not enough training in society. Firstly, many boys, indoctrinated by the patriarchy, need to know how to behave better, that abuse is wrong. For example, when they discriminate against girls because of their sex. Secondly, the reporting of paedophile behaviour in schools needs to improve. Pathways to protect vulnerable students need to be clear – who can report and to whom – and school principals need to be accountable.

Judge Pizan: In your first appearance before this court, you presented a *Time* magazine with Mother Teresa on the front cover. Have you come out of your dark night of the soul?

Me: Yes, Your Honour, I believe I have. I have spoken the truth, rather than surrender to the silence and I have written my story.

Judge Pizan: Your grandmother was a victim of backyard abortionists?

Me: Yes.

Judge Pizan: You testify it drove her mad and she took it out on you?

Me: Yes, she suffered in a world constructed by patriarchal values. She wanted me to suffer for it too.

Judge Pizan: How have you overcome this?

Me: I have analysed my nightmares and harnessed my feminine power to overcome the abusive patriarchal system. Society is filled with voices of the patriarchs and their sexist values and attitudes. We need to make room for voices of the matriarchs and their values and attitudes, before it is too late, and their voices are lost forever in time.

Judge Pizan: If the matriarchs could speak, how do you propose to have their voices heard?

Me: In schools, workplaces and all public and private spaces where we can share discussions and seek a common ground in search of harmony between the sexes.

Judge Pizan: When you were a child you were beaten and persecuted by the people who are supposed to protect you, which led you to question the existence of God?

Me: Yes. I was alone and I had no one to speak to. I reached out to Jesus but I wasn't sure if he heard me.

Judge Pizan: How did you overcome your suffering alone?

Me: Recently, I wrote a letter to God for answers. The Ten Commandments have been broken by humans since the beginning of time. Now that I have written through litanies of despair and soul searching, I can see more clearly. I must find it in my heart to forgive the adults who persecuted me in the madhouse.

Judge Pizan: I see on your application that Lady Macbeth has testified as a witness. How so?

Me: Lady Macbeth has been recognised by the collective unconscious as an archetype. Parallels existed between Lady Macbeth and my witchy grandmother and witchy mother's behaviour.

Judge Pizan: Can you explain that further?

Me: They were worn down and brainwashed to act like violent marauding men. Each one of them entered the gates of madness and lived a miserable life until their deaths.

Judge Pizan: How has this knowledge helped you move forward in your life?

Me: The wearing down of their psyches further caused them to act like chaotic forces of nature, each played at the forefront of the drama, subverting the identity of the main culprits. In the case of Lady Macbeth, it was Macbeth. In my mother and grandmother's case it was my father. I came to understand they were not biological women at all, but rather a feminine archetype required by my father to continue his sordid behaviour.

Judge Pizan: I have a witness statement from your physician, Dr Nuha. She confirms that your complex PTSD is consistent with soldiers and people who have suffered under a military regime.

Me: Yes, Your Honour. My panic attacks, uncontrollable shaking and heart palpitations occur when I am reminded of the torture inflicted on me.

Judge Pizan: What have you learnt?

Me: Men will continue to fight wars. It is a 'civilising force' which they will experience repeatedly to define themselves. Women and daughters get in their way and obstruct them from moving forward in space and time. Mum tied herself to my father's success and consequently we both lost our personhood. Mum never recovered from it. Writing my book has helped me to develop a sense of female worthiness.

Judge Pizan: I have before me written testimony from the late Marilyn Monroe. She says that the second-wave of feminists adopted her because she spoke about a mother's madness, child abuse and victimisation.

Me: Yes, Your Honour, Christine.

Judge Pizan: How does Marilyn's testimony help you and the women's movement today?

Me: Marilyn wrote poems and prose to seek her truth in a time when the issues of objectification and violence against women were not recognised by a society dominated by masculine values. Her familial network was broken and she had no pathway to seek balance and compromise. Violence against women, family breakdowns and coercive control are still happening today. It is vital to keep the pathways of communication open between men and women in homes, families, workplaces, schools, armed services, Parliament House, and all others, and put an end to sexual discrimination. Marilyn continues to be an icon for our movement.

Judge Pizan: You met Demeter, then? The goddess of the cycle of seasons, no less.

Me: Yes, I did. She will appear in person if you summon her. I have some pumpkin seeds, sweet-smelling plumeria and wheat stalks from her crown as evidence of our encounters.

Judge Pizan: What is that she would have you say as evidence for your truth?

Me: She says that the world has not changed since the time of the Gods on Mount Olympus to the present day. The instinct to remain silent in my family was part of the foundation of society but it should not be tolerated any longer.

Judge Pizan: How do you respond to this advice?

Me: She inspired me to keep searching for my lost child and not to give up. To do this, I had to write the truth and dispel the false belief of our loving family unit.

Judge Pizan: I will allow Sappho's poem, To her Brother Charaxos, to be presented as evidence even though she is our jury leader. Sappho's writing is eternal, she is a woman of discretion and moral conscience; therefore, it will not prejudice the outcome of this court.

Me: Thank you, Your Honour, Christine. This makes for strong evidence coupled with a transcript of former Prime Minister, Julia Gillard's speech about sexism and misogyny in modern Australia, since it refers to men in high office.

Judge Pizan: How do you intend to use this evidence to support your story?

Me: Since the time of Sappho until our present day in modern society, the dominant male behaviour toward women is poor and without respect for woman and children. Prime Minister, Julia Gillard's speech substantiates this to this day.

Judge Pizan: Based on this evidence, how do you propose we go forward?

Me: We can educate our children and the community on proper manners towards women, but not excluding men and other vulnerable people. Awareness of the patriarchy would also help men to free themselves of the burdens of inflicting pain on women or for themselves being the victim of it. I believe this would fit well with the new 'consent' legislation.

Judge Pizan: You have an Instagram page and quote women's writing to connect with women on a subconscious level?

Me: Yes, Your Honour, Christine. Social media is dominated by men and their opinions. Since more men follow my account, I quote women's voices to subvert the status quo.

Judge Pizan: I see that you have referenced The Two Fires by Australian poet Judith Wright. Her work predates this century, but I must say I like her forthrightness when it comes to speaking the truth.

Me: That is true. When I was tortured, my body was on fire and I was breathless. The Minneapolis fires during the George Floyd riots sparked deep anxiety and life-threatening flashbacks, all linked to fire and destruction. When world leaders enter nuclear deals, I only see fire, death and destruction, and in time, these powerful men will go rogue on us. These devices of mass destruction will cause unimaginable human suffering. Have they no conscience after Hiroshima? It's my hypervigilance, Your Honour – there is no separating child abuse, torture, racism, war, hatred, abuse of power and toxic masculinity.

Judge Pizan: You say you dread washing days.

Me: Yes. I 'helped' Mum with the household chores since I could remember. From six years of age, I scrubbed the linoleum floors and then polished them with wax on my hands and knees. My mother and grandmother stood over me, hands on their hips, forcing me to do it. I did this hard labour after I poured the pungent phenol down the outside dunny and collected Grandad's newspaper scraps from the dirty, spider-ridden floor. I was trained in the wash house to do the family washing by hand. When I was older and physically able, around puberty, I did all the washing by myself.

Judge Pizan: Did your mother or brothers help you?

Me: Never. Mum was busy smoking cigarettes and my brothers were sleeping or out with their mates. Of course, my father never lifted a finger – except on me!

Judge Pizan: What is your objective here?

Me: Your Honour, Christine, I offer up written testimony from Goddess Persil. It reads,

'You shouldered most of the unpaid housework – washing and cleaning for your family in the name of a scarcely acknowledged patriarchal tradition. The media gods of capitalism, dominated by male executives, constructed the stereotype to keep women in their place.'

Judge Pizan: In other words, your mother exploited you because you were child labour, she did not challenge the stereotype. Further, she held a long-term grudge and resented you because she could not accept your father was a paedophile. The housework was another form of punishment. Child abuse comes in many forms. On a finishing note, I hope your washing detergent-induced dermatitis clears up. We shall have a short break and resume in the thirteenth hour!

I seated myself on the wooden bench outside the courtroom and ate my sandwich – tomato, sprinkled with chopped basil from the community edible garden, on crispy rye. It was a bright cold Orwellian day in April and I was pleased that Judge Pizan called into question everything previously presented to the court. Normally, clocks strike twelve and then start over with one strike. What this court needed was a malfunction in time because old time, embedded in toxic masculinity and patriarchal values and attitudes, could not be trusted.

We resumed in court.

Judge Pizan: I trust our witness and members of the jury are sufficiently rested.

Judge Pizan's eyes flashed to Sappho and her circle of jurors, dressed in elegant white robes and garlands of wild blossoms. Soft plumes of frankincense drifted from their gallery and administered healing to the wounds opened by my testimony.

Judge Pizan: It is clear from your testimony that your father used psychological manipulation and torment to dominate you to his will. You had no means of escape from the abuse in your home.

Me: That is true, Your Honour. Even though he is dead, I would like to bring his crimes to justice.

Judge Pizan: Did your psychologist help you?

Me: To a point. My wellbeing improved but I could not block out the childhood memories.

Judge Pizan: How did you go forward?

Me: I resolved to write my story even if I trembled, reddened and bled. I needed to write the truth to restore balance to my life. I owed it to my child within and to the women's movement to help bring change to society.

Judge Pizan: I see Judge Lear called your case a mistrial. What reasons did he give?

Me: Several, including, I was a hippie, liar, in need of a psychiatric report, unreliable witness and a dumb blonde.

Judge Pizan: How have you resolved to go forward after that tirade on your character and feminine identity?

Me: I must look beyond the tyranny of oppressive structures that uphold toxic masculinist values. I will continue to chronicle my 'truth' and gift my creative energy to the women's movement, in honour of my abused child within.

Judge Pizan: You have cried a landslide of tears caused by your childhood trauma and suffering! What steps have you taken to heal this?

Me: I have looked beyond modern psychology and relied on feminist-based philosophy which subverts the male-centred narrative that women cry over nothing. Instead, for women and men too, tears are a non-verbal process by which they can speak and empower themselves. Demeter herself knows tears hold wisdom and truth.

Judge Pizan: How can this philosophy benefit society going forward?

Me: Rather than being quick to dispense antidepressants, which emotionally blunt trauma victims, take time to get to the bottom of the tears. Seek out the story, the truth behind the tears and then allow the healing to take place.

Judge Pizan: What actions by the women's movement do you suggest?

Me: We should march on Parliament House on a regular basis, sit on the lawn outside and cry. It's okay, we have a lot to cry about. Always hashtag 'let her speak' to expand our social media audience and get more reach. And we must keep writing our stories, our lived experiences of child abuse and violence to women, to keep them alive in the collective consciousness and bring much needed changes to society, for the benefit of everyone.

Judge Pizan: Isn't it true the Aboriginal Tent Embassy has been outside Parliament House since 1972, fifty years, protesting land rights, indigenous sovereignty and self-determination? Successive governments have challenged the validity of the embassy. Why should governments treat women's issues any differently?

Me: That is true, Your Honour, Christine. But we must continue the battle, alongside our Indigenous friends. Your book was published in 1372 and went out of circulation two hundred years later. In 1986, five hundred years later it resurfaced and helped feminists to understand that this fight is long and arduous – the male auctors have been relentless in silencing the opinions and values of women. We still have a lot to accomplish to protect ourselves from society's violence towards women and children. I hope that my story will help bring much needed change.

Judge Pizan stared at me, actually right through me. For a moment it felt like I didn't exist. And then her gaze refocused, it was like I stood there naked. I had bared all for her to judge as she may. I put my trust solidly in her elegant slender hands.

She turned toward the jury and spoke like a powerful queen.

"You are now to reach your conclusions for the court, based on the evidence as presented in the trial. To each and every one of you, I ask what you say?"

For most of the time, I had forgotten the jury were there. I had been so consumed in telling my truth to Judge Pizan. Now, I turned toward them and met Sappho's gaze. The jurors behind her, obscured from my vision, sat there in a violet haze. Sappho stood elegantly in her white Grecian robe, a garland of blooming hyacinths upon her golden hair. One or two bell-like flowers fell to her dawn-sandalled feet, at which her ubiquitous letters lay.

"Based on the evidence put forward by you—" Her voice was as musical as a lyre. "—I have listened to you speak of the meanness of others, sadly your parents and grandmother. I myself have written letters to my brothers admonishing them for their darkness which brought pain and suffering on my family. You have done what everyone must do, to speak out so to be heard, otherwise society will never change. Abusers must be held to account for their crimes. I conclude that I forgive you for not speaking out earlier because you were once a child and could not come 'sing these things and talk to us then and give us your grace.'"[2]

My heart thumped hard in my chest. Sappho's kindness flowed through the courtroom like frankincense. She sat down and the violet haze lifted from over the other jurors. Behind her appeared a golden-haired child making garlands from peach blossoms scattered about her on the floor. I remembered the young girl from the garden at the mental hospital. She wasn't a figment of my imagination. She was alive and well, here in the female-dominated courtroom.

"Based on the evidence put forward by you—" Her 'violet-robed voice had put aside her anger.'[3] "I have listened to you speak of the atrocities done to me. You think I am dead – that I am in exile and that your memories of me are terribly wasted." Her small nail-bitten hands kept on weaving the peach blossoms. "I forgive you for letting go of me at Black Rock. I agree the sadistic memories were too much for a child to bear."

The young girl, my child-self, held the peach blossoms close to her chest, her Betty Cuthbert hair swept upward by a light breeze descending the aisles, bringing relief to her black torment and suffering of early days.

"I am committed to keep making this garland as the one beautiful memory of my childhood. I pray you live out the rest of your life 'unharmed and accomplish all that is in your heart.'"[4]

My legs started to give way and I held on to the witness stand rail to keep me up. My child had forgiven me, she had absolved me of the lifelong guilt I carried. But it was hard to accept, it had taken me so long to find the courage to speak out to defend and protect her. All I could feel was the guilt of an adult who turned her back on a vulnerable child.

Next to her was a woman holding a scroll. It was my graduation certificate. She stood up and straightened her academic gown before she spoke.

"Based on the evidence put forward by you—" her voice sounded like a French feminist holding vigil for 'others'. "I have listened to you speak of your desire to further educate yourself as a way to understand what causes child abuse. You thought that toxic masculinity and misogyny were only confined in the household you grew up in until you realised it is embedded in institutions in our society, including the university where you strove to find your voice to speak out about child and sexual abuse."

She was staunch and adversarial. Even though my academic career was defeated by a misogynist professor she spoke 'with a voice like an echo of thunder'.[5] "I forgive you because the force of patriarchy was too strong for you to fight alone. You built trust with your feminist network only to have that trust violated by the institution. This, no doubt, sent you into panic like anyone suffering abuse from childhood. I am proud that you have used feminist thought and philosophy to unpack western culture that cut us off from our natural roots and contributed to the issues of child and sexual abuse. This abuse has alienated millions of children from their parents and caregivers in a most unnatural way for too long."

I witnessed myself in the prime of life connect with such wisdom and understanding for what had held me captive and silent at that time. No longer was silence speaking in the lulls between threats and intimidation.

Still holding the witness stand for support, my chest began to swell as another figure emerged from the violet haze of the jury box. The fog lifted and a smartly dressed woman in boots and an A-line skirt topped with a pretty white blouse appeared to me. She was holding her Joan of Arc teacher diary. My heart was about to burst.

"Based on the evidence put forward by you—" her sweet voice sounded like the mother I never had. "I have listened to you speak of the many atrocities of your childhood and link them to the numerous influential texts you have taught to your students over the years. I have great faith in your unrelenting search for the truth and justice for child and sexual abuse and to make the world a better place. I have met many of your students in recent years and they have commended you for open classroom discussions and encouraging them to identify injustice with critically thinking minds. You set an example by standing up to the school paedophile even if it meant losing your job. Our society has not come to terms with the culture of silence which harbours abusers and punishes those who speak out. I forgive you because you did not stay silent, condoning the perpetrator's abuse as the other adults did. It was not your fault, you did all you could."

The violet mist had fully lifted, the jury had spoken. Each and every one of them forgave me for being my own witness, speaking out to be heard by society, by those who have suffered abuse and by myself.

It was official.

There was no need for more paper or another rough draft. The words which were all mine, were laid out, trustingly and without further reproach. I let go of the witness stand with a new, deeper appreciation of what it was to be understood. I had turned to so many, desperately seeking forgiveness and freedom from the shame put upon me by those who had tortured me, but no one had the power to release me as I had within myself. This was the legacy of writing my memoir and speaking my truth, unleashing the goddess within myself.

Further Reading

Clarissa Pinkola Estes, Ph.D., *Women Who Run With the Wolves: Myths and Stories of the Wild Woman Archetype* (New York: Ballantine Books, 1997).

Clementine Ford, *Fight Like A Girl* (New South Wales: Allen & Unwin, 2018).

Clementine Ford, *Boys Will Be Boys* (New South Wales: Allen & Unwin, 2020).

Julia Banks, *Power Play: Breaking through bias, barriers & boys' clubs* (Melbourne: Hardie Grant Books, 2021).

Julia Gillard, et al., *Not Now, Not Ever: Ten Years on from the Misogyny Speech* (Vintage: Random House Australia, 2022).

Judith Herman, M.D., *Trauma and Recovery: The Aftermath of Violence- From Domestic Abuse to Political Terror* (New York: Basic Books, 2015).

Bessel van der Kolk, *The Body Keeps the Score: Brain, Mind, and Body in the Healing of Trauma* (Penguin Books: Penguin Random House, 2015).

Dr Nicole LePera, *How To Do The Work: Recognise your patterns, heal from your past + create your self* (United States: Harper Collins, 2021).

Helen McCabe and Jamila Rizvi (ed), *Work. Love. Body. Future Women* (Sydney: Hachette Australia, 2021).

Grace Tame, *The Ninth Life of a Diamond Miner: A Memoir* (Sydney: MacMillan, 2022).

Endnotes

Introduction

1. Anonymous, *Female Transport*, circa 1788, [retrieved 3 December 2022] https://allpoetry.com/Female-Transport

2. Dave Pelzer, *A Child Called 'It'* (London: Seven Dials, 2019, first published 2000).

3. Bravehearts, *Prevalence of child sexual abuse*, 2016 [retrieved 25 August 2022] https://braveheart.org.au/research

4. Blake Antrobus, *More than 100 Queensland children killed by parents, carers over past 16 years, figures reveal,* 19 June 2022 [retrieved 25 August 2022] https://www.news.com.au/lifestyle

1. The Arrival

1. Emily Bronte, *The Complete Poems* (London: Penguin Book, 1992).

2. Kirli Saunders, *Kindred* (Broome: Magabala Books, 2019).

3. Tom Lowrey and Jack Snape, *Scott Morrison's 'bullets' for protestors comment stuns Australian UN representative,* 16 March 2021 [retrieved 3 December 2022] https://abc.net.au/news/2021-03-16/bullets-women

4. Judith Lewis Herman , *Father-Daughter Incest* (Cambridge: Harvard University Press, 2000).

2. The City of Ladies

1. Mary Shelley, *Mathilda* (Random House UK: Penguin, 2016).

2. Nuala Ní Dhomhnaill, *Pharaoh's Daughter* (Wake Forest University Press, Tenth printing, 2018).

3.   Letter to My Brother

1.   Sappho, *The Complete Poems of Sappho* (Colorado: Shambhala Publications, Inc., 2009).

2.   Rupi Kaur, *Home Body* (New South Wales: Simon & Schuster, 2021).

4.   In the Beginning: The Dark Night of the Soul

1.   David Biema, *The Secret Life of Mother Teresa, Her Agony, A decade after Mother Teresa's death, her secret letters show that she spent almost 50 years without sensing the presence of God in her life. What does her experience teach us about the value of doubt?* (*Time*, 34, 23 Aug. 2007).

2.   Mary Shelley, *Mathilda* (Random House UK: Penguin, 2016).

5.   Grandmother: Too much Information

1.   Oodgeroo Noonuccal and Kabul Oodgeroo Noonuccal, *The Rainbow Serpent,* Spring 1988 [16 April 2022] https://meanjin.com.au/poetry

2.   Natasha Cica, *Laws and Bills Digest Group, Research Paper 1, 1998-99. Abortion Law in Australia – Parliament of Australia.* [retrieved 9 October 2022] https://www.aph.gov.au/about_parliament

3.   Luce Irigaray, *Quotes.* 2022 Goodreads Inc. [retrieved 3 December 2022] https://goodreads.com./author

4.   Luce Irigaray, *Quotes.* 2022 Goodreads Inc. [retrieved 3 December 2022] https://goodreads.com/author

5.   Anthony Albanese, *#March4Justice – Responding to the Prime Minister.* Speeches, Monday, 15 March 2021. [retrieved 16 October 2022] https://anthonyalbanese.com.au/media-centre/march-4-justice

6.   Luce Irigaray, *Quotes.* 2022 Goodreads Inc. [retrieved 3 December 2022] https://goodreads.com/author

6.   God is Dead

1.   Anna Akhmatova, *Requiem* and *Poem without a Hero* (Ohio: Swallow Press, first published in England 1976 by Elek Books Limited, London).

2. Steve Vai, *Steve Vai Discusses Devin Townsend and New Album, 'Sex and Religion*,' in 1993 Guitar World Interview/Guitar World. https://www.guitarworld.com/gw-archive/steve-vai-discussess-devin-townsend-and-new-album-sex-and-religion-1993-guitar-world-interview

3. Florence + The Machine, *Big God* (2018). Spotify, Licensed by Musixmatch.

4. Clara Jones, *Queensland police response to domestic and family violence inquiry hears of ugly comments, crews avoiding call outs*. 14 July 2022. [retrieved 15 October 2022] https://www.abc.net.au/news/2022-07-14/qld-police-responses-dfv

5. Friedrich Nietzsche, *Quotes*. 2022 Goodreads Inc. [retrieved 3 December 2022]https://goodreads.com/author

7. The Outside Dunny

1. William Shakespeare, *The Tragedies, Macbeth* (Great Britain: Octopus Books Limited, 1986).

2. Nuala Ni Dhomhnaill, *Pharoah's Daughter* (Wake Forest University Press, Tenth printing, 2018).

3. William Shakespeare, *The Tragedies, Macbeth* (Great Britain: Octopus Books Limited, 1986).

8. Torture by Light

1. Edna St Vincent Millay, *The Selected Poetry by Edna St Vincent Millay*. Neeland Media, 11 June 2018.

2. Dave Pelzer, *A Child Called 'It'* (London: Seven Dials, 2019, first published 2000).

3. Clara Jones, *Queensland Police Commissioner Katarina Carroll questioned at inquiry over senior officers' misogynistic comments*. 18 August 2022. [retrieved 18 August 2022] https://www.abc.net.au/news/2022-08-18/dfv-inquiry-qld-police-commissioner-carroll-misogynistic.

4. Monique El-Faizy, *As grassroots feminist movement takes hold, Egypt moves to restrict women's rights even further*. 1 April 2021. [retrieved 8 October 2022] https://www.france24.com/en/middle-east/20210401-as-grassroots-feminist-movement-takes-hold

9. The School Visit

1. Marilyn Monroe, *Fragments: Poems, Intimate Notes, Letters* (New York: Farrar, Straus and Giroux, 2012).

2. Marilyn Monroe, *Fragments: Poems, Intimate Notes, Letters* (New York: Farrar, Straus and Giroux, 2012).

3. Gail Garriger, *The Heroine's Journey* (Gail Carriger LLC, 2020).

10. The Strip Search

1. Marina, *Man's World.* 2020. Spotify, Licensed by Musixmatch.

2. D.H. Lawrence, *Quotes.* 2022 Goodreads Inc. [retrieved 3 December 2022] https://goodreads.com/author

3. Marina, *Man's World.* 2020. Spotify, Licensed by Musixmatch.

11. Shopping Day

1. Audre Lorde, *Quotes.* 2022 Goodreads Inc. [3 December 2022] https://goodreads.com/author

2. Clara Jones, *Queensland Police Commissioner Katarina Carroll questioned at inquiry over senior officers' misogynistic comments.* 18 August 2022. [retrieved 18 August 2022] https://www.abc.net.au/news/2022-08-18/dfv-inquiry-qld-police-commissioner-carroll-misogynistic

3. Sappho, *The Complete Poems of Sappho.* (Colorado: Shambhala Publications, Inc., 2009).

12. Keen's Mustard

1. Judith Wright, *Collected Poems 1942-1985* (Sydney: Angus & Robertson, 1994).

2. John Leicester, *'Dangerous': Around the world, police chokeholds are being scrutinised.* The Sydney Morning Herald, 2 June 2020. [retrieved 16 October 2022] https://www.smh.com.au/world/europe/around-the-world-police-chokeholds-are-being-scrutinised-20200603

3.   Judith Wright, *Collected Poems 1942-1985* (Sydney: Angus & Robertson, 1994).

4.   Nidal Majdalani, Instagram @nidal.majdalani. Award winning journalist, *Lonely Planet* author, tourism expert, photographer, heritage and environment advocate.

5.   Judith Wright, *Collected Poems 1942-1985* (Sydney: Angus & Robertson, 1994).

6.   Judith Wright, *Collected Poems 1942-1985* (Sydney: Angus & Robertson, 1994).

7.   Nuala Ni Dhomhnaill, *Pharoah's Daughter* (Wake Forest University Press, Tenth printing, 2018).

13. Washing Day

1.   Sappho, *The Complete Poems of Sappho.* (Colorado: Shambhala Publications, Inc., 2009).

2.   Julia Gillard, Transcript of *Julia Gillard's Speech.* 10 October 2012. [retrieved 15 November 2021] https://www.smh.com.au//politics/federal/transcript-of-julia-gillards-speech-20121010

3.   Anna Laetitia Barbauld, *Washing Day* (circa 1770). *Seven Centuries of Poetry in English, Fourth Edition*, ed. John Leonard (Melbourne: Oxford University Press, 1998).

14. What He Brought Home

1.   Sylvia Plath, *Cut* and *Ariel, The Restored Edition: A Facsimile of Plath's Manuscript, Reinstating Her Original Selection and Arrangement* (Great Britain: Faber and Faber, 2004).

2.   Oodgeroo Noonuccal, *Municipal Gum. The Penguin Anthology of Australian Poetry*, ed. John Kinsella (Victoria: Penguin, 2009).

3.   Helene Cixous, *Quotes.* 2022. Goodreads Inc. [retrieved 3 December 2022] https://goodreads.com/author

4.   Melina Marchetta, *Looking for Alibrandi* (Penguin Australia/Orchard Books, October 1992).

5. Grace Tame, TweetDeck Feb 9, 2022 @10NewsFirst

6. Matt Coughlan, *Minister labelled ex-staffer 'lying cow'*. The Canberra Times, Mar 4 2021. [retrieved 16 October 2022] https://www.canberratimes.com.au/story/7152115/minister-labelled-ex-staffer-lying-cow/

7. Sashka Koloff et al., *'Parliament House security guard describes finding Brittany Higgins on night of alleged rape in minister's office.' Four Corners* 22 March 2021. [retrieved 8 June 2022] https://www.abc.net.au/news/2021-03-22/four-corners-security-brittany-higgins/13259262

15. Leaving School

1. Dorothea Mackellar, *My Country. The Penguin Anthology of Australian Poetry*, ed. John Kinsella (Victoria: Penguin, 2009).

2. *'Rape': the penetrative sexual offence, Family Violence-A National Legal Response (ALRC Report 114), Australian Government, Australia Law Reform Commission,* 11 Oct 2010. [retrieved 8 October 2022] https://www.alrc/gov.au/publication/family-violence-a national-legal-response-alrc-report114/25-sexual-offences-3/rape-the-penetrative-sexual-offence/

3. Dorothea Mackellar, *Arms and the Woman. The Poems of Dorothea Mackellar* (Adelaide: Rigby, 1971)

4. Mary Wollstonecraft, *A Vindication of the Rights of Woman* (London: Penguin Pocket Hardbacks, 28 April 2020).

5. Sylvia Plath, *The Bell Jar* (London: Faber and Faber, 1999).

6. Marina, *Man's World.* 2020. Spotify, Licensed by Musixmatch.

7. Sylvia Plath, *The Moon and the Yew Tree* and *Ariel, The Restored Edition: A Facsimile of Plath's Manuscript, Reinstating Her Original Selection and Arrangement* (Great Britain: Faber and Faber, 2004).

8. David Attenborough, *A Life on Our Planet: My Witness Statement and Vision for the Future* (UK: Penguin Random House, 2020).

16. Crying: A Child is Dead

1. Renate Blumenfeld-Kosinski, about Christine de Pizan, *The Selected Writings of Christine de Pizan* (New York: A Norton Critical Edition, W.W. Norton & Company, Inc, 1997).

2. Christine De Pizan, *The Selected Writings of Christine de Pizan.* Ed by Blumenfeld-Kosinski, Renate (New York: A Norton Critical Edition, W.W. Norton & Company, Inc, 1997).

3. Clementine Ford, *Fight Like a Girl* (New South Wales: Allen & Unwin, 2018).

17. The Final Judgement

1. Virginia Woolf, *A Room of One's Own* (London: Penguin Modern Classic, 4 June 2020).

2. Sappho, from Fragment (27), *The Complete Poems of Sappho.* Colorado: Shambhala Publications, Inc., 2009.

3. Sappho, from Fragment (103), *The Complete Poems of Sappho.* Colorado: Shambhala Publications, Inc., 2009.

4. Sappho, from Fragment (5) *The Complete Poems of Sappho.* Colorado: Shambhala Publications, Inc., 2009.

5. Anna Akhmatova, *The Year Nineteen-thirteen*, Line 300, *Requiem* and *Poem without a Hero* (Ohio: Swallow Press, first published in England 1976 by Elek Books Limited, London).